My Grandmother's Secret

My Grandmother's Secret

Laura Sweeney

bookouture

Published by Bookouture in 2025

An imprint of Storyfire Ltd.
Carmelite House
50 Victoria Embankment
London EC4Y 0DZ

www.bookouture.com

The authorised representative in the EEA is Hachette Ireland
8 Castlecourt Centre
Dublin 15 D15 XTP3
Ireland
(email: info@hbgi.ie)

Copyright © Laura Sweeney, 2025

Laura Sweeney has asserted her right to be identified
as the author of this work.

All rights reserved. No part of this publication may be reproduced, stored in any retrieval system, or transmitted, in any form or by any means, electronic, mechanical, photocopying, recording or otherwise, without the prior written permission of the publishers.

ISBN: 978-1-83525-941-2
eBook ISBN: 978-1-83525-940-5

This book is a work of fiction. Names, characters, businesses, organizations, places and events other than those clearly in the public domain, are either the product of the author's imagination or are used fictitiously. Any resemblance to actual persons, living or dead, events or locales is entirely coincidental.

For Mum and Dad

PROLOGUE
LILY

June 1945

The path to the post box at the end of Beachfront Road was littered with streamers and crumpled party hats. A folded trestle table leant against Seafoam Cottage's white-washed front garden wall, which was lined with stumps of cast iron. One day the railings would be replaced, now peace had come.

The buggy I was pushing quickly got caught in a line of discarded red, white, and blue bunting lying across the pavement, forcing me to come to a standstill to untangle the string from around the wheels. Sheila Jones stepped out of the cottage next door, her hair still in curlers. I shoved the envelope I was holding into the pocket of my skirt and patted my short, blonde curls that were blowing about in the breeze.

'Morning, Lily,' Sheila wheezed, her lungs permanently damaged from a lifetime of chain-smoking Woodbines. The waft of smoke from the one dangling from her nicotine-stained fingers triggered a memory which I blinked away.

'Morning, Sheila. Did you enjoy the party?'

She took a long drag. 'Not had a good old-fashioned knees-up in a while, have we? We should be grateful we're able to, I suppose. Richard well?'

I nodded.

'Good, good. Anyway,' she eyed my hand which was inching its way involuntarily towards my pocket, 'I won't keep you.'

'I'll see you at church on Sunday.' The letter was burning a hole in the fabric of my skirt. I could swear it was giving off enough heat to scorch my leg.

'You certainly will. My Betty might be able to come along too, if she can spare a moment from her books,' Sheila said, her beady eyes glancing at my pocket.

Once Sheila's front door slammed behind her, I let out a breath and pulled the envelope out into the open air again. It flapped in my hand as a gust of wind blew up from Dovecote beach a few yards away. Specks of salty spray dotted the paper like tiny teardrops. My writing was small on the front of the envelope, smaller than usual, as though I'd been afraid of running out of space. I ran my thumb over the words, careful not to smudge the ink.

Mr. H. Benoit

4 rue de Lyon

Paris

<u>*FRANCE*</u>

The line I'd scored under 'France' wasn't straight. I kissed his name and raised the letter to the post box. The edge of the envelope touched the side of the opening before I wrenched my hand back and stuffed the envelope into my pocket.

. . .

I was home and leaning against the hallway wall before my breathing returned to normal. I couldn't do it; I couldn't send it. What good would it do anyway? It was too late. Bridges had been crossed and burnt, the water under them long flowed away. I scolded myself for writing the damned thing as I stomped up the stairs and into my bedroom. Opening my knicker drawer, I pulled out the large white envelope hidden beneath an old girdle. I untied the white ribbon around the envelope and stuffed my unsent letter amongst the stack of paper inside. I buried it. And with it the secret my husband and I would take to our graves.

ONE

GRACE

August 2015

Grace just needed a moment's respite from the chatter and clink of teaspoon on porcelain filling the church hall next door. She also needed a break from the sympathetic nods and apologetic smiles. But alone in the coolness of the sixteenth-century church, she was unable to settle. Standing or sitting still allowed too much space for her grief. She wandered the south aisle before leaning against a mullioned window. She stared out at the arched stone bridge over the railway line that ran parallel to the bustling Dovecote High Street, and the pebbly beach and rolling waves beyond. The sea was grey and flat, not unlike the heaviness in Grace's heart that somehow still beat under her black dress, despite it being in several pieces. She'd been through some tough times in her thirty-three years, but today seemed the bleakest of them all. Restlessly she pulled her golden-blonde hair from the bun at the base of her neck and ran her fingers through it, letting it settle across her shoulders. With a sigh, she turned her back on the framed snapshot of Dovecote, sat down in the back pew, and buried her face in her hands.

An hour earlier, the church had been filled with the respectful low voices, kind words, and favourite hymns of her grandmother Lily's funeral. Now there was only silence, and it was so heavy that it sat on Grace's shoulders like an old blanket.

At the creak of the door, she wiped fresh tears from her cheeks and turned to see Ben's tall frame silhouetted against the afternoon sun. He sat down next to her, undoing the button of his black suit jacket.

'Here you are,' Ben said gently, running his fingers through his short, auburn hair.

'Sorry, I just needed a bit of a break. It's been a tough day,' she said, shifting her gaze up towards the altar. The solid, sturdy bulk of her ex-husband was the only thing that seemed real. His elbow nudged hers and Grace looked down from the ceiling to meet his blue-grey eyes. The kindness in them forced fresh tears to bubble up. She dabbed her eyes with an already sodden tissue and fought the urge to bury her head in Ben's chest and melt into the security of his strong arms. He probably wouldn't mind if she did, but it wouldn't be right. It had been a little less than a year since they'd reached the mutual decision that they were better off apart. As if sensing her predicament, he put his arm around her, and she laid her head on his broad shoulder.

'Thank you,' she said, and he squeezed her arm ever so slightly.

'You're going to get through this, Grace,' he said.

'I don't know. I mean it's just so real now that she's gone, forever. And I don't know how I'm going to cope without her. She was more than my grandmother; she was my everything. After Mum died and Dad walked out, Nanna became my surrogate mum, my best friend, my secret keeper, my rock, the inspiration for my silly little magazine column. Everything I ever learnt about anything important, I learnt from her. And now she's gone. There's so much more I needed her for.'

'Hey, come on now. You don't need inspiration to write

about being a good mum, you do that because you are one. I know it might not seem like it now, but you will be alright. You've got friends like Rachel, and your grandad, and me.'

Grace sighed and pulled herself out of Ben's embrace. 'Except I don't, do I?' Her shoulders chilled quickly without the comfort of his arm around them.

Ben laced his hands together on his lap. 'Yeah, I know, it's complicated. But I am still here for you, you know that. And, hey, there's always our Harry.'

Grace smiled through her tears. 'Yes, at least we've got Harry.' She was going to say something else about their son, but the church door groaned open again.

'Sorry to disturb you, Grace, but I think it's time we took Richard back to Bayview.'

Grace looked towards the doorway at Heather, one of the carers at her grandad's care home. She was a wiry young woman, with a wicked sense of humour and endless patience.

'Oh, of course. Thanks, Heather.' She turned to Ben. 'I'd better go and see him off.'

As they walked through the gothic doorway at the church entrance, Ben nudged her elbow again. 'This old church has seen a lot of people pass through these oak doors, but I bet it's never known a nicer lady than Lily. She was one of a kind.'

Grace looked up at the grey stone of St. John's Church, its steeple towered above her head, pointing towards the heavens.

'She sure was,' Grace sighed.

Grace waved at the car window as Heather efficiently and expertly tucked Richard's plaid blanket around his knees to keep him warm. She swallowed the hard lump in her throat as the car pulled away from the kerb and disappeared through the church gates. Her grandfather didn't turn to wave. Why would he? He didn't know who she was any more. It must have been a confusing day for him. It wasn't likely he remembered that the Lily Morrison they had buried had been his wife for nearly seventy years. There were times Richard didn't know who he himself was, never mind anyone else.

A stiff breeze rustled through the apple trees dotting the edges of the church car park. Grace looked to the blue sky, scattered with cotton-wool clouds and seagulls riding the swirling coastal thermals, hoping that gravity would pull back the tears gathering again in her eyes.

'He's not well, is he?' Ben observed beside her.

'No, he isn't. The doctors say his dementia is quite advanced now. I've known for a while how bad it was getting. The last time I took Nanna to see him at the care home, he didn't know who she was. Grandad hasn't recognised me for a long time.'

'That must be hard on you.'

Grace shrugged. 'Stop that,' she said, picking at a loose thread on the sleeve of her jacket. 'Stop being so nice to me, you'll set me off again.'

'Come on, let's get you home,' he said softly.

'Grace,' Reverend Clive called, half-jogging down the path from the church and through the lychgate, his bald head catching the sun and his round face full of kindness. She had meant to go and thank him for everything he had done.

'How are you doing?'

Grace managed a weak smile. 'Fine. I'll be fine. Thank you, Clive, for everything. You've been a rock these past few weeks, I couldn't have got through it without you.'

Clive reached out and clasped her hand in his. His skin was soft and warm, he oozed comfort from every pore.

'I'll be thinking of you, Grace. You know where I am if you need me.' He released her hand and gave Ben a pat on his upper arm. Neither man said a word, but Grace caught the look that passed between them and the slight nod of both their heads. She was lucky to have people looking out for her, especially now she had to navigate a future without the person who had been her anchor, preventing her from drifting out to sea.

TWO

GRACE

August 2015

As Ben drove them up over the railway bridge and down the High Street, Grace gazed out of the window at passing houses and shops. She'd lived in the small seaside town of Dovecote, just a few miles east of Brighton, for most of her life and even now in her darkest hour it filled her with a warm glow. The rows of independent shops adorned with hanging baskets were beacons of resilience, prospering despite the best attempts of market forces and soulless chains. She could almost taste the crispy battered fish and vinegary chips from her favourite chip shop. The sudden memory of her grandmother meeting her outside the chip shop after school on a Friday and buying paper-wrapped parcels of chips to eat on the beach sliced through her chest. Dovecote was more than a town, it was a community – big enough not to be claustrophobic, but small enough to be filled with plenty of familiar faces. Each place – Harrington's Bookshop, The Seaside Café, Aoife's Hair Salon, Crawford's Opticians, The Royal Oak pub, The Promenade, the beach, the cliffs, Victoria Park – was a part of her history, and her family's history.

It was only when Ben slowed to navigate the mini roundabout outside the train station at the bottom of the High Street that Grace turned to him.

'Do you think I did the right thing, not letting Harry come to Nanna's funeral?' she asked.

'It was your decision but, for what it's worth, I think you were right. He is only ten,' he said, a slight frown creasing his forehead as he turned into Beachfront Road.

Grace nodded slowly and let the silence fall between them again. It was a nice silence – easy and comfortable, and far from the tense atmosphere of the waning days of their marriage.

Ben pulled up outside the detached double bay-fronted cottage that had been Grace's childhood home, and the home she and Harry had returned to a year ago. For Lily and Richard, it had been home for a lot longer than Grace's lifetime. Her grandmother had often told her the story of their first night together in Seafoam Cottage, the night after their wedding, when they had only the barest of bare essentials; she said it was the best night of her life.

The heavy green curtains in the bay window of the sitting room were still closed, as Grace had left them. She stood on the pavement staring up at the white-washed walls, pale blue window surrounds, and matching pastel blue door. Her hand gripped the front gate so hard that the wave motif carved into the wood imprinted itself on her skin. Her grandmother was in all of it: the gate, the pittosporum tree in the front garden, the creamy-white daisy bushes lining the path to the front door, the sloping red-tiled roof and matching porch canopy. Even the chimney held the memory of her grandmother telling off her grandfather after he'd made a mess of the sitting room rug while sweeping out the fireplace.

She was lost in comforting memories when Ben's warm hand came to rest on her arm.

'Why don't I go and pick Harry up from Jake's?' he asked softly, almost as if he knew Grace was deep in memories and didn't want to disturb them. 'You go in and get yourself a stiff drink.'

The click of the front door echoed around the terracotta-floored hall. She stared at the tiles for a moment. They were original, a couple of centuries old. How many footsteps had they absorbed? How many comings and goings, entrances and exits? Everyone who had ever been in the cottage had left an invisible imprint on those tiles, like the imprint everyone she'd ever loved had left on her heart.

The air was so still that Grace could hear her own heartbeat as she made her way into the kitchen. She put her bag down on the kitchen table and sank into a chair, kicking off her black court shoes. There was a pile of unopened post on the table, some addressed to Mrs Grace Curtis, some to Miss Grace Lyttleton. She really needed to sort that out, the two identities were jarring. The letter addressed to Mrs Lily Morrison made Grace push the bundle out of reach. She eyed her laptop. The next fortnightly column she wrote for a national women's magazine wasn't due for a few days. There was no need to worry about that for now.

Hauling herself up from the table, she went into the sitting room to open the curtains. She paused a while at the window, resting her forehead against the cool glass. Her heart skipped a beat at the pair of blue eyes that looked back, but it was just her reflection. As far back as she could remember, people had told her she had her grandmother's eyes. Beyond the low stone wall on the other side of the road, the beach narrowed to a point where the chalk-white cliffs met the sea. On stormy days, the occasional wave jumped the wall and splashed the road. There had been more cottages to the right of Seafoam Cottage, but a tumultuous storm at the turn of the last century had washed two into the sea. The remaining four had stood firm, protected by the wall and Beachfront Road, until the one on the town end, Seaview Cottage, had succumbed to age and dereliction and been demolished in the 1960s to make way for an extension to the train station car park. There were just three cottages left, huddled together on the road nestled at the base of the cliff, watching over the sea, while the rest of Dovecote grew towards the east and back inland. Grace closed her eyes and held her breath to listen for the rush and fizz of sea over pebble – the soundtrack to her life.

There was a hint of her grandmother's perfume on the curtains and cushions. Grace could still see Lily's hunched shadow at the square table in the bay window, meticulously working on a jigsaw puzzle or writing letters, as she had done right until the end.

Her grandparents had modernised the house, putting in central heating and updating the décor as fashions changed. The kitchen had been redone twice in Grace's lifetime and the bathroom fixtures had once been avocado coloured. The conversion of the storeroom off the kitchen into a downstairs loo in the 1990s had been a huge relief. They never did get round to replacing the iron railings on top of the front garden wall, though. The stumps of the old railings, sawn off during the war, the only witness to their existence. Despite all the changes, the house had kept its fisherman's cottage charm, and the sitting room in particular still had an old-fashioned ambience, with white linen antimacassars on the floral-print sofa, green and cream wide-striped wallpaper, and an art deco-style cream and brown tiled fireplace added at some point in the 1920s. All that was missing was the faint whiff of Woodbine cigarettes and men's Brylcreem that Grace imagined everywhere had smelt of in the past. In time, she would update the room and bring it into the twenty-first century, but for now it would exist as a sort of shrine to those who were no longer here.

There was a definite sense of ending sitting heavy on her shoulders, and the future was shrouded in a grief that dulled any prospect of light.

Grace had dried her eyes for the umpteenth time that day and was unloading the dishwasher when Harry's key turned in the lock. He barrelled down the hall and threw his skinny arms around her waist. She held him tightly and inhaled his scent. He was hot and out of breath and she looked up at Ben, who was leaning against the door frame, his suit jacket slung over his arm, his tie loosened, and the top button of his shirt undone. He looked wrecked.

'I figured you needed a bit of time, so we had a kickabout in the park,' he said, puffing his cheeks out. 'I'm getting old.'

Harry extracted himself from Grace's hug.

'Can I go and play on my computer now?' he asked, giving Grace his best puppy-dog eyes. He was still young enough to get away with playing cute.

'Just until dinner time, then I'm sure you've got homework to do.'

Harry's reply was lost in the whoosh of air that followed him up the stairs. Grace flinched slightly at the banging of his bedroom door.

'How are you doing?' Ben asked, taking a mug from Grace's hand and placing it down on the countertop.

Grace reached for the cutlery caddy. 'I'm alright.'

'Do you want me to take Harry back to mine? I don't mind shifting our days around if you need a bit of time and space.'

Grace glanced up at the ceiling. Tinny computerised music filtered through the floorboards.

'No, it's fine. I want the company. I don't think I could cope if the house was too quiet.'

'Alright, but if you change your mind just give me a call.'

Grace nodded.

'I'd better go,' Ben said, and Grace followed him to the door.

'Thank you for coming today, and for, well, everything. It was nice to have you around.'

'No worries, I wanted to come. Lily was always so lovely to me.'

'She liked you.'

'I'm a likeable guy,' Ben quipped, coaxing a small smile from Grace. 'See you at the weekend.' He gave her arm a brief squeeze. The touch of his hand unleashed a thousand warm, happy memories that widened Grace's smile just a fraction.

'See you.'

Ben reached the front gate at the same time Rachel pulled up in her cherry-red Fiat 500. She wound down the window and Ben bent down to talk to her. Her ex-husband and her best friend couldn't have made it any more obvious that they were talking about her if they'd tried. Grace's right eyebrow gave an involuntary twitch, and she supressed a smile. There was a lifetime of love and care between all three of them. They'd known each other since primary school after all.

Eventually Ben drove off and Rachel climbed out of her car. She was dressed in her work uniform after a long day of cajoling people to read eye charts but, as always, her hair and make-up were immaculate. In the thirty years Grace had known her, she'd never seen Rachel with a single strand of her chestnut-brown hair out of place. If only Rachel could say the same about Grace. One of them had to be the one with untameable hair and an allergy to most cosmetics, and it wasn't Rachel.

'Oh sweetie. How are you? I'm so sorry I couldn't be there. It was just impossible to get anyone to cover the shop,' Rachel said, enveloping Grace in a warm bear hug. 'Come on, let's get the kettle on and you can tell me all about it.'

'Oh God no. I've drunk enough tea to sink a ship today. There's a bottle of white in the fridge though.'

Rachel grinned. 'Just one small one for me. You deserve the rest of the bottle.'

With a glass of cold Chablis in front of her, and having updated Rachel on the long day's events, Grace pushed an envelope across the table.

'This came.'

Rachel picked up the envelope and opened it. She pulled out an unremarkable sympathy card with white lilies on the cover and opened it. Her eyes widened and she looked up at Grace.

'Your dad sent a card?'

Grace raised her eyebrows. '*He* sent a card. Talk about kicking someone when they're down.'

'He probably didn't mean...'

'I've heard nothing from him for nearly thirty years since he abandoned me the week my mum died, Rach. Nothing when I got married. Nothing when Harry was born. I wasn't even sure he was still alive, turns out he is. How about that?' There was a heavy undertone of sarcasm in Grace's voice and Rachel looked up from the card with a sympathetic look.

'He's written his email address,' Rachel said. 'Are you...'

'No! I'm not getting in touch with him. I know nothing about him, I wouldn't recognise him if I bumped into him on The Promenade.' Grace took the card back and glanced at the unfamiliar writing. The fact that he'd signed it 'Tony (Dad)' made bile rise in her throat. He had no right to claim that title. He'd ceased to be a dad to her when she was five years old. She stuffed the card into the envelope and tossed it onto the pile of cardboard waiting to be put in the recycling bin. 'Too little, too late.'

Rachel reached across the table and patted Grace's hand. There were a lot of words in the gesture and Grace was grateful for it.

'It's been a tough day for you all round. Will you be alright?'

Grace squared her shoulders and drained her wine glass. 'I'll manage.'

'Of course you will.'

As she got into her car, Rachel blew Grace a kiss. 'Night, darling. Call if you need anything.'

'Bye,' Grace replied with a little wave.

Once Rachel had gone Grace climbed the stairs and knocked on Harry's bedroom door before going in, mindful of his recent request for increased privacy. She crossed the wooden floor to the white desk by the small window where he was, to her surprise, engrossed in maths homework.

'Hi, Mum. I thought I'd better do my homework without you having to nag me seeing as you've had a hard day. How was it?' Harry's voice was gentle, and he looked up with such innocence in his brown eyes that Grace couldn't resist putting her arms around his shoulders. Unusually, he didn't try to wriggle out of her grasp. His skinny arms squeezed her waist. He was at that stage where he was all limbs, as if the rest of his body hadn't quite caught up.

'It was tough, sweetheart,' she said into his soft, thick, chestnut hair.

'Don't be sad, Mum. I'll look after you,' he said, causing the tears that pricked the back of Grace's eyes to flow freely down her cheeks.

THREE

LILY

April 1940

'Oh,' I said, my hand automatically going to my chest which was rising and falling at an alarming rate. 'I don't quite know what to say, Richard.'

Richard leant on the garden bench and hauled himself up from his one-kneed position.

'The traditional answer is "yes".'

I looked away, biting my lip. I paced the lawn under the cherry tree, my thin fingers tugging at the fabric of my favourite peach day dress. Richard said the dress complemented my complexion and brought out the blue in my eyes. The grass was littered with pink blossom that was falling, rather ironically, like confetti. A droning noise made me look upwards at the clear spring-blue sky, but I couldn't make out the source of the low whine. Relieved that we weren't about to be hit by a rogue bomb, I turned back to Richard and forced a polite smile on my lips. He did look awfully nervous, and a little crestfallen.

'Perhaps I may have some time to think about it? Marriage is a frightfully big step, Richard. We are so very young still. I'm only just nineteen, you're barely much older and...' My voice faltered as I glanced up at the back of Mummy and Daddy's house. The slight flicker of the net curtain in the dining room window gave away that Mummy was watching. Presumably Daddy had given his blessing to Richard which had led to this, rather unfortunate, situation. Mummy would have been delighted and supportive, not that Daddy would have given her a say. Women did not get to have opinions in Daddy's world. I returned my thoughts to Richard, waiting patiently for me to say something. But what on earth could I say? It wasn't that I didn't love him; of course I did. I had fallen for him the instant I saw him across the ballroom of his parents' house in Hove at a party in the spring of '38. He looked quite dashing in his tail-suit that night, with his tall, slim figure and broad shoulders. I was smitten. The moment our eyes met, my heart had simply melted. I had thought it so grown-up to have a chap at the tender age of seventeen. Had it been anyone but Richard, the eldest son of Daddy's former commanding officer in the last war, it would have been forbidden. And now here he was proposing marriage. I suppose I should have seen it coming. But... My musings were interrupted by Richard coming over to me and taking my hand in his. It was warm, soft and gentle. The sun sparkled in his grey eyes and reflected off the Brylcreem in his sandy-coloured hair.

'Lily, if you need some time then you can have it. Please forgive me for getting a little emotional, but I do love you. And I do think that I would rather like to have you as my wife.' I nodded dumbly, and Richard released my hand. 'Please do not take too long, I sail for Singapore next Friday, and I should like to know before then.'

'Do you really have to go?' Maybe if he could stay, we could have a little more time together. More time for me to work out whether I wanted to spend the rest of my life with him.

'You know I do, Lily. My father's company has been requisitioned by the War Office and they are relying on me to go and oversee the rubber production, to ensure supply keeps up with demand. I know some of our friends think badly of me that I am not in uniform, marching up and down, rifle in hand, but this *is* important war work. We need rubber, and my father is trusting me to make sure we do not let our armed forces down.' He had gotten quite het up while speaking, his cheeks were flushed, and he drew a shaky breath. I nodded even though he had completely misunderstood the reasoning behind my question.

'I will think on it,' I whispered, not able to meet his eyes.

He straightened and shook his head slightly, his eyes losing their softness. I had upset him and, possibly even worse, embarrassed him. He gave me a modest, light kiss on the cheek. Even at a time like this, when he was asking me to give him my entire life, he was still adhering to the ideas of propriety from the last century that had governed our parents' lives. If only he would fling all that aside, take me in his arms, kiss me properly, and make me swoon.

'If you cannot give me your answer before I go, perhaps it would not be too impertinent of me to ask you to wait for me to return?'

All I could do was nod again. My voice had deserted me entirely.

'Maybe it would be best if I were to leave.' He glanced up at the house. 'If you would be so kind as to give my regards to your parents.'

I nodded once again, aware that I probably looked like a duck, bobbing my head up and down. I watched him walk up the garden, through the side gate, and out onto the square of terraced stucco-fronted townhouses that were ubiquitous in these more affluent areas of west Brighton.

I crumpled down onto the bench and looked at my fingers, knotted in my lap. A seagull squawked overhead. Dear reliable, stable, safe, sensible, respectable Richard who had not pressed upon me a desire for anything more intimate than a chaste kiss on closed lips. He was no Cary Grant, but he was a good man, if maddingly lacking in passion. Was that enough? Oh, why couldn't he have kissed me. And marriage? I sighed, not looking forward to having to tell Mummy I'd not said yes. She wouldn't understand how much the idea of marriage made my insides ache, how the mere thought of a wedding band on my finger felt like being locked in a prison. I yearned for more out of life than being tied to the kitchen sink. Daddy was going to be furious. No doubt he would say that I am being selfish and disobedient and bringing shame on the family. That was one of his favourite admonishments. I was staring down a dead-end road and it was rather bleak.

FOUR

GRACE

August 2015

Organising her grandmother's funeral had given Grace the perfect reason to put off sorting through Lily's personal things. A few days later, with Harry packed off to Ben's for the weekend and her column sent to the editor, she was all out of excuses. She braced herself as she stepped into her grandmother's bedroom. The room had smelt the same for as long as Grace could remember – lily-of-the-valley and rose, with undertones of cold cream and hair spray. It was this room she had run to after her grandparents had sat her down on the flowery sofa in the lounge and told her, with red-rimmed eyes, that her mother would not be coming home. There had been an accident and Mamma had gone to live with the angels in Heaven. Five-year-old Grace had thrown herself face down on the soft comforter on the bed and sobbed herself to sleep. The urge to do the same now was overwhelming. It was irrelevant to Grace that Lily had had a long life, it was still desperately unfair that she was gone. It still seemed too soon.

Another memory of this room, another dark night. The

memory wasn't as sharp as the night her mother died but she remembered the softness of the blanket she had snuggled under and the cool cotton of her grandmother's nightdress that absorbed her tears. Her enduring memory was of the intense confusion that had led to the question she had asked in her five-year-old innocence. 'When will Daddy be coming back, Nanna?' Lily had stroked her hair and pulled her closer, almost smothering her. 'Don't worry, pet,' she had whispered, 'you'll always have me and Grandad.'

The vision of the cheap card sitting in the recycling box amongst envelopes, pizza cartons, and assorted junk mail made Grace shiver. Her dad's name hadn't been uttered in the house, at least not within her earshot, for decades and now the card had reopened an old wound that suppurated anger and resentment. She shook herself down and dragged herself back to the present, looking around the room for the best place to start.

'Just get on with it,' she said as she opened the wardrobe – surely she could manage to fold clothes into charity shop bags.

Two hours later the hanging rails and shelves of the wardrobe were bare, and Grace sat down on the floor amongst piles of skirts, dresses, coats, blouses, jumpers, and cardigans, exhausted and too hot. She opened the window to allow a blast of summer air into the room. The breeze brought with it the scent of the sea that mingled with the sweet floral fragrance of the room.

The corner of a squat, cream-coloured cardboard box poked out from under the pile of shoes, boxes, and handbags at the bottom of the wardrobe and Grace pulled it out. The lid was decorated with a swirly gold pattern, faded by time. Carefully lifting the lid, Grace pulled back the thin, yellowish paper. Inside was a large, square, and very heavy photo album with a cream cover and a gold embossed border. She lifted the album from the box and leant back against the plump softness of the bed.

The first photograph was of a bride and groom under the familiar gothic arch at St. John's Church. Dovecote hadn't changed much. She ran a finger over the picture, over her grandmother's V-neck dress that demurely covered her knees. The dress was lovely, if rather plain, with half-sleeves and gathering over the shoulders and around the bust that gave the illusion of a large bow at the front. There was a flash of metal at the waist, maybe a belt. The black and white photograph made it impossible to tell what colour the dress was. She wore a small skull-cap type hat with a tiny wisp of netting rather than a veil. It was a world away from the silk and lace froth Grace had worn on her own wedding day, carefully chosen to obscure her swollen belly. Her grandfather's suit was single-breasted and looked like a regular work suit, no morning dress or fancy top hat in those days. There was a small bouquet of greenery in her grandmother's hand with a few roses poking out amongst the foliage. They had been incredibly good-looking in their youth. The best thing about the photo was the smiles on their faces that radiated warmth and happiness.

Flicking through the photographs it dawned on Grace that many of the people in them were probably dead by now. She looked into the faces of the young men, presumably friends and colleagues of her grandfather's. How many of them had fought, and died, in the war? Goosebumps formed on her arms, and she turned the page quickly.

Over the page was a picture of the bride, flanked by women all dressed up in their Sunday best. Straight knee-length skirts poked out from underneath winter coats and gloved fingers clutched boxy handbags. A couple of them were in uniform, possibly nurses, with stiff-looking caps perched on their heads. A tall, thin nun stood out in her wimple and habit. In the arms of an older woman with tight curls was a small girl, not quite two years old by the look of her. She had her thumb wedged into her mouth and her head snuggled against the woman's neck. With a long exhale Grace put the album back into the box and returned the lid.

Later that afternoon, Grace drove the short, but steeply uphill, distance to Bayview Care Home, parking at the top of the winding driveway. The severity of the two Edwardian red-bricked bay-fronted houses was softened by the recently constructed glass entrance linking them. Window boxes crammed with dahlias and chrysanthemums added a splash of welcoming colour. A warm, salty breeze swished through the leaves of the sycamore tree at the edge of the sloping lawn and caressed Grace's skin as she got out of the car. When her grandad had become too ill to live at home the previous summer, her grandmother had been reluctant to move him to Bayview. She hadn't said why, just that she'd rather there was somewhere else he could go. In the end, the specialist dementia care offered at Bayview was too good to turn down and it meant her grandad wasn't far from Seafoam Cottage. Her grandmother had always been tense when they'd visited though, and often would seem as lost in faraway memories as Grandad was. Funny how that was what came to mind as Grace pushed open the front door.

The instantly recognisable smell assaulted Grace's nose as she signed the visitor's book on the front desk. The pervasive chemical floral perfume, sprayed in the air with a heavy hand to mask the aroma of incontinence and bleach, and the stifling heat of the recreation room were two things Grace would never get used to. She would forever associate them with a helpless sadness that sat heavy in the pit of her stomach.

Richard was in his usual chair, a high-backed, cherry-red armchair with wipe-clean upholstery, by the far window that overlooked the front lawn and the sea. He had told her once that he liked that chair because it was the 'farthest one from Brenda, who talks to herself and smells of wee'. Not for the first time Grace wished she could take him home. Away from Brenda and the others. Away from the overpowering smell and the overbearing heat. But she knew she couldn't look after him herself. He was far too unwell for that now. He had gotten thinner, if that was possible, in the last few days and his shoulders were more hunched. Even so, he had an air of authority about him, which was impressive in jogging bottoms, slippers, and a dressing gown. He had a full head of hair that old age had turned fine and white. But his grey eyes were still those of the young groom in the wedding photos, although now nestled within folds of wrinkled skin.

'Hi, Grandad.' Grace smiled as she dropped her bag on the floor and sat down in the vacant chair next to him. He inclined his head very slightly towards her, his eyes glassy and devoid of recognition. This wasn't unusual; it had been a while since he had remembered her. The first time he asked her who she was, she'd cried in her car for an hour.

'I've got something to show you.'

This seemed to get his attention and his withered hand curled and unfurled in his lap.

Grace withdrew the photo album from her bag and watched as Richard's face brightened and his eyes focused. He recognised the album. She placed it on his lap and watched silently as he traced the gold embossing on the cover with a bony, crooked finger.

'Where did you get this?' His voice was a hoarse whisper and Grace hesitated. Heather had warned her that if anyone tried to tell him his wife was dead, he got very upset.

'Lily gave it to me to show you,' she lied.

'I expect she'll be along soon to see me,' he said. The light in his eyes was a dagger in Grace's heart.

'Yes, I expect she will,' she lied again. 'Shall I help you?' At Richard's nod, she opened the album.

'Hoo, hoo,' Richard exclaimed with a chuckle, 'quite the looker, wasn't I?'

Grace laughed too. 'Indeed, you were.'

'And still are,' added Heather as she passed by.

Grace and Richard leafed through the photographs. Some drew a comment from Richard, others left him tight-lipped. At some of them a shadow crossed his wrinkled face, and Grace didn't ask about the young men whose images clearly brought back painful memories. Richard was beginning to tire, his head lolled to one side and his eyes were misty, so Grace took the album from his lap and put it back in her bag. By the time she turned around to say goodbye, he was already asleep.

Afternoon had morphed into early evening by the time Grace got home. Having poured herself a large Merlot, she flopped down on the sofa. The house was always so quiet without Harry, and it was even more so now Lily had gone too. Her mobile pinged with a message:

Hi Mum. I asked Dad if I could go to the cinema with Jake and for a sleepover at Jake's after. He said it would be fine if you said yes. He says he'll pick me up tomorrow and bring me home. Can I go? Please? X

Grace sighed; her baby was growing up too fast.

It's fine with me. Thank you for asking and have a good time! Love you x

Thanks Mum. Luv u 2 x

How much longer would he put kisses on his texts? How much longer did she have before it became uncool for him to tell his mum he loved her? He was changing, growing so quickly. He would always be her baby, even when he, inevitably, outgrew her. Her phone pinged again. It was Rachel this time.

Hey, how are you doing? X

I'm keeping it together. Been sorting out some of Nanna's things. I found their wedding album, so I took it to show Grandad. He was thrilled. X

Ah lovely! I was just messaging about tonight.

In a moment of weakness, she'd agreed to go with Rachel to a speed-dating night at their local pub, The Royal Oak. She groaned. Going out would mean having to find something to wear that didn't make her look like a thirty-three-year-old-divorced-mother-of-one. She read the rest of Rachel's message.

The thing is, I'm really sorry but I'm going to have to cancel. Something's come up.

Grace frowned; it was most unlike Rachel to be so evasive. But, if it meant getting out of making small talk with random, desperate, needy, and probably weird, men, she'd take it. Clearly Rachel had got a better offer. She waited a moment before replying.

Oh no, and I was so looking forward to it!! Is everything alright?

Fine. Just some work thing I have to go to. Talk later. Xx

Something was definitely up; since when did Rachel go on 'work things'? She usually avoided them like the plague. Whatever it was Rachel would tell her in her own time. At least getting her evening back meant she could push on with sorting out the mess she'd made in her grandmother's bedroom *or* she could just sit on the sofa and watch some mindless television...

Three episodes of *Love Island* later, the wine glass in her hand was empty and, although tempted to refill it, there was a dull ache starting behind Grace's eyes. What she needed was an early night. Sleep had been hard to come by in the weeks since Lily's death, and the nights spent tossing and turning were beginning to take their toll.

Up on the landing, Grace paused outside Lily's bedroom door. Unable to help herself, she pushed open the door and stepped into the room. The open curtains allowed a shaft of moonlight to fall on the bed and on the photo album that Grace had left there after getting back from Bayview. She sat on the bed, cradling the album and rocking back and forth gently, as though trying to lull a baby to sleep. Was this all a part of grief? This soul-crushing fear of letting someone go without committing every second of their existence to memory. She tapped the lid of the box firmly. She needed to get a grip of herself. That's what her grandmother would have told her to do. Let it go, move on.

Grace opened the wardrobe door and leant down to place the album back where she'd found it. There was no need to clear everything out yet, it wasn't going anywhere, and neither was she. Her eye caught the edge of another box, larger than a shoe box, tucked amongst the tangle of stuff at the bottom of the wardrobe. Grace lifted it out and put it on the bed before flicking on the light.

The box was crammed with wallets of photographs and on

top was an A4 envelope folded in half and tied with a blue ribbon. Grace untied the ribbon and put her hand into the envelope. She drew out a bundle of thin paper that may have once been white, but that had yellowed with age. Letters. Grace separated the first letter and held it up to the light. The writing was neat and masculine and instantly recognisable from over thirty years of birthday and Christmas cards. Then she saw the date on the top – Singapore, May 1940.

It was very sweet that Lily had kept these letters from Richard. It must have been hard for them both, being so far away from each other, literally half a world, and a war-torn world at that. Richard loved seeing the wedding photos. Maybe it would be nice for him to see his letters again? She could read them to him. It would keep Lily alive just a little longer.

FIVE

LILY

June 1940

'Lily Mulholland, whatever has gotten into you? You can't go out on the ward looking like that, Matron will have a fit.' Dilys tutted, as she fussed with straightening my apron and adjusting my starched cap, so it sat squarely on my blonde curls.

Dilys had got the hang of a perfectly presented uniform early on in our nursing training and had frequently come to my rescue when I wasn't up to scratch. 'That's what friends are for,' she'd say with a smile on her round face, while rearranging my cape or smoothing my hem. I would like to think I'd improved with practice over the past two years, but when my mind was elsewhere, I did occasionally lapse. When I didn't respond, she put her hands on my shoulders.

'Are you still thinking about Richard?'

A long deep sigh seemed to come up from right down inside my standard-issue black laced Oxford shoes.

'I know I should have said yes, Dilys. Mummy and Daddy were most upset that I didn't.'

'But you didn't say no either.' Dilys paused at the door to

the ward, her freckled hand on the brass plate. 'So, there's nothing to worry about. When he comes back you can say yes then.'

'*If* he comes back. What if something happens to him in Singapore? What if he meets someone else?'

Dilys's hand dropped from the door, and she folded her arms tightly across her chest.

'Do you want to marry Richard Morrison or not?' she said, exasperation writ large on her wide forehead.

'Of course I do. Who wouldn't? He's well-off, has a good job and prospects. He's kind, caring, smart, handsome, steady, dependable, the perfect gentleman. But...'

'But what, Lily? Why didn't you say yes?'

'Because I'm frightened.'

Dilys's foot started tapping on the corridor's stone floor, like it did anytime she was impatient.

'I'm scared that I'm too young to settle down. What if I miss out on something big, something spectacular? What if...' I stopped as Dilys held up her hand.

'You daft goose,' she said with a grin. 'You've got yourself a solid, nice man, Lily, don't let him get away.' A haunted look fell across her eyes. I knew she was thinking of her Archie away at training camp in the Highlands, waiting for the day he'd be called upon to do his bit for King and Country. 'Once all this madness is over, good men might be in short supply the rate the Germans are going. Now, come on, pull yourself together. We better get in there before Matron notices we're late. She'll have our guts this time.'

I nodded feebly. Dilys was right – Richard was too good to lose, and I had been a fool to let him go to Singapore without accepting his proposal.

There was an ominous hush across the ward. Young, freshly trained nurses, mostly probationers like Dilys and me, moved silently from one bed to the next, scribbling notes and giving reassuring smiles to the injured men in their care. The past week had been the worst we'd seen at Brighton Municipal Hospital. Matron said it was good for our training; we felt entirely overwhelmed. We had very little time to prepare for the influx of injured soldiers rescued from Dunkirk. On the pre-operative ward, nurses had been reduced to laying mattresses on the floor, as the need outstripped the supply of beds. I gave Dilys what I hoped was an encouraging look and set off towards the far end of the ward to start my round.

We were lucky as most of the chaps on our ward were post-operative; clean, bandaged and confined to bed rest. Some had more serious injuries than others. Some seemed to be physically fine, with nothing more than cuts and bruises, but their eyes were blank and lifeless. It made me shiver when they looked at me. There was just nothing there.

Matron's booming 'Good morning' stopped me in my tracks. I turned towards the ward's double doors, fearing I was about to be reprimanded for daydreaming, or walking too slowly, or a wrinkle in my stocking. It wouldn't have been the first time.

'Nurse Mulholland, Nurse Franklin,' Matron hollered. Dilys and I caught each other's eyes. 'We need to get these men moved on. There's another batch coming in from surgical and we do not want to be holding things up. We need five beds, so determine the five most suitable candidates that can be relocated to the convalescent home. Quick smart, girls.'

She didn't have to ask us twice.

The young man in the bed halfway down the ward had come in with the first wave of soldiers a few days earlier. He couldn't have been much older than me and he didn't have frightening, dead eyes. No, Henri Benoit's brilliant blue eyes sparkled when he smiled. The way they glistened as I approached made my stomach flutter just a little.

'*Bonjour*, good morning,' he said. His accent elongating the vowels making the words stretch as though made of treacle.

'Good morning. You certainly sound as though you're in good spirits.'

He looked at me slightly blankly.

'Feeling well,' I clarified.

He tapped the thick bandage on his right thigh gently. 'Today, I cannot complain. I am one of, as you say, the "lucky ones".'

His eyes were fixed on me as I fussed around him, checking his temperature, taking a blood pressure reading. Being under his watchful gaze was what I imagined it felt like to sit for a portrait. He was studying me, and I rather liked it. I jotted down his vitals in his folder.

'You're in good health, Mr Benoit,' I said, blushing slightly as I glanced at his handsome face. 'I think you are well enough to move into convalescent care. There's not much more we can do for you in hospital.'

'Ah, but I fear not seeing your lovely face every day will make me very unwell. I think it is for the best I stay here under your care.'

My cheeks flared and I supressed a shy smile. He was such a smooth talker. No doubt he was the same with all the nurses, although Dilys had never mentioned it.

'I shall be coming with you. They're short of staff at Bayview, so Dilys and I are being lent out to them for a while.'

Henri let out a short chuckle. 'Ah, *bien*. In that case, I think I should absolutely go.'

It was most uncomfortable in the rickety old bus as we bumped our way along the twisty coastal road from Brighton to Dovecote, where Bayview Convalescent Home was situated. Albert, the elderly hospital porter at the wheel, was having trouble steering the bus and each bump and jolt was accompanied by pained moans and groans from our patients.

'Why do we have to go to Dovecote? I shall hate having to get on the train every day and we won't get back to Brighton before the blackout. I shall miss the start of the cinema shows,' Dilys complained as we sat together at the back of the bus.

'The first twenty minutes are just news reels and silly cartoons anyway, you won't miss much,' I replied. I didn't mind being transferred away from the hospital. I dearly loved nursing, I couldn't think of anything I would rather do, but it would be nice to get a bit of a break from it all and spend time in the pretty seaside town of Dovecote. I'd been there a few times with Richard for picnics on the cliffs and it was a rather charming place, with a darling little bookshop. And maybe Dovecote beach wasn't off-limits like Brighton's was. It would be lovely to dip a toe in the sea again.

'Blimey, Albert,' I cried as the bus bounced over a hole in the road and I nearly banged my head on the roof. 'We would really rather not have to take these men back to the hospital.'

'Sorry, Miss,' came the distinctly unapologetic muttered reply. Henri Benoit, who was in the seat in front of me, turned and winked at me causing my temperature to go up a notch. He then turned to his fellow Frenchman and said something to him which resulted in a scrap of paper and a pencil being handed over.

Miraculously the bus arrived at Bayview Convalescent Home with all its wheels still attached. We wound our way up the steep driveway, passing sloping lawns dotted with benches and a couple of large sycamore trees. Two figures were waiting outside the front of one of the imposing red brick buildings. I was glad it was sunny. On a dark, stormy day the houses with their large bay windows, high roofs, and mock-Tudor-fronted eaves would have looked foreboding and intimidating. A few window boxes would have cheered the place up, but I supposed there wasn't time or funds for such frivolities.

'Nuns?' Dilys whispered as the two women approached. 'We shall have to be on our best behaviour.'

I rolled my eyes. 'Oh Dilys, don't be silly. Nuns aren't all as fearsome as people say.'

The nun was tall and thin, her blue habit failing to disguise her stick-like figure. I couldn't immediately guess her age, perhaps around Mummy's age, so early forties. She had beady eyes; the kind of eyes that saw everything, not unlike Matron's. I was instantly as petrified of her as I was of Matron.

The other lady was an altogether friendlier prospect. She was short, round, and wore a tweed skirt and beige blouse. Half-moon glasses hung on a chain around her neck. Her red hair had just a few flecks of grey and was set in pin curls. She had the air of someone's kind, doting grandmother, and I estimated she was probably around sixty or so.

'Good morning, ladies. I'm Sister Margaret and this is Mrs Macnamara our manager. Might I suggest we get these men inside and settled in their rooms and then I can get you acquainted with how we do things at Bayview.'

'Yes, Sister,' I replied reaching to help one of the men down from the bus. My heart nearly exploded when Henri gripped my hand. When he was safely on firm ground, I withdrew my hand to find a folded piece of paper in my palm. I looked down at it and back up at him. There was an intense look in his eyes. Something fluttered inside me, like a very tentative butterfly. I began to unfold the paper.

He shook his head. '*Non*. Read it later, just before you go to sleep tonight.'

I must have been blushing furiously; my face was so hot. As we walked through the doors into the men's house, I tucked the note in the breast pocket of my uniform and nodded, I couldn't do anything more.

SIX
GRACE

September 2015

Harry had refused to let Grace drive him to school on the first day of term. Now that he was in Year 6, it was mortifyingly uncool to be dropped off by your mum, apparently. At the first sign of a wet morning he'd be begging for a lift. She'd been the same. As she waved him off from the gate of Seafoam Cottage, she blinked back tears. How was her baby starting his last year at primary school? In a year, he'd be off to secondary, and she was not ready for him to be that grown-up yet.

The cottage was too quiet after six weeks of having Harry around during the day. Thankfully a short-lived outbreak of norovirus at Bayview was over, so she could visit her grandfather again. She couldn't have held out much longer without reading the letters that were smouldering in her handbag. Waiting just a week had been hard enough.

The sycamore tree in the car park was starting to shed its leaves and the sunlight filtering through the branches was casting a dappled light across the tarmac.

'He's not in the best of moods today,' Heather whispered to Grace as she crossed the recreation room, heading for Richard's favoured bay window. The bad days were beginning to outnumber the good ones and Grace heaved a heavy sigh. Grace waved at Betty Jones as she passed. Her grandparents had been friends with Betty for years, since she and her mother, Sheila, had lived next door in Seaglass Cottage. Grace remembered Betty popping in occasionally for tea before she'd had a fall and had to move into Bayview, leaving Seaglass Cottage empty. Neither Betty nor her grandfather remembered any of that now.

'Hi, Grandad,' Grace said.

No response. He didn't even turn his head towards her. He continued to stare, glassy-eyed, at the orange and red leaves tumbling from the sycamore outside the window. Thanks to Bayview's location on the slope of the hill, the window offered a panoramic view of the town below. At a glance, Grace could pick out the train station, the tiled roof of The Seaside Café, Victoria Park, the sports pavilion, the lighthouse beyond the headland, and the row of shops along the High Street that led down to the beach. She couldn't quite spot Seafoam Cottage. The sycamore obscured her view.

'How are you today?'

Finally, a slight head tilt in her direction.

'I bumped into Reverend Clive yesterday, he said he'll come to see you soon. And Janice from the café said she'd been in the other week and brought you one of her sticky buns. That was nice of her, wasn't it?'

There was still no response from Richard, he just continued to stare out of the window. Grace pulled at a loose button on her cardigan. These days, when he was so closed off from the world and his damaged mind took him so far away from her, were the hardest. Would the stack of letters in her bag cheer him up? Or make him worse? She watched as his watery eyes stared blankly at the window. She had to try, even if she could give him just one moment of happy reminiscence. She reached into her bag and pulled out the envelope. Without any explanation she began to read out the first letter.

Singapore, May 1940

My Dearest Lily,

I have finally arrived. The journey was rather long and rough in places. I was grateful that you did not have to endure it. As first impressions go, Singapore seems to be an efficient kind of place, although I have not had a chance to explore extensively yet. The heat is quite remarkable and so unlike even the hottest summer day in England. The Syce (that is the name given to drivers here) who met me off the boat said it is the humidity that makes the difference. I shall need to purchase some additional climate appropriate attire. Cotton and linen seem to be customary in these parts. Certainly, there is no need for wools or tweeds.

I will be able to provide you with further details regarding the office and my permanent living arrangements when I write next. For the interim, I have been billeted in quarters in the Singapore Club which occupies part of the same building as my office. It is very agreeable and has a splendid view of the Anderson Bridge.

On a personal note, I do wish you had given me a response to my question before I left. It would provide me with some comfort while being parted from you. I do, however, appreciate you giving my proposal your deepest considerations. Although I am not prone to emotional outbursts, I do hope you know that I am very fond of you, and you would be doing me the utmost honour in consenting to be my bride. You shall be ever present in my thoughts while we are apart. I will offer nightly prayers that you are kept safe in these wretched times and that we are reunited before too long.

Do write soon, I shall be waiting for word from you.

Ever yours,

Richard

The formal tone of the letter was familiar and quite comforting. Richard showed no signs of even having heard her read his words. She paused, disconcerted. From this letter it seemed like he'd proposed to Lily before he'd left, but not received an answer.

'Bit cheeky of Nanna to make you wait the whole time you were away before accepting your proposal, Grandad.'

He didn't reply.

She turned to the next letter.

Singapore, July 1940

Darling Lily,

Thank you for your letter. It brought me much comfort to know that you are well. I am settling in nicely here. I am even finding that I am becoming accustomed to the heat! The chaps in the office are fine fellows and have introduced me well into Singapore society. I have joined both the YMCA Tennis Club and the Singapore Cricket Club. I am also being nominated for membership of the Tanglin Club. I understand it to be the most exclusive private club in Singapore and they have the finest swimming pool and the best dance floor on the island. Not that I shall be doing much dancing, my dear, not without you.

Work is going rather splendidly; rubber production is

steady and the supply chain quite uninterrupted. We are ready for an increase in export should it be required. Although, I may have to see if I can get a decent secretary. The poor lamb I have at my disposal is quite out of her depth and I fear for her health at times. If you were able to join me, there would be plenty of work here for a clever girl like you.

I do hope this tiresome war isn't getting you down. There is very little hint of any unpleasantness out here. Nasty business at Dunkirk by all accounts. I shouldn't fret; with Churchill in charge all will be well. I can't see it going on much longer. I am proud of you for doing your bit. I am sure the wounded at the hospital will be much cheered by your ministrations. Do stay safe though and stay out of London. Our air defences are good enough to keep the Luftwaffe away from the city, but better safe than sorry.

I look forward to hearing from you, although I know you are busy.

Yours eternally,

Richard

When Grace stopped reading and looked up, the expression on her grandfather's face had shifted ever so slightly. His head was inclined towards her, and his eyes seemed more focused. He slowly lifted his hand and made a 'carry on' gesture. Grace rapidly flicked to the next letter.

Singapore, August 1940

Dearest Lily,

Just time to write you a short note today for we are rather busy, and I have much to do before an important event this evening. I am to meet the Governor of Singapore, Sir Shenton Thomas, at a gala dinner hosted by one of the wealthiest and most influential local British families, the Carsons. It is a charity fundraiser organised by Lady Thomas to do with evacuated children or some such worthy endeavour. Maya Carson, the daughter of the family, is very keen to be doing her bit for the war effort. I do not wish to give the impression that I am spending all my time socialising. I am only attending as it will be a good opportunity to meet some of the key players in the rubber industry at local level. It is vital I get to know these people if we are to continue to work efficiently and expand our efforts should increased demand require a greater co-operation between all interested parties. My apologies, I should not be worrying you with the minutiae of my work, I don't wish to be one of those frightfully dull husbands who witter on about the office long after the end of the working day.

I should like to be able to tell Lady Thomas that my future wife will soon be travelling to join me out here, and I will delight in doing so the instant you give me your answer.

Yours in eternal hope,

Richard

There was the faintest hint of a smile now, so Grace carried on. The next letter was months later. The war must have begun to disrupt communication lines, or perhaps the distance between Richard and Lily was starting to take its toll on the relationship.

Singapore, January 1941

Darling Lily,

Please accept my apologies for the delay in writing to you. I have been in Malaya meeting with the suppliers of the sap we use as the base product in our rubber with my colleague, Neil Thompson (or Tommo as we call him). The work that is done there really is quite fascinating. It is reassuring to see that the jungle is indeed as impenetrable as we have been told. It would certainly be a demanding undertaking to attempt to get an army through by land, and the lack of fortification along the northern coast of Singapore Island does appear justified.

Life carries on here largely uninterrupted by the war. The parties and dancing continue. Last week, I attended a very lively gathering at the Tanglin Club; it was jolly good fun. Maya Carson, the daughter of the people who hosted that gala last summer, was there. She is tremendous fun. All the chaps and girls out here are good sports. The girls do marvellously well at keeping up with fashion trends and always make an effort to look their best. I do wish you could be here. I long to introduce you to the many friends I have made.

I do hope the war is not getting you down. I am very proud of the nursing work you are doing; we must all do our bit.

Do keep writing, I do so look forward to hearing your news.

Yours always,

Richard

A very light, soft chuckle escaped Richard's mouth. He was fully listening now, and a warm glow spread across Grace's chest. He was back with her.

Singapore, June 1941

Dearest Lily,

I write with the sad news that my dear old school friend David Wilkinshaw has been killed in North Africa. It's such a devastating loss. He had agreed to be my best man (should you accept my proposal). This war is taking too many young men, and we all hope and pray that it will end soon.

I am relieved to hear that you have fully recovered from your bout of tonsillitis. It can be a nasty thing. My secretary, Gregson, a fine chap from Durham, is spending much of his free time looking after his wife who suffers badly with inflamed tonsils. I have encouraged him to take her to hospital. We have a fine hospital here, the Alexandra. My friend Maya does the odd shift there as a volunteer nurse. You would have much in common with her.

You are quite right that it is not wise for you to travel here currently, even if it were possible. We are increasingly cut off from supplies and communications and, as the Japanese army continue through Malaya, it may become rather fraught. I do not for a moment expect them to take Singapore. We are heavily protected by the jungle to the north and the guns of Fort Siloso to the south, but we may have to give them a bit of a fight. We've had the odd stray bomb fall on us but nothing too severe, mainly it is an inconvenience. Not like the poor blighters in London. I cannot imagine how frightening it must be for those wretched people. I have heard stories of them having to shelter in underground stations which must be terribly uncomfortable.

I will close, as always, by wishing you be kept safe and with the promise of continued prayer that we be reunited as soon as possible.

Your loving friend,

Richard

Richard's face had become blank again; perhaps the mention of the death of his friend had been too much for him. Maybe she should have read the letters first, to avoid upsetting him. That was the last of them anyway. She leant forward, resting her elbows on her knees.

'Grandad, tell me about your time in Singapore,' she said very quietly.

Richard turned slowly towards her, confusion and disorientation clear on his face. Her heart sank.

'My dear, I don't know who you think I am, but I am not your grandfather. I never had any children of my own, you see. As for Singapore, there is nothing I can tell you, I have never been. But it sounds like a marvellous place, judging by that chap's letters, whoever he is. Now run along, I have important visitors coming for tea.'

Grace's heart thumped and her stomach twisted into a writhing mass of knots. All the same a wry smile caught on her lips.

'Oh, how lovely. Who's coming to tea?'

'Why, the Governor of Singapore and his wife, of course. I'm sure you must know Sir Shenton and Lady Thomas.'

Grace crept away from Richard's chair as his eyelids fluttered and he fell into a fitful sleep. In her car, she wiped tears from her eyes and put the letters back in the envelope. She'd been close, so close to getting him back and then just like that he was gone again.

'Ouch,' she said, as her cuticle caught on something inside the envelope. She pulled out the offending piece of paper. It was smaller than the letters, which explained how she'd missed it. It wasn't actually a letter; it was a typed Post Office telegram. The stamp said Dovecote and was dated 15 Feb 42.

EVACUATING STOP BOMBING INCREASING STOP AIMING FOR CEYLON STOP

WILL SEND WORD STOP
R STOP

Even though Grace knew Richard had survived and made it home, the sense of panic in those few short words made her blood run cold.

SEVEN

GRACE

September 2015

The following day was unseasonably beautiful. The autumn sunlight dappled the pavement through the thinning leaves and a warm, gentle breeze carried the smell of the sea. Every corner and street of Dovecote was like a well-loved blanket – familiar and comfortable. Grace had moved away to study journalism at university in London but retreated to the safety and security of Dovecote not long after graduating. As she closed the gate to Seafoam Cottage and walked along Beachfront Road, she banished the memories of how and why she'd come home from her head. They were best kept locked away.

It was a perk of being a self-employed magazine column writer that she could take off on a long walk if she fancied it. There couldn't be anything worse than being stuck in an office, tied to a desk all day. It was fine for Ben; he liked the structure of his accountancy firm. Grace preferred the flexibility that her work gave her.

There was something calming in the natural, earthy beauty

in the greys and blues of the pebbles and tempestuous waves. Even in autumn when the holidaymakers and day-trippers had fled, taking their deck chairs and beach towels with them, the scent of suntan lotion and ice cream lingered, mixing with the salt of the sea. Staring out to sea helped put things into perspective and the ever-present wind blew away any cobwebs that might have gathered. The sea didn't care whether you were anxious, lost, sad, happy, excited, or confused. It just swept in and out, over and over, like a heartbeat.

Grace strolled along The Promenade, with its Victorian, turquoise-painted, filigreed wrought-iron railing, running the length of the stony beach. Wide flowerbeds filled with bright red, pink, and yellow flowers separated the pedestrian walkway from Queen's Parade, the road parallel to the beach. Here and there, the path was dusted with sand and dotted with pockmarks and footprints imprinted by curious seagulls before the concrete dried. In the distance, the white, chalky headland and the lighthouse shimmered in the autumnal sunshine. Halfway along The Promenade, beyond the edge of Victoria Park and just before Dovecote Museum, was The Seaside Café – a small, steamy tearoom that sold very strong tea and the best sticky buns in town. Grace pushed open the pink-painted door and stepped inside. Janice was, as always, behind the counter. Her grey bob was clipped away from her face and her reading glasses hung from a chain around her neck. Janice was as much a Dovecote institution as the café itself and was still going strong in her seventies. There wasn't a time Grace could remember when Janice wasn't there, doling out gossip and advice along with the tea and buns. A few of the tables inside were occupied by elderly ladies drinking tea from mismatched flowery teacups.

'Afternoon, Janice,' Grace called as she approached the counter relieved to see the mound of sticky buns under the glass dome had been replenished. There was nothing quite so disappointing as coming all the way down to find Janice had sold out. It could ruin a whole day.

'Hello Grace, love. How's Richard?'

Grace shrugged. 'Much the same. I sat with him for a good long time yesterday and there were times I thought he was aware of what I was saying. But then, well, it was like a cloud passing over the sun, and he was gone again.'

Janice nodded sagely. 'Just keep talking to him, love. I'm sure he's glad of the company.'

'Yes, even if he doesn't know who I am, I know who he is and that's important, I guess. Oh, before I forget, Heather asked next time you smuggle in a sticky bun for Grandad, could you bring her one too?'

Janice laughed. 'I thought I'd gotten away with it. Richard's face was a picture when he saw it though. He always had a sweet tooth. I presume you're having one with your tea?'

'Of course, Janice.'

At one of the outside tables, under the pink awning with a mug of tea, a bun in front of her, and a few fat seagulls for company, Grace watched the waves roll over the shingle. Lost in thought about her grandfather and the unfairness of the illness that was taking him from her, it took her a moment to realise that the woman in the red coat coming towards her was Rachel.

'Well, hey you,' Grace called, waving. Rachel's smile seemed oddly forced, but she came over and sat down.

'Grace. Hi. I wasn't expecting to see you.'

'It's far too nice a day to waste indoors, so I thought I'd come out for some fresh air. Also, I'm putting off sorting more of Nanna's things.' She shook her head. 'I can't say why, but I'm really not looking forward to clearing out her knicker drawer.'

Rachel didn't seem to have heard her; she was glancing around, her left leg bouncing rapidly.

'Sorry, what?' Rachel finally said, eventually turning her attention back to Grace.

'I was just saying, never mind. Come on, what's up with you? First you cancel our speed-dating night and now you're like a cat on a hot tin roof!' Grace gave Rachel a narrow-eyed stare and put down her cup. 'Are you meeting someone?'

The tips of Rachel's ears turned blush pink.

'No. No, nothing like that,' she said, taking out her mobile and glancing at the screen before hastily putting it back in her pocket.

'Oh, come on, Rach. This is me you're talking to. We don't keep secrets from each other, we never have.' Rachel didn't reply. 'You're starting to worry me now. You're not sick, are you?' A wave of panic washed over Grace. 'Rachel, please.' But Rachel was already back on her feet and looking at Grace with weirdly startled eyes.

'I have to go. See you.'

'Rachel,' Grace shouted, but her friend was gone, hurrying down The Promenade, her phone at her ear. She rubbed her eyes as a particularly large seagull landed on the railings and tilted its head at the crumbs and currants on her plate. What had all that been about? Grace got up from the table, gathered her bag, exchanged smiles and waves with Janice, and headed back along the seafront. Harry would be home from school soon and dinner wouldn't make itself.

Grace looked up from her phone at the sound of the front door slamming. An email from the solicitor dealing with Lily's estate had distracted her from making a start on dinner. She'd have to ask Ben to have a look – he was the accountant. She put her phone down on the table as Harry bounded into the kitchen, heading straight for the fridge.

'Well, hello to you too,' she said, with a grin.

'Oh, sorry. Hi, Mum.'

'I'm going to put dinner on in a bit, so don't eat too much now.'

'But I'm starving. Can I have one of these?' He pulled a Cornetto from the freezer and waved it at her.

'Yeah, go on then. Here, pass me one too.' If her son was going to have his pudding before dinner, then so was she. Just once wouldn't hurt. Life was too short to be strict all the time. 'Good day?' she asked, as he joined her at the kitchen table.

'It was alright,' he said with a nonchalant shrug. 'We're doing a play after half-term. All the parents have to come and see it.'

'Oh, that sounds exciting. Have you got a part?'

'Just a small bit,' he shrugged.

'Well Dad and I will definitely come along to watch. Have you got much homework?'

Another shrug. 'Some.'

Grace supressed a sigh. Some days it was like she already had a teenager on her hands.

'Why don't you go upstairs, make a start, and I'll call you for dinner?'

Harry got up from his chair and thudded his way up the stairs.

'And no computer games,' Grace called after him. The only reply was a slammed door. With a groan she roused herself from the table and started gathering pans and ingredients for dinner. She was about to start chopping an onion when her phone buzzed.

Hey, sorry about earlier. Are you still up for coffee on Friday? Usual time and place?

She'd almost forgotten Rachel's earlier odd behaviour and typed an immediate reply.

Sure. If you need to chat in the meantime, you know where I am. Xx

There was no reply so with a shake of her head, Grace got back to making dinner. But there was an odd swirling in her stomach. Something wasn't right.

EIGHT

GRACE

September 2015

When they were teenagers Grace, Rachel, and Ben had occasionally bunked off Friday afternoon lessons for Dovecote beach. They had been good times; hanging out with her two best friends. As Rachel discovered boys and they discovered her, Grace and Ben were left on their own to fall in love. Ben had been the centre of her world and, back then, she had no intention of ever breaking free from his orbit. It was funny how, despite some of them floating away, they'd all ended up back on the same beach. They were like homing pigeons, or salmon, or pieces of flotsam washed around the world by the tide only to end up back where they started. These days it was just Rachel and Grace that met every Friday lunchtime for a hot drink and a chat. At the mini roundabout at the junction of Beachfront Road, the High Street, and Queen's Parade Grace made her way down the stone steps to the pebbly beach, the breeze ruffling her hair. The trepidation on Rachel's face banished her warm memories in an instant.

'Oh dear,' she said, sitting down on the stone bench and

taking the takeaway cup of tea Rachel handed her. 'I know that look. What is it this time? He's married but only technically; both he and his wife know it, but getting a divorce is so expensive and time-consuming? He described all his exes as "psychos"? He still lives with his mother? He wears dodgy little y-fronts? Or is he perfectly nice but his idea of foreplay is squeezing your boobs like he's trying to milk a cow?'

The edge of Rachel's mouth twitched upwards at Grace's all-too-accurate summary of Rachel's recent dating experiences.

'No, nothing like that,' Rachel eventually said, turning away from Grace and looking out over the beach. The sea seemed angry; waves crashed on rocks at the end of the beach sending spray into the air, blurring the view of the lighthouse.

'So, I was right, you are seeing someone. Come on then, tell me everything. If he's responsible for making you look like you're thinking of throwing yourself into the sea, then point me in his direction and I'll sort him out.'

Rachel took a long drink of her coffee and chewed her top lip for a minute before replying. 'We've only been seeing each other for a couple of weeks, but it's gotten serious pretty quickly.'

'You've slept with him, then?'

Rachel didn't need to reply, the deepening red of her cheeks did that for her.

'The problem is he's perfect. No, that's not true, he's not perfect but he's perfect for me. And he feels the same about me.' She gave Grace a glance out of the side of her eye. 'Even though it's only been a couple of weeks, I think he might be the one.'

'Wow, Rach, that's great. I'm well chuffed for you. But why is that a problem? Look at me, would you? What's going on?' The look in Rachel's eyes as she turned to face her did nothing to relieve the strange churning in Grace's stomach.

'This is really hard to say to you. Promise me you won't go mad?'

'Honey, this is me. Come on, just tell me. Whatever it is, it can't be that bad.'

'Alright. So, the thing is, the guy I've been seeing, and who I have completely fallen in love with, is Ben.'

Grace's stomach divebombed into her boots and a cold wave rippled over her skin. The paper cup slipped from her hand and landed on the ground. The white plastic lid popped off to release milky tea that seeped slowly between the pebbles. For a long moment, there was nothing except the rhythmic crash and rush of the waves, and the squawks of the circling seagulls. A loud thumping was coming from Grace's chest. After a long look out to sea, Grace broke the silence, her voice quivering.

'Ben? My Ben?'

'We didn't set out to end up like we have. We kept bumping into each other in random places, and on nights out, and when we started spending more time together, it just kind of happened.'

'Right,' Grace murmured. Her head was numb; she struggled to process what she'd been told.

'And I'm so sorry we kept it from you. I wasn't sure how serious it was going to get, but after the weekend when...'

'Don't. I don't need to know.' The rolling in Grace's stomach intensified. This couldn't be real. It couldn't be happening. 'It was him, wasn't it?' she croaked, finding her voice. 'On Tuesday, at the café. You were meeting him.'

Rachel swallowed and nodded.

'That's why you were so jumpy. You were meeting him, and you didn't want me to know.' The nausea was subsiding, leaving room for a burning anger to spark into life. 'And when you cancelled our night out?' It made so much sense. 'He palmed Harry off on Jake to go out with you instead.'

'Grace, honestly, that was a coincidence. Harry arranged that himself. But yes, when Ben found himself with a free evening, he called me and asked me if I'd go for a drink with him. One thing led to another and...'

'I said I don't need to know.' Little black spots swam at the edges of Grace's field of vision, making her dizzy.

'Grace?'

Rachel was watching her closely, probably surprised at how calmly Grace was taking this news. Inside, she was anything but calm. Her heart was pounding and every muscle in her body seemed to be shaking. She got to her feet slowly, wrapping her coat tighter around herself to ward off the biting wind that was coming up the beach from the sea.

'I should go,' she said, forcing the words between gritted teeth. She turned and walked away, the crunching of pebbles under her feet competing with the rushing sound in her ears.

'Grace,' Rachel called, and Grace turned slowly. 'I'm not sorry that Ben and I are in love. But I am sorry if it hurts you.'

Grace didn't trust herself to open her mouth to reply in case all that came out was the very unpleasant word that was bouncing around in her head. She wanted to scream it so loudly that everyone in Dovecote would hear.

As per usual Harry inhaled his dinner that evening and was waiting at the front door, bag and portable games console in hand. He was always like this on the days when Grace ferried him across town and deposited him at Ben's front door. She and Ben had managed, despite the slow dissolution of their marriage, to remain friends. It could have very easily gone the other way, but neither of them wanted to exist in vitriolic toxicity, mostly for Harry's sake. But, for the first time, Grace was dreading coming face-to-face with her ex-husband.

She wished she had some time before seeing Ben to give the wound Rachel had inflicted on her a chance to scab over. It would never fully heal. She didn't trust herself not to say something she'd later regret. How could he? How could either of them? She drummed her fingers nervously on the steering wheel as she drove up the High Street, down Courcey Road, and into Branwell Close.

Grace pulled up outside Ben's 1960s semi-detached house on the eastern outskirts of Dovecote. The salty spray from the sea didn't reach this far inland. Only the wind that funnelled through the streets gave a clue that they were near the coast. The builders had taken advantage of the location and added wooden cladding to the front upper half of the house. Any closer to the sea and the salt would have weathered it horribly. Even still, painting the wood white was an annual job, and one that Ben constantly moaned about.

Harry leapt from the car, dragging his bag behind him. He stopped halfway to the door and looked back. Grace reluctantly clambered out. There was always a slightly weird disconnect about walking up to her former marital home, like going back to visit your old school; as though you should still belong, that it should still be home, but you don't, and it isn't. Grace's stomach churned as she glanced up at the window of the master bedroom, almost expecting Rachel to be peering through the venetian blinds like a suburban Mrs Danvers.

'Dad,' Harry cried, throwing his arms around Ben's waist at the door.

'Hey, mate,' Ben replied, giving Harry's hair a tussle. She'd have to take Harry for a haircut sooner rather than later. Harry vanished inside, leaving Grace and Ben face-to-face on the front step. An uncomfortable minute stretched into eternity before Grace turned on her heel and walked away. She had reached the kerb when Ben caught up with her.

'Grace.'

'Don't, Ben. You can't land something like this on me and expect everything to be the same as it was before. I haven't worked out what to think about it all yet.' She massaged her temples. 'That's not true, I'm sickened and livid. I just don't know whether I'm angrier about you and her getting together or you both lying to me about it.'

'I wanted to tell you sooner.'

'Does Harry know?'

Ben shook his head. 'No, and I won't tell him unless you're happy with it.'

A short, sharp, hollow laugh escaped from Grace. 'Ben, I am never going to be happy with this. I mean, how...' She stopped and looked around the cul-de-sac of family homes. The kerb outside a semi-detached house on a quiet suburban street was not the place to be having this conversation. 'Harry needs to be at cricket practice at ten o'clock in the morning.'

Ben ran a hand through his hair. 'I know.'

He sounded weary. Grace was less than sympathetic. She was tired too. An afternoon of furiously scrubbing the bathrooms, while seething about your ex-husband and your best friend lying to you for weeks, would exhaust anyone.

'And he needs to be back on time on Sunday. He's got an early start on Monday for his school trip.' She leant closer to him. 'And if I hear one mention of Rachel when I ask Harry what he's done this weekend, he won't be coming anywhere near this house again.'

'You can't do that,' Ben snapped, his face stormy.

'I can and I will.' The slamming of the car door reverberated around the cul-de-sac.

Somehow Grace managed to get across town, park her car neatly on Beachfront Road, open the front door of Seafoam Cottage, and fall onto the sofa in the lounge before dissolving into tears.

NINE

LILY

June 1940

'Ah, it is so good to finally be out in the fresh air after being inside for so long,' Henri said, taking huge gulps of summer-scented, salt-tinged air. 'So, Nurse Mulholland, where are you taking me?' he added with a wink.

'I'm not going to make you walk far, don't worry,' I said, nodding towards the bench at the top of the sloping front lawn of Bayview. I'd sat on the bench a few times and it had a lovely view of the town and the beach. You could see right over to the chalk cliffs and the lighthouse and watch the smoke from the steam trains as they chugged in and out of Dovecote train station. 'Just over there. Can you manage that?'

'*Mais oui*, of course. I have been practising.'

I knew he had, I'd watched as each day he paced the recreation room from the bay window to the piano and back again, slowly getting stronger, his limp less pronounced. He still leant on a stick, so I offered him my arm, which he took, wrapping his long fingers around my elbow. His touch ignited a warm glow in my chest, that I quickly tried to extinguish. It was not the first time he'd thrown me into emotional disarray.

In the two weeks I had been at Bayview, Henri and I had stolen a few, all-too-brief, moments alone in the recreation room or in the bright sunroom at the back of the house. We talked about silly, inconsequential things, and we laughed. His blue eyes, dark hair, defined jawline, and bushy eyebrows were imprinted on my brain and kept me company on the short train ride back and forth to home in Brighton. He had continued to press secret notes into my hand if we passed in a corridor, or at times when there were too many people around to talk freely. The last one had sent me into quite a flutter. Of course, I was ashamed to even have any such thoughts about him; what with dear Richard loving me from half a world away. He had asked me to give him an answer to his proposal again in his last letter from Singapore. He'd also asked me to go out there. At least I was able to bat that one away with some rambling about U-boats and the government's advice against any travel; thank you Mr Churchill.

Henri's tightening grip brought me back to Bayview's sloping garden and I guided him to the bench under the sycamore tree. He looked grateful to be able to sit down, his leg must have been giving him more trouble than he was letting on.

'You are sad?' he said looking directly at me, his eyes boring deep down into my soul.

'Am I?'

'If you are not, you are doing a very good impression of *une femme triste*. I know you are missing your fiancé.'

I wished I'd never told him about Richard.

'He is not my fiancé. I haven't said yes yet,' I said with a wry smile.

Henri replied with a slow, yet expressive, shrug.

'The truth is I'm not really missing him, and I am ashamed of that.'

'I do not like seeing you sad. A woman with such a beautiful face should not be sad.'

I couldn't help the girlish giggle I let out.

'Ah, that is better,' he laughed. He put his hand to his chest and closed his eyes.

'Are you alright?' I asked, suddenly concerned. His eyes opened and he turned towards me again.

'I am just trying to capture this moment so that I remember it forever,' he said, dropping his hand from his chest down onto the bench between us. His little finger grazed mine, sending fireworks shooting up my arm into my head. He turned towards me, moved a fraction closer, closed his fingers around mine, and brought my hand, now held in his, up to his lips.

'My darling Lily,' he said, his voice low, 'I have seen so much, lived through so much, but when I am with you all the dark memories scatter like dandelion seeds in the wind. I cannot put into words the feelings I have.'

I tried to respond, to form coherent sentences, but found my voice was gone as if swept out to sea on the same wind as his dandelion seeds. He was still holding my hand. I wanted him to never let go.

'Lily,' he whispered, drawing closer to me. 'I should very much like to kiss you.'

I barely had a fleeting moment to register that I would quite like him to before it happened.

TEN

GRACE

September 2015

Back in Lily's bedroom the next morning, Grace was determined to tackle the collected jumble of belongings. She'd cried herself to sleep the previous night, following her row with Ben. Of course she'd never stop Harry from seeing Ben; that would be monstrous. Her grandmother would have been appalled that she'd said it even as an empty threat. *She* was appalled that she had. Life happened, things happened, people moved on. But it still hurt that both Ben and Rachel had lied. She wasn't going to cry over it any more though, she'd done that, and enough was enough. There was a chest of drawers by the window, and that was where she began.

Pulling open the top drawer she grumbled to herself, there wasn't anything worth saving. She grabbed an armful of M&S knickers, Playtex 'Cross Your Heart' bras, and restrictive-looking girdles, and threw them down on the bed. As she reached for an errant nylon slip that crackled with static, her fingers brushed against something papery. A white envelope with yellowing corners, tied with a white ribbon was camouflaged against the bottom of the drawer. Untying the ribbon, she reached into the envelope. Her eyes widened as she found herself holding another bundle of letters. These were not in Richard's familiar handwriting. These were written in a loopy, almost flowery, script. The first few weren't even letters; they were short notes seemingly scribbled in haste on scraps of yellowed paper with ragged, curling edges.

Lily,

When I saw you leaning over me that first morning, with your halo of blonde curls and your sparkling blue eyes, I was sure you were an angel. I have since come to realise that my first impression of you was true, you are indeed an angel. You have given me such pleasure with your cheerful company over the past few days that I no longer suffer with my wounds.

Henri

Lily,

What a joy it was to spend time with you today. Your skills as a nurse are only eclipsed by your beauty and tenderness as a friend. I wait with impatience for our next opportunity to sit awhile and talk of all things, and nothing.

Henri

Lily,

To exchange words for kisses as we have makes my heart sing. I have tasted beauty on your lips and, although you say you are promised to another, I still yearn for more. I find my heart full of you, unable to think of anything else but you. When can we meet again, my love? I pray it is soon for each passing second without you in my arms is torture.

Henri x

Grace's mouth fell open at what she was reading. Who? When? How? What the actual? She grasped for the next piece of paper, but the shrill ring of her mobile made her curse and reach for it instead. She hesitated to accept the call when she saw Ben's name on the screen. If Harry hadn't been with him, she probably would have hit the red icon. Instead, with her heart thumping, she made the split-second decision to press the green one.

'Grace?' Ben sounded frantic. 'Don't panic.'

If there was one thing guaranteed to make a mother panic, it was the adult in charge of her child telling her not to panic.

'I'm taking Harry to A&E in Brighton. He's had a bit of a knock at cricket. I think his wrist might be broken.'

'Is he alright?' Grace asked, already on her feet and heading down the stairs.

'He's a bit shook up and in a lot of pain. But he's conscious and everything...'

Grace could hear the fear in Ben's voice. He cared about and loved Harry as much as she did.

'I'm on my way. I'll meet you at the hospital.'

Ben poked his head out of the A&E department doors just as Grace arrived. His face was a sickly grey.

'He's been taken into triage, there's a nurse settling him now. I'm so sorry.'

'What happened?' she asked, as he led her through the double doors.

'A mis-timed googly. Bounced up off a tuft of grass and hit

him square in the wrist. I heard the crack from where I was. The poor bowler looked horrified.'

'Hey, sweetheart.' She rushed to the side of the bed where Harry was sitting cross-legged, cradling his arm. His eyes were red raw and there were wet tracks down his cheeks. She enveloped him in a tight hug, pulling him into her chest and stroking his hair.

'It's alright, it's alright,' she whispered. There were tears brewing in her own eyes and she gulped them away. It broke her heart to see him in pain.

The young red-haired nurse standing at the foot of the bed closed the folder she'd been writing in and gave Harry a smile.

'See, we said your mum wouldn't be long.' She turned to Grace. 'Hi, I'm Mandy. We need to get some pain relief into him. Any allergies?'

Grace shook her head.

'Lovely. Okay, give me a minute and I'll be back. Then once the pain's eased off a bit we can sort out getting an x-ray.' She gave Harry a reassuring smile as she left.

Grace and Ben sat down on either side of Harry's bed. Grace's initial panic had subsided, letting her anger at Ben back in.

Time ticked by and Harry, having perked up once the painkillers had kicked in, was playing on Ben's iPad one-handed. Occasionally Ben looked at Grace and opened his mouth as if to say something but closed it again without uttering a word. The longer they sat in silence, the more Grace's anger waned. It was awful not being able to talk to him. Maybe she could forgive him. Maybe she could find it in herself to accept his and Rachel's relationship. Maybe she could even find it in her heart to wish them well. Maybe.

Nurse Mandy came back. 'Time to get that x-ray,' she said cheerfully.

'Can Mum and Dad come?' Harry asked.

'We usually say one adult,' Mandy said, glancing from Grace to Ben. Ben nodded and Grace stood up.

'I'll get us some coffee while you're gone,' he said, and Grace managed a grateful smile.

By the time Grace and Harry returned from the x-ray department, the coffee Ben had bought was cold.

'I'll go and get you a fresh one,' Ben said when Grace grimaced.

'No, it's fine. Don't worry. Oh look.' Harry had fallen asleep on the bed. She climbed up next to him and hooked her arm around his shoulder, letting his head rest against her chest. 'He's had a tough day.'

'Yeah,' Ben said with a soft chuckle that made Grace miss him even though he was only a couple of feet away.

'Ben,' she whispered, not sure what the next words out of her mouth were going to be. 'About you and Rachel.'

'You want to talk about that now? Here?'

Grace nodded. 'Yeah. Here I have to keep my voice down and can't shout at you. Look it's messed up, the whole thing. In all honesty, it really hurts that you'd both act in a way that shows a monumental lack of concern for my feelings.' She waved away his burgeoning protestation. 'But it is what it is. I know neither of you would have set out to hurt me. If you're serious about her and about the two of you being together, I've no right to get in your way.'

Ben let out a long breath and glanced at the ceiling. When he looked back down his eyes were shining.

'Thank you. And you're right, we didn't set out for any of this to happen. It just sort of did. And I know it's weird. I think it's weird too, but I can't help the way we feel about each other.'

'I get that. It just might take a bit of getting used to, but I guess I can at least try. I just need to know one thing.'

'What's that?'

'Did you think about her in that way when we were together? Have I kept you from her all these years?' Grace stroked Harry's dark hair. 'I guess what I'm really asking is whether you married me out of a sense of obligation while all the time wanting, loving, her?'

Ben's hand on her knee was warm. He shook his head as he spoke. 'Not at all! Grace, I asked you to marry me because I loved you, nothing more, nothing less. And my God, I loved you so much. Part of me still does, and probably always will.'

'I'm sorry.'

'What for?'

'Everything.'

'You don't have to be. I don't regret a single minute of any of it.'

It was on the tip of her tongue to tell him about the letters she'd found that morning when Harry stirred.

'Mum?'

'I'm here, sweetie. You just fell asleep for a bit.'

'Are they going to cut my arm off?' he asked sleepily.

Grace ruffled his hair. 'No, honey. I don't think it will come to that.'

When Grace, Harry, and Ben emerged from the hospital, it was already getting dark. With a sprained wrist in a splint and a letter excusing Harry from P.E. for a few weeks, the three of them walked to Grace's car and she bundled him in.

'So,' Ben mumbled, looking rather unsure of himself.

'So?' Grace replied, shutting the car door.

'Are you and Rachel...'

Grace's fingers drummed an uneven rhythm on the roof of the car. 'I'll have a chat with her.'

'And are you alright with me telling Harry?'

She screwed up her face. 'Can you give him some time? Let him get over today first.'

Ben nodded. 'Sure. There's no rush, I guess.'

'Well, I'd better get him home.'

'Yeah. See you.'

'See you.' There was an odd lump in Grace's throat as she drove away. She missed Rachel.

ELEVEN

LILY

June 1940

The day was bleeding into evening as I pulled the heavy Bayview entrance door behind me at the end of my shift. I was going to have to hurry if I was going to catch the last train back to Brighton. Dilys had bunked off early to go to the pictures with her cousin. I didn't mind that it was getting dark, although it did mean I'd have to watch my step on the walk down the hill and through the town. There were a few loose paving slabs that were hazardous in the nightly blackouts. I didn't see what difference a few streetlights would make; Dovecote was hardly at the top of the German Airforce's bombing list. But it was probably better to be safe than sorry, even though the only places being hit so far were airfields. What was bringing my mood down was that Sister Margaret had moved me to the women's house away from Henri. She didn't say that she'd seen us on the bench the week before, but it wouldn't have surprised me. Nothing much escaped her watchful stare. My head was saying it was for the best that I was delivered from further temptation, I was spoken for after all, but my heart didn't agree. It was akin to torture not to see Henri. It made my chest ache to admit that I didn't experience the same pain at being separated from Richard.

My hand closed around the folded scrap of paper Dilys had pressed into my hand with a mischievous grin when she'd snuck into the women's house before bolting for the train station. I pulled the paper from the pocket of my cape and leant into the yellow light of the frosted-glass window. Someone should have pulled the blackout curtains. I was glad they hadn't. There was just enough light to read the words written in a loopy, elegant script. There was a single x at the bottom of the page, and I drew the paper up to my lips and kissed it.

'Lily.'

I turned, startled by the voice from the shadows.

'Henri?'

He stepped into the light and my heart thudded against my ribs.

'What are you doing out here? You should be in bed. If Sister Margaret finds out you've escaped your room, she'll have a fit.'

He looped his arm around my waist, drawing me into him. He smelt faintly of Brylcreem and Woodbines. He leant down and kissed me squarely and deeply.

'I don't care. I had to see you. I have missed you. Where have you been?'

'Sister Margaret moved me to the women's house,' I replied, trying to steady my trembling voice.

'Will you walk with me? I have something I wish to show you,' Henri asked. I nodded my reply and he lifted his arm from my waist and draped it across my shoulders instead. I gave no thought as to where we were going. I would have walked to hell and back with him.

A light drizzle began to fall, and Henri turned up the collar of the overcoat he was wearing. I knew his uniform had been laundered and patched up for when he was ready to be discharged from Bayview. In the meantime, Henri, like the others who were well enough to be allowed out of bed, had been given civilian clothes donated by the residents of Dovecote. They were mostly articles left behind at home by young men who'd joined up. A slight shiver passed through me as I wondered who the previous owner of the overcoat had been, and where he was now.

'What's wrong?' I asked, looking up at his furrowed eyebrows.

He shook his head and rearranged his features into a slight smile. 'Nothing.' He glanced up at the sky. 'Apart from this weather. Where I am from, it is possible to go for a moonlit stroll with a pretty girl without getting so wet.'

'Ah, yes. Welcome to England. We have excellent hospitals and marvellous tea, but rather inclement weather. You never did tell me where you are from.'

'I did not? Usually, I talk about home a lot. Perhaps the blue of your eyes distracted me.'

I gave him a light, playful slap on his arm.

'I am from a small fishing town west of Nice.' He sighed, lacing his fingers through mine. 'We have beautiful beaches, superb wine, and the best seafood you could ever hope to find.'

'And lots of pretty girls?'

'I suppose.'

'You miss it?'

'Very much. I miss my family, my home.'

'The pretty girls?'

We stopped at the entrance to Victoria Park. The rain had stopped so I had no objection to lingering. I had visited the park the previous summer with Richard and remembered there being tall, ornate, wrought-iron gates at the entrance. They must have been taken down to be melted into aeroplane parts or some such thing, as only a wooden gate now marked the way in.

A single streetlight had been left burning; the bulb shielded to deflect the light downwards in accordance with blackout regulations. In the faint orange glow, I could see an intensity in Henri's eyes that stole my breath. He stroked my cheek and brushed a loose curl of blonde hair back behind my ear. With his hand resting on the back of my head, he drew me into him.

'None of them are as beautiful as you,' he whispered.

Victoria Park wasn't the sort of place I would have ever considered going in the dark on my own. Even in the daylight, the gangs of youths that gathered amongst the dense undergrowth and clumps of trees were intimidating. Dilys and I had ventured down to eat our sandwiches one lunchtime but turned around sharpish and retreated to Bayview's garden. But when Henri took my hand and led me through the gate, I was fearless. As we walked around the edge of what had once been the cricket pitch, but was now a series of allotments for growing vegetables, I could hear the sea rushing over the pebbly beach. I had been most disappointed to find Dovecote beach just as barricaded and inaccessible as Brighton's. I longed to stroll along the shoreline with the sea tickling my feet. I brushed away the thought as we approached Dovecote's Victorian pavilion. With most of the local cricket team having been called up, the pavilion had been converted into a storeroom for sandbags and other Home Guard paraphernalia. The windows were dark and the door was shut, or so I thought. I gasped when Henri pushed the door and it swung open, revealing the pitch-black interior.

'After you,' Henri said. There was an invitation in his eyes. I should have experienced a twinge of trepidation, or at least a touch of nervousness at entering an unlit room, late in the evening, with a man I had only known for a few weeks. Instead, in a rather intoxicating and liberating way, I felt entirely safe and completely unafraid. Henri closed the door behind us, shutting out the faintest glimmer of silvery moonlight. I held my breath as my eyes adjusted to the lack of light. There was a scratch and a whoosh, and I watched Henri's face in the dancing light of the match he'd struck as he transferred the flame to a collection of candles. Soon a warm glow filled the room, throwing peculiar-shaped shadows across the walls. Henri beckoned me over to where a red tartan blanket had been spread on the floor. There was also a bottle of wine and two glasses.

'How on earth did you arrange this?' I asked.

The edges of Henri's lips twitched upwards. 'I promised the gentleman who agreed to be negligent in his duty to lock the door that I would not reveal his identity. Come. Sit.'

'You are a dark horse, Henri Benoit,' I chuckled as I unhooked my cape, throwing it on a nearby chair, before sitting down on the blanket, and tucking my skirt around my knees.

'A dark horse? That is a phrase I do not know.'

'Oh. It just means you're surprising. It's a good thing.' I was smiling in the dim light. 'If I had known you were planning something like this, I would have changed out of my uniform.'

The look in Henri's eyes made my heart beat a fraction faster. Richard had never looked at me like that – the way Cary Grant looked at Katharine Hepburn. Henri's eyes held a trace of hunger and a flash of desire. The longer he looked at me, the louder my pulse thundered in my ears and the more fleeting my thoughts about Richard became. My heart was winning the war against my head, far more convincingly than we were fighting the Germans. He held my glance as he reached for the bottle, only looking away to uncork it and pour two glasses.

'You know, you really shouldn't be drinking, not with the pain medication you're on,' I cautioned.

He grinned and leant close to me. 'I won't tell Sister Margaret if you don't.'

'I should certainly not want her to find out that I am here like this with you.'

'It is not right for two people to have a glass of wine together in England?'

I shook my head when, really, I should have nodded. 'Some people, like Sister Margaret, and Mrs Macnamara, would consider it improper for a young man and woman who are not married to be alone, without a chaperone, at night.'

'Do you think this is improper?' He said the word as though it left a bad taste in his mouth.

I could only smile and pray silently that the moment would not be interrupted by an air raid siren. Not tonight, please.

'It depends.' I blushed, looking at him from under my eyelashes, fully aware that Mummy and Daddy would be of the same opinion as Sister Margaret. There would be serious repercussions at home if they ever found out about this.

'On what does it depend?'

'On whether you are going to behave like a gentleman.'

Henri lifted the wine glass from my hand and put it down on the blanket. Once again, he cupped the back of my head with his hand and drew me towards him. He leant close to my ear, his warm breath on my neck making my skin tingle.

'*Absolument pas*,' he whispered.

'Thank God for that,' I breathed before he kissed me, deeply and urgently. I reached out and entwined my fingers in his thick, dark hair. The force of the kiss made me lean backwards. Without breaking away Henri gently guided me down until I was lying on the blanket with him. Our lips separated and he kissed my earlobe sending ripples of electricity through my body. Even if an air raid had sounded, I would have completely ignored it. He murmured my name into my hair before kissing me again, with even more urgency. I knew what he wanted to do, and I knew I was undeniably prepared to let him. More than that, I very much wanted him to.

TWELVE
GRACE

September 2015

It didn't take Grace long to settle Harry when they got back from Brighton General. He was shattered and, even with the bulky wrist support, he was fast asleep as soon as his head touched the pillow. She sat with him, just watching him sleep for a bit, the light from the hallway illuminating his face. Was it her imagination or was his jawline becoming more defined, less childlike? Already? But he was her baby.

Down in the kitchen, Grace added a dash of tonic to the large measure of gin she'd poured and climbed back upstairs, bone-tired and longing for her bed. There was a glint of light seeping under Lily's bedroom door and Grace tutted; she must have left it on when she rushed out to the hospital earlier. Pushing open the door, she saw the scattered pile of letters from the mysterious Henri that she'd been reading before Ben's phone call. Balancing her gin and tonic between thumb and forefinger, she scooped up the pages and flicked off the light.

She pulled the comforter she'd moved from her grandmother's bed to her own tightly around her chest, took a long sip of gin, and began reading the letters.

Bayview, Dovecote, June 1940

My sweet Lily,

Thank you. That is the most I can say. I understand what you gave me last night and I thank you for it. You have given me something so precious, so beautiful, and I am humbled and deeply in love with you. The soft caress of your skin on mine haunts me. I can still taste your sweetness on my lips. Oh, my love, you have awoken such deep passion in me that I fear I shall go mad if we two are not one again soon.

Your devoted lover,

Henri x

Grace read the note twice, blinking hard, not quite believing what she was reading. At least this letter had a date on it. A date which firmly established that while Richard was halfway around the world, Lily was carrying on with some random guy called Henri who, despite having a French name, seemed to have no problem fully expressing himself in English. And a place. Bayview? Here in Dovecote? Surely not? How? Grace took an even bigger sip of gin.

Salisbury, July 1940

My darling,

I should be grateful that I am deemed sufficiently well to have been declared fit to go back into battle. I have been sent to

Salisbury to prepare to return to France, but my heart is broken. Not seeing you every day, not being able to touch you, to caress your body, to be one with you, is a torture no man should have to endure. It is a pain that not even the prospect of returning to my beloved homeland can soothe. I will continue to write words of love to you until that glorious day when we can, at last, be together.

For now, my love, with deepest affection,

Henri x

Salisbury, August 1940

Lily,

As my day of departure grows ever nearer, I am watching the sun descend over the gardens of this grand house, all at once refreshed and melancholy. My wounds from Dunkerque are now fully healed, but the one in my heart remains. I can still feel the shadow of your touch on my skin, the trace of your lips on mine. My God, Lily, you have infiltrated every part of me and I long to be part of you once more. I long to feel your hot breath on my neck, to experience your body move with mine. The look in your eyes when we made love is seared on my brain. You have healed my body with your nursing skills and my mind with your love. How much longer must I endure being parted from you? Damn this war. Even a second is too long to wait to touch you once again.

I will go and pray you visit me in my dreams so at least there I may know you.

Yours with impatient passion,

Henri x

Grace's face burned with a mixture of shock and embarrassment. This man, this Henri, was clearly quite unabashed in displaying his emotions. These letters were passionate, almost to the point of being erotic. At least now there was some clue as to how Henri had come into Lily's life. It sounded like he had been wounded at Dunkirk and been treated very close to Lily's home. Her grandmother had talked a bit about the time she spent as a nurse in one of the big hospitals in Brighton. Had she meant during the war? Yes, hadn't a couple of Richard's letters made reference to her nursing work? But how did Bayview fit into it? If she'd also worked there and had carried on her affair with Henri there, no wonder she'd been reluctant for Richard to move in decades later. Grace made a mental note to look into the history of Bayview Care Home and find out its role in the war. So, Lily had nursed Henri and they had fallen in love, had a steamy passionate love affair and then what? What had happened to Henri? Grace grabbed hungrily at the next letter on the pile.

London, September 1940

My darling Lily,

It is thanks to you that I am restored to full physical health as you know. Alas the time that we both feared has come. I am being sent back to the front line, back to France. Although I am keen to see my homeland again, I am dying at the thought of being even further away from you. The thought of the sea being between us hurts my heart and makes me weep. I am full of joie de vivre since knowing you, and without you this life of mine, however long or short, would have no meaning. I beg of you with all my heart that you wait for me, my precious darling. Once the horrors of war have passed, I will return to you, my beautiful angel, and I will make you my wife and we shall be together forever. My love for you is eternal and I am sure that our union is one designed and blessed by Heaven itself. There is no other explanation for the way I love you, and for the magic our combined bodies create. My love, mon amour, I must go now, my train awaits. I will see you again. I will love you again. That is the vow I make with each and every part of my body and soul.

Until we meet again my love,

Henri x

The sole tear that dripped down Grace's cheek brought her crashing back to the present and she wiped it away with a shaky hand. She could imagine Henri, dashing in his uniform, frantically scribbling the last note to his true love before boarding a boat back to the front line. In his letter, he had sworn to come back for her. Why hadn't he? Or had he? What had happened? There was one more letter.

4 rue de Lyon, Paris, May 1945

My dearest darling Lily,

Praise to God, it is over. I am sorry I have not been able to write for such a long time. I have been deep underground, working for the war effort and have been unable to contact anyone, even you. As I promised in my last letter, I am now able to come back to you, if you will still have me. I know many years have passed and I have no doubt that a woman of your beauty and nature would have had many suitors, but I have held in my heart all this time the hope that you will still be mine. With all my soul I beg you, please send me your word and I will come to you with all possible haste. I do so long to take you in my arms and smother your whole body with kisses.

With hopeful expectation,

Henri xx

So, Henri had survived the war and written to Lily asking her if she still wanted him to come for her. By 1945 Lily was married to Richard. Grace drained her glass and rested her head against the headboard. Her grandfather must not have known. That had to be it, there was no way he would have married her if he'd known she'd been unfaithful, would he? It was quite a shock to find out her grandmother, a woman who had been so upright, and moral, and stable, had a colourful past.

'Oh Nanna,' she whispered into the night sky. 'What I wouldn't give to be able to talk to you about this and all the other parts of my life that seem to be falling apart.' Returning the letters to their storage envelope, the paper snagged on something. Grace reached in and pulled out a small white envelope, slightly thicker than a normal letter. It was addressed, in her grandmother's neat handwriting, to Mr. H Benoit, 4 rue de Lyon, Paris, France, and it was sealed.

Grace read the address again and gasped. She was holding a letter from her grandmother to Henri with no postmark on it; a letter her grandmother wrote, but never sent.

She slipped her finger under the flap but stopped before separating the stuck down paper. Something was stopping her from opening the letter and a small thought flickered at the edge of her mind – what if?

Grace put the letter down on her bedside table and flicked off the light. She laid her head on the pillow. There was one person she could talk to about what she'd discovered, one person who would tell her if her thoughts were entirely insane. But she wasn't currently speaking to her.

THIRTEEN

GRACE

September 2015

Harry hadn't stopped chattering since Grace picked him up from school the following Monday afternoon. As much as she loved her son, his constant stream of excited babbling was starting to grate just a fraction. She was still reeling from finding those letters, and their contents. She silently counted to ten as Harry waffled on about some computer game or other.

'Mum?' His plaintive cry dragged her attention back to her son. 'Are you listening?'

'Yes, I'm listening. I'm also trying to find a parking space.'

'There's one right there. Next to that green car.'

'Thank you,' she said through gritted teeth, cursing herself for not spotting it.

'Is Rachel going to be doing my eye test?' Harry asked, practically skipping along beside her. They made their way down Dovecote High Street, past Harrington's Bookshop and Dovecote Décor that sold seaside-themed knick-knacks and homewares, to Crawford's Opticians where Rachel worked. Harry had been inching closer and closer to the television, so it was probably a good idea to get his eyes looked at before he started having issues at school. She'd booked the appointment well before Friday's big revelation. Now the prospect of seeing Rachel was causing a squirming, writhing, mass of nerves in the pit of her stomach.

'Yes, of course. Why would we go to anyone else?' she replied, her insides knotting as they pushed open the glass door under the hand-painted green and gold sign and stepped inside.

'Hey, you,' said Rachel, stepping out from behind the desk just inside the door, a clipboard in her hand.

'Hi, Rachel,' replied Harry with a grin. 'Are you going to check my eyes?'

'I sure am, buddy. How's your wrist?'

Harry held up his splint, which had been covered in marker drawings and scribbles by his classmates that day. 'It's alright. I hope it'll be better by half-term.'

'That would be great.' Rachel turned to Grace. 'Can you fill this in?'

The switch in Rachel's tone of voice was like a shard of ice, stabbing between Grace's ribs and lodging itself in her heart. Grace avoided Rachel's eye as she took the clipboard, concentrating instead on the questionnaire in front of her.

'Harry, you ready?'

'Do you want me to come in with you?' Grace asked.

'Mum,' Harry groaned, rolling his eyes. 'I'm nearly eleven. I don't need you holding my hand all the time.'

'Oh,' said Grace, her stomach contracting sharply. Obviously Harry had to grow up, but quite so soon, and with quite so much cheek?

'Harry, if your mum wants to come in, that's fine,' Rachel offered in a thin attempt at compromise. 'Grace?'

Grace looked at Harry who flashed his best puppy-dog eyes at her.

'Why don't you see how you get on by yourself? Shout if you want me to come in, or if there are any questions you need me to answer.'

Harry beamed with satisfaction.

She watched Harry and Rachel disappear down the corridor and into the consulting room. Rachel was part of Harry's life now. She always had been, as her closest friend, but now... she was kind of his stepmum, even if he didn't know it yet. She glanced out of the shop window at the tapas restaurant opposite. Las Gaviotas had been their place to go, leaving Ben at home to mind Harry, to drink red wine and scoff garlic prawns. Grace's knees crumpled at the memories and she fell into the plastic chair, knocking against the overgrown potted plant next to her and nearly sending it crashing into the display of glasses in the shop window. There had always been the chance that, at some point, Ben might meet someone. Would the idea of Ben and a strange woman be easier to stomach than the image of him and Rachel together in her former marital home? With a sigh, she forced the hypothetical, unhelpful question out of her consciousness. She needed to focus on rebuilding her shattered friendship. If she didn't, her relationship with Ben would suffer, which in turn would affect Harry. Ultimately, her need for Rachel's support and friendship was greater than her anger at Rachel for replacing her at Ben's side.

'Mum, guess what?' Harry's excited yelp yanked Grace from her introspections. 'Rachel says I need glasses. Isn't that so cool?'

Grace looked up at Rachel.

'He's a little bit short-sighted in both eyes. He could probably get by without glasses, but it might start affecting his schoolwork, especially with the amount of computer work they do in Year 6. So, I'd recommend a pair to give him a bit of a hand and to prevent any damage from overcorrection.'

'And you're happy about it?' Grace asked, giving Harry a light punch on the arm.

'Yeah. All the cleverest people have glasses and Jake's cousin Alice Jackson said guys with glasses are really cute.'

'Oh, so this is all about a girl, is it?' Grace shook her head. She hadn't expected to be asking him that for quite a few years yet. She had been well into her teens before she developed her first crush, on a certain Ben Curtis.

'The ones that will fit you are over there,' Rachel said, pointing to a stand on the other side of the shop. 'Why don't you go and pick out a few pairs you like the look of?'

'Awesome,' Harry breathed as he raced across the room.

'Grace,' Rachel started.

'I better go and help him,' Grace said, only a little more frostily than she'd intended. Taking the first steps towards reconciliation was going to be harder than she'd expected.

Harry was trying on a pair of round metal-rimmed glasses and shaking his head when Grace joined him by the mirror.

'I look like something from the olden days,' he laughed, taking the glasses off and putting them back on the display.

'I don't know, those were all the rage when I was young,' Grace said.

'Yeah, the olden days. I like these ones. These are cool.'

Grace's stomach did a little flip when Harry reached for a pair of black-rimmed specs. She pushed away the sudden thought that leapt at her the minute he put them on and tried to look at her son objectively. The glasses really suited him.

'Can I get these?'

'If they're the ones you want, then sure,' she said trying to keep her voice steady.

Rachel didn't meet Grace's eyes as Grace handed over her credit card to pay for the glasses.

'I'll let you know when they're ready for collection,' she said, handing back the card.

Grace's heart thudded and her eyes brimmed with tears. God, how she longed to throw her arms around Rachel, forgive her for everything, and go back to how they had been. She'd promised Ben she'd speak to Rachel but now she couldn't do it. Something was holding her back. Pride? Stubbornness? Wanting Rachel to apologise first? Whatever it was made her turn and usher Harry out of the shop without another word.

FOURTEEN
GRACE

September 2015

In the days following Harry's eye test, Grace had tried, and failed, to compose several texts to Rachel. She wanted to say she was sorry about how things were, and that she wanted Rachel to be happy, but she couldn't form an appropriate sentence. *Hi, do you want to meet up for a chat?* looked insufficient, shallow. Grace had started typing again when the doorbell of Seafoam Cottage chimed, nearly making her drop her phone.

'Hi,' Rachel said, holding out a plastic box. 'Harry's glasses came in and I thought I'd drop them round.'

'Oh. Thanks.' Grace's throat turned dry. 'Do you need to check them on him?'

Rachel hesitated. 'I should do. But...'

'You'd better come in, then,' Grace said. 'Harry,' she called up the stairs. 'Rachel's here and she's got your glasses. Can you come down please?'

Harry bounded down the stairs and into the kitchen.

'Awesome. Alice was asking when I'd get them,' he said excitedly.

'I'm hearing an awful lot about this Alice,' Grace said with a smirk. 'I think I should have a chat with her mother.'

'Mum,' Harry groaned. 'Please don't.'

Rachel opened the box and passed the black-rimmed glasses to Harry. When he slipped them on that odd tugging started up in Grace's chest again, and it wasn't just because they made him look far too grown-up.

'Mum, this is amazing!' Harry gasped, looking around the kitchen. 'I can even read the words on Nanna's cookery books.'

'Just take it steady for a couple of days, Harry,' Rachel urged. 'You might find things a bit full-on now that you can see clearly. And don't sit so close to the television any more, or you'll be needing square glasses for your square eyes.'

Harry nodded earnestly and Grace had to laugh.

'Go on, see how you get on with your homework. You've got that history project due tomorrow that you need to finish. Be careful on the stairs.'

Harry rolled his eyes at Rachel. 'Mum's no fun.'

'What do you say to Rachel?' Grace said, giving him a light play-punch on his arm. 'She came round especially to bring your glasses.'

'Thanks, Rachel.'

'You're welcome, Harry. I needed an excuse to pop over.'

Grace glanced away as Rachel gave her a look. When Harry had run back upstairs and slammed his bedroom door, Grace and Rachel were left at the bleached pine kitchen table in an awkward silence.

'I could do with a glass of wine,' Grace admitted, getting up and going to the fridge. Without waiting for Rachel's reply, Grace poured two glasses and put them down on the table. They both took a large mouthful and their glasses landed back on the table in perfect synchronicity.

'I'm sorry,' they both said at the same time. Their words hung in the air for a moment before they both laughed.

'I'll go first, I have more to apologise for,' Grace said, investigating the contents of her glass closely. 'I'm sorry I've been ignoring you, and for how I reacted.'

'No, I'm sorry for the way I landed it on you. I probably could have done it better. Maybe Ben was right, and we should have told you together.' Rachel looked down at her hands. 'Are you still furious at us?'

'How did you know I was furious?'

Rachel gave her a lopsided smile. 'I would have been.'

'I'm not going to lie, I'm not thrilled about it. It's just a bit weird. But,' Grace drew a long breath and let it out slowly, 'you're both good people, who deserve a good person in their lives. Lord knows, you've had shocking luck with men.'

'Made bad choices you mean,' Rachel replied with an arched eyebrow.

'Maybe a bit of that too. And Ben, well, he's one of the good ones. I guess what I'm trying to say is that it bothers me, but not enough to lose my best friend over.'

Rachel reached across the table and took Grace's hand in hers. 'Thank you. And hey,' she said with a grin, 'at least you know I'll get on with Harry.'

Grace chuckled. 'Yeah, God forbid he'd end up with an evil stepmother.'

'Hold your horses. Let's not get carried away. Ben and I have only been together a month, don't go buying a hat yet.' Rachel's smile faded. 'You've had a rough time of late with everything. How are you doing, really?'

Grace let out a sigh. 'You don't know the half of it. Wait until I show you the letters I found hidden in Nanna's knicker drawer.'

Grace refilled their wine glasses while Rachel read Henri's letters. Her friend's eyes widening as she turned each page.

'Flipping heck, Grace!' Rachel let out a puff of breath as she put the last letter down on the table. 'These are... wow, I mean... wow.'

'Tell me about it. That was pretty much my reaction. I have so many questions.'

'Me too. Like what happened to him, this Henri?'

'And did Grandad ever know?'

Rachel's hand went to her chest. 'Oh, I hadn't thought of that. Poor Richard. I mean, fair play to your nan for pulling a fit French soldier, but poor Richard.'

Grace flinched. 'Can you not use the word "pull" in relation to my grandmother, please.'

'Sorry,' Rachel said, leafing through the letters again. 'But that's totally what happened, right?'

Grace leant forward, picking up a letter and putting it back down again. 'It does sound like it.'

'This guy was pretty keen on her. I mean, this last letter, when he says he wants to come back for her. That's like Hollywood movie levels of romance. I wonder why she said no?'

'Probably because she was married to Grandad by then.'

'Oh yeah. That would make sense.'

'I'm guessing Nanna waited for Henri to get in touch, but he never did. She must have thought he'd met someone else, or changed his mind, or even been killed. And when Grandad came back from Singapore, I guess she fell for him again. He wrote to her too, and she also kept his letters. I took them to Bayview and read them to Grandad. For a moment I thought he remembered, but...' She shook her head sadly.

Rachel squeezed her hand. 'I'm sure on some level he did.'

Grace sighed. 'Maybe.'

'Were Richard's letters as hot as these?'

Grace laughed. 'Oh God no, his were very English. Very formal, and definitely no mention of any rumpy-pumpy which I'm very glad about. There is one other thing. I also found this.' She handed the last envelope to Rachel. 'It's a letter from

Nanna to Henri,' she said, her voice reduced to a breathless whisper.

'How come you've not opened it?'

'I can't. I mean it feels wrong to.' She looked up at Rachel, who was staring at her with amusement in her eyes. 'Rachel, what if he's still alive? What if I can find him?'

'Grace, honey, be serious. He'd be well into his nineties, if not a hundred. Sorry to say this, but it's quite likely he's no longer with us.'

'But what if he is?'

'And what? You track him down, give him Lily's letter and what?'

'I don't know. But...'

'Or you could just open the letter.'

Grace shook her head. 'I have to try, Rachel. I don't know why, but something is telling me finding this letter wasn't an accident. I need to find him.'

It was a little disconcerting, being the third wheel, sat around a table with Ben and Rachel in The Royal Oak a week later. It was a rare chance for the three of them to get an evening out together, as Harry was at Jake's. The Royal Oak was a handy place to meet, being slap bang in the middle between Ben's house and Seafoam Cottage. And where else would they go? They'd been regulars in the pub since they were legally allowed to be, if not before. The oak panels and worn fabric were comfortable and homely. In the winter many a Dovecote resident warmed their hands over the roaring fire. It wasn't cold enough for that yet, being only mid-September, but it wouldn't be long. Ben and Rachel were doing their best to make it as unawkward as possible and were keeping their hands off each other. Now that she'd got to the bottom of a large Malbec, Grace was finding that she cared less about it. There were bigger things in the world to worry about, like her so far fruitless search for her grandmother's wartime sweetheart. She'd been searching online for a week and was getting nowhere.

'No joy, then?' Ben asked, coming back to the table with the next round that Declan, the perma-tanned, baby-faced barman, had placed on the bar without Ben needing to ask. Grace claimed her glass of red.

'Nothing. I did find a couple of Henri Benoits on Google, but they can't be him. One's a Canadian politician, the other a forty-year-old nuclear physicist.'

'Bummer,' Rachel said solemnly.

Ben shook his head. 'I don't know. I mean, maybe it's for the best.'

'You're not suggesting she give up, are you?' Rachel shot Ben a horrified look.

'I just mean, maybe it's a sign,' said Ben, shrinking back slightly from Rachel's glare. Grace tried not to smile.

'A sign of what, exactly?' Rachel countered.

'That maybe it's not meant to be.'

Grace sighed. 'Maybe you're right, Ben. Maybe I should let it go.'

Rachel slammed her hand down on the table making them jump. 'Absolutely not. Grace, last Friday, when you showed me the letter, I was a bit like what's the big deal? But the more I think about it, the more I think you're right. You have to find him.'

'Rach, the odds are like a billion to one that he's even still alive. I just don't think Grace should get her hopes up.'

'Oh, where's your sense of romance? Grace, listen to me. Don't give up. You're meant to find him, to give him Lily's letter. I know it, in here.' She put a hand to her chest.

'I think you've had quite enough wine,' Ben chuckled, shaking his head and giving his pint his full attention.

'Whatever,' Rachel said, giving him another withering

glance. 'Anyway, Grace. So, you've found nothing on Google. What's next?'

Grace shrugged. 'I'm not sure.'

'What about the Royal British Legion, you know, the poppy people? Don't they reunite war veterans with long lost relatives?'

'I'd not thought of that,' Grace said, smiling. 'But I'm not a relative, am I? They probably won't be able to help.'

Rachel let out a soft grunt. 'Oh yeah. Well, you'll think of something.'

A thought formed in Grace's head, like a butterfly emerging from its chrysalis but she pushed it away almost as it was growing. There was someone who might be able to help, but no; it would mean dredging up too much of the past.

'So anyway,' Ben said, breaking into the thought that made Grace's insides liquify. 'Can we tell Harry now. You know, about us?'

Grace sat back in her seat. It was a big step for her to agree for them all to take. Once Harry knew, there would be no going back and whatever the outcome of Ben and Rachel's relationship, it would affect him. Was she ready to expose him to that? However, he was a sensible kid and, while he might think it was a bit weird, most likely he'd just be happy that Ben was happy. There was such a hopeful look on Ben's face, mirrored on Rachel's, that Grace's heart melted a fraction.

'Oh fine, go on then,' she conceded. 'Just be gentle with him.' She caught the look that Ben gave Rachel, and the movement of his hand onto her knee. The smallest shard of jealousy spiked in her. It would be nice to have someone who looked at her the way they looked at each other, but what were the chances of that happening?

FIFTEEN

GRACE

September 2015

It had been so long since Grace had come up to London from Dovecote that it surprised her how easy the journey was. She'd have to do it more, maybe bring Harry up one weekend. There was so much he'd love to see and do. She stood outside the Imperial War Museum in Lambeth on Thursday morning for a long moment, looking up at the portico and the copper dome-topped tower. It was a seriously impressive building, but it was who was waiting inside that had turned Grace's stomach into a bubbling pit of nerves.

It took Grace no more than a couple of seconds to spot James at the table by the window of the Imperial War Museum café. The thought that came to her while having drinks with Ben and Rachel had refused to leave her head over the weekend. A quick search of the museum's staff page had confirmed her ex-boyfriend James Rutherford still worked there. He was Dr James Rutherford these days. Grace had no idea what a curator did, but whatever it was warranted a bio on the website, and a contact email address, but no photo. She'd emailed him before she lost her nerve and spent the rest of the weekend wishing she could turn back time. His reply, when it came on Monday morning, gave no hint as to his emotional state. What must he have thought when her name appeared in his inbox?

Her heart was beating double time as she covertly watched him. Would she have sent the email if a photo had forewarned her that he hadn't changed a bit in nearly twelve years? He was a little more filled out than he'd been the last time she'd seen him; his face was a little rounder. It suited him as he'd always been a bit on the skinny side. His dark hair was still the same, right down to the floppy fringe falling into his eyes as he leant over the book he was reading. The urge to turn and run away was hard to resist, and the memories and emotions flooding over her threatened to engulf her. She was a heartbeat away from giving into the temptation to flee when he put the book down and saw her. Oh God, he even had the same glasses. The colour of his eyes still reminded her of melted chocolate. He got slowly to his feet. Grace moved as though through treacle towards him.

'Hi,' she said.

'Hi,' he replied. 'It really is you. I've been wondering whether there are two Grace Lyttletons in the world.'

There was a seemingly endless silence as they worked out how to greet each other. Should she hug him? He didn't look like he wanted to be hugged. As though by silent mutual agreement, there was no physical contact and Grace's heart rate began to return to normal, although her palms were still clammy. She sat down opposite him, and he put the book into his bag.

'I'm sorry about your grandmother,' he said.

'Thank you. Yes, I'm going to miss her.'

Another silence.

'How have you been?' he asked.

'Good. You?'

'Yeah fine. Busy.'

Good. Fine. Busy. Vanilla responses offering a condensed summary of over eleven years. This was a mistake. She never should have emailed him. The silence was laden with unasked questions. Perhaps she should apologise for what she had done all those years ago. Perhaps it would be better to just mention the elephant in the room. Grace opened her mouth and closed it wordlessly.

'Tell me about this person you're trying to find. You didn't put much detail in your email. I don't know how much help I can be.' The leaden atmosphere lifted, and Grace was grateful James had reminded her why she was there in the first place, before she had a chance to make the meeting even more awkward.

'When I was tidying out some of Nanna's things, I came across some old letters. There were some written by Grandad from when he was in Singapore during the war, but there were also some from someone called Henri Benoit. From what I can make out, he ended up in hospital in Brighton after being evacuated from Dunkirk, where he met Nanna. He was then moved to Bayview Convalescent Home, in Dovecote.'

James's left eyebrow flicked slightly.

'I know, what are the chances?'

James didn't laugh and Grace swallowed awkwardly. 'From the letters, it is pretty clear that they were, well, more than friends.'

James gave her a brief, questioning look, his left eyebrow now fully raised. 'And it's him you want to find?'

How many times had he given her that look? Mostly there had been amusement behind it, but this time he just looked a little concerned that she might be a bit unhinged.

'Yes.'

'Why?'

'There's a couple of reasons.' Grace withdrew Lily's unsent

letter from her bag and put it on the table between them. 'Including this. That's Nanna's handwriting.'

James reached for the letter and pulled it closer. No wedding ring. No indent either. Suddenly conscious of the pink mark that ran around her own ring finger, she clasped her hands together on her lap.

'A letter she wrote but never sent?'

'Uh huh. I'd love to know what happened between him and Nanna, and I think this letter might give me some answers.'

'Why don't you just open it and read it?'

'I don't know, I just think it'd be wrong to without knowing whether he's still alive.'

He shrugged. Another wave of memories flooded Grace; such was the familiarity of the slight movement of his shoulder.

'I get that.' He jotted down the address in his notebook and handed the letter back to her. 'So, if I can track him down, and he's still alive, what then?'

'I'd like to meet him.'

'Gracie, he'll be over ninety years old. He probably won't even remember your grandmother.'

'I know, I know.' The way James said her name sounded like home. No one else had ever called her Gracie, and hearing it again was all at once comforting and uncomfortable. 'But I've read his letters. He was mad about her. I've never read anything like them. They're so full of passion and love. If she felt the same way about him, then I'd like to meet him.'

His eyes searched her.

'I'll see what I can do. We know he survived the war and ended up in Paris in 1945. It might be hard to find out what he did, or where he went from there, but I'll give it a go.'

'Thank you.'

James checked his watch. 'Sorry, I have to go, I've a meeting to get to.'

Grace tucked a strand of her golden-blonde hair back behind her ear. 'Sure, no worries.'

Another, slightly less awkward, silence.

'It's good to see you again, it's been a long time,' he said haltingly.

'Yes, it has,' she replied, her voice strangely quiet.

James cleared his throat. 'Anyway, I'll let you know what I can find out.'

He had turned and walked away by the time Grace formulated a reply.

Left alone amongst the hubbub of the café, Grace tried to get her head around the vivid, harsh, unnameable emotions that seeing James had left her battling. It had been a little disconcerting to see him, and to see that he hadn't changed, but it had also been quite nice. He was looking well, that was the main thing. He was still the bookish young man she'd known but with an added confidence and presence. Their reunion had rekindled a deep sadness, and a lingering guilt about what they had been, and what, thanks to her, they had lost. But she was one step closer to finding Henri, and that was what she'd come for.

There was a long queue at the café's counter now and, aware of the pointed looks she was getting from people searching for an empty table, she got up and wandered out into the main hall. On the other side of the glass entrance doors, rain splashed the stone steps, so she opted for a wander around the museum.

The first floor was dedicated to the turning points of the Second World War. Towards the back of the displays of flying suits, flags, ammunition, and model ships, there was a tableau of black and white photographs labelled 'Escape from Dunkirk'. The first was heart-rending: hundreds, maybe thousands, of men lined up on a beach looking like penguins huddling together against the Antarctic winds. The line stretched far into the distance, far beyond the point where the beach ended, and the sea began. Grace stared at it for a long time, wondering who each of the men in long coats were, and how many of them made it home.

The last photograph momentarily winded her. It was of a group of French soldiers who had been rescued from Dunkirk and brought to relative, if temporary, safety in England. They were leaning out of a train window giving thumbs up signs to the photographer. They were smiling but their eyes held a strange, haunted blankness and looking at each young man in turn sent a shiver down Grace's spine. It was impossibly unlikely that any of the men in the photograph were Henri Benoit but, all the same, Grace examined each face closely just in case.

Surprisingly unsettled and growing tired of battling crowds of unsupervised school children, Grace headed for the doors. The earlier rain shower had passed, leaving puddles and dripping leaves for Grace to navigate as she made her way towards Lambeth North tube station. The sun came out as she was about to pass under the red-tiled station entrance and the sudden burst of warmth encouraged her to keep walking. She strolled up past St Thomas' Hospital, around the back of County Hall avoiding the crowds of tourists on Westminster Bridge, emerging from the maze of office buildings into the green space of Jubilee Park. She shielded her eyes from the beaming sun as she looked up at the glistening white and glass of the London Eye.

Passing under the railway bridge and on to Southbank, Grace stopped for a moment to look at the river. It was greyer and murkier than she remembered, but maybe that was because the last time she'd walked along the wide path, the whole world had shone with that special glow that only those in love can see.

With twelve-year-old memories weighing heavily on her,

she carried on under Waterloo Bridge, pausing a moment to cast a quick glance over the rows of second-hand books laid out on trestle tables. She'd been here with James too, looking for cheap copies of classic books, trying to stretch their student budgets as far as they could. They'd been so young, just second-year university students, when they'd met at a cheesy 80s night at the Student Union bar. James hadn't even planned on going out that night, but his mates had persuaded him to put down his essay on the Franco-Prussian War and go for a pint instead. Grace had spent more time in the bar than she probably should have, but it was pretty much a given that the journalism students liked a drink or two. Her group of friends certainly lived up to the stereotype. A memory broke the surface of her mind: a song, a dark-haired, bespectacled, bookish young man catching her eye across the dancefloor and holding it. Grace wiped away a stray tear that was making its way slowly down her cheek and moved away from the book tables.

Her heart beat a little faster as she came across a short, wooden pier jutting out into the Thames. She was blindsided by a sudden vivid memory. It had been late, dark, and they'd been walking around London a bit worse for wear after a house party somewhere. James had taken her hand and led her down this very same pier. At the end he'd held her face gently in his freezing cold hands and said that he quite liked the idea of growing old with her, if she didn't mind. She'd said that would be fine.

Tearing her watery eyes away from the pier and dragging her mind back to the present, Grace looked around. She could go back to Waterloo and get the Northern Line all the way to Camden and find their flat. The rent was probably a lot more now than it had been when they'd moved in, just a month after graduating. It hadn't been a tough decision, or even a conscious one, to move in together. It just kind of happened organically, a natural progression from living in each other's pockets in their final year. She could go back and revisit the street where they'd lived, but maybe she'd had enough of looking at the past today. Maybe James's unchanged hair and glasses had been all the flashbacks she could cope with. Was this inexplicable tug towards the past, this burning desire to revisit what had been and gone, all a part of grief? She needed to return to the comfort blanket of Dovecote. With her chin tucked into her chest to ward off the biting wind, she crossed the river to catch the train home, so she'd be back in time to pick Harry up from school.

SIXTEEN
LILY

August 1940

The weather was atrocious. I found it hard to believe it was the middle of summer. For a week low clouds had blanketed the sky, and rain was never far away. While the terrible weather had meant a decline in the number of air raids, it did nothing to help my mood. Every morning I trudged from home to Brighton train station, jostled for a seat on the packed train, and stared out of the window at the grey. Then I trudged up the hill from Dovecote station to Bayview, stopping only for a quick peek in the window of Harrington's Bookshop. Today I didn't trudge though, I nearly ran, my gas mask case banging against my leg. I was late.

I pulled my cape off and adjusted my cap as I barrelled through the Bayview doors. Sister Margaret had moved me back to the men's house, after Henri and his colleagues had been moved on. If I were being uncharitable, I'd have suspected it was out of spite, as each day I was faced with having to see his shadow everywhere he used to be. I had asked to be sent back to the main hospital, but my request was denied. As a probationer,

I couldn't really kick up much of a fuss, so I kept my head down and tried to get on with it.

Dilys cornered me as I hung my cape up in the little cloakroom set aside for the staff.

'Lily, where have you been? You're an hour late. Mrs Macnamara's on the war path and Sister Margaret's been looking all over for you.'

'I know, I'm sorry. There was a problem with my train. I think there was an unspent incendiary device near the track. You know how long it takes the disposal people to clear those.'

'Well, there is a war on, I suppose. Come on, we'd better get a move on. I'm just doing the wound dressings before I clock off. I'm exhausted. I hate the night shift. Be a dear and carry these.'

Dilys thrust a bundle of rolled up bandages into my hands as another wave of nausea rolled through my stomach. That had been happening a fair bit recently, but I put it down to having to get that rickety old train every morning, and not having time to have a proper breakfast. I did miss the days when I could take my time in the mornings and have a leisurely breakfast with Daddy, before strolling along the seafront to the hospital. I did so enjoy Daddy glowering at me in my uniform over his morning paper. He really hadn't got used to seeing women in uniform. He'd only agreed to me becoming a nurse to stop me running off and joining the Auxiliary Territorial Service. I delighted in reminding him that he needed to keep up with the times, and that after the war things weren't going to go back to the way they were before. These days, I barely had time to grab a piece of bread and margarine (how I missed real butter) as I ran out the door to get the train. In a way, I didn't mind avoiding Daddy and Mummy as much as I could. I thought they'd somehow be able to tell what Henri and I had done in the cricket pavilion that night. That they'd notice a change in me, be able to spot that I wasn't a young girl any more.

I trailed along behind Dilys trying to put on a brave face for the injured men in our care, but it was unbearable. I missed Henri so much. It was like a part of me had been cut off the day he left. I had cried myself to sleep that night, clutching his beautiful letters to my chest. I could have kept crying for days, but I had to carry on as though my heart wasn't in a million pieces. While it was good of him to write, Richard wasn't helping with his jolly letters filled with stories of parties and balls. He could probably still get eggs for breakfast. At least one of us was having a good time.

'What?' Dilys asked, turning around.

'Nothing,' I said, not sure what part of my thoughts I'd inadvertently said out loud.

'Look here,' Dilys said, pausing outside the room of a Polish airman who'd been shot down over the English Channel. He'd had fourteen pieces of shrapnel removed from his left leg. 'I don't know what's gotten into you, but you're bringing me down with your moping around like a wet blanket.' Her face softened and she placed a gentle hand on my arm. The ring on her left hand sparkled in the overhead light. She and Archie were going to get married the next time he got leave. 'Tell you what, why don't you come to the pictures with me after you finish this evening? And you can tell me what's on your mind. If you dash to the station, we might even have time for a spot of tea before the show.'

I shook my head. I was so dreadfully tired. 'Thank you, Dilys, that's very kind. But I don't feel quite the full ticket at the moment.' I gave her as jolly a smile as I could muster. 'It will pass.'

She patted my arm. 'I know, the war is getting to us all. Especially now the ports are being bombed, it's all getting a bit too close for comfort.'

'Dilys?' I asked, pulling her to one side. 'Can I ask you something?'

Her eyes widened and she nodded.

'Your monthlies, are they usual?'

'Oh. Well, yes. Why?'

I checked over my shoulder to make sure there were no men within earshot, they were ever so funny about such things. 'It's just that mine are a bit... off.'

'My sister is the same; ever since the bombing started, she's not had a single one. Lucky for her, I say. They're such a nuisance. I expect you're the same. If you relax and try not to fret, I'm sure things will start up again.'

I breathed out slowly. She was probably right, it was the stress of the war, that was all.

'Yes, I expect so. Come on then, let's get on with it, before we both end up getting an earbashing from Sister Margaret.'

It was easy for Dilys to tell me not to fret, but I had no idea where Henri was or whether he was being shot at. For all I know, his ship could have been sunk by a U-boat. If only there was some way of finding out where he was, and that he was in one piece. All I wanted, and all I would ever want, was to know he was alive.

SEVENTEEN
GRACE

September 2015

The click of the front door of Seafoam Cottage on Sunday afternoon roused Grace from her laptop. She hadn't heard Ben's car pull up outside or the creak of the gate. She closed the computer and nudged it across the kitchen table. She'd sent in a couple of her columns since her grandmother's funeral, but they were ones she'd written beforehand. Now she was staring at a blank page, not knowing where to start. In the few days since she'd been to London, she'd tried very hard not to think about James, and to turn her attention to the future, but it was hard to fight the pull of the past.

'Hey, honey,' she said as Harry dropped his bag on the terracotta tiles in the hallway and gave her a limp hug. 'You okay?' When he didn't reply Grace looked up at Ben standing just inside the front door. 'Go on, go get yourself a snack and you can play on your computer for a bit,' she said, ruffling Harry's hair.

'Is he alright?' she asked Ben when Harry had slunk off down the hall into the kitchen.

'He was fine last night, bouncy and talkative as usual, but this morning he just woke up like... that,' Ben said, waving a hand in the rough direction of the kitchen.

'You told him, didn't you? About you and Rachel. What did you say to him?' There was a sharpness to her questions, but if Ben and Rachel had made her little boy unhappy, then she'd never forgive them.

Ben ran his hand through his hair and puffed out his cheeks. 'I told him last night. I just said that I'd started dating someone, and that it was Rach. Honestly, Grace, he wasn't fazed at all. He asked whether you knew and if you were okay.' Ben looked down at his feet. 'I said that you were.'

'And did you check with him this morning? You know how he thinks about things?'

Ben rolled his eyes. 'For pity's sake, Grace, you're acting as if I don't know him. Of course, I did, and he said he was fine. Then he went back up to his room looking at his phone, and when he came back down, he was all mopey.'

Grace glared back at Ben. How dare he take that tone with her. The glare worked and Ben stuffed his hands into his jacket pockets and slumped against the white door frame, the fight gone from him.

'Sorry. I didn't mean to snap. But I need you to know that the way Harry and I are around each other hasn't changed. I'm not a different kind of dad.'

Grace folded her arms and examined the floral pattern on the wallpaper. 'No, I'm sorry. I do know that. It's just...'

'I know. It's an adjustment and we're still working it all out, aren't we?'

'Yeah, we are. I guess that's what parenting is all about at the end of the day. It would be so much easier if kids came with instruction books.'

'Or if life did,' Ben added with a half-smile.

'Indeed. I'll have a chat with him in a bit. He's growing up. I think it's probably just hormones.'

'Already? It seems like only yesterday he grew out of the terrible twos.'

'Yeah, time flies, doesn't it? It feels like five minutes since we brought him home...' Grace's voice trailed off. Ben was giving her a look that held many years of shared memories. She couldn't meet it.

'I know. He's fine, Grace, we've done the right thing. It's better for him to have two happy homes than one stressful one.'

'Yes, I know. I guess everything is catching up with me. I'm just a bit emotional. Any chance of a hug?' she sniffled. It was best Ben thought she was emotional over the impact of their divorce on Harry, instead of him finding out she was preoccupied with her ex.

A soft smile pulled at his mouth. 'Come here, you,' he said pulling her into his broad chest. 'You'll be fine, we'll all be fine,' he said softly as Grace snuffled slightly into his shoulder. 'Have you had any more luck with finding your elusive French soldier?' he asked, as she pulled away.

Grace glanced down at the tiled floor. There was a draft coming in through the wooden front door and she supressed a slight shiver. She could say nothing, say she was still looking. She didn't have to mention that she'd roped James into the search, let alone that she'd met him. But, seeing the concern in Ben's blue-grey eyes, she couldn't lie. Not to him.

'No,' she said eventually. 'But I have asked someone to help with the search.'

'Oh, fair enough. Who?'

Grace swallowed and braced herself for Ben's reaction to her next words. 'James.'

'James?' Ben hissed, the concern slipping from his face, replaced with thunder. 'You got in touch with James?'

Grace's hands were trembling, so she knotted them together. 'Yes. And I met up with him on Thursday.'

Ben rubbed his face slowly. 'Damn it, Grace. Why him? I hope you know what you're doing.'

'I can handle it.'

Ben didn't say anything else, he just huffed and walked out. He looked back at Seafoam Cottage as he opened the wooden gate, as if he wanted to say something else. He shook his head and got into his car without another word. Grace watched as he drove away, shielding her eyes from the sun. She leant against the door frame for a moment, listening to the waves crashing against the sea wall, taking deep breaths of salty air, and trying to regulate her heart rate, before shutting out the world and turning her attention to Harry.

There was a football in the flowerbed that ran the length of the back garden from the beech tree outside the kitchen window to the sloping foot of the cliff at the bottom of the garden. Harry had been kicking it against the fence again. She'd asked him repeatedly not to as the thud of the ball against the fence sent the next-door neighbour's dog into a frenzy of yapping. As there was only silence from the garden of Seaspray Cottage, she wouldn't tell him off this time. Harry must have gotten bored of that game as he was laid down on the grass, starfish style. His eyes were closed against the glare of the low sun, so he didn't see her approach and lie down next to him. She should have put a coat on, Harry was still wearing his. But there was just enough warmth left in the sun to take the edge off the sea breeze.

'What's up, love?' she asked.

He opened his eyes at her voice. 'Nothing,' he replied turning over onto his stomach and picking at the blades of grass.

'Are you sure? You're not upset about Dad and Rachel seeing each other, are you?'

'No,' he said.

'What is it, then? Something's clearly not right.'

He sighed dramatically. 'I didn't get an invite to Jake's birthday sleepover,' he said, his bottom lip beginning to tremble. 'The other kids in my class were talking about it today on WhatsApp. They all got their invites in the post, but I didn't get one.'

With a jolt, Grace remembered the stack of letters she picked up from the doormat on Saturday that she hadn't had a chance to look through. They were still on her grandmother's square table by the bay window.

'How do you know?' she asked. 'It might have come while you were at Dad's. There's some post in the sitting room. Why don't you run in and check if it's there?' The spark of hope that lit up his face as he got up and ran inside, caused her to cringe inwardly. 'Please let it be there,' she whispered.

She sat up as she heard his fast footsteps in the kitchen and he emerged through the back door, a small blue envelope in his hand.

'It's here, it's here!' Harry exclaimed, ripping the envelope open.

'See, nothing to worry about,' Grace said, picking up the discarded envelope. Should she have ripped open Lily's unsent letter the way Harry had ripped open the invite? She still could.

'Great, I'm going to text Jake.' At the kitchen door, he paused. 'I can go, can't I?'

Grace chuckled. 'Of course you can.'

'Yes! Thanks, Mum.'

Grace lowered herself back down onto the grass. It was nice just to lie amongst the daisies and stare at the sky. There had been many a long summer's day she and her grandmother had sat on the grass having a picnic, making daisy chains, or forming shapes in the clouds. She'd sat out here in the garden with her grandad too; him in his deckchair snoozing after a Sunday roast, while she read about the exploits of girls at boarding schools, or children going on adventures and solving mysteries. A soft smile pulled at her lips; they'd been happy days. She was trying to work out whether the cloud above looked more like an elephant or a rabbit, when her phone buzzed in her pocket. She nearly dropped it on her face as she held it up to read the text message.

Hi Gracie. Just wanted to let you know I'm working on finding your mysterious Frenchman. I've a few leads to follow up on but I think I might be getting close. I'm sorry we didn't have much time to talk the other day. It was good to see you and I was wondering whether you wanted to have a proper catch up. I could come down to you if it's easier, or you can come up here. Maybe we can meet somewhere a bit nicer than the IWM cafe. I'd like to hear what you've been up to. Anyway, let me know. James.

She sat up slowly, her mind racing. She'd only meant to involve James to help her find Henri. Meeting up with him socially had not been in the plan. There was a part of her that really wanted to, but a bigger part was terrified of where that might lead.

EIGHTEEN
GRACE

October 2015

The click-clack of the train wheels provided a background rhythm to the questions ricocheting around Grace's head like a ping pong ball in a washing machine. Was she overdressed? Did she have too much cleavage on show? Why had she agreed to this? Was she a bad mother for sneaking off to London while her son was having a sleepover at his friend's house? Was it time to tell James everything?

Her thoughts drifted back to her journey many years ago, her one-way ticket clasped firmly in her hand. She remembered it all so clearly: the middle-aged man who lifted her suitcase onto the luggage rack more out of impatience at her dithering, than out of any sense of duty or helpfulness. The shaking of her hands that the old woman across the aisle spotted and raised her eyebrows at. The ache in her chest at the thought of James's face when he got back to the flat that night to find her note stuck to the fridge by the magnet they had bought in Amsterdam.

The jolt of the train dragged Grace back to the present. She rolled her shoulders, trying to release the tension that had stiffened them.

No, she couldn't tell him. Not yet.

By the time she arrived in London and found her way to the tube station, Grace was a little calmer. All she had to do was keep the conversation neutral, just talk about Henri, avoid anything that might bring up her history with James.

Her hand was shaking as she pushed open the door of the trendy bar in Vauxhall where James had suggested they meet. Her eyes met James's and his wide smile caused her stomach to swoop involuntarily. She had to keep it together.

James kissed her cheek in greeting.

'This is very fancy,' Grace said, looking around the art-deco bar. 'A bit of an upgrade from the pubs we used to drink in.'

'Yeah, just a bit,' James chuckled. 'What was the name of that pub near our flat?'

'Quinn's?'

'That's it, Quinn's! Awful place, so dodgy. I don't know why we loved it so much.'

'I think it was cheap,' Grace laughed.

'Sounds about right.'

Their laughter died, replaced by a heavy silence. So much for keeping the conversation neutral; the first thing she'd said had flung open the portal to all those years ago. The memories of the dingy pub were almost physical. She remembered the sour smell of spilt beer, the fug of cigarette smoke that found its way into every fibre of clothing, the glasses that were never sparklingly clean. And James. His arm around her shoulder, or his hand resting on her thigh. The little looks he used to give her; silent communication between the two of them that no one else ever understood. The way he would whisper things in her ear that made her blush. The walk home from the pub which took forever because every few steps he would stop, take her in his arms, and kiss her deeply and passionately. That one time they couldn't wait until they got home and...

'I'm sorry you had to come up to London. I would have come down to you, but work is manic at the moment. I just never know what days I'll be able to get away early. Saturdays are the worst. I don't have to work them often, but when I do they're chaos.' James's voice broke into her memory and her brain shifted back to the present.

'It's fine. Not a problem.'

She hadn't agreed to come to London out of kindness. It was out of a fear of being seen with James. Dovecote was too small to hide in, everywhere she went she saw people she knew. Never mind Janice who would be very interested in her liaising with a strange man. The fallout from Ben discovering she'd gone for a drink with James didn't bear thinking about. And if it all went horribly wrong, she could get up and walk away, consigning James and London back into the depths of her memory. There were already so many ghosts in Dovecote, the last thing she needed was to add James to the mix. She could cope as long as the two worlds didn't collide, not yet anyway.

Grace took a long sip of her wine just to have something to do. Her mind raced trying to find something to say. All that was in her head were memories – warm, soft memories that wound themselves around her like an old blanket and drew up old feelings she thought she had locked away and buried deep.

'So, um, how are you getting on with finding Henri?' she asked once the silence had become unbearable.

James looked up from his pint, his soft, brown eyes searching Grace's face. 'Good. I've found his service record and evidence that he was evacuated from Dunkirk. He was treated for a minor gunshot wound to the right leg and various cuts and bruises in Brighton and Dovecote, before being sent to the redeployment station in Salisbury. After that the trail goes a bit cold, I'm afraid.'

Grace deflated a little. James was her last, and only, hope to find Henri. If he couldn't, then there was no chance.

'But,' James continued and Grace perked up a little, 'I have found a photograph of some Dunkirk survivors taken at the 75th anniversary commemoration event earlier this year, and a related newspaper article that mentions him. I'm just working on translating it.'

Grace beamed. 'That's brilliant news. Thank you so much.'

James's face relaxed. 'No problem.' A heartbeat passed. 'So, anyway, tell me what's been going on with you for the last decade.'

Grace bit her lip and swirled her wine glass, watching the liquid run down the inside of the glass. 'Nothing very unusual. Just, you know, stuff.'

'Did you ever get married? You were pretty keen on the idea once upon a time.'

The moisture in Grace's mouth evaporated and her stomach constricted painfully.

'Um, yes,' she mumbled, unable to meet James's gaze.

'You're not wearing a ring now.'

Damn it, he'd always been too observant. Grace automatically ran her thumb across the base of her ring finger, still discomfited by its emptiness.

'Ben and I separated about a year ago.'

'Oh. I'm sorry to hear that.'

Grace couldn't speak, all she could do was wave away his sympathy with a shake of her head. There was a hot pressure in her sinuses, and she clenched her jaw, willing the tears to stay away.

'Wait, the Ben you were dating before you moved to London? You guys got back together? Any kids?'

'One. Harry. He's just started his last year at primary school.' Grace could see James doing some mental arithmetic.

'You didn't hang around.'

'Yeah well, sometimes these things just happen.' Why did her voice sound so wobbly?

'Shall I get us another drink?' James was already on his feet when he asked. Grace nodded.

By the time he returned she had composed herself.

'Thanks,' she said as he put another glass of red down in front of her. 'So, what about you? Did you take the university up on their research grant offer? I remember it was a massive amount of money.'

A faraway look clouded his eyes. 'I did. I spent three glorious years travelling around South-East Asia doing research on the Vietnam War. It was a dream come true, that job. I even managed to get a book published out of it.'

'I'm glad it worked out for you,' Grace said, avoiding looking at him. Her instincts had been right, she would have held him back. He'd known she hadn't wanted him to go, and she had known she couldn't stop him.

'Well, the timing worked out,' he said with a slight flick of his eyebrows. 'It made things a little easier, being half a globe away from all the places that reminded me of you.'

Grace's stomach twisted in a tight knot.

'You wrote a book?' she said, grasping any chance to steer the conversation back from the precipice.

'It wasn't exactly a bestseller, it's a bit niche. Although it is available in the IWM gift shop,' he replied with a chuckle.

'That's brilliant. I did a bit of writing after, you know, but then Harry came along, and I never really went back to it. Just recently I've picked it up again. I write a semi-regular column in a women's magazine. It's hardly Pulitzer Prize winning journalism. I'm sure my university lecturers would be appalled, but it's something to do I guess.'

'Yes, I know. I've read a few of them.'

'Oh God, you haven't.' Grace's face burned.

'I did, and they're good. Pretty funny too. And some serious topics, under the fluff. You always had a lovely way with words. Did you ever think about writing short stories, or even a novel? I reckon you could.'

Grace shook her head. 'No, not seriously anyway. Don't think I'd have time now.'

'Hmm,' said James with a smirk. Grace cleared her throat. There was a question she was dying to ask, even though she wasn't sure why she needed to know.

'So, um, what about you? There's no ring on your finger either.'

James looked down into his glass again, his smirk replaced with a frown. 'No. I guess I never met the right person.' There was a trace of bitterness in his voice that caused a sharp stab of guilt to pierce her chest. Had she really broken his heart that much?

They both gave their drinks their full attention for a long minute before James spoke again. 'Gracie—'

'Don't,' Grace interrupted, knowing what he was going to say. 'Please don't ask. It was a long time ago.'

James sighed sadly. 'Yeah, you're right it was a long time ago. I just... never mind.'

'If it helps, I am sorry. I've thought a lot about what I did. I'm not proud of it.'

'It doesn't help, but thanks.'

'Maybe I should go,' said Grace.

'Please don't,' James begged. 'I'm sorry, I shouldn't have brought it up.' He pursed his lips and glanced up at the ceiling. When he lowered his eyes, they met Grace's. 'You know, I imagined this conversation a million times. What I would say to you if I ever saw you again or if you ever replied to the messages I sent or returned any of my calls. Now that you're here, I don't really know what to say.'

'I'm sorry, James. I did what I thought was for the best at the time.'

'I guess I understand. We were quite intense, weren't we?'

'Yeah, a little.' The swirling in Grace's stomach subsided a touch at the increasing lightness in his voice. 'Go on then, tell me all about South-East Asia.'

The sky was an inky black when they emerged from the bar. They walked together towards the tube station.

'Here we are,' James said, rubbing his hands together to try to warm them.

'Yep,' Grace replied, curling her fingers around the ticket in her pocket.

'Thanks again for coming all the way up to London.'

'Thank you for inviting me. I had a great evening.'

'Me too.' They stood, wordless, as the crowded pavement pulsed and thronged around them. It was a relief when he put his arms around her and hugged her tightly, causing her skin to tingle beneath her jacket sleeves.

'It was good to see you again,' he said.

Grace's voice had deserted her, so she simply nodded and smiled.

'I'll let you know as soon as I have news on Henri.'

'Thanks,' whispered Grace. 'See you.'

'Yeah, see you.'

At the bottom of the tube station steps she turned to wave to him, but he was already gone.

NINETEEN

GRACE

October 2015

It had been a week since Grace's sneaky trip to London, and she'd heard nothing more from James. He'd given her hope that he was close to finding Henri; it was a little frustrating that there had been no further development. On the other hand, it was probably a good thing that she had time to get her head straight. She still had that weird instinct that something was calling her to find Henri. It was one of those feelings that if she tried to grasp hold of and interrogate it, it would vanish like smoke from an extinguished candle.

The other thing she had time for was finally dealing with the last of Lily's things. Her room was a lot tidier now; all the cupboards were empty, the books returned to the bookshelves in the sitting room, the various lotions and potions from her dressing table gathered up and binned. It pained her to do this, but her grandmother had always been a stickler for tidiness, and the idea of tubs and bottles gathering dust would have irritated her. So, Grace had steeled herself and chucked the lot. She kept Lily's favourite bottle of perfume and the gilt-rimmed hand mirror that Grace had been allowed to touch when she was very small and had always loved. Grace had washed the quilt that had lain across the foot of her grandmother's bed and placed it on the bottom of her own. It didn't smell right though, so she regularly gave the quilt a spritz of Lily's perfume. It was probably completely psychosomatic but breathing in the scent of lily-of-the-valley every night seemed to be helping her sleep a bit better.

A thin film of dust had settled on the photograph of Lily and Richard on the dresser, and she wiped it off with her sleeve. It must have been taken in the winter, they were both bundled up in heavy coats and Lily's curly blonde bob was tousled by the wind. They were standing in the front garden of Seafoam Cottage, the shape of the distinctive bay window and the mottled plaster of the cottage's walls was unmistakable. They were smiling widely and holding hands. They had held hands all the time, right up until Richard moved into the care home and stopped recognising Lily. That was the only time Grace had ever seen her grandmother cry, the day he'd refused her hand. They had always looked so happy together. Grace replaced the photograph and pulled open the dresser drawer.

The drawer was inches deep with necklaces, earrings, bracelets, and rings. None of it was valuable in monetary terms, but each piece was a memory, and just chucking it out was inconceivable. Pushing aside a strand of chunky orange beads, Grace's fingers brushed against soft velvet. She had never seen the dark-blue pouch before, and she tipped the contents into her palm. The thin wire necklace was crude, and most certainly handmade with an odd-shaped piece of thick glass with smoothed edges tied to it. Holding the glass up to the light it looked like a piece of broken bottle. She turned it over in her hand. Why was this rustic piece of junk wrapped so carefully in a velvet pouch while gold and gemstones were left to become tangled in the general melee of the drawer? It must have been special to her grandmother. But if it had been, why had she never worn it? Grace gently caressed the rounded edges of the glass, and, without thinking, fastened it around her neck.

The shrill buzz of her mobile roused her from her thoughts.

Hey, I don't suppose you're free tomorrow? I'm popping down to Dovecote to see Mum and Dad and I have news for you. J.

Once again, October couldn't decide what season it was in, weather-wise, and Grace regretted wearing a jumper and a jacket as she waited outside Dovecote's pretty train station. She had passed it, and passed through it, thousands of times throughout her life but hadn't ever really stopped to look at the building that closely. The decorative wooden pelmet that hung from the sloping slate-grey roof had been given a fresh coat of green paint that matched the window surrounds and stood out against the grey stonework. The original entrance now served as the exit and a new way in had been added by the car park at some point before Grace's memory of Dovecote began.

She heard the click-clack of an approaching train and the sigh of the brakes as it drew to a stop. Dovecote was the end of a branch line that had survived the cuts of the 1960s, a relief to those who otherwise would have to suffer a twisty, bumpy bus ride from Brighton. A trickle of people began to spill from the narrow exit. She saw James before he saw her and waved. This time there was no hesitation and they embraced warmly.

'Hey, how are you doing?'

'I'm alright, thanks. You?'

'Yeah good.'

'How long have your parents lived in Dovecote?' Grace said as they started walking towards the beach. When she'd seen James's message and realised what he was saying, a cold dread had seeped through her bones. Why hadn't he mentioned that his parents lived in Dovecote? Had she ever seen them? Passed by them in Victoria Park or on the beach? Been sat at a table next to them in The Seaside Café? She'd only met Gordon and Veronica Rutherford once, when they'd come down to London to see James towards the end of third year. They'd gone for dinner and Grace had felt like a piece of meat in a butcher's window under Veronica's intense scrutiny.

'They moved down from Aylesbury a couple of months ago when Dad retired. Of all the seaside towns on the south coast they had to move to yours, huh.'

Grace didn't comment on that. At least they'd only lived in Dovecote for a few months, rather than years. What would it have been like to bump into James, or his parents, in The Royal Oak? The idea made her throat hurt.

'Dad's a bit under the weather. Mum begged me to come down and see them. I haven't been down as much as I should have, what with work being busy and stuff.'

'Oh, nothing too serious I hope?' Grace asked.

James shook his head. 'I doubt it. He's a massive hypochondriac. It's probably just a head cold.'

The strong wind down on the beach whipped Grace's hair around her face. She dug in the pocket of her coat, found a hair tie, and pulled her hair back into a ponytail.

'Now that's the Gracie I used to know,' he said quietly. 'You always had your hair tied back.'

'Did I?' Grace replied. 'I don't remember.'

'I do,' said James. 'I remember all of it.'

Grace glanced at him from the corner of her eye. He was staring down at the pebbles and there was a slight pink tinge on his neck. They walked along the beach in silence. The clatter of the stones under their feet was accompanied only by the call of the seagulls and the soft swish of the waves. James cleared his throat, stopped walking, and turned to Grace.

'Gracie, I need you to be honest with me,' he said.

Her insides clenched. 'Yes,' she said warily. Was he going to ask the question she desperately wanted to avoid?

'What are your intentions with regards to Henri?'

Grace's heart skipped a beat. 'Does that mean he's alive and that you've found him?'

'Yes, I have, and yes, he is still alive.'

Grace let out a little squeal and clapped her hands together.

'But I need to know what you intend to do before I give you his details. He's a very old man.' There was a touch of caution in his voice.

'James, just tell me what you know,' she begged, pulling Harry's favourite trick and giving him her best puppy-dog eyes. 'Please.'

James sighed. 'Alright,' he said, a weary expression on his face. 'Like I thought, it was a little difficult to trace him after Dunkirk. There is no record of him going back to France and rejoining the army. It is possible that he joined the Free French Army in England. Charles de Gaulle was recruiting heavily around that time. Anyway, when I found that photo, and the article I mentioned, I got in touch with a charity that specialises in reuniting friends and families with veterans. They confirmed that he was still an active member.'

A bubble of excitement burst inside her making her face light up. 'Wow. That's fantastic news. I can't believe he's still alive. I mean what are the chances?'

'Yeah, I was dubious, there aren't many Dunkirk veterans still with us. He must be one of the last.'

Grace chewed the inside of her cheek and glanced out at the sea. She was thrilled that James had tracked Henri down, but now she had no choice but to decide what to do about it. Should she get in touch with him? Should she tell him who she was? Would he even remember Lily? James was looking intently at her.

'You look like you're deep in thought?'

'Sorry. Thank you so much, it really means a lot to me to know he's alive. I was just thinking about what I should do. What do you think? Should I get in touch?'

James bent down and picked up a small stone from the beach, rubbing it between his thumb and forefinger. Without a word, he walked down to the edge of the sea and flicked the stone into the water. It bounced twice before sinking below the waves. She joined him at the water's edge. He didn't look at her when he spoke.

'I don't know. Sometimes the past is best left where it is. Sometimes resurrecting it just brings difficult memories and pain to the surface.'

There was a sadness in his eyes and a firm set to his mouth. Was he still talking about Henri and Lily? Before she could stop herself, she asked a question that had all the subtlety of a nuclear bomb.

'Is that what I've done by getting in touch with you?'

James took a piece of paper out of his pocket and held it up. He didn't pass it to Grace. 'I have the name of the town in the South of France where Henri lives. I can give it to you if you decide that you really want to meet him. Just remember Henri is a very old man, and maybe *he* doesn't want to be reminded of what he lost.' James turned and walked away up the beach, towards The Promenade. Grace was left reeling from the bitterness of his words, and with a sense of dread that he had just got his revenge by walking out of her life, just like she had walked out of his all those years ago, but with the added bonus of taking Henri with him.

The fresh air tingled Grace's skin and she gulped it down into her lungs. It was the sort of day her grandmother would have loved. A sharp stab struck Grace's chest. She missed Lily so much. She missed having her around to bounce ideas off. She missed being mothered by her, the way she had been from the moment a car crash had stolen Grace's mother from her. She missed the way she used to talk her through recipes step-by-step over the telephone. When Harry was a baby she was always there, even in the middle of the night when Grace rang her with some new-mum panic or worry. When Harry grew, she was still there offering reassurances that Grace wasn't totally screwing up. She wished she could talk to her now, tap into that seemingly limitless well of wisdom and sanity, or even just ask her again whether she was screwing everything up. Most of all, Grace wished she could ask her about the past.

The sun disappeared behind malevolent clouds that had blown in and her hands, despite being stuffed into her coat pockets, had gone numb thanks to the relentless frigid wind coming off the sea. Grace turned her back to the waves and clambered up the beach in the opposite direction to where James had gone. There was no point in chasing after him; it would only end in tears. Maybe she could cheer herself up with some chips from the chip shop for lunch.

She had just crossed The Promenade and was about to turn into the High Street when two familiar figures came into view. Grace smiled as Ben released Rachel's hand the instant he saw her.

'Hey,' said Rachel, giving Grace a tight hug when they drew close enough. 'What's up?'

'Nothing,' Grace sighed. Clearly, she wasn't doing as good a job of hiding the maelstrom inside her head as she'd hoped.

'Are you sure?' asked Ben.

'I'll tell you about it some other time,' Grace said.

'We were just going to get some lunch. Come with us,' said Rachel, her hand still on Grace's forearm.

Grace looked from Rachel to Ben and back again. 'Oh no, I don't want to intrude,' she said.

'Nonsense,' said Rachel firmly, looping her arm through Grace's. 'Ben?'

'Absolutely. Actually,' he added, giving Rachel a look that she nodded at in response, 'there was something we wanted to ask you, so why not over lunch?'

A small twist of regret tugged at Grace's stomach. How many times had she and Ben communicated silently to each other like that? She forced the jealousy and discomfort away. It would drive her mad to analyse every interaction between Ben and Rachel and compare them to hers and Ben's. She had to let it go. There was her grandmother's voice again. As for joining them for lunch, having some company would prevent her from tying herself in knots trying to dissect James's parting words.

'Alright, if you're sure you don't mind,' she said.

The Seaside Café was heaving, and they nabbed the round table by the net-curtain-covered window. Grace fiddled with the pink carnation in the white bud vase and looked around as they waited for Ben to bring over their teas. He was having a lively chat with Janice. She'd always had a soft spot for him, and he loved to play up to her with a bit of harmless flirting. It seemed like a lifetime since she'd last been in the café and had that weird conversation with Rachel. So much had happened in the intervening weeks.

'Come on, then,' said Rachel as Ben put down a tray of mugs of tea, 'what's got you looking like all those dear to you have died? Sorry, that came out wrong.'

Grace grinned at the look of abject horror on Rachel's face.

'Sensitive as always, Rach,' she joked. 'I've just been talking to James.' She shot a look at Ben. 'Not now,' she said wearily, and Ben pursed his lips and looked away. 'I presume Ben told you that I'd asked James to help me find Henri?'

'Yeah. I did think you'd have talked to me about it though,' Rachel said, a touch of annoyance colouring her voice.

'Sorry.' Rachel was right, she should have told her directly, not relied on Ben to fill her in. 'I guess. I don't know. I just...'

'I get it,' Rachel said, giving Grace's hand a squeeze. 'It's a learning curve for us all. I'm still your BFF though, so don't ever think you can't talk to me about stuff. Even if it's stuff you don't want him,' she jerked a thumb at Ben, 'to know. Mates before dates, you know that.'

Ben inhaled a long breath and held it for a moment before releasing it slowly while rubbing the back of his neck. 'For crying out loud,' he muttered.

'Anyway, Grace. You were saying you'd seen James. Has he found Henri?'

Grace reached for her cup of tea but didn't pick it up. 'He has. Henri is alive and living in the South of France. James won't tell me exactly where until I decide whether to try and meet Henri.' She paused and glanced out of the window. The grey clouds covering the sun made the light outside dusky and ominous, like there was a storm approaching. 'And I don't know quite what to do.'

'I think you should go. Definitely. I mean, otherwise what was the point of looking for him in the first place. By the way, is that a new necklace? It's unique,' Rachel said, cradling her mug of tea.

Grace's hand went to her throat. 'I found it in Nanna's dresser. I don't think I ever saw her wear it. I don't know why I put it on, I just did.'

'It suits you. Anyway, Henri.'

Grace picked at a loose bit of cuticle on her thumb. 'What do you think, Ben?'

There was a slight frown on Ben's forehead. 'I think you'll do whatever you want to do no matter what anyone says. But, seeing as you asked, I don't think you should.'

'Why?' Rachel asked.

'Let's say Grace goes all the way to France and finds this old guy and he doesn't want to meet her, or he doesn't remember Lily. Or what if he does and reminding him of Lily stirs up difficult feelings? Would you be comfortable about potentially upsetting an old man, Grace?'

Grace swallowed a mouthful of tea. It was so typical of Ben to be the sensible voice in all of this. 'I don't know.'

'I know you'd feel guilty about it forever. I don't think it's worth the risk.'

'But what if Henri has been wanting to know why Lily never wrote to him all these years?' Rachel asked. 'What if Grace going could give him closure, and the answers he's been waiting seventy-odd years for?'

Grace suddenly broke out laughing, making Ben and Rachel turn to her in surprise. 'Sorry,' she said. 'Listening to you two is like watching my own brain argue with itself. You both make excellent points, the same ones I've been making to myself. I'm going to sleep on it.'

'Whatever you decide, you know we'll support you. Won't we, Ben?' Rachel raised an eyebrow and Ben sighed.

'Yes, of course we will. And we'll be here to pick up the pieces when it all goes belly-up.'

The conversation halted as Janice brought over their cheese toasties. Just as impressive as her sticky buns, they were next best thing to chips.

'Alright, my loves?' Janice asked. 'Looks like there's a bit of bad weather on the way.'

Rachel pulled aside the net curtain and looked out of the window. 'Yes, the clouds do look rather menacing.'

'It's more my knees, dear,' Janice said. 'I can always tell when a storm's brewing by my knees.'

'Fine looking knees they are too,' Ben said with a grin and Janice pretended to cuff him round the ear.

'Less cheek from you, young man,' she said, making Ben laugh. 'Wish Harry a happy birthday from me tomorrow, won't you.'

'We will, Janice, thank you,' Grace said.

'Enough about me, what was it you wanted to ask?' Grace asked once Janice was out of earshot and Ben had stopped laughing. It was never a good idea to discuss anything potentially private around Janice; she spread gossip like an out-of-control forest fire. It was a standing joke that if there was something you needed everyone to know, you could save yourself time by just telling Janice. Reverend Clive had spread many a parish notice that way. Rachel gave Ben a nudge and he skewered a cherry tomato before speaking.

'It's just that, well I, I mean we, were, um.' Ben looked helplessly at Rachel as he floundered, and Rachel groaned.

'What mister articulate here is trying to ask is would you be happy with us taking Harry away for half-term? We were thinking of going down to Porthcawl.'

'Ah,' said Grace raising an eyebrow. 'Spending time with the family?'

Rachel grinned back. 'Well, they've not seen Ben in years, and I thought it was time to let them know we're, you know, more than friends now. And I'd like them to meet Harry too.'

Grace glanced at Ben, some of the colour had faded from his cheeks. 'You're not nervous, are you?' she asked, with a smirk.

'No. Of course not.' Ben looked from Grace to Rachel. 'Fine, maybe a little.'

'How are they doing? I bet your dad's loving retirement and being back where he grew up,' Grace said.

'He was always banging on about going back to Wales, wasn't he?' Rachel said. 'They're doing great. I don't think they're missing me at all.'

'I'm sure that's not true, but I'm glad they're well.' Grace took a long drink of tea. Rachel wanted to introduce Harry to her family. That was a pretty big deal in Grace's book, and it made her stomach go a little tight. She had no issue with Ben taking Harry away. She trusted Ben. There would be no question that Harry would be safe. So, what was it that was bothering her? Was it that Rachel wanting to introduce Harry to her family was evidence of how serious things were between her and Ben? If Ben and Rachel were going to go the distance, then there would be a hundred milestones like this. They were on a road for which Grace had no map, no reference points, and no idea how to navigate. But if she kept interrogating each turn, bump, and crossroads, she'd drive herself slowly mad. She had to give in and just go with it. It was either that or risk losing everything. She drew a breath and put her empty mug down on the table.

'Go on then, take Harry with you. He'd love a week on a proper sandy beach. Actually,' she said, 'that could work out really well. I could go to France that week if I decide to try to meet Henri.'

'Ah brill. Thanks. Even if you don't go and meet Henri, why don't you get away yourself for a bit. A change of scenery might do you good,' Rachel said.

'You know, Rach, I like the sound of that,' said Grace. Maybe a change of scenery wouldn't be a bad thing. She needed a break from everything that reminded her of everyone she'd lost or was losing.

TWENTY

GRACE

October 2015

The next morning Grace lay in bed, listening to the branches of the tall beech tree in the back garden tapping on her bedroom window in the wind. She'd left Lily's letter to Henri propped up against her bedside lamp, so it was the first thing she saw. As the white envelope glinted in a shaft of watery sunlight coming through a gap in the blue and white dotted curtains, she knew what she had to do. Knowing Henri was alive meant she had no choice – she had to get the letter to him. She could just contact Henri and ask for his address and post the letter to him, that would make perfect sense. But if she did that, there was no guarantee that he would contact her once he'd read it; she might never get to know what was in it. And Rachel was right: a week in the South of France, whatever the outcome, sounded like a very good idea.

Her finger poised over the send icon as she re-read her text to James:

Hi. I want to try and find Henri, so I can give him the letter in person. Can you let me have all the info you have, please?

That sounded fine, friendly yet detached. The last thing she wanted was to evoke another emotional outburst from James. The moment she hit the send button, Harry barrelled into her room and flung himself down on her bed. She pulled him close and wrapped her arms around him. He smelt deliciously warm and sleepy.

'Happy birthday, Harry,' she said, softly.

He tolerated one kiss on the head and a minute of hugging before he extracted himself from her embrace.

'Are my presents downstairs?'

She had to laugh. 'Yes, on the kitchen table where they always are. Do you want me to make birthday pancakes?'

'Oh, yeah! Thanks, Mum.' And he was off like a shot, thundering down the stairs. Grace tucked her mobile into the pocket of her dressing gown and followed. By the time she reached the kitchen, Harry was already ankle-deep in ripped wrapping paper. Grace had been extra generous to make sure he was compensated for the presents he would have received from his great-grandparents. Of course, there would be another mountain of gifts waiting for him at Ben's, so there was no way he'd be short-changed.

'Oh wow, Mum. This is awesome!' He'd unwrapped his main present, a new mobile phone. 'Thanks.'

'Dad's going to help you set it up when you go over there later,' Grace said, gathering pancake ingredients. 'He'll sort out moving all your numbers and things across and set up the parental controls. We've had a long chat about it, so no trying to tell him I agreed to anything that he says you can't have access to. He's going to link it to my bank account and my mobile account, so I'll be able to see if you make any sly purchases.'

'No worries. I'll be careful with it too. I know you're trusting me to be grown-up with it, so I'll try.'

Grace gave him another kiss on the head. 'That's all I can ever ask of you, sweetie. Now, chocolate or golden syrup on your pancakes?'

Harry tilted his head slightly to the left and considered his options. 'Chocolate,' he said at last. 'Can I have chocolate chips as well?'

'It's your birthday, Harry. You can have whatever you want.'

Grace was loading the breakfast things into the dishwasher when her phone buzzed in her pocket.

Meet me at Dovecote station at eleven and we can talk. J.

Grace did a bit of mental gymnastics. Harry was going to be at Ben's until eleven, before Ben would be taking him to the football pitches at the secondary school for his party. She didn't need to meet them there until half past eleven. James had picked the busiest day of the year, but she just about had time to stop at the train station after picking up the party decorations to get Henri's address off him. What she didn't have time for was another of James's cryptic speeches. And definitely no deep and meaningful conversations. She was surprised he was willing to speak to her at all after what he'd said on the beach.

James was sat on the stone bench outside the train station when Grace pulled into a drop off space and indicated at him to get into the car.

'Don't let any of the balloons escape,' she said as he pulled open the passenger-side door.

He looked into the back of the car. 'Balloons?'

'It's Harry's birthday. He's having a football-themed party run by Dovecote's Football in the Community team. They hire a pitch for a few hours and do a training session and a match, and then take the kids for food afterwards. I have to drop these off at the burger bar over on Churchill Drive so they can decorate it for him.'

'Nice. Into sport then, is he?'

Grace nodded. 'He's pretty much an all-rounder. He loves football and cricket, which is how he ended up with a sprained wrist last month, but he's no slouch in the classroom either. How's your dad?'

'As I expected it's nothing too serious. Just a bout of sinusitis. Some meds from the pharmacy and he'll be right as rain.'

'That's good.'

'So, you want to meet Henri, then?' James asked, giving Grace a side-eye glance. 'What made you decide?'

'It's the right thing to do. Ben is taking Harry away for half-term so I can't pass up the chance for a week in the sun. So where is Henri?'

James pulled a folded piece of paper out of the inside pocket of his jacket. 'This is the translation of that article I told you about. It shows a picture of Henri at a VE Day commemoration in the town where he lives.' Grace reached out for the paper, but James pulled it out of her reach. 'Before I give it to you...'

'Stop playing games, James,' Grace snapped, rapidly running out of patience.

James tutted. 'See this is the problem, Grace. You're way too desperate for this. Have you really thought all this through? Have you considered that Lily's letter might upset him? And how you'd feel about that?'

'I'd just have to cope, wouldn't I?' It was quite touching that both James and Ben had raised the same concern.

'What would you think about me coming with you?'

Grace shrank back in her seat. 'You? To France? With me? Why?'

'Couple of reasons,' James said, counting on his fingers as he spoke. 'One, I am worried that if you don't get what you want, you'll do something weird, or illegal, or just go too far. You need someone there to rein you in if you overstep the line, or to bail you out of a French police cell. Two, as a historian, I'd quite like to meet Henri too. We're rapidly running out of Dunkirk survivors, and I've never met anyone who was there. I'd love to hear his account of his experience. Also, that area of the South of France is where Operation Dragoon took place. I happen to be writing a chapter on it for a book about overlooked World War Two events, so it would be useful to have a look around, get a feel for the place.' He paused and raised an eyebrow at her. 'Lastly, you don't speak French. I do. And we don't know whether Henri speaks much English.'

'That's more than a couple,' Grace huffed. How could she agree to him coming with her? The two of them spending time like that together. What would they talk about? A bead of cold sweat ran down between her shoulder blades. 'I don't know, James. I mean...'

'I know, it's a big ask. I can understand why you'd be reluctant. I mean, we've not spent a significant amount of time together in twelve years. And, no, forget it. It was a stupid idea.'

Grace stared out of the window for a moment. Something James said actually made sense, and it was something she'd not thought of. Although Henri's English had been good enough to write those letters, what if it no longer was? It would be pointless going to meet him if they couldn't understand each other. She tapped the steering wheel for a minute.

'Fine, you can come along. In the official capacity of translator.'

He passed her the paper. 'We'll need flights to Nice and a hotel in Neuville-sur-Mer.'

The paper rustled in Grace's quivering hands. 'Neuville-sur-Mer?' The words sounded clumsy in her mouth. 'Is that where he lives?'

James nodded. 'It was when that article was written. It's about an hour's drive west of Nice. It's our best shot.'

'I'll book it and let you know dates and times, and how much you owe me,' she said, rolling her eyes at him. 'You better go, or you'll miss your train.'

'And you better go, or your son won't have any birthday balloons.'

She pulled out of the station with a frown creasing her forehead. How was she going to explain this latest development to Ben?

As ten panting, muddy, wired kids descended on the reserved area of the burger bar, Rachel tapped Grace on the arm.

'Have you decided?'

Grace leant closer to Rachel and lowered her voice. 'Yes, I'm going to go and see if I can find and meet him. I've told James and he's given me the name of the town where Henri was last known to have lived.'

'That's great. Good luck.'

Grace glanced over at the table of kids. Satisfied that there wasn't anything she needed to do, she turned to Rachel and ushered her away, out of Ben's earshot.

'There's just one thing. And please, Rachel, don't tell Ben. I don't like asking that of you, I know it's not exactly the foundation of a good relationship.'

Rachel frowned slightly but nodded.

'The thing is, James is coming with me.'

Rachel let out a low whistle. 'Hmm, I can see why you're not mad on Ben knowing. He's not going to like that.'

Grace bit her lip. 'I know. I'm not entirely enamoured with

it myself. But, as James pointed out, I need him in case there's a language barrier. James is pretty much fluent in French. And also,' she paused and let out a short huff, 'in a way I'm glad I'll have someone with me, in case anything goes wrong. Promise you won't let on to Ben?'

'Grace, is there anything going on between you and James? You're not, like, you know?'

Grace shook her head vigorously. 'Hell, no. We're barely even friends. So much time has passed since I felt like that about him. I can't see us ever going there again. Absolutely not. It would be weird.'

'Stranger things have happened,' Rachel said with a sly grin. 'My lips are sealed.'

'Thanks. It's going to be so bizarre.'

'I'll say. At least you'll have plenty of time to catch up.'

'That's what I'm worried about,' Grace said. She caught Ben glancing over at them. 'Best get back to it.'

'I want to know if anything happens. You know how it is, all that sun, wine, beautiful scenery.' There was a mischievous glint in Rachel's eyes.

'Oh, shut up,' Grace hissed, giving her a dig in the ribs. They were just going to meet Henri, that was all. If she had her way, she wouldn't be spending any time at all alone with James. She certainly wasn't going to be sharing a bottle of wine or having any cosy tête-à-têtes with him. One drunken slip of the tongue could be disastrous.

TWENTY-ONE

GRACE

October 2015

A week later, Grace pushed Harry's feet off the pile of folded laundry on her bed making him look up from his mobile phone.

'Why can't I come to France with you?' he asked, giving her a round-eyed stare.

'Because you're going to Wales with Dad and Rachel,' Grace replied, giving the same answer she had the previous ten times he'd asked her. The chime of the doorbell interrupted his protestations, and he raced down to let Ben in.

'Hey, buddy. All packed and ready to go?' Ben's voice floated up the stairs as Grace made her way down.

'Hi,' she said. 'Harry, can you go and put those last few things on your bed into your bag please?'

Harry groaned and trudged back up the stairs.

'So, when do you go?' Ben asked, brushing a lock of auburn hair from his forehead. In times gone by, Grace would have used that gesture as a prompt to remind him to get his hair cut, but that was no longer her job, or her place.

'Tomorrow morning. The flight's at half ten, so I should be

in Nice by half twelve, well half one French time. By the time I pick up the car, I guess I'll get to Neuville-sur-Mer by three-ish,' Grace replied.

'I hope it goes well.'

Grace searched his face for some hint that Rachel had told him about James, but all she could see in his eyes was a slight disapproval overlaid with concern. He probably thought she was crazy. 'I'm sure it will all be fine.'

'You know that whatever happens...' he faltered.

'That meeting Henri won't bring Nanna back? That I might end up causing trouble for an elderly man and his family? That you think I'm being selfish? I know all that, Ben. But I still think I'm doing the right thing.'

'I was going to say that whatever happens, I'll be here for you.'

'Oh, thanks.' A small pang of guilt spiked through her. It was for his own good that she was keeping James's involvement a secret. Knowing the truth would only spoil his holiday. Harry thumped down the stairs and dropped a large rucksack at Ben's feet.

'Right, I'm ready. Can we go now?'

Ben ruffled Harry's hair and picked up the bag. 'Come on then, buddy. Give your mum a hug and then we'll head off.'

'Bye, Mum,' Harry said, throwing his skinny arms around her. 'I'll miss you.'

'I'll miss you too, sweetheart,' Grace replied, giving him a kiss on the forehead, which he wiped away with his sleeve. 'Be good. Don't lose your phone, and don't break your glasses.'

Harry rolled his eyes and headed out the door.

'See you next week,' Ben said. 'Call me if you need a chat.'

'Have fun,' called Grace. She stood by the gate, running her fingers over the wave motif carved into the wood, until Ben's car disappeared around the roundabout at the end of Beachfront Road.

. . .

At visiting time that same afternoon, Grace drove up to Bayview and parked under the sycamore tree outside the window her grandfather would be sitting at. She had long given up hope that he'd recognise her car and give her a cheery wave from the window, like he used to do when she popped round to Seafoam Cottage after dropping Harry to school. She also knew he wouldn't miss her if she didn't come to see him for a week. She was right, he was at the window staring blankly at the car park and the gardens beyond.

'That tree is dying, they need to cut it down,' he grumbled as Grace sat down next to him.

'It's not dying, Grandad. It's just losing its leaves because it's autumn. You'll see, next spring there'll be green leaves on it again,' Grace replied with a touch of sadness in her voice. She was under no illusion that not only was he a very old man, but he'd been ill for a few years now, to the extent of needing professional care over the last year. He wasn't going to get better. It was possible her grandfather wouldn't be around to see the spring. The thought of losing him made her heart heavy. They sat in companionable silence for a little while before Grace spoke again.

'Grandad, I'm going away tomorrow for a few days, so I won't be able to come and see you.'

His only response was a slight huff.

'But I've spoken to Reverend Clive and Janice, and they said they'll pop in.'

'I don't like her,' Richard said with the sullenness of a toddler.

'Janice? Why not? Everyone loves Janice.'

'She keeps telling me I'm doolally.'

Grace patted his arm gently. 'Well, you just ignore her,' she said in a tone she hadn't heard herself using since Harry was a small child. Janice would never say something like that to Richard. She might be a gossip, but she wasn't mean. It was this that was so cruel about his illness – she could never be sure whether what he was telling her was real, or whether it was in his muddled head.

'Will Lily be able to come? I'd like to see her. She's a very pretty lady.'

Grace struggled to swallow the huge lump that formed in her throat. 'We'll see, Grandad,' she said softly.

As Richard's vacant gaze turned again to the bare sycamore outside the window, Grace made her way quietly across the room. It was only when she was in the solitude of her car that she put her head in her hands, let out a heavy sigh, and rubbed her eyes. When had she become so exhausted?

TWENTY-TWO
LILY

September 1940

I didn't dare look up from my hands, folded in my lap. The drawing room was stuffy, I could barely breathe. Mummy always kept this room too warm. I couldn't bring myself to look at their faces, to see the effect of what I'd just said marked on Mummy and Daddy's features. The silence pressed down on the back of my neck like a lead weight. My stomach churned and I placed a protective hand over the very slight outward curve of my belly. I hadn't expected to see that yet. I'd thought I had more time to plan, to come up with a solution. But I'd already had to deploy a safety pin to hold the waistband of my skirt together. This baby was growing at an alarming rate, and I couldn't put off telling my parents any longer.

'Have you told him?' It was Daddy who spoke first.

Obviously, he meant Richard. I shook my head.

'Look at me, you stupid girl,' he hissed.

Holding my breath, I raised my head. Daddy was standing at the fireplace, his right hand gripping the mantlepiece, his face a deep red, his greying moustache actually twitching. Mummy was perched on the edge of her reading chair, staring into the middle distance with wild eyes, a hand clutching a hanky to her mouth, her chest rising and falling rapidly. It wasn't fair on Richard to let Daddy's presumption stand. None of this was his fault and I couldn't let him take the blame. I cleared my dry throat.

'It's not Richard's,' I said, in a voice that sounded as though it was coming from somewhere outside of my body.

All hell broke loose. Daddy lashed out, sending photo frames and vases crashing from the fireplace onto the hearth below. Mummy screamed, a high-pitched, blood-curdling scream that echoed around the sitting room. Daddy crossed the room in two strides and grabbed hold of my hair and pulled me to my feet. There was a raw, animal fury in his eyes, the likes of which I'd never seen. I couldn't hold back the tears, his grip on my hair and his hand around my arm were hurting me.

'I'm sorry,' I tried to say. All that came out of my mouth was a whimper.

'You disgusting little trollop, you filthy little whore.' He was pushing me out into the hall now. My pulse quickened as he pulled open the front door and launched me through it. Mummy had dissolved into loud wailing. The door banged behind me.

I stayed where I had landed, shaking and scared. The grass was damp with early-evening dew. From behind the front door, I could hear my mother's wails and my father's heavy footsteps up and down the stairs. An unending stream of hot tears poured down my face. I wasn't so foolish as to have expected my news to go down well, but I had thought they might have understood, or at least given me a chance to explain. I certainly never expected to find myself on my rear-end in the front garden of my home. The rest of the street was silent. It was a quiet neighbourhood away from the centre of Brighton and the residents were mostly people my parents' age. A street of closed doors behind which very little was happening.

The door opened again, and yellow light flooded the otherwise pitch-black street. Somewhere in the darkness a cat yowled. I got up and took a tentative step towards the house. A small bag landed at my feet, followed by my coat and hat, my gas mask case, and my ration book.

'You have destroyed this family and shamed us all. You are a disgrace,' Daddy growled. 'You will never set foot in this house again.' The letter box rattled as he slammed the door shut. His words were like punches to my chest.

I had a quick rummage in the small bag, thank goodness Henri and Richard's letters were there. I wrapped my coat around my shoulders despite the warmth of the evening, stuffed my ration book into my pocket, and wedged my blue felt hat on top of my curls. I made my way down the garden path, my knees shaking, the rest of me completely numb, my heart in pieces. As I pulled the gate behind me, I stole a glance at the sitting room window. I could just about make out Mummy's thin face through the lace. She was looking out at me, wiping her eyes with her silly little linen hanky. Daddy came up behind her and drew the blackout curtains. That was the end of that.

I turned down the hill towards the beach, not that I could walk along it. It had been closed for a year and mined since July, but it was a straight road to the town centre. At least the kerbs had been painted white to provide some guidance in the dark. I set off towards town, not really having any idea where I was going, but hoping to avoid the attention of any Air Raid Precautions wardens. There was a low droning overhead and the searchlights lancing the sky began to sweep, highlighting the dark outline of a plane where the beams crossed. The wail of the air raid siren pierced the night air. That was all I needed. I sighed, being blown to smithereens or crushed by a falling house would solve all my problems. The steady thump of the guns at the anti-aircraft artillery station by the sailing club reverberated in my chest. I wanted to go down and tell them to stop, not to bother shooting down the bomber, to let him come and put me out of my misery.

I passed the Grand Hotel, which had been requisitioned by the Ministry of Defence just a few months earlier, and turned inland, away from the beach. The road ahead was closed anyway. The path underfoot became steeper and as I climbed, it truly dawned on me quite what a mess I was in. I had been thrown out of home, I had no money, nowhere to live. Reaching Brighton train station, I operated on autopilot, showing my pass to the familiar guard and boarding the waiting train to Dovecote. Daddy was not the sort of man to go back on his word, so whatever the future held, I could no longer call Brighton my home.

TWENTY-THREE
GRACE

October 2015

'Here we are, then,' Grace remarked, getting into the driver's seat of the hire car.

So far, the journey had been manageable even though she'd been on edge since they met at Gatwick Airport, early that morning. James had barely said a word to her in the airport, dashing off to pick up some last-minute bits and pieces. On the plane, he'd put in his headphones. She'd willed the window seat to remain empty so she could scooch over and put a little distance between them, but her hopes had been dashed by the late arrival of a passenger who had headed, naturally, for 14A. Her thighs ached from the effort of preventing her knee from resting against his.

James fastened his seatbelt as Grace adjusted the mirror and made herself familiar with the car's controls, which were the opposite way around to at home.

'Yes, here we are.'

They gave each other a sideways glance.

'Look, Gracie,' he said with a sigh, 'thanks for letting me tag along. And I know this is a bit weird, so would it help if we established some, I don't know, ground rules?'

'Like what?' Grace asked, whipping around to look at him. He wasn't going to suggest a *dinner à deux* was he?

'I'm here to help you find Henri, and that's it. I also have work of my own that I need to get done.'

'I know that. I'm not expecting to hang round with you the whole time. In fact, that's the last thing I want. I'm here for a break too and, not to be funny about it, spending a week with you isn't what I would call a break.' She'd gone too far. He looked a touch offended. 'Sorry, that came out more harshly than I meant. Look why don't we just agree that we are under no obligation to spend every minute with each other. If we want to eat alone, go for a walk alone, or do whatever else we want, that's fine.'

'Yeah, I guess that's what I meant.'

'And we won't take offence at being told to buzz off for a bit.'

James laughed. 'Agreed.'

As soon as they were on the road out of Nice Côte d'Azur Airport, James put his headphones in again, leant back in his seat, and closed his eyes. Grace's shoulders released from somewhere around her ears as she drove along the sun-bleached highway. The sky was an unbroken blue, and the trees swayed gently in the breeze. Even though it was mid-October, there was no sign of autumn on the French Riviera. They had left behind leaden skies and persistent, miserable drizzle to land in brilliant sunshine.

As the outskirts of Nice fell away, replaced by rolling, tree-covered hills, James began to snore softly. Grace's thoughts wandered to what she'd left behind in Dovecote: the empty cottage, the remnants of Lily's things that she still hadn't finished sorting out, Ben and Rachel's fresh, loved-up happiness, the sheer heartbreak of watching Richard's decline. She wouldn't allow herself a shred of guilt for taking a break from it all. The only person in her life that she didn't want to run away from was Harry, and he was growing up and away from her.

Shaking away these thoughts, Grace refocused on the road ahead, the sun streaming in through the car windows. She refused to linger over any of it. She'd have enough on her plate looking for Henri and dealing with being in close proximity to James.

The hills were behind her, and she pulled off the highway onto twisty roads lined with pine trees. As she rounded a headland, she caught her first glimpse of the sea. It wasn't the steel-blue of Dovecote's English Channel. This was the Mediterranean and it was sapphire, with hints of turquoise, teal, and topaz. Here and there, the waves were white-tipped as they slapped partially submerged rocks. There were no sharp cliffs or stony beaches, only green hills and yellow sand. Grace rolled down the window and pulled the salty air deep down into her lungs. The warm air flooding the car woke James from his nap.

'Nearly there,' Grace whispered, keeping her thoughts about the colour of the sea to herself.

The Hôtel Provence was an imposing white-walled, red roof-tiled, three-storey building with pale blue shutters at the windows set back from the road that ran parallel to the beach. The raised outdoor terrace of the bar provided a prime people-watching spot. A large plane tree, with fairy lights draped across its branches, provided shade to the white-clothed tables in a courtyard that served as both restaurant and hotel reception.

'This is me,' Grace said stopping at a pale wooden door

halfway along a cream-painted corridor. 'I think I'll unpack and then go for a wander. I want to check out the town and the beach.'

'Sounds like a plan.' He flashed her a smile. 'I've got a few emails to do, so I won't ask if I can join you. See, I get the hint, you don't even have to tell me to buzz off.'

Grace rolled her eyes at him as he dragged his suitcase along the corridor, the wheels muffled by the burgundy carpet. He didn't look back.

Grace's room was bright and airy, with a huge bed piled high with squishy pillows. The peach walls matched the bed spread and the curtains. There was a desk in the corner and a cream sofa next to the balcony doors. The bathroom was completely white and spotless. She looked longingly at the free-standing bath that was just crying out to be sunk into.

Having hurriedly unpacked, Grace pulled back the voiles at the balcony doors and stepped out into the warm afternoon sun. Her balcony offered an uninterrupted view of the bay. Beyond the path, lined with pine trees bent almost double in the wind, on the other side of the main road was the beach; a ribbon of sand laid down in stripes of various shades of white, yellow, and brown marking the reach of the tide. Short stone piers punctuated the beach, at the end of which men patiently waited for something to bite at the lines they had cast into the white-capped waves. Neuville-sur-Mer was nestled in the middle of a sweeping bay embraced by tree-covered headlands dotted with houses of various shapes and sizes, all either painted pink or white and covered with purple and pink bougainvillea. In the distance, behind the headland, the foothills of the Alps shimmered blue-green and sage in the heat haze. On the horizon, where the azure-blue sea met the powder-blue sky, a cruise ship sailed majestically eastwards towards Monaco.

Grace was roused from staring out at the sea by a beep from her mobile. It was a video from Harry of Ben driving down the

M4 in lashing rain. She chuckled as the phone panned around to reveal Harry giving the camera a thumbs up in the back of the car. Rachel was giggling in the background. Having replied, resisting the urge to send a picture of the sun-dappled beach, she threw her mobile into her handbag and headed out.

The delicious aroma of warm garlic and herbs filling the hotel's courtyard caught Grace's attention, and she stopped to peruse the restaurant menu mounted on the wrought-iron gates. The *moules frites* sounded very appealing.

The row of shops next to the hotel wasn't terribly exciting: a pharmacy, a bank, and an estate agent. There wasn't a soul in any of them. There was a bit more life in the next row along. On the corner, a bakery emitted enticing smells of pastry and fresh bread. There was a trinket shop with a window full of seaside-themed knick-knacks. At the end of the row, the pavement opened onto a large square with a war memorial at the centre. She walked up to the fin-shaped statue, with an old anchor in front of it. The inscription explained that at 6.30 a.m. on 15 August 1944 an allied liberation army had landed in the area. The monument was dedicated to the 45th American Division. A group of old men played *boules* on a dusty pitch under the shade of plane trees, the clack of the balls a staccato rising above the muted chatter.

With a contented sigh, Grace crossed the street and paused at the railings overlooking the beach. It was wider than she had thought, expansive enough for there to be restaurants built into the sea wall along it with wooden decks almost reaching down to the water. The narrow steps leading down to them, and the A-Frame menu boards dotted along the path, were the only clues to their existence. Neuville-sur-Mer was clearly more geared up to catering for tourists than Dovecote. A small tiki bar complete with palm trees offered two-for-one cocktails decorated with paper umbrellas. While she may not be able to find a sticky bun or a cheese toastie as good as Janice's, the delicious smells of garlic and seafood wafting up from the beach restaurants and the warm sugar emanating from the *boulangerie* hinted at a myriad of delights waiting to be discovered.

Towards the hotel end of town, there were a couple of bars, another estate agent, and a small supermarket. Beyond, a low stone wall stretched as far as Grace could see, behind which the sea pounded dark, sharp rocks. Grace wandered down the road that hugged the coastline. High walls and wrought-iron gates hid the houses along the road. Was Henri, and the answer to what had happened between him and Lily, lurking beyond the stone and rhododendron barricades? A rumble from Grace's stomach forced her back to the present and back towards the town.

As Grace passed her hotel's terrace bar, she spotted James at one of the tables. She hesitated long enough for him to look up from his phone and see her. He gave her a wave.

'Coffee?' he asked, as she approached. 'Or something stronger?' He gave her a look. 'Of course, under the ground rules you're free to say no to either.'

Grace pulled out a chair and sat down next to him, giving him an exasperated look.

'A coffee will do just fine.'

'Well,' he said once the waiter had set down Grace's espresso. 'Now what?'

Grace looked up at him, stirring her coffee. 'I don't really know,' she said slowly. Now she was here, what was the next step? 'And I can't think on an empty stomach.' She glanced at her watch. It was getting close to six o'clock, no wonder she was hungry. 'Ground rules notwithstanding, did you have any plans for dinner?'

James grinned at her. 'No. The hotel restaurant looks good though.'

'It really does.'

'And seeing as we need to work out our strategy, surely it falls under the "finding Henri" criteria?'

'Which makes it perfectly acceptable.' Grace laughed. 'Alright. I need to finish unpacking and have a shower. Meet you back here at seven thirty?'

'It's a date.'

Grace gave him an exaggerated shake of her head. 'No, it most definitely isn't.'

'Do you think Henri might be listed in the phone book?' Grace asked, putting down her fork and sitting back in her chair, stuffed to the gills with *moules* and chips, as well as a few glasses of the lightest, most delicious rosé she'd ever tasted. Despite dinner being supposedly about discussing Henri, they'd mostly chatted about James's work, his parents, and mutual friends neither of them had spoken to in years. They had relaxed into the conversation, and the tension that had knotted Grace's neck eased slightly. Yes, she'd broken her own rule by having a few drinks with James, but she could handle it. She was not going to let her guard down.

James took a sip of his beer and shook his head. 'I've already checked the online one, and there's no sign of any Benoits.'

Grace pulled the newspaper article from her handbag. 'What about his niece? What was her name?' She found the paragraph in the article. 'Here. Sophie Laurent. The article says she's Henri's only living relative. And he's quite old, so maybe he lives with her?'

'I'll have a look,' James said. While he tapped on his phone, Grace looked up at the fairy lights in the tree. They were twinkling as the leaves fluttered in the very light breeze that rippled through the courtyard. 'Here.' He turned his phone screen to her. 'Nice work, Sherlock.'

Grace traced Sophie's name with her index finger. 'No address?'

'Nope. Just a phone number. You'll have to call her.'

'Me? Can't you do it?'

James shot her an indulgent look. 'Ha! No. I'll text you the number.'

Grace fidgeted with her napkin. She'd not actually thought about what she would say to either Henri or Sophie, and now that she had the means to contact them, the prospect of doing so filled her with a strange sense of dread.

'Is this insane?' she asked, as James put his phone back in his pocket.

'Definitely,' he said with a slight shake of his head. 'But then you always were a bit reckless.' Grace turned away to hide the panic in her eyes, if he only knew how accurate that innocent statement was. A tall woman with dark hair, pulled into a tight chignon, walked past the hotel entrance. There was something familiar about the shape of the woman's nose and the sharp angle of her chin. Grace quickly pulled the article out of her bag again and looked carefully at the picture. She was already on her feet when James's hand closed around her arm.

'Hey, where you going? What's up?'

Grace wrenched her arm from his grasp. 'It's her.'

'Who?'

'That woman who just walked past. It's Sophie.'

James grabbed her arm again, a little more firmly.

'Gracie, no. You can't just go up to her randomly in the street.' He gently pulled her back down into her chair.

'I wasn't going to speak to her, I just wanted to see where she was going,' she said, petulantly.

'You were going to follow her?' James hissed. 'See Gracie, that's exactly why I said I wanted to come down here with you. To stop you doing something stupid like that. What if it hadn't been her and you'd followed some poor random woman home?'

Grace let her shoulders droop; he was probably right. Not that she'd let him know that. 'Alright, I'll call Sophie tomorrow.'

'That's better. And when you call her try not to be weird.'

Grace scowled and drained her wine glass. It rankled that he was right. It was irritating that he was here at all. If he hadn't been, she would have known where Henri was by now. She'd been sure that was Sophie.

He was annoying and yet that was somehow comforting in its familiarity. As much as she hated to admit it, it was nice to have him back in her life.

TWENTY-FOUR
GRACE

October 2015

Grace held her breath as the phone on the other end of the line rang a third, and then a fourth time. She exhaled when there was no fifth ring. Instead, an incomprehensible stream of fast French in a woman's voice rattled down the line, followed by three piercing beeps. It took her a moment to register the silence expectantly waiting to be filled with her voice.

'Oh. Um. Hi. Um. I. Um. My name is Grace Curtis, I mean Grace Lyttleton. I was. Um. I was hoping to speak to Henri Benoit. If this is the correct number, um, maybe you, I mean he, could call...' and the line went dead. 'Urgh,' she groaned, throwing her phone down on her bed in frustration. It had taken her all morning to build up the courage to make the call and she'd screwed it up. She'd not even left her number.

As she stood looking out to sea, the water that lapped Grace's toes was warm and instantly relaxing. It wasn't the end of the world; she could call Sophie back. She had to, otherwise she'd look like a complete idiot to James. She crossed her arms. Why had she agreed to let him tag along when there had always been a risk that she would fail? She should have put her foot down, told him to swivel, and given herself the chance to fail in private. With a deep sigh, she stepped back into her sandals and turned away from the sea. She claimed a table right on the edge of the wooden terrace outside *Pieds dans l'Eau,* a restaurant with a white, sail-shaped awning. She was perusing the menu (very kindly provided with an English translation) when a shadow fell across the table.

'You can of course invoke the prime ground rule and tell me to sod off, but I can't walk past without giving you the option to have lunch with me.'

She looked up at James smiling at her. His eyes were hidden behind his sunglasses, but they were probably flashing with amusement.

'I should have told you to sod off back in the car park of Dovecote train station. Oh, for God's sake just sit down, would you?'

'Thanks. So, what have you been up to this morning?' he asked, swapping his sunglasses for his regular ones. He held up his hand. 'Sorry, does asking that contravene the ground rules?'

Grace shook her head. 'I spent most of the morning psyching myself up to call Sophie.'

James's eyebrows flicked up over the rim of his glasses. 'And?'

'I got an answer machine. I don't even know if it was Sophie.'

'Did you at least leave a message?' he said, with a grimace.

Grace laid her arms on the table and rested her head on them. 'I tried. But I got flustered and I think I just spouted gobbledegook.' She raised her head. 'I didn't even leave my number. Don't look at me like that.' He was giving her the kind of look she gave Harry when he'd done something utterly idiotic.

The waiter came to the table and Grace managed to pull herself together long enough to order some grilled prawns, while James opted for calamari. It may have only been lunchtime but, by unspoken agreement, a bottle of local rosé was also requested.

'And what have you been up to?' she asked, keen to steer the conversation away from her disastrous morning.

'I could say that I spent the morning trying to convince the gorgeous redhead I met in the bar last night to leave my room, but I'd be lying.' He scrunched up his nose. 'I've been working on my book chapter and doing some local research online. I know, I'm a boring old fart.'

'Did you at least meet a gorgeous redhead in the bar?'

He let out a short, sharp, laugh. 'I wish. I did go for a nightcap, but it was just me and a couple of old guys drinking pastis and playing cards. I got chatting to one of them and he said he'd give me a tour of the beaches and take me to see the monument to Operation Dragoon on Saint-Tropez beach.'

'That's good. I don't know much about Operation Dragoon.'

'It was part of the Allied invasion of Europe on D-Day. Everyone knows about the Normandy landings, but you don't hear much about the landings all along this area in August 1944. It was a pretty big deal, and successful too. It was only on one of the landing beaches, Saint-Raphaël, that the Allies came up against any serious defences. In conjunction with the parachute regiments that landed a bit further inland, the operation paved the way for the French forces' liberation of Marseille and Toulon – important ports for the Allies.' He gave her a stern look. 'Stop trying to distract me from you messing up a simple phone call. You are going to try again, aren't you? Or is this whole, very expensive, trip going to be a waste?' James stabbed a piece of calamari.

'Of course I am,' Grace said indignantly. 'I just don't have any clue what to say.'

James put down his fork. 'Do you want me to try?'

Grace looked down at her prawns. 'As much as I hate to say it, yes, I do.'

'Alright. I'll give her a call this afternoon.'

Grace didn't look up in case his eyes gave away that he was laughing at her.

An hour, and half a bottle of wine later, Grace was trying to pick a souvenir for Harry from the charming little gift shop when her phone buzzed with an incoming message.

All sorted. We're going to meet Sophie and Henri tomorrow afternoon.

Her hand was shaking as she typed her reply.

Thank you. Are we meeting at their house? Did Sophie give you the address?

She could imagine James rolling his eyes at that.

Yes, and yes. The address is 6 rue St Sebastien. I'm telling you this now on the promise you won't do anything daft. I had to negotiate pretty strenuously to get Sophie to agree to meet us. Don't make me regret it.

Grace bristled slightly at his insinuation and then put the address into the map app on her phone. She put the seashell-studded photo frame back on the shelf and left the shop.

. . .

The walk along the coastal road was longer than she anticipated but Grace was distracted by the blues and greens of the sea splashing the rocks that lined the shore. The sea breeze was chillier than the day before and she pulled her cardigan a little tighter around her shoulders.

Reaching a dusty car park, she followed the map on her phone and turned into the road highlighted in yellow. A blue plaque with a white 6 identified Henri's house to be the third house on the left, almost at the end of the road. A high, pink-painted concrete wall and green iron gates blocked the view of the house from the road. Grace stood on the opposite side of the road and looked at the gates for a long moment. The sound of a car engine startled her, and she ducked out of sight behind a large tree. The car stopped outside the gates of number six while they opened, and then disappeared inside. The gates closed again before Grace could get a good look at what lay beyond.

There was a little beach in the cove beneath the deserted car park at the end of the road. Would there be a view of the house from there? Lifting her long skirt to avoid treading on the hem and sending herself tumbling down the steep, narrow steps, she made her way down into the cove.

The beach was butter-yellow sand and slate-grey shingle, and crystal-clear water lapped it with a lazy, unhurried rhythm. At the far end, dance music thudded from speakers on the wooden deck of a beach restaurant. Settling herself down on a large boulder, she looked for the house, shielding her eyes from the sun. There it was. A little, red-roofed bungalow with coffee-brown stone walls. There were palm trees in the garden and a spindly, metallic structure that looked like a pergola of some sort. The house was right on the tip of the cove and waves crashed on the rocks at the end of the garden. It looked like a very peaceful place and Grace imagined Henri sitting there tucked in blankets, like he had been in the photo in the newspaper, staring wistfully out to sea. It must have been what Seafoam Cottage had been like, before the sea wall had been built, with the waves pounding the rocks right outside the front door.

Grace sat and stared at the house, transfixed by its dark walls and low, heavy roof until the shadows lengthened across the beach and the chill of the sea breeze became sharp. With a last long look, she climbed back up the steps and walked into town. She was going to wake up soon and find this was all a dream. Except the sand in her shoes and the tightness of her sun-warmed skin were real. This was all real.

Sitting still for so long in the little cove had chilled Grace's bones and she struggled to get warm, despite the lengthy walk back to the hotel. She sank gratefully into a very hot bath and closed her eyes. Her thoughts drifted to the reception she and James could expect the following day. Hopefully James was wrong, and Henri would be glad to be reminded of Lily.

Her musings were interrupted by the shrill ring of her mobile phone. Damn it. She dried her hands and reached for the handset, but she smiled when she saw who was calling.

'Hello, sweetie,' she said brightly.

'Hey, Mum. You alright?'

'I'm fine, how's your holiday going?' It was lovely to hear his voice.

'Mum, it's been amazing. Rachel's mum and dad are *so* cool, and they have a Labrador called Monty and we played fetch for hours. We're at the beach now, and it's stopped raining.'

'That sounds lovely. Are you getting on with Rachel? You don't mind that it's not just you and Dad?' Grace asked, drumming her fingertips on the edge of the bath.

'Oh, yeah, she's been pretty cool. She's only had to fix my glasses once.'

'Harry Curtis, don't tell me you broke them already?'

'It wasn't my fault. I forgot I was wearing them, and Monty jumped up and they kind of slid off. It's okay though, Rachel put the arm bit back on. You can hardly see the little scratches on the frame. There is one thing though.'

Grace sat upright at the change in his tone.

'What, sweetie?'

'It's just a bit gross, Rachel and Dad are always holding hands and smooching. You and Dad never did stuff like that.'

'Oh honey, I know. It's just that when you first start going out with someone, it's all exciting and new. Don't worry, it will wear off. Do you want me to say something to Dad?'

'No, it's okay. I'll just keep pulling sicky faces when they do it. That will put them off.'

'Yeah, you do that,' Grace said with a chuckle. Oh, to be young and innocent.

'I'd better go. We're going out for dinner.'

'Alright, honey. Thanks for calling, it was a lovely surprise.'

'That's okay. Love you, Mum,' he said almost whispering as though afraid someone might hear.

'I love you too, Harry. See you soon.'

'Bye, Mum.'

'Bye, sweetheart.' Grace inhaled a lungful of perfumed steamy air and sank back down into the bubbles. Maybe she could give James a call, see if he fancied going for a drink. It was a fleeting thought because as soon as she thought it, she brushed it away, remembering the ground rules.

TWENTY-FIVE

GRACE

October 2015

Grace nervously patted her hair as James pressed the buzzer of 6 rue St. Sebastien. She could see a sliver of the bungalow's stone walls in the gap between the gate post and the wall.

'What did you say to Sophie to get her to agree to this?' questioned Grace as the green gates creaked open and they stepped onto the palm tree-lined, roughly paved driveway. 'Did you tell her about Nanna?'

'I may have overemphasised my role in all of this, a little,' he replied, giving her a hesitant glance. 'I said I had come across Henri as part of some research and was interested in speaking to him, and that there might be a personal connection with your family. I was deliberately vague.'

Grace didn't get a chance to reply as a middle-aged woman came to the door. Her elegant black, ankle-length dress was a little formal for a warm October afternoon, and she was definitely the woman Grace had seen walking past The Hôtel Provence. There was a pinched look on her severe face, not relieved by the tight chignon of dark hair at the base of her neck.

She was imposing, and a little terrifying. At least in the sunlight she looked younger than she did in the newspaper article photograph. When Grace had read the article, she'd supposed Sophie was in her seventies, but seeing her in the flesh, she was probably closer to mid-sixties.

'Welcome, Doctor Rutherford.'

Grace shot James a loaded look, simultaneously impressed and infuriated that he'd clearly used his academic credentials to good effect.

'I am Sophie, Henri's niece. He is looking forward to meeting you.'

James shook Sophie's limp proffered pale, slim hand. 'This is Grace Lyttleton, who has unearthed a connection between your family and hers.'

'Hello,' Grace said, giving Sophie a polite smile. Her nerves were starting to ramp up from mildly nauseating to full-on panic. The expression on Sophie's face made it abundantly clear just how warm the welcome really was. 'It is an honour to be here and to meet your uncle,' Grace continued, consciously matching Sophie's formal tone. 'I am hugely—'

'Please come through. My uncle is in the garden,' Sophie interrupted.

'Grateful,' she muttered to herself. Grace fell into step behind James as he followed Sophie through the house. 'After you, Doctor,' she whispered, giving him a poke in the ribs. The inside of the house was cool and surprisingly light, considering how dark and foreboding it looked from the outside. Despite the heavy farmhouse-rustic wooden furniture and exposed, red-tinged stone walls, it was fresh and airy. There was a large brick fireplace with two cream leather wing-back armchairs arranged in front of it, and a farmhouse kitchen with French Grey painted cupboards. A set of glass double doors, the likes of which Grace could only dream of getting planning permission to install in the Grade II listed Seafoam Cottage, allowed the sun to shine into the room and led out to a large, unevenly paved patio. The clack of her heels on the terracotta tiles reminded her of home.

As they reached the patio doors, Sophie turned to James, blatantly ignoring Grace.

'My uncle has a bad chest, and the doctors say that the sea air is good for him.' The stone-paved patio area was boarded by coarse, spiky shrubbery and large rocks, but beyond that there was nothing but open sea.

'You're certainly in the right place for plenty of sea air,' said Grace, her eyes falling on the tiny figure wrapped in blankets, sitting lopsidedly in a wheelchair in the middle of the patio. The withering look Sophie shot her cut to the bone.

She followed a few steps behind Sophie, her knees trembling slightly as they approached the old man. His eyes were closed, his head bowed. There was a short, bosomy woman with a wide, smiley face, wearing blue dungarees and a bright yellow t-shirt, around the same age as Sophie, sitting next to him. The woman stood as Sophie, Grace, and James approached.

'This is my friend Jenna,' Sophie said, but Grace caught the look the women exchanged. There was something in the way their eyes spoke to each other that made Grace wonder whether 'friends' was an entirely accurate description of their relationship.

'Hey, y'all,' Jenna said with a sunny smile, her broad Californian accent a complete surprise. 'I guess you folks are here to see Henri.' She glanced at Sophie whose scowl deepened. 'I'll leave you to it,' said Jenna, some of the brightness gone from her voice. 'I'll be inside,' she added, addressing Sophie, as she ran her fingers through her grey, curly bob.

'*Oncle*, the people I told you about from England are here to meet you.' Sophie spat the words as though uttering a curse. At her voice, the old man's eyes fluttered open and he lifted his head. It only took a second for the drowsiness and confusion of an interrupted nap to fade from his face. Grace had a sudden mental image of Richard, whose face was forever frozen in hesitation and bewilderment.

'Ah Miss Lyttleton, Doctor Rutherford,' Henri said, extracting a thin, weathered hand from the folds of countless blankets.

'Grace, please,' Grace said, taking his hand gently. 'It's lovely to meet you, Monsieur Benoit.'

'*Non, non.* Henri, please. Sit, sit. We have things to discuss do we not? Sophie, *du thé.*'

As Sophie marched back into the house, Grace and James settled into wicker armchairs next to Henri. He was looking at her intently, almost as if...

'We have met before, no?' he asked, interrupting Grace's thoughts.

'No, never,' she said gently.

'Oh well, perhaps not,' Henri shrugged slightly. 'Although your eyes are very familiar.'

Grace's mouth dried up. People often told her she had her grandmother's eyes.

After a moment's pause, Henri turned to James, his expression shifting from curiosity to mild weariness. 'You want to know about Dunkerque,' he said.

'In all my years researching wars, I've never had the opportunity to hear a first-hand account of the events at Dunkirk. It would be such an honour to hear your story.'

'So says everyone I meet for some reason. Well, alright, I will tell you.' Henri steepled his fingers, his elbows resting on the arms of the wheelchair, closed his eyes, and began to speak. 'I do not fear death because I have already seen hell. I was a boy in 1940, just twenty-one years of age, a soldier in the 32nd Infantry Division of the French First Army. The division was formidable, full of keen, young men eager to protect our beloved France. We advanced north to attempt to halt the German invasion but ended up surrounded at Lille. We were determined not to go down without a fight, but there were only about forty thousand of us left and we fought against seven German divisions for three days. We were hugely outnumbered; we could not win. British and French forces were trying to hold the port at Dunkerque so that there could be an evacuation. Our job was to hold back the advancing forces for as long as possible. The longer we held out, the more likely it was that we would be too late to be rescued ourselves. It was chaos. There were abandoned vehicles blocking the roads and injured and exhausted refugees coming the other way in a constant stream. It was very difficult to see one's countrymen so beaten and distressed.'

Henri turned towards Grace. His eyes were shining, and he patted her knee gently.

'I don't mind saying that I was scared and worried about what we might find when we got to Dunkerque. I was sure there would be no one there to rescue us. I was right to be frightened. What we found when we got to the town was nothing less than hell itself. Fires burned everywhere. There was no water to put them out. I can still smell the burning oil and taste the ash in the air. There were bodies lying in the streets where they had fallen. Men, women, and even children. Houses and shops had been reduced to piles of matchsticks. There were bottles of brandy in the road from the shops that had been burnt. I picked one up, we all did.

'And still they came, the Stuka bombers, even when there was nothing left for them to destroy, except our way out. There were bullets too, they came from all directions. There were no boats in the harbour for us. We found any shelter we could and waited.'

'How long were you waiting?' James asked, his eyes wide. He was clearly in his element.

'I have no idea,' Henri answered, shaking his head slowly. 'The shockwave from an explosion had stopped my watch but I was in that ditch a long time. Night fell and the fires continued to roar around us. Word filtered through that some boats were coming. I ran toward the beach where tiny rowboats were coming to take us to the larger ships further out in the harbour. A bullet caught me in the thigh. I fell, dropping my bottle of brandy. It smashed and I watched the golden liquid run down the road. For many days, I cried about my bottle of brandy.' Henri's eyes fluttered shut, as though asleep. His voice was hoarse when he spoke again, his eyes still gently closed.

'Somehow, I staggered on. I think some others were dragging me. I was lifted from my feet and loaded like a sack of potatoes into a boat. I remember staring back at the town and thinking about the men, women, and children being left to the mercy of the Germans. France had been lost, and we were leaving her. I was so full of sadness that I might never see my country, or my family again. I must have blacked out at some stage; I have no memory of arriving in England or how I got to the hospital. The next thing I knew, I was being woken up by a nurse in a hospital in Brighton.'

Henri opened his eyes as Grace blinked hers. A tray of tea and madeleines rested, untouched, on the table beside them. Sophie must have brought them out and now hovered nearby, pretending to tend to the bushes in the flowerbed.

'There you have it. My Dunkerque story.' Henri reached for a handkerchief and blew his nose.

James blinked a few times and shivered. 'Thank you, Henri. Really, thank you. It is an incredible story. Have you ever thought about writing it down, getting it published even?'

'I don't think so. I was one of hundreds, thousands. My story is not so special.'

'It is though,' James said, shaking his head. 'Every story from that time should be recorded for posterity. Each story deserves to be told, and studied, and learnt from.'

'Well, perhaps one day. Maybe you could help me with it?'

'It would be a tremendous honour,' James said, blushing slightly.

Grace tried to speak but found her throat and mouth dry. All the moisture seemed to have gathered in her eyes which were brimming. She searched frantically in her handbag for a tissue and wiped her eyes carefully, trying not to smudge her mascara. He had been so young and had seen so much death and destruction. Her chest ached for the ones that hadn't made it, young men she knew nothing about other than that they had been his comrades, his friends. She chewed her lip and tried to compose herself. There was still so much she wanted to talk to him about, and she still had the letter. Yet there was something telling her not to disrupt this old man's peaceful existence. He was looking at her again, with that same searching curiosity.

'And when you got to England,' James said, pulling Henri's attention away from Grace. 'After your recuperation in hospital, what did you do then?'

Grace scowled. Why had James skipped over the most important part of Henri's story? Was he leaving it up to her to mention the woman that nursed him back to fitness, and with whom he'd clearly fallen in love? Maybe he too was doubting whether it was a good idea to bring Lily back into Henri's life.

'I was treated in Brighton before being taken to a convalescent home in a pretty little town by the sea called Dovecote. Do you know of it?'

Grace and James shared a look and Grace smiled. 'Yes, we do.'

Henri beamed. 'I was looked after so well. Being by the sea was the next best thing to being home here in Neuville. As soon as I was passed fit, I was sent to a muster point in Salisbury to prepare to return to the front. I did not want to go. I wanted to stay in England.' He paused glancing at the pendant of the necklace Grace was wearing. 'I should be ashamed of that, but I was a young man and very afraid. I thought I had been very lucky to still be alive but going back to war meant asking for trouble, pushing my luck.

'In London a fellow I knew said I could volunteer for the Free French Army, under General de Gaulle. I could stay in England and help train women at the military school in Bournemouth, all very secret. It helped that I had good English, thanks to a formidable tutor from Canterbury my mother insisted on hiring when I was a boy. The other men could barely order a cup of tea. *Maman* always insisted that being able to speak English was the way to succeed in the world. It certainly helped prolong my life by keeping me away from the front line.

'Naturally, I signed up straight away and caught the train from Waterloo. Soon I was involved in all sorts of things, secret things. It was hard not to be able to tell my family.' He looked at Grace again. 'Or anyone, where I was, or what I was doing. I did end up back in France eventually, but as I was working deep within the Resistance, I could not contact anyone.'

Grace's chest ached. All that time, he'd only been a couple of hours away in Bournemouth, not across the sea in France. He had been so close, and yet unable to tell Lily. That must have been so hard for him. Instinctively, she raised her hand to touch Lily's glass pendant.

He turned back to James. 'Then I became involved in the FFI and Operation Dragoon, which brought me home for a short while. I was in Paris for liberation day.'

'You were involved in Operation Dragoon, with the FFI?' James said, almost vibrating with excitement. He turned to Grace. 'The FFI was the French Forces of the Interior, de Gaulle's formal name for the resistance fighters.' He turned back to Henri. 'Were you involved in the landings then? Forgive me, I'm researching Operation Dragoon and it's incredible to get to meet someone who was there.'

Henri smiled. 'I was one of the liaisons between the FFI and the Allied forces, again my good English was useful.'

James asked another question that Grace barely heard. She got up and wandered to the end of the garden where the sea crashed against the rocks sending a seagull squawking into the sky. Grace watched the bird swoop and dive in the thermals. The letter was in her handbag and her fingers itched to pull it out and hand it to him. But he was a frail old man with a traumatic past. Were Ben and James right? Could she risk upsetting him, reminding him of something he'd lost that maybe he didn't want to be reminded of? What would her grandmother want her to do? She turned back to find Henri watching her while James scribbled frantically in his notebook.

'Henri,' she said hesitantly, sitting back down next to him.

He reached out and patted her hand.

'My dear, I was told by my niece that you know of an old friend of mine, yes?'

Grace nodded. A gentle approach was required. 'Henri, you mentioned the nurses that looked after you. Do you remember a young nurse...'

'That is enough questions.' Sophie's stern voice cut in. 'I think you should go now.'

Henri glanced up at his niece and back at Grace. There was a look of regret but also resignation in his eyes. It was clear Sophie wasn't often disobeyed. James got to his feet, and Grace followed.

'Thank you for your time, Henri. It was very kind of you to agree to meet us, and it has been an honour to hear your stories,' said James. 'I'm going to visit the Dragoon beaches tomorrow but, if you will allow me to, I'd like to come back and talk with you some more about it.'

'You are welcome,' Henri said, reaching out to take James's hand again. 'And of course, anything I can do to help I will.' He turned to Grace. 'We will meet again. I think there are things we need to discuss.'

Sophie snorted dismissively but Henri ignored her.

'In fact, I think you should come again tomorrow at ten o'clock. Yes, I would like that.'

'Really? Oh yes, that would be wonderful. Thank you.' She glanced at Sophie who sniffed loudly. 'If you don't mind?'

Sophie sighed. 'I suppose not.'

At the front door, with a warm breeze ruffling her hair, Grace turned to Sophie. 'Is tomorrow...?'

'If my uncle insists.'

'Sophie, I...' Grace paused, unsure of what it was she was trying to say and withering under the older woman's glare. 'Thank you.'

Grace shared a look with James as Sophie shut the door firmly.

'She's a barrel of laughs,' James joked. 'But he's amazing. And to find out that he was involved in Operation Dragoon.' He puffed out his cheeks. 'Incredible.' He checked his watch. 'It's five o'clock, and I don't know about you, but I could do with a drink.'

'I think that's a very good idea,' Grace said, letting out a long breath.

Henri Benoit had turned out to be a far more remarkable person than Grace could ever have imagined. What right did she have to break his heart all over again?

TWENTY-SIX
GRACE

October 2015

Approaching the edge of the town they stopped at *Le Bord de Mer*, a bar with a red awning Grace had seen from her hotel room balcony. The large wooden deck under the awning extended out over the beach. It was like being on the bow of a ship, with the waves lapping against the struts below. The view was of an unending sky and sea.

'Thank you, James, for sorting out today. It means the world to me.'

James blinked a couple of times, a shy smile pulling at his lips.

'You're welcome,' he said softly. 'I get the impression Sophie isn't going to be home when you go round tomorrow.' James reached for the bottle of wine. Grace's first glass of rosé had vanished disturbingly quickly.

'I did assume so, which is good. I don't think she'd let me talk to Henri about Nanna if she were there. To be honest, I'm not sure I want to, now I've met him.'

'What do you mean? Isn't giving him Lily's letter the entire reason for coming?'

Grace put her glass down and looked out across the water. The sun was just dipping down to the horizon, painting tendrils of orange and pink across the sky. 'I know but there's just something telling me I shouldn't disturb him.'

'What makes you think that talking about Lily and giving him the letter is going to disturb him?'

Grace shot James a look. 'I thought you said I should bear in mind that he might not want to be reminded of something he lost.'

It was James's turn to gaze out over the white-tipped waves. 'I'm not sure I meant that,' he said after a long moment. 'Having met him, I think he can handle it. I mean, he talked today about the worst thing he's ever been through. I don't think being reminded of an ex-girlfriend is going to faze him.' He swirled his wine glass, watching the liquid slosh against the sides. 'It's not as if *she's* going to suddenly reappear, is it?'

'No, she's not,' Grace said, a wave of sadness washing over her.

'So, you'll give him the letter?'

Grace puffed out her cheeks. 'Probably.' Her mobile phone pinged, and she picked it up, smiling at the picture that had come through. It was of Harry and Ben standing next to a bright orange lifeboat, both grinning like idiots.

Nearly had to send this out when Dad had a go at windsurfing!

That sounded like Ben alright. He'd give anything a go, regardless of talent or experience, or fitness. The number of times he'd given himself a minor injury doing something daft like rock climbing or trampolining, was too many to mention.

'Something wrong?' James was looking at her with curiosity and she locked the screen before he could see the photo.

'No, no. Just a message from Harry. He's having a great time on holiday by the sounds of it.'

'He's gone with his dad?'

'And his dad's girlfriend.'

'Oh. Is that not a bit weird? For you, I mean. It must be hard to trust someone new coming into his life.'

Grace swallowed the last of her wine. 'Yes, and no. Ben's girlfriend is someone Harry knows well, so it's fine for him and I know he's safe with her. She's been my best friend since kindergarten.'

'Rachel?'

'Yes. I can't remember if you ever met her. She came down to visit me once in London, but it was in first year, before you and I got together.'

'You told me about her, but no, we never met.'

A silence fell between them as they watched the sun sink down out of sight and the sky turn from blue to navy.

'Do you mind me asking you something?' James said as the first stars came into view.

Grace shook her head warily. What was he going to ask her now?

'What happened with you and Ben? How come you separated?'

'You can say the "D" word, James,' she said. 'I don't really know. I think we just ran out of steam. By the end, last summer, we found we didn't really have much to say to each other. We were snapping at each other a lot, and generally not getting on. It was a mutual decision.' She lifted her drooping shoulders. 'It was the right thing for us to go our separate ways. We're conditioned to think that parents should stay together no matter what, for the sake of their children. But I think it's far more damaging for kids to live in a toxic environment, watching their parents snipe at each other constantly. I suppose I kind of wanted Harry to see that there's no shame in admitting that sometimes we make mistakes. That sometimes we do things we wish we hadn't. And, in a way, it worked out for the best all round. Grandad had just been moved into Bayview, so Nanna was glad of the company when Harry and I rocked up at Seafoam Cottage.'

'Do you regret it? Marrying Ben, I mean.'

'Not for a second. But I also don't regret calling time on our marriage either. I don't like regrets. At the end of the day, we make the decisions we do based on our circumstances at the time. There's no point looking back and wondering whether you could, or should, have made different ones. You're never the same person as you were when you made your choices.'

Their eyes met and he held her gaze for a long moment.

'Please don't ask,' she pleaded, breaking eye contact and looking away.

'Are we going to not talk about it forever?' he asked.

'Not now.'

'Then when?' he said, crossing his arms. Grace chewed her lip and didn't reply. James got up from the table. 'Fine. But we need to talk about it, Gracie. I need to talk about it. And if... Never mind.'

He walked away across the wooden deck and out of the bar. Grace watched as he crossed the road and headed for the hotel a few yards away. She'd lied to him. She did have regrets, lots of them, and they were all about him.

Having finished the bottle of wine and settled the bill, Grace wandered back to the hotel herself. She could give James a call but if he was in the mood to discuss their past, it was better that she left him alone.

Back in her bedroom, Grace slid open the balcony doors and stepped out into the night. The sea and the sky had become indistinguishable, just one black velvet curtain bejewelled with sparkling stars and the lights on the masts of the boats bobbing on the current. Neuville-sur-Mer was still, quiet, drowsy. Her mind kept wandering back to James and what he'd said about needing to talk about what had happened all those years ago. It was bound to have come up. How could they spend a week together and it not? So far, she'd kept it at bay, but the conversation was looming, getting closer, and the prospect of having it sent a shiver down her spine. She just needed to deflect it a little longer. Her thoughts were interrupted by the ringing of her mobile from where she'd dropped it on her bed.

'Ben. Hi,' she said, a touch of anxiety in her voice as there always was when he called her when Harry was with him.

'What the hell are you up to, Grace?' He sounded furious and Grace's heart sank, Rachel must have told him.

'Ben, listen.'

'No, Grace, you listen.'

She could hear waves in the background, he must have gone to the beach to call her.

'I don't know what you're thinking, going on holiday with James. How do you think that looks? I can't believe you'd do this and not tell me.'

'I didn't have much choice. I needed him to help me meet Henri.'

'I'm fed up to the back teeth of hearing about Henri, Grace. Seriously, I don't know what's gotten into you. Just answer me one thing – have you told him?'

'No,' Grace snapped, appalled that Ben could ask that. Didn't he know her at all? 'Of course not, and I wouldn't. Not without discussing it with you first.'

'You'd better not.'

Grace shuddered at the venom in his voice. There was a pause as they each waited for the other to say something. She heard Ben draw a breath.

'Are you sleeping with him?'

It was one thing for Ben to have a go at her for not telling him about James, but this? Blood pounded in her ears.

'That's none of your business, Ben. Don't you start getting all narky about who I get involved with, I'm not the one who's bedded my ex's best friend.' She paused. She had been about to deny his allegation, but why should she? She didn't have to justify herself, or what she did, to him. He had no right to dictate anything about her life. 'Oh, just...' She bit back the word she wanted to say, swearing at him wouldn't help. 'Naff off.' She hung up.

With rage still bubbling in her veins, she threw her phone down on the bed only to pick it up again when it beeped. It was a message from Rachel.

I am so sorry, it just kind of slipped out xx

Grace let out a short, sharp huff. She'd been stupid to think that Rachel wouldn't tell Ben at some point. It also made it very clear that her relationship with both of them had changed, forever. She drew a couple of calming breaths. It wasn't Rachel's fault; it was hers for expecting Rachel to keep it a secret. She typed a response.

It's done now.

Back out on the balcony, Grace drew a couple of deep breaths of evening-warm salty air. The situation with Ben and Rachel would need to be dealt with head-on. Boundaries needed to be established. They couldn't just bumble their way through it, or she'd end up losing them both. And she couldn't do that to Harry. She pushed all of that to the back of her mind; that was a Dovecote problem to be sorted out in Dovecote. Her job in Neuville was to give Henri her grandmother's letter and get home without letting James get too close.

TWENTY-SEVEN
LILY

September 1940

I stumbled off the train into the darkness of Dovecote. The sirens weren't sounding here, so the bombers must not have ventured this way. I made it as far as the stone bench outside the station before I crumpled and buried my face in my hands, sobbing.

The whistle of a train startled me, it was the last train coming in. I had been crying on the bench for over an hour. I needed the bathroom, so I peeled my exhausted body off the bench. The instant I stood up, the now-familiar nausea rolled over me. I hurried to the toilet inside the station, retching as my empty stomach tried to turn itself inside out.

Placing one shaky hand over my belly and wrapping the fingers of the other around the pendant at my throat, I chanced a look at myself in the mirror. Unsurprisingly, I looked quite a state. My eyes were red raw, my hair limp, my usually plump cheeks drawn and hollow. But beneath it all, there was something else, a light in my eyes, a sort of glow.

'Hullo,' said a rounded west-country accent I recognised from behind me. 'What are you doing out this late?'

'Mrs Macnamara,' I said, startled, turning sharply and banging my hip against the sink. Of all the people I could have bumped into, I would never have expected to see the manager of Bayview at Dovecote station, in the middle of the night.

'Heaven's above, girl, whatever is the matter? I hope you don't mind me saying but you look rather peaky.'

I couldn't hold it in any longer, I broke down and Mrs Macnamara put her chubby arms around my shoulders and drew me into her ample chest. Her cardigan held the faint smell of Bayview, clean and slightly clinical but there was a hint of rose water on the wool.

'Come, come now child,' she said softly, stroking my head. It was the kind of show of affection I was not familiar with. Mummy hadn't ever held me like that. 'Come on, whatever it is it can't be that bad.'

She released me from her embrace and looked into my eyes.

'I was just heading home. You've missed the last train back to Brighton, so why don't you come with me and stop for the night? In the morning, you can tell me what this is all about. Things always look better in the light of day.'

All I could do was nod.

The next morning, I awoke in a soft bed with sunlight streaming through a small window. The memory of the night before came back as I looked out at a beech tree and a garden that was entirely dug over and planted with vegetables. Beyond the garden, a cliff face rose steeply, and I could hear the sea. The night before, in complete darkness, I had barely registered arriving at Mrs Macnamara's home. I think she said it was called Seafoam Cottage? It hadn't been a long walk from Dovecote train station, and it was the opposite way to Bayview. I did remember the sensation of the sea nearby, and, of all things, that there was a post box at the end of the road.

I dressed and made my way gingerly down the stairs into a terracotta-tiled hallway. I could hear the low hum of the radio and followed the sound.

'Ah, there you are, Lily.' Mrs Macnamara was stood at the sink, the sleeves of her pink flowery housecoat rolled up to her elbows. 'I thought I'd let you sleep, you seemed to need a rest.' She came over and patted my arm. 'Go on into the sitting room and I'll bring you in a cuppa.'

I gratefully wrapped my fingers around the hot cup as Mrs Macnamara sat down on the sagging couch next to me. The sun coming through the net curtains on the bay window cast fine shadows on the carpet and across the green wallpaper on the walls. It was a cosy room, and clearly well-loved.

'Well now,' Mrs Macnamara said, giving me a warm, but intense stare. 'What were all the tears for?'

I had to tell someone, I had to say the words.

'I'm in trouble, Mrs Macnamara,' I said, falling back on that old euphemism that elderly church ladies used to describe girls like me. When Mrs Macnamara didn't say anything, I clarified. 'The "in the family way" kind of trouble.'

'Oh dearie, you aren't the first, and I very much doubt you'll be the last. That's one in the eye for Herr Hitler, I suppose. Your young man away, is he?'

I nodded. 'Singapore, and he's been gone more months than I can account for.'

I glanced up at Mrs Macnamara, the shape she'd made with her mouth made me think she understood what I meant. There was a short pause.

'And your other young man?'

'Shipped back to France a few weeks ago.' Had it really only been a few weeks since I got his letter telling me he was leaving for France? It felt like a lifetime. 'I know, I know. I've been so stupid and careless. Other girls say it can't happen on your first time, but I'm a nurse, I should know better.'

'So how come you ended up wandering around Dovecote late at night?'

'I had nowhere else to go. I told my parents yesterday evening. It didn't go down well. Daddy called me a string of names I couldn't possibly repeat and threw me out the front door. He said I'd brought shame on the family, and that I wasn't ever to set foot in their house again. Mummy didn't say anything, she just screamed and wailed. So here I am, with nowhere to live and a baby on the way. It's all looking rather bleak.' I paused as a sickening realisation dawned on me. 'I shall have to give up nursing, won't I? They won't let me keep working, not in my condition.'

Mrs Macnamara shook her head gravely. 'No dear, they won't.'

We sat in silence for a moment, sipping our tea, listening to the seagulls squabbling outside. Mrs Macnamara was twisting her wedding ring around her finger, her eyes fixed on the photograph on the cream and brown tiled fireplace. I returned my gaze to my cup.

'You know dear, since my Bill was killed and my daughter, Catherine, went to live in Aberdeen, I've been a little lonely. I could do with some company. You could take Catherine's old room and we could clear out the box room for a nursery.'

I'd known Mr Macnamara had been killed in an accident at the munitions factory right at the start of the war. Sister Margaret told us so we didn't inadvertently say something and put a foot in it, but I didn't know Mrs Macnamara had a daughter. A pinch of guilt twisted my gut. It was so easy to get caught up in one's own life and forget that other people around you also had their troubles. It dawned on me what Mrs Macnamara was offering.

'Do you mean for me to come and live with you? Here in your cottage? I have some savings which I could make last a couple of months, but after that without a job, I won't be able to pay any rent or...'

'I get by alright, dear. My widow's pension covers most things, and my salary tops things up. It will work out. Do you have your ration book?'

I nodded earnestly; it had hit me square in the face when Daddy had thrown it at me.

'Well then, we'll get by. And I'm sure I can get my hands on plenty of things for the baby from the church jumble. I daresay Catherine's old cot is still up in the loft. Bill never did like to throw anything away. I might even get my knitting needles out. I'll speak to your parents, let them know you will be living in Dovecote with me. Despite what you think, they will be worried about you. And we'll get you to the doctor, just to make sure everything is as it should be. Come here, pet,' she said, opening up her arms and beckoning me to lean into her. She held me tight. 'In these wretched times we all have to look after each other,' she said quietly. 'God knows that's the truth.'

A trickle of tears escaped my eye, brought on by relief rather than despair. One thing was for certain, Richard wouldn't want anything to do with me now. To my shame, that thought didn't upset me. All I could think about was that I was going to be alright. My baby, Henri's baby, was going to be safe. I could only hope and pray that Henri would be too, and that one day we might be able to be a family.

TWENTY-EIGHT
GRACE

October 2015

The gate of 6 rue St. Sebastian had been left open and Sophie's car wasn't on the driveway. That was a relief. After Ben's phone call, Grace had had a restless night and was too tired to have to deal with Sophie's particular brand of hostility. The front door was ajar, but she couldn't bring herself to just walk in, so she tentatively knocked.

'Is that you, Grace? It is open. Please, come in.'

Grace found Henri in the kitchen still wrapped in his blankets, not in a wheelchair this time, but in one of the wing-backed chairs by the stone fireplace. The chair opposite was empty, and Henri gestured for her to sit down.

'Sophie has had to go to Saint-Raphaël for an appointment, she should be back soon. She doesn't like to leave me alone for too long.'

'She looks after you well.'

'Oh yes, she has been wonderful to me. It has not been easy for her, to move away from her friends, her job, her life in Paris, to come back home to Neuville to look after me. I'm getting old and each year another part of me stops working.' He sighed. 'One of these days I am going to run out of parts and then that will be the end of me.'

'I hope that won't be for a long time.'

Henri laughed. 'I have been around for a long time. Perhaps too long. But I am here for now. Where is your friend this morning?'

'James? He's gone to Nice this morning, to the Resistance Museum. He met a man in our hotel bar who is going to give him a tour of the local battle sites this afternoon.'

'It is good that people are taking interest in some of the less well-known events from that time.'

'He was delighted to meet you. I don't think he can quite believe that you were there.'

'Ah, there are some days when I do not believe it myself and I wonder if my old brain is making it all up. But, my dear, yesterday we did not get to talk much about why you have come to find me. My niece called an end to our meeting as you were asking me about the nurses who looked after me in England.'

Grace swallowed hard. 'Yes. Do you remember a young nurse by the name of Lily Mulholland?'

Henri's eyes flicked again to the piece of glass hanging on thin wire around Grace's neck before they misted over. He looked away from Grace into the empty fireplace.

'Lily Mulholland. I have not said that name out loud for many, many years. Oh yes, I remember, I remember very well. My dearest Lily. She was the most beautiful woman I have ever laid eyes on, and to this day I have not met another to match her beauty. She was my first, and only, true love. She had a wonderful smile. It shone brighter than the sun, and eyes the colour of the sea; a sea a man could easily drown in. I was very much in love with her. But how do you know of her?'

Grace cleared her dry throat. It was now or never. 'She's my grandmother.'

'*Mon Dieu!*' gasped Henri. 'Child, look at me.'

Grace turned her head and looked into his eyes.

He gasped again. 'Yes, but of course, I knew I had seen your eyes before. The blue is the same. Please tell me she is still alive.'

Grace bowed her head. 'No, I'm so sorry. She died a few months ago.'

Henri sighed. 'It is the way. When you live to be as old as I am, you lose many of your friends.'

'When I was tidying out some of Nanna's things, I found some letters. Letters that you wrote to her.'

Henri looked up at Grace suddenly, a startled look upon his face. 'She kept my letters?'

'Yes, she did. And I can see why. I hope you don't mind but I read them. If I hadn't, I never would have known about you. Henri, I know you wrote to Nanna at the end of the war, and I can see from your letters that you were very much in love with her. What happened?'

Henri rested his hands on the blanket and looked towards the ceiling. 'There was so much celebration in Paris the night the war was over. We danced in the streets, we sang, we drank too much wine, but my one thought was that now I could go back to England and to Lily. A friend said I should write to her first, just in case something terrible had happened, that she was no longer alive, or that she had moved on from me. I wrote to her. I told her that I was still in love with her and that I would come for her if she asked me to. I never got a reply. I was heartbroken for a very long time. My friends could not understand. I was sure she had met someone else. Or perhaps the fine young English gentleman who had once proposed marriage to her had returned from his far away posting and reclaimed her heart. Some of my friends tried to help by suggesting that perhaps she never got my letter, but I was inconsolable. I have often wondered in the years that have passed how she was, what had happened to her.'

Reaching into her bag for Lily's letter, Grace pulled it gently out into the daylight. She leant forward and placed it on Henri's lap, a lump in her throat. 'She got your letter. I have read it. I know it is about seventy years too late, but I found her reply. The letter she wrote but never sent.'

His hands closed around the letter and Grace watched, not having the faintest idea what he was going to do. Slowly he raised it to his lips and kissed it.

'It is still sealed?'

'Yes, I didn't want to open it. It would have been wrong to read it before you. She meant for you to have it, I'm sure, but I don't know why she never sent it. This is why I wanted to find you, to give you this.'

'Thank you.'

Sophie appeared, spectre-like, behind Henri, removing her coat. 'I think my uncle is tired now.'

Grace understood the subtext of Sophie's statement.

'I will leave you to read it in private, Henri.'

'Perhaps you could come back later. This afternoon?' Henri asked. 'We have not had much time this morning.'

Sophie shot Grace a menacing look and said something to Henri in French. He made a dismissive gesture with his hand.

'My niece is concerned because she will be out again this afternoon.'

'Oh. Well maybe another time, then?' Grace said, attempting a conciliatory smile towards Sophie.

'Nonsense,' Henri said with a snort. 'All the more reason for you to come back. To keep me company.' He turned to Sophie and said something else Grace couldn't understand.

'It is fine,' Sophie said through clenched teeth.

'Good, that is settled. I will see you later, around three o'clock, if that is good for you.'

'Of course. I look forward to it. I can see myself out. Thank you, Sophie,' she added giving the woman another smile, and getting a fresh scowl in return.

Grace couldn't face lunch; knowing that Henri was reading the letter made her nauseous. Instead, she'd walked the length of the beach, from *Pieds dans l'Eau*, past the stone piers, all the way to the marina filled with boats of all sizes covered and tidied away in preparation for winter. It was still as warm as a decent English summer's day. The weather app on Grace's phone said 23°C, but she supposed for the locals this was definitely autumn. There were only a handful of hardy swimmers daring to venture into the sea. Even the tiny dogs seemed to pull on their leads with more ferocity, keen to get their business done and get back to the warmth of their soft beds as quickly as possible.

There was also the matter of that 'conversation' with Ben. How dare he ask whether there was something going on between her and James. She shouldn't have snapped at him though. And then there was James. What was going on there? Had he really pushed to accompany her on this trip just to meet Henri, or was there more to it? His comment that Henri shouldn't have an issue with talking about Lily because she wasn't going to suddenly burst back into his life, made her nervous. After all, hadn't she suddenly appeared back in his? Was he hoping that spending time together might make them closer, even bring back something of what they had been before? But it had been over a decade ago. Love like that, which has been buried for so long, can't just be resurrected on a whim. Lightning doesn't strike twice.

. . .

The afternoon had turned breezy and, as Grace stood on Henri's doorstep, she wished she'd packed a proper coat. The sky was loaded with heavy grey clouds. She could hear the rapid click-clack of heels on the tiles and, before she had a chance to knock, the door was flung open. Grace found herself face-to-face with Sophie. The woman's lined face was puce, and a vein pulsed in her forehead.

'You have some nerve coming back here,' Sophie almost spat at her.

Grace opened her mouth to protest but the fire in Sophie's eyes made her close it again without uttering a syllable.

'Stay away from my family. Do you not realise what you have done? That letter could have killed him.'

Grace's heart pounded. 'Sophie, I...' Her voice faltered.

Sophie was now wiping her eyes with a linen handkerchief and sniffing loudly. When she looked up at Grace, there was undiluted hatred in her black eyes.

'Your grandmother ruined his life all those years ago and my uncle never wants to see or hear from you ever again.'

Grace's head dropped. 'I see,' she said quietly. As she turned away, Henri's voice came from somewhere inside the house.

'*C'est* Grace?'

She wanted to shout back that yes it was her, and she was about to when Sophie cut across her in a clear, bitter voice.

'Your grandmother was no better than a common whore.'

Grace inhaled sharply. 'How dare you!' she shouted, as Sophie slammed the door in her face.

The banging of the door was drowned out by a crack of thunder overhead. Fat drops of rain tumbled onto Grace's face as she stood, stunned, looking at the closed door. A fork of lightning split the sky and she stumbled down the driveway, splashing through puddles, raindrops pelting her face.

The road into town was deserted, and Grace ran the whole

way, only stopping to pull off her high-heeled sandals that were slowing her down. Her dress was soaked through, and her wet hair whipped her face. Flashes of lightning illuminated the pavement. The air seemed to glow green and purple and fizzed with electricity. At *Le Bord de Mer* she sank down on the stone wall outside the bar. The sea was angry, and spray from the waves crashing against the rocks splashed onto her feet. She held her face in her hands and cried and cried as everything that had happened in the past months overwhelmed her.

By the time her tears had stopped, so had the thunderstorm and weak sunlight filtered through the gloom. Grace watched the heavy clouds float away across the bay and out to sea, wishing she could do the same. She scrambled up from the wall and walked towards the steps that led down to the beach. Wet sand oozed between her toes and waves lapped her feet as she walked at the water's edge. What on earth was in that letter? If she couldn't speak to Henri, she would never know. What she needed was someone who could sweet-talk Sophie, someone who Sophie didn't hate with the burning fury of a thousand suns. She pulled her phone out of her bag and called James.

James arrived at Grace's hotel room bearing a bottle of wine, for which Grace was massively grateful.

'What happened?' he asked having poured them a large glass each.

'Just what I said. Sophie called Nanna a whore and slammed the door on me,' Grace sniffled.

'And she didn't give any hint to what was in the letter that upset her so much?' James's frown forced his eyebrows closer together.

'Nope. Whatever it is must be huge. Sophie said it could have killed him.'

'Something that would have come as a shock, then. Do you have any idea what it could be?'

'None. You know as much as I do.'

James swirled his wine around his glass for a moment. 'Let's go over what we know, then. Talk me through what you know of Lily's life around the war.'

'Well, from Grandad's letters we know he proposed to Lily before he left for Singapore, but she never gave him an answer. From Henri's letters, and from the conversation I had with him this morning, we know that he met Lily at the hospital in Brighton, was nursed back to health by her, and they had a brief love affair in Dovecote. Then Henri disappeared out of her life, working undercover with the French Resistance. Henri wrote to Nanna at the end of the war saying he would come back for her, but he got no reply.'

'And we know that sometime after Henri left, Richard, your grandfather, came home and married Lily in 1943. They had one child, your mother.'

'Yeah. What?' Grace paused catching James's eye. 'You don't think? No. Definitely not.'

James shook his head. 'I mean the thought did occur to me. Are you sure your mother was born after your grandparents got married?'

'She died when I was five, James, there's a lot about her I don't know. Just as I told you years ago, she was killed when a tree fell on her car in a storm. She had gone out to pick up my dad who'd been out with his mates and was so drunk no taxis would take him.'

Grace swallowed the ball of anger that formed in her throat. She hated him, her so-called father, who was not only responsible for her mother's death, but abandoned her when she needed him most. But now was not the time to rake though all of that. This was about Lily, Richard, Henri, and that blasted letter.

'The accident tore Nanna and Grandad apart. Even mentioning her name caused bucket-loads of tears. We did mark her birthday, but only quietly. Come to think of it, I'm not sure her age was ever mentioned. And it's not as if there's a gravestone or anything.'

She hesitated, that sounded very cold and detached.

'Mum was cremated, and her ashes were scattered in the sea from the rocks around Dovecote lighthouse. When I was old enough to question it, I asked why there was no memorial to Felicity Lyttleton, to my mother, but Nanna just said it was too painful to talk about. I didn't ask again.'

James's eyes were softer now, and he was looking at her with deep sympathy.

'It was a long time ago,' Grace said, clearing her throat. 'But I'm not convinced. Nanna wasn't the kind of person to keep something like that a secret.' Her own words caused her stomach to do a nauseating roll.

'I know, I'm sorry. I shouldn't have even suggested it. It was a dumb thing to say.'

'Yeah. So, what could be in that letter to cause such a reaction? It can't have been Nanna telling Henri that she married Grandad. Surely, he would have presumed she got married, considering he knows I'm her granddaughter?'

'I'm stumped,' James sighed.

'Me too. But I really want to know. That letter came from my grandmother. If there's something in it about my family that I don't know, I think I deserve to.' She looked up at James. His gaze was soft but intense and might have held a thousand meanings. 'I should have just read the letter, shouldn't I?'

He shrugged. 'I'm not going to lie, that thought did occur to me,' he said, reaching for the wine bottle and topping up their glasses.

'Any ideas on how we get Sophie to let me see Henri?'

James could only shake his head. They sat in silence for a

while. Grace drank her wine quickly and before long the bottle was empty. A warm fuzziness seeped through her, numbing her fingers and dulling the ache in her chest. The loud sob that erupted from her startled her, as it did James who moved from the chair by the table to sit next to her on the sofa. She couldn't speak through the tears, so didn't object when he put his arm around her shoulders and drew her into him, gently rubbing her back and slowly rocking her.

Her sobbing eventually receded. 'Sorry,' she muttered, extracting herself from his embrace.

'Don't be.'

'It's been a tough couple of months what with Grandad getting so ill, Nanna dying, Ben and Rachel becoming a couple, finding out about Henri, and seeing you again.'

She sniffed and turned away. James reached out and gently cupped her chin in his hand, turning her face back towards him. The space between them got slowly smaller until it vanished, and their lips touched. Grace was aware of letting go, of melting into his kiss. So familiar, yet not. Somehow right, but so, so wrong. A sudden spark of clarity pierced the wine-soaked fog of her brain. She pulled away abruptly.

'James, I...'

'Sorry,' he murmured, getting up. 'I shouldn't have...' He turned and walked out of the room, leaving Grace to wonder how far they might have gone.

TWENTY-NINE
GRACE

October 2015

Grace blinked in the brightness of another clear morning and put the events of the night before down to a surfeit of emotion and wine. Thank goodness she'd come to her senses when she had. She was enjoying James's company and getting to know him again, but there was no way anything like that could happen between them; it was far too dangerous. And if he had a different agenda, a different idea as to the direction of their relationship, then it was probably a good idea to avoid him for a bit. Unfortunately, that meant she was on her own when it came to trying to work out how to deal with Sophie. She had to find out what was in her grandmother's letter, absolutely had to. She just needed to get Henri alone.

Grace was sitting at a table in the hotel courtyard under the shade of the plane tree, absentmindedly stirring her coffee, when a flash of yellow caught her eye. Before she could second-guess herself, she was out of her chair and chasing the woman in the yellow jumpsuit down the street.

'Hey, Jenna,' she called, having caught her up.

Jenna turned, saw who was behind her and looked around nervously.

'Grace?'

'Yeah. Hi,' she mumbled, suddenly tongue-tied.

'Soph will freak out if she sees me talking to you, honey. She's furious about that letter, and right now you are public enemy number one.'

Grace frowned and looked around, there was no sign of Sophie.

'Do you have a minute, maybe we could grab a coffee?'

Jenna twirled a curl of hair around her index finger for a moment. 'Sure, I guess it can't hurt. But before you ask, I don't know what's in the letter. Soph wouldn't tell me, she said she couldn't. And Henri refused to let anyone, apart from Soph, read it.'

Grace led the way to the courtyard and back to her table. Two coffees appeared without Grace having to ask for them and she gave the young waiter a grateful smile.

'I *need* to know, Jenna,' Grace begged. 'I mean if there is something in my grandmother's history, then surely Sophie must see that I have a right to know what it is.'

'You don't have any clue?'

Grace sighed. 'Nope. I've been through everything I know about the relationship my grandmother had with Henri, and my grandfather, and I can't work out what she could have put in that letter that would cause such a ruckus.'

Jenna shook her head. 'A ruckus is a good word for it. Soph is scared about something, honey. I've never seen her like this before.'

'And Henri?'

'He keeps his thoughts to himself. He doesn't talk much.'

'Is there anything you can do to get Sophie to agree to me meeting Henri again? Or if not, then maybe to get her to meet with me to talk about it.'

Jenna reached across the table and patted Grace's hand. 'I don't know, honey. I can see how important it is to you. But I don't know how much influence I have in this.'

'You and Sophie aren't just friends, are you?'

Jenna blushed slightly. 'She doesn't like to tell strangers, but sometimes love is hard to disguise, I guess. Sophie studied film history in Paris, but she took a gap year to L.A. where I was training to be a make-up artist. We met and fell in love. I returned to Paris with her. I mean who in their right mind would pass up the chance to live in Paris? We moved down here to Neuville when she had to come back to look after Henri. It hasn't always been easy; she can be a handful at times. And we grouch and snipe at each other like all couples do, but I can't imagine my life without her.'

Grace looked down at the table. What did this lovely, sunny woman see in the miserable, grumpy, downright cold Sophie? How could they be compatible?

Jenna sighed and stood up. 'I better be getting back. Don't be too hard on Sophie. She's devoted to, and very protective of, her uncle. And she's not a bad person. Under that tough exterior, she's very sweet.'

'Will you ask her if she'll change her mind and let me see Henri, or at least call me?' Grace asked, pulling a scrap of paper from her handbag and scribbling down her phone number.

Jenna took the piece of paper and looked at it for a moment.

'She's also stubborn. But sure, honey, if a right time comes up, I'll ask.'

'Thank you,' Grace said, a hint of sadness in her voice. She wasn't going to hold out much hope that Jenna could get Sophie to change her mind, but it was better than nothing which, without Jenna's intervention, was exactly what Grace was left with.

. . .

Two strong coffees in quick succession were affecting her nervous system and, once Jenna left, Grace found herself unable to sit still. She paced the pavement on the other side of the road, from the entrance of *Pieds dans l'Eau* and down to *Le Bord de Mer*. She was turning around at the bar for the second time when she collided with someone. Looking up, she found the solid mass she'd walked into was James. He put his hands on her arms when she tried to duck around him.

'Hey,' he said, dipping his head to catch her eyes. 'I've been watching you pace up and down here like a caged animal. What's up?'

Grace gave him a look. Could he really not guess?

'Look,' he said, averting his gaze a touch, 'I'm sorry about last night. Can we put it down to too much wine and forget it happened?'

Grace softened her hard stare. 'Sure. Yeah, that's fine by me.'

'Phew. So now that's out of the way, will you let me in? Let me know what's going on in there?' He gave her forehead a gentle poke and Grace couldn't help but let her shoulders droop, releasing some of the tension in her neck.

She turned away from James and looked out to sea. She was still jittery from too much caffeine and a torrent of words were pushing to be let out.

'It's just all too much. Meeting Henri, the letter, what Sophie said, the not knowing. It's driving me mad. I spoke to Jenna earlier and I'm hoping she'll be able to convince Sophie to speak to me. Oh, by the way, she and Sophie aren't just friends, they're a couple and yet they're so different. Jenna seems so jolly and sunny, and Sophie is, well, just so mean.'

James's lips twitched but he didn't say anything, not that he could have; Grace barely paused to draw breath. Now that the words were spilling out, she couldn't stop them.

'I never thought the letter would, I mean, I only wanted to

give a man a letter he should have received a lifetime ago. I thought I was doing the right thing. But all I've done is cause hurt and pain. Before I gave Henri the letter, I thought it must just be a sweet little thanks-but-no-thanks kind of thing, but now I know there's something big in it. And that something is something to do with my family and now I may never know what it is. On top of all of that, Rachel is sending me photos of Ben and Harry on holiday with little comments about the things they're enjoying doing and how lovely they are together, as if I don't already know. As if I haven't watched Ben be the best dad to Harry for the last eleven years. As if I don't know that Ben had to carry Harry over seaweed because Harry used to be scared of walking on it. As if I haven't seen the way Harry looks up to him, the way he collapses with uncontrollable giggles when Ben does something funny. And that's something else I've done by coming here, I've upset Ben.'

She finally paused and James gave her a startled look.

'Why is Ben upset about you coming here?'

'It's not that I've come here, it's that you're here with me. I didn't tell him, but I made the mistake of telling Rachel, and trusting that she wouldn't tell him. But she did. She says it was an accident. That she didn't mean to, that it just slipped out. I won't be making that mistake in the future.'

The words were tumbling out even faster now.

'So of course as soon as Ben found out, he rang me, completely going off on one. He now thinks there's something going on between us. Of course, he's only worried that I might tell you about Harry, but it's still incredibly rude of him to ask whether we're sleeping together. What?'

The look on James's face made her stop. She instantly wished she could take back the words she'd let escape, the words she'd so desperately tried to keep inside for so long. James's face had gone a shade of greyish-white and his previously folded arms were hanging limply at his sides, although his hands were balled into tight fists.

'Tell me what about Harry, Gracie?'

'What? Oh, nothing,' she said with a nervous giggle and a slight wave of her hand. Her heart was doing double time.

'Gracie?' James's breaths were coming faster now, and his usual colour was coming back. A little too much colour, if anything. It was spreading up from his neck, across his forehead.

'It's nothing, James. Drop it.'

'You can't say something like that and then ask me to drop it, Gracie. What is it about Harry that Ben is so worried about me finding out?'

His voice had gone up a notch in volume and Grace shrank back from him slightly and shook her head. She pressed her lips tightly together as if to physically prevent any more words from being set loose.

'Gracie...' his voice trailed off and he ran his fingers through his hair.

Grace's mind whirred. She could just tell him. No, it would do far too much damage, not just to him, but to her, and Ben, and most importantly to Harry. She just couldn't do that. If she wasn't going to tell him the truth, she'd have to lie. No credible lie came to mind. She was tired of lies, and secrets, and pretending. Maybe the best thing to do would be to walk away, but her feet were rooted to the spot.

'I'm waiting, Gracie.'

'I can't,' was all Grace could manage.

'Oh. You're all "I deserve to know what's in my grandmother's letter because it's about my family" but when I ask for the truth about something that you're hiding from me, then I don't have that same right? You're no better than Sophie.'

'It's not that simple. Nanna is dead. Nothing that can come

out about her now can hurt her. I will hurt so many people, not least of all my son. I can't.'

James began to shake; his breaths were shallow and rapid. His lips were pressed tightly together, and his jaw muscles were working overtime.

'Gracie. Seriously. I'm not stupid, and I can count. But, if what you're hiding is what I think it is, then I need to hear you say it.'

'You can think what you like, James, that's not my problem.'

The sniffy, dismissive, nonchalant bravado was an act. Inside, Grace was shaking like a leaf caught in an autumn wind.

'Just say it,' he shouted, attracting looks from people around them. She knew from the sheer horror and fear in his eyes that he knew.

She closed her eyes momentarily and listened to the swish of the waves on the sand, to the squawk of the seagulls, to the thrum of the cars on the road. This was the moment she'd been dreading for eleven years, the moment when her world was going to implode. She opened her eyes and drew a breath.

'Ben isn't Harry's father. You are.'

THIRTY

LILY

March 1941

Another breath-stealing pain shot through my back and lower abdomen, like something had grabbed hold of my insides and was twisting and stretching me. The wave of pain across my bump made me curse, for the umpteenth time in God knows how many hours. At least I was at home. Mrs Macnamara, and the midwives, had tried to convince me to move into the women's house at Bayview. They said it was safer, in case of bombs. But I'd told them if a bomb were to fall on Dovecote it would probably flatten the whole town, Bayview included. Now, gripping my bed frame so tightly my knuckles had turned white, I was glad I had dug my heels in. There was nowhere I'd rather do this than in Mrs Macnamara's white-washed cottage. Over the last few months, Seafoam Cottage had become a real home to me, the warmest, kindest home I'd ever known.

I panted through the next contraction, pushing out short, sharp bursts of air. I felt like I was being ripped apart from the inside. I stopped panting and gave in to my body's demand for me to push.

At that moment, the bedroom door was thrown open.

'The cavalry has arrived, Miss Mulholland.'

I let out a long sigh of relief at the familiar, no-nonsense voice of Sister Margaret. I was in safe hands.

'Right.' Sister Margaret pulled on a gown and a pair of gloves and clapped her hands together. 'Mrs Macnamara, towels and hot water if you please. Let's see how you're doing, my dear.'

'Oh, I say,' she muttered a moment later, having lifted my nightshirt and had a bit of a poke around. 'Well, the bad news for me is that we're too late to give you an enema. So, I shall have to deal with the consequence of that should it arise,' she said, giving the small of my back a firm rub. 'But the good news is that the night is far too cloudy for any bombers to make an appearance and interrupt, and more importantly, baby is the right way around, the clever thing, and we'll have this over in a jiffy. Up on the bed with you, my girl, and let's get on with it. Right, on your next contraction, I want you to give it all you've got.'

I nodded. It was building.

'That's it, come on now, a bit more.'

I pushed down as hard as I could, the searing, burning pain forcing a tight scream from my throat. Sweat dripped from my forehead into my eyes.

'Keep it up. Come on. We're nearly there.'

'I can't,' I said, my voice small and wavering. 'I'm too tired.'

'You're doing wonderfully,' Mrs Macnamara said gently, giving my hand a squeeze. When she'd first taken hold of it, I'd imagined it was Henri's. The thought of him, out there somewhere in a mucky trench or worse, triggered something deep down inside me, something basic and primitive. A surge of strength washed over me, and I pushed as hard as I could.

'That's it. Head's out,' Sister Margaret cried. 'One more and we'll have the rest.'

I held the vision of Henri's smiling face in my mind and pushed for all I was worth.

'Got her.' Sister Margaret's triumphant call seemed to come from somewhere far away.

My head dropped back against the pillow as a wave of relief washed over me. A loud, plaintive, thoroughly outraged newborn cry wrought a loud sob from me.

I don't remember how I ended sitting up in bed, propped up against my pillows, but somehow that's where I was when Sister Margaret handed me a tiny bundle wrapped in towels.

'You've a little girl,' she said, beaming at me. 'Well done, poppet.'

I looked down and saw the singularly most beautiful thing I had ever seen: my daughter's tiny, scrunched up face.

'Hello, little one,' I whispered, not wanting anyone, not even Mrs Macnamara or Sister Margaret, to hear. 'We're going to be just fine you and I. Maybe one day, if we're very lucky, your daddy will come home.'

THIRTY-ONE
GRACE

October 2015

Grace stood, frozen to the spot, as James stormed across the road and vanished into the hotel. She held a trembling hand to her mouth, as if doing so could somehow stuff the words she'd said back inside. The undiluted shock, fear, and hatred that twisted his usually soft features, would be seared in her memory for eternity. She rested her head against the trunk of a nearby palm tree and let tears flow freely.

A buzzing from her handbag stirred her from her self-pity and she numbly reached for it. It was a call from an unknown number, with a French prefix.

'Hello,' she said, trying to disguise the wobble in her voice.

'Grace, honey, it's Jenna.'

Something snapped in Grace's head. 'Jenna. Hi.'

'Grace, it's Henri. He's been taken ill, and he's asking for you to come and see him. It's looking bad, honey. Can you come quickly?'

Grace had already started walking quickly down the footpath. 'What about Sophie?'

'She's not thrilled but she'll obey her uncle's wishes. I'll meet you at the door.'

'Thanks. I'm on the way.'

As she broke into a run, she frantically rifled through her handbag in search of a tissue to wipe her puffy eyes. Not finding one, she rubbed her sleeve across her face. A brief glance in the reflective screen of her phone confirmed she looked a mess. But more than that, she looked frightened. Something in Jenna's tone had hit her like a shard of ice, stabbing deep into her chest. She couldn't lose Henri, not yet. Not until she knew the truth.

The lightness was gone from Henri's stone bungalow. There was a different atmosphere in the cool hallway now, and it made Grace shiver with dread. It was the same heavy silence that permeated through Seafoam Cottage in Lily's last days, as her tired body succumbed to the inevitability of old age. It was death and she was not ready to face it again. When Jenna indicated wordlessly towards a door, Grace steeled herself and pushed it open.

The small, dark room was dominated by a high, wrought-iron bed, in which Henri sat, propped up by several pillows. At his side, in a hard-backed wooden chair, sat Sophie, clutching Henri's hand. Without his nest of blankets, Henri seemed even smaller, and impossibly frail. Sophie stood and stepped silently from the side of Henri's bed. She shot Grace a look of pure hatred as she slunk silently past. She pulled the door behind her but left it ajar. Henri's hand reached out and Grace clasped it in hers and gave it a gentle squeeze. There was no flesh on it, he was merely skin and bone.

'Ah, Grace. I am sorry to be leaving so soon after meeting you.' Grace opened her mouth, but Henri shook his head slightly. 'Shush now, I have much to say to you and, as you can see, perhaps not much time left. Grace, thank you for bringing

Lily back into my life. Reading her final letter has healed me in ways I could not have imagined.' He paused and took a few brittle gasps.

Grace tried to speak but her throat had tightened, trapping her words. She wanted so much to ask him if she could read the letter, but somehow, she found she couldn't. Perhaps he didn't want her to know, perhaps he intended to take Lily's last letter to him, and the secrets it contained, to his grave. That was his right, however much it hurt. She shooed the thoughts away, determined to focus on Henri, to enjoy what could be the last moments she got with him. He had been an important part of her grandmother's life, even though their love affair seemed to have been doomed, and she owed it to Lily to be present in the moment.

'Grace, I know why you came to find me.'

'You do?'

'You wanted to find the man who was in love with Lily, and who she loved too.'

Grace could only nod.

'As you no doubt worked out from my letters to Lily, yes, I remember every word I wrote, your grandmother and I were lovers. What I did not know until I read her letter, is that when I left Dovecote, I did not only leave Lily with a pendant I made from a fragment of a broken brandy bottle.'

Grace's hand flew to the glass at her throat.

'I found that piece of glass in my uniform pocket when I was on the boat leaving Dunkerque. It was all I had the night I asked Lily to be my wife. I wanted to give her diamonds, but all I had was glass.' The regret in his voice wrapped around Grace's chest and squeezed.

'She never wore it,' Grace whispered. 'I found it in a velvet pouch amongst her jewellery.'

'I am glad she kept it. You must wear it for her. As for the other memento she found herself with from that same night, I am sorry I never knew. But I do now. I know that I have a daughter.'

'A daughter?' Had James been right all along? Grace blinked and released her hold of Henri's hand.

'You did not know?'

Grace dumbly shook her head. Henri reached for the piece of paper on the table by his bed. He unfolded it but did not give it to Grace. He looked at her, his eyes shining.

'What Lily didn't tell me before I was sent back to the war, was that she was expecting a child. My child. Perhaps she did not know until after I had written to tell her I had to leave, and after that, she had no way of contacting me. She put it all in her last letter. Your mother, her name is Felicity, yes?'

Grace nodded, a numb coldness seeping up from the ground into her feet.

'Ah yes, so it is true, then. You see Felicity, your mother, is my daughter.'

Grace stood up from the chair, her knees shaking, and walked to the window. The late afternoon sun was glistening through the fronds of the palm trees that were swaying slightly in a light breeze. Her thoughts were jumbled, confused. If Felicity was Henri's daughter, that meant her grandad wasn't Felicity's father. Felicity was born while he had been in Singapore. A sudden memory popped into her head: a small girl with her thumb in her mouth, resting her head against a plump woman's shoulder in a photograph. A photograph in her grandparents' wedding album. That child was Grace's mother. She turned from the window to find Henri looking at her with a soft, gentle gaze and it finally dawned on her. Richard Morrison wasn't her grandfather, Henri Benoit was. Her brain refused to process that information. Instead, it fired fragments of memories, conversations, and unanswered questions at her. Eventually she found her voice.

'I always thought Mum had been born after Nanna and

Grandad got married, after he got back from Singapore. But she wasn't, was she? She was born while he was away.'

'In March 1941. You will have to ask her to confirm it.'

Grace's hand flew to her chest. If she'd known, if she'd had any inkling that this was what was in the letter, she would never have come. Because now she was going to have to tell him the rest of the story.

'I can't,' she said, moving slowly to the chair and sitting back down. She took hold of Henri's hand, swallowed, and bit her lip. How was she going to tell him?

'I'm sorry, Henri, my mother, your daughter Felicity, died nearly thirty years ago. She was killed in a car accident when I was five years old.'

His face crumpled.

'I am so sorry. If I had known about any of this, I would never have given you the letter. I should have read it before I came here. I didn't have to do this to you.'

'No, no,' he said, shaking his head slowly. 'I am happy to finally know, even though I am sad that Lily is gone and I shall never meet Felicity. It is as though a part of me is brought back, no those are the wrong words. I am complete.' He put a shaky hand to his chest. 'In here, there has always been something missing. But not any longer.'

'Nanna should have told you,' Grace cried. How terribly hypocritical was that?

'How could she? She had no way to contact me. And by the time she had a way to reach me, she was already married. I think I understand why she did not post this letter. There would have been no reason to. What could I have done? What could she have done? Even if she still loved me, and I think perhaps she did, she was married.'

'She shouldn't have married Grandad, she should have waited for you,' Grace said, a tear dripping down her cheek.

'Now, now. Don't cry, little one. I do not think she should

have. She did the right thing. You have to understand, Grace, that in those days, there was a terrible shame in having a child when you were not married. I am grateful to Richard that he took care of her, and of Felicity. She could not have waited for me. As far as she knew, I could have been dead myself. Do you see?'

Grace saw all too well. 'Yes, I do understand. It's just a bit hard to find out that she lied to me too, for all those years. And that my mother never knew. If only we could go back in time.' She let out a long breath. 'I wonder what Grandad thought when he arrived back in England to find Felicity.' She sighed heavily. 'I can't ask him because he is very sick. He doesn't remember anything any more.' Her voice stuttered.

'The illness that robs people of their memories is the most vicious of all. I would suffer endless physical pain so long as I have my mind,' Henri said, releasing Grace's hand and wiping away the remnants of her tears.

'He loved her very much. I think he still does, although his memory of who she was has gone. He talks about her often, even though he doesn't remember she was his wife. They had many happy years together. I grew up surrounded by love,' Grace said slowly, emotion bubbling in her voice. It was true; when she looked back all she could see was the love her grandparents gave her.

'You have made me happy, Grace. Yes, I have learnt that the only woman I have ever loved has died and that I had a daughter I never knew about, and she is also dead. But I have found a granddaughter. It is comfort to me to know that I have descendants left in a world that I am not long for. Now Grace, what about you? Are you surrounded with love now? I see no ring on your finger, but I hope you are happy.'

Grace pursed her lips and let out a long breath. 'I can tell you this, Henri, my story is not all that different to Lily's.'

'*Mon Dieu*, little one! Tell me.'

A light laugh escaped from Grace's mouth at his tone, and she looked away slightly embarrassed.

'I was married to a lovely man called Ben, but we got divorced just over a year ago. I have a son, Harry. He is eleven. But, like Nanna, my husband was not the father of my child. I never told Harry's father about him at the time, even though I loved him very much. I had my reasons for doing that, and at the time I believed I was doing the right thing.'

Grace paused, as the image of James's enraged face swam into her mind. She pushed it away, that was something she needed to deal with at another time. She jerked her head as something from years earlier suddenly made sense.

'Do you know,' she said with a slight chuckle, 'it's only now that I understand why Nanna didn't go mad at me. I have always been a bit confused as to why she was so understanding and supportive when I told her I was pregnant. I suppose the times had changed and it wasn't such a big deal to be an unmarried mother as it was in her time. Still, she must have been disappointed to see me in the same situation she had been in herself.'

'In her letter to me, Lily explained that when she told her parents of her condition, they were very angry and banished her from their home. That is why she reacted the way she did towards you. She did not want you to feel unloved and ashamed like she did.'

'That is awful, poor Nanna.' Grace drew a breath. 'Well, Harry and I certainly always felt loved.' She glanced away to wipe a tear that had leaked from her eye. When she looked back at Henri, there was a broad smile on his face and a glint in his eye.

'What?' she asked, mirroring his smile.

'You named your son after a great-grandfather you did not even know he had.'

'My goodness,' she managed to say, as a wave of giggles broke through her.

Henri was laughing too. His was a tight, rasping laugh that shook his fragile body. 'It is a good strong name.'

'But I didn't choose it,' she said, shaking her head. 'Ben and I couldn't decide on a name, and it was Nanna that suggested we name him Harry, well Henry officially. Nanna gave us your name to give my son.'

Henri didn't say anything, but his eyes were watery and the pressure of his hand on hers increased slightly. Grace sniffed, wiped her eyes, and returned his grasp. Henri let out a rasping cough and laid back against the pillows. The effort of talking seemed to have exhausted him. When he turned his head towards her, there was a seriousness in his eyes.

'Grace, you must promise me something.'

'Anything,' she said, dropping her voice to a whisper.

'You must promise me that you will look after my great-grandson and tell him of his namesake. Tell him my war stories, but more importantly tell him that I once loved as though there was no tomorrow. You know, Grace, the heart is a wondrous thing. It is fragile enough to break, to shatter, but it is also strong enough to heal. The thing that mends it the most is the truth. I never knew my daughter, and I may not have much time to get to know my granddaughter. Oh, what I would give for that chance. Your son should know his father, who should know his son. Family is built by flesh and bone. There is no stronger bond and with that bond comes love. Where you have blood, you will always have love, and you will always be family here.'

Grace let his words sink deeply into her brain, storing them away to be called on at a later date. He let out a rattling breath, and Grace held his hand a little tighter. Henri's eyes began to droop, and his face relaxed into sleep, exhausted by his long speech. Grace drew his hand up to her lips, and gently kissed it.

. . .

There was a tense atmosphere hanging over the terrace as Grace stepped through the sliding doors. Sophie was standing under the metal-framed pergola at the far end, looking out over the sea. Jenna was beside her, holding her hand, with her head resting on Sophie's shoulder.

'Sophie?' Grace said as she approached the pergola. 'Henri is sleeping now. Thank you for letting me see him. It means a great deal to me.'

When Sophie released Jenna's hand and turned, Grace could see lines of dried tears on her pale skin.

'I won't let you take him away from me,' she hissed before pushing past Grace and walking quickly back towards the house.

Jenna placed a hand on Grace's shoulder. 'Give her some space, this is all very hard on her. She's told me what was in the letter. I'm guessing you didn't know.'

'That Henri, her uncle, is my grandfather? That she and I are, what? Second cousins? No, I had no idea. My whole life I've known someone else as Grandad and now...' She sighed. 'I'm sorry to upset her. And please let her know that I don't want to take Henri away from her or change anything between them. Can you let her know that, please?'

Jenna squeezed Grace's shoulder. 'Okay, honey. I'll tell her. Why don't you slip out the gate, huh?'

'Yeah, I think that's a good idea.'

At the gate, Grace turned. 'Thank you for calling me. Will you let me know how he is?'

'Sure thing, honey,' Jenna said with a small nod.

Walking back to the hotel, Grace had the intense urge to talk to someone about all of this; to tell someone that she wasn't who she'd spent her whole life thinking she was. A month ago, she wouldn't have hesitated to call Rachel, but now, even though Rachel had been the one most in favour of her finding Henri, she couldn't do it. Nor could she call Ben. She was still mad at him for his outburst, even though she'd proved his fear to be well-founded. She'd done the one thing she promised him she wouldn't. She shuddered. And James? Oddly enough, if there was one person who might understand what it was like to have your entire world turned upside down, it was him; albeit for reasons that were entirely her fault. She paused at the palm tree where she'd spilled her secret and leant against it. The sea didn't look beautiful any more, it didn't sparkle in the sunlight. Instead, it was a vast, empty void. She rubbed her face.

'Oh, Nanna,' she said softly. 'How did I get myself into this mess? I could really do with your help.'

Having watched the sun dip below the horizon from her balcony, Grace shivered in the cooling air and turned her back on the sea. She sat down on her bed, a large glass of wine in her hand and, against her better judgement, typed a text to James.

> *Just been to see Henri, he's very unwell. He told me what was in Nanna's letter. You were right. My mother was his daughter. He never knew, Nanna never told him. He's my grandfather and I don't know how to feel about it.*

She raised an eyebrow when her phone lit up with a response.

> *Sorry to hear about Henri. Now you know what it's like to find out you've been lied to. Not nice, is it? Sudden surprises can really mess with your head.*

Grace downed her wine and refilled the glass, before making the only good decision she'd made in months: she turned off her phone before she could reply.

THIRTY-TWO

GRACE

October 2015

Grace raised her hand and knocked on James's door, wincing at the pounding in her head. She'd been only partially surprised to wake up to find the wine bottle empty. She needed to talk to James but not about Henri, that was her problem to sort out in her head. No, she needed to talk to him about Harry. The prospect of driving back to Nice and being wedged next to him on a crowded flight filled her with dread.

'Oh,' he said, as he opened the door. 'If you've come looking for sympathy then sorry, but I'm all out.'

'James, please,' she begged. 'We need to talk.'

He grunted.

'Can I come in? I want to try to explain. Please.'

He looked at her for a long time, clearly debating whether he wanted to listen to her explanations. Eventually he huffed, pursed his lips, and stepped aside to allow her through the door.

His suitcase was open on the bed and was half full of clothes. There was a half-empty bottle of scotch and a tumbler on the bedside table. Clearly, she wasn't the only one with a pounding head.

'I was putting some of Henri's story down,' he said, catching her glancing at his laptop open on the desk.

'He'll be delighted. You're packing?'

James scowled and flipped the suitcase closed. 'Yeah, changed to an earlier flight. I'm heading back this afternoon.'

'I'm glad I came to see you, then.'

'You wanted to explain, I'm dying to hear you try.' He scowled, crossing his arms and leaning against the desk.

Grace sat down on the end of the bed opposite him. She struggled to look at him, so instead focused on her hands, twisted together in her lap.

'Do you remember the day you told me that your research grant application had been approved?'

'How could I forget?' He unfolded his arms and rested his hands on the edge of the desk.

'And we had that massive row.' Grace looked up from her folded hands, their eyes met for an instant before James looked away.

'You mean the row where you said you didn't want me to go to South-East Asia and you didn't want to come with me, but you *also* didn't want me to stay with you in Camden? I offered every solution I could think of but none of them were good enough for you.' James huffed.

'It wasn't quite like that.' Or perhaps it had been, and Grace had rewritten it in her head.

'Gracie, I was confused and had no idea what I was supposed to do. All I knew was that I wanted to be with you.'

Grace sighed. 'I know, I'm sorry. Looking back, I don't think I knew what I wanted. I was scared of losing you, of living somewhere new, of being so far away from home. But most importantly, I didn't want to prevent you from chasing your dream and have you hate me for it. In my defence, my hormones were probably all over the place.'

'Wait, you knew during our row that you were pregnant?' James gasped.

'No, of course not! I promise I didn't. If I had known then, maybe everything would be different.' Grace shook her head. 'Anyway, we had that argument and I told you we were at different stages of our lives and that it was better if we called it a day.'

'And I was so angry at you for making me confused that I agreed. I didn't think we meant it though. I thought it was just something we'd both said in the heat of the moment. When I got home the next day and you'd left me I couldn't believe it. You didn't even tell me where you'd gone. I was completely gutted.' There was a dark shadow across James's eyes and the fissures in Grace's heart cracked open a fraction.

'I know, I was pretty broken too.'

'It was your choice.' He thumped the desk. 'So how long was it before you discovered you were pregnant?'

'About a month. You'd gone by then. You were already on the other side of the world.' Her voice faltered as a lump formed in her throat. She swallowed it down.

'And Ben? Don't tell me by then that you and he were...?'

Grace shook her head again. 'No. We'd rekindled our friendship but nothing more. So, before you ask, there's no way Harry's not your child.'

'Hearing you say all this is just so hard, Gracie. Seriously, I'm a mess right now. I don't understand any of this.'

'And I can't really explain it either.'

They sat in silence for a moment. Grace could see James wrestling with what she'd said. He looked like there were questions he wanted to ask but was afraid to. She started to reach out, to put a hand on his but pulled back. At that moment, the couple of feet between them was as wide as an ocean.

'Can I ask a question? One that, as a man who has never had, and will never have to make that choice, I don't really have a right to ask.'

'If you're going to ask why I went ahead with the pregnancy, then the answer is I don't know. I agonised over what to do. I was only a couple of years out of university, trying to make a start in the cut-throat world of newspaper journalism. A baby was not a part of the plan. But maybe I wasn't as ready to let you go as I'd thought I was.'

'And why, Gracie, *why* didn't you tell me? It wasn't like I was uncontactable.'

'I know, I know. Again, I thought so much about it, I went over and over it in my head. But I couldn't get past that comment you made about not being ready to settle down, that you had so much you wanted to do, that you weren't ready for marriage, or children. And you were right, at that age, we should have been having adventures without a care in the world.'

James paced to the window, his face contorted in confusion. 'Wait, hang on. When did I ever say I didn't want children?'

'You used to say it loads. Remember when that friend of yours got married and you said you couldn't get your head around why. You said you couldn't imagine being ready yet, that there was so much you wanted us to see and do.'

'Exactly, "yet". I didn't mean ever.'

'Well, James, I didn't have "ever" to wait for. I was having your baby then and there. I know what would have happened if I'd told you. You would have come straight back and done the right thing, but you would have ended up resenting me for it. I couldn't destroy your dreams like that. I couldn't bring myself to put you in that position.'

James crossed the room again and he gave the desk another light thump with his fist. There was fire in his eyes, but it was tinged with sadness.

'That wasn't your decision to make. Gracie, seriously, you should have given me the choice.'

'I know,' Grace said in a small voice.

'And Ben? He had no issue with being tied down?'

Grace released a slow breath. 'It was his idea. We'd been spending more and more time together and when I told him I was three months pregnant, he said that since I'd returned to Dovecote, he'd fallen back in love with me. He said he never actually stopped loving me, and he wanted to make everything right. He wanted to look after me. It wasn't easy, but he had a good job by then. Nanna and Grandad and his mum and dad helped us out and we managed to scrape together enough for a house. It was a wreck, but Ben worked really hard, we both did, and we made it into a home. When Harry arrived, we settled into a happy little routine, the three of us. A little family. I'm sorry, James. I truly am. All I can say in my defence was that I did what I thought was best for both of us at the time.'

James raised his eyebrows briefly and huffed. 'Well, it's done now. We can't change the choices that were made.'

'No, we can't. That doesn't make them right though.'

'If you could...' He paused. 'No, there's no point in asking that.'

'What?'

'I was going to ask, if you could go back whether you would make the same choices.'

'I don't think I can answer that. I know that if I were in that position now, I wouldn't make the same choice. Because I'm older, wiser, and not that scared young woman I was then.'

'And Harry doesn't know?'

It was Grace's turn to shake her head. 'No.'

James turned away and looked out of the window.

'No, as far as he's concerned, Ben is his dad. And he's been a brilliant dad.'

'Do you think you'll ever tell him?'

'I don't know,' she said. 'You know, having met Henri and seeing the regrets he has about never knowing his child, I do wonder whether it's ever right to keep secrets from other people. In the beginning, I always said I would tell Harry when the time was right, but as he grew and the bond between him and Ben became so strong, I couldn't bring myself to do it. I don't know is the honest answer. I suppose it would depend on...' She stopped, reluctant to say what she had been about to.

'On what?' James asked, his gaze shifting until he was looking directly into her eyes.

Her resolve weakened at the intensity of his look. There was only one way to right the wrong she had inflicted on him.

'Years ago, I took away your right to choose how to react to having a child. I'm giving you that choice now. If you want to be a part of Harry's life, then I won't stand in your way. I will have to tell Ben, obviously. He's going to have strong opinions on all of this. He won't want to lose Harry or hurt him in any way by telling him the truth.'

'I need to think long and hard about this, Gracie. Seeing you again after all this time has confused me. One of my reasons for wanting to come on this trip was to spend time with you, get to know Gracie now; to see if she was still *my* Gracie, the Gracie I loved so much. I never expected to have something like this land on me. Now I don't know what to feel or think. I'm just numb.'

'I can understand that.'

Their kiss flitted into her head. They were at a crossroads. James could walk out of her life, like she had walked out of his, and she may never see him again. But she didn't want that to happen without knowing whether he regretted their kiss.

'Can I ask you something? The other night, when we kissed, was that really just down to too much wine?'

James rubbed his forehead and let out a puff of air. 'In all honesty, while we're doing that, no.'

'Oh.'

'The truth is, I've found that you *are* still my Gracie. You're still chaotic, hopeless, impetuous, head-strong, stubborn, foolhardy, funny, sweet, and kind. You're still all the things that I loved about you. I don't know whether those old feelings I had for you have come back, or if they never went away but, God help me, I found myself falling for you all over again.'

'But now?'

He heaved a weary sigh. 'Now? Now, I have absolutely no idea. It's going to take a lot for me to forgive you, Gracie. All this time, I've had a son. I don't know if I'll ever get my head around this.'

'I understand. I'll leave you to finish your packing. And maybe, well, let's just leave it like that for now.' Grace stood up and walked to the door.

'Gracie?'

She looked back at him.

'How are you feeling about Henri?'

Grace gave him a weak smile. 'I need to smooth things out with Sophie. I just hope he lives long enough for us to get to know him better. I'd like Harry to meet him.'

'Yeah, that would be nice.'

'One last question,' he said, as Grace pulled open the door.

'Go on.'

'If you hadn't found your grandmother's letters and found out about Henri, do you think you would have ever contacted me?'

Grace stared down at the burgundy carpet for a long time before raising her eyes and looking at him.

'In all honesty, probably not. Not unless Harry had found out the truth and asked about you. Maybe then.'

'Do you regret getting in touch with me?'

This time Grace didn't hesitate before replying.

'No.'

And with that she stepped out into the hall, letting the door close with a click behind her. She stood there for a long moment before trudging back to her own room. She was grateful he'd listened to her attempted explanation. But would she ever see him again?

Not daring to leave her room in case James stopped by on his way out, Grace sat on the balcony and just let her mind wander. Although there was more autumn than summer in the air now, and the breeze from the sea was stronger and cooler, there was still a warmth in the sun that seeped into her tired muscles.

It was a quiet day in Neuville-sur-Mer with only a handful of people walking along the road, pausing to look at the menus of the few beach restaurants that were still open, or to let their dogs sniff around the trees. The navy-hulled boats that ferried people from Saint-Tropez to Cannes were less frequent, and fewer yachts sailed past.

Mesmerised by the waves surging in and out over the rocks, like the waves that lapped the rocks at the base of Dovecote lighthouse, Grace lost herself in thoughts about everything. About Ben and the consistent love she'd had from him, and everything he had done for her and Harry. About Ben and Rachel and how she honestly hoped they made it. About Harry and his resilience and maturity through all the recent changes in his life. About Henri and how easily he forgave Lily for keeping such an immense secret from him and how readily he had accepted Grace into his life. Most of all, she thought about James and the sadness in his eyes that would haunt her forever.

The rhythmic roll of the waves called to her, and she got up from her chair with a stretch and answered the call.

The tall, thin bartender leaning against the bamboo counter of the tiki bar across the road from the hotel, looked so bored Grace couldn't bear to walk past.

'*Madame?*' he asked standing up straight and visibly brightening.

'*Un Kir Royale, s'il vous plaît,*' she replied.

She was technically on holiday, so three in the afternoon was a perfectly acceptable time for a drink, but perhaps it was too early for two cocktails for the price of one.

'*Merci,*' she said as the bartender placed the flute of blackcurrant-infused champagne down in front of her. Could she convince Janice to start selling cocktails at The Seaside Café? She turned to face the sea and spotted a familiar thin figure in black at a table in the corner. As though sensing Grace's eyes on her, Sophie looked up. There were tear lines on her face and Grace's heart went out to her. As if her beloved uncle falling ill hadn't been hard enough, she'd found out she had a cousin she knew nothing about. There wasn't any malice in Sophie's eyes now, if anything the look she gave Grace was one of embarrassment and regret. Grace stepped down from the stool and made her way over to the table, Sophie watching her every step of the way.

'Hi,' Grace said. 'May I?' she added, indicating the empty chair opposite Sophie.

Sophie hesitated but then nodded, and Grace sat down.

'How is Henri?'

A sliver of a smile cracked Sophie's pinched face. 'He is much the same, which is the best we can hope for. He seems to be a little better even.'

'That's good. Look, Sophie, I understand how tough this must be for you.'

Sophie let out a slight huff, but Grace ploughed on. There were things that needed to be said.

'I'm sorry to have upset you. Please understand I have no wish to take Henri away from you. I wouldn't, couldn't, do that.

He's your family. But he's my family too and I want to get to know him and to be a part of his life. Fate, and decisions made decades ago, have meant that we didn't know about each other until now, but I would like us to be friends.'

'I am sorry, Grace. I have not been very kind to you. It has been a difficult time. I gave up everything to come back to Neuville and look after my uncle. I once escaped from this little town, where you can't do anything, or be anything without the whole village knowing.'

'Where I grew up is like that too, but it's what I love about it.'

'It is perhaps a different experience if you are unlike other people, if you know what I mean.'

Grace nodded; she did get that. Dovecote was small but its residents generally had a live and let live approach. She wasn't so naïve as to think everywhere was the same.

'Anyway, I left many years ago and worked hard to build myself a good life, first in Los Angeles and then in Paris. I had to give it all up after my mother died, leaving Henri without anyone to care for him. When you arrived, I was frightened I had sacrificed everything in vain. I convinced myself he would care for you more than me and I would no longer be needed. I don't know. God forgive me, I even worried he might want to leave the house to you. That is very shallow of me, I know.'

'You have to believe me, Sophie. I want nothing from Henri, other than to know him. My life is not in Neuville, it is in Dovecote. Of course Henri needs you! And you didn't sacrifice everything, you still have Jenna.'

Sophie's thin lips parted in a slightly brighter smile this time. 'Yes, I do. Every day I count my blessings that she has stuck by me, even though it is hard for us to be together here. There are a lot of judgemental people, people who don't think it's right.'

'That's awful and must be so difficult for you. I don't know what to say, except that I hope things change and you can both live as your true selves.'

Sophie sighed. 'I am glad I got this chance to talk to you and to say I am sorry.'

Grace smiled. 'Me too.'

'Will you come and see Henri before you leave?' Sophie asked.

'We've said our goodbyes for now already,' Grace said. 'And I don't want to tire him out, or get in your way.' Despite Sophie's optimism about Henri's condition, his frailty and pallor hinted that he might not have long left. She wouldn't steal Sophie's precious time with him.

'If you change your mind, you would be very welcome,' Sophie said as she got up from the table.

'Thank you,' Grace said simply. She watched as Sophie walked away, her head bent low, and didn't envy her one bit. She knew from her grandfather's slow decline how painful it was to see someone you love slip away.

THIRTY-THREE
GRACE

October 2015

Having checked out of the hotel the next morning, Grace set off along the coastal road out of Neuville-sur-Mer. She had left early on purpose, so she could make a pitstop on the way. Sophie's greeting wasn't yet warm, but at least it was civil.

'I am glad you have come. He is doing much better today, and he'll be happy to see you,' she said as Grace approached the front door. Sophie touched her arm lightly and indicated towards Henri's bedroom. 'Take as long as you want. Spend as much time with him as you can. Each time he is ill, I see a little more of him fade away. There will not be much left soon.' There was deep sorrow in her eyes as she turned away, leaving Grace standing in the hallway.

She pushed open the door, unsure of what to expect to see. Just like when she had previously visited, Henri was still sitting up in bed, leaning against several large pillows but his face was a more natural colour. There was some redness back in his cheeks. His skin was a little less papery and his eyes once again sparkled.

'Ah, Grace, it is good to see you.'

'It is very good to see you too. You are looking much better than when I last saw you.'

'Yes, every so often the grim reaper comes knocking, but I am strong enough to fend him off for now. I am glad you have come. I wanted to tell you again how much joy your visit has brought me. I have been reading Lily's letter again. Her words bring me great peace. I am not yet done living. I am even more determined to stay around for a while longer if it allows me time to get to know my granddaughter, and my great-grandson.'

'I have been thinking about that. What would you say about me bringing Harry down during the next half-term break, in spring? I would say sooner, but Christmas might be a bit tricky, so the half-term is the next holiday.'

'Oh yes, that would be wonderful. I will be here, do not doubt that. I had another visitor yesterday afternoon.'

'You did?' There were no prizes for guessing who.

'You failed to tell me that your son's father is the man who came with you to find me.'

'James told you?'

'I think he needed some advice from someone who, by chance, has been through a similar situation. And I will tell you what I told him. You are the lucky ones; you have time on your side. You have a second chance to make things right. Do not make decisions when you are angry or hurting. Give yourself time, and space, and listen to what your heart tells you. Your heart is never wrong.'

That was all good advice.

'I will tell you something else. Something you may not know.'

'What is that?'

'He loves you still.'

'James?'

Henri nodded. 'Indeed. He didn't say it as such, but I could see it in his eyes when he spoke your name. He calls you Gracie.'

A lump formed in Grace's throat. 'Yes, he does. He always did, and he was the only one I ever let call me that.'

'It is very sweet. Give him time, Grace.'

'And my ex-husband? What do I tell him?'

'Yes, that is going to be a difficult conversation. But if I have learnt anything this past week, it is that we must not underestimate the power of the truth. Secrets and lies only cause damage and hurt. The truth? Oh yes, that can hurt too, of course. But in the end, it can also heal. Perhaps the bigger question is whether you are going to tell your son?'

'I don't know. I'm not sure whether to wait to see what James says or whether to tell Harry anyway. I'm tired of carrying such a heavy secret. I wonder if Nanna was tired too. As far as I know, she never told Mum. I suppose maybe if you and Nanna had ever met again, it might have been a different story. It will also depend on what Ben says. I may no longer be his wife, but I still care about him, and I don't want to hurt him.'

'You have some difficult times ahead. But as long as you make your decisions based on love, and listen to what your heart is telling you, you will not go too far wrong.'

'I'm not going to pretend that I'm not a little scared.'

Henri leant over and picked up the paper from his bedside table again. 'Come, let me show you something.' Henri must have seen her eyes light up. 'Yes, that is Lily's letter. For now, I should like to keep it just for myself, if that is acceptable.'

'Yes of course, it is your letter after all. You don't have to share it with anyone.'

Although initially she had been dying to inhale Lily's words, just knowing the truth was enough; it didn't matter if she never got to read the actual letter.

He picked up another small rectangular piece of paper and held it out to Grace.

'She included this with the letter.'

Grace looked down at a sepia photograph of the blushing bride from Lily and Richard's wedding album, and on her lap was the chubby little girl with light-coloured curly hair. Felicity didn't have her thumb in her mouth in this picture and the rosebud shape of her mouth was instantly familiar to Grace.

'Harry has the same mouth as my mother,' Grace said softly, her heart swelling. 'But he has his father's eyes.'

'And you have your grandmother's,' Henri said, giving Grace's hand a gentle squeeze.

She handed the photograph back to him. He didn't put it down, but kept it gripped tightly in his hand.

'I very much look forward to meeting him,' he said.

Grace reached for her handbag to retrieve her phone so she could show Henri a photo of Harry when the clock on the wall chimed the hour.

'I'm going to have to go,' she said sadly.

'It is not goodbye, Grace. Merely *à bientôt*,' Henri said, squeezing her hand again. 'Good luck. Remember your heart is usually right. Trust it.'

'Thank you,' Grace said, leaning forward and kissing Henri lightly on the cheek.

She left the bedroom and went into the kitchen. Jenna was flicking through a newspaper and Sophie was putting a lot of effort into kneading a loaf of bread. She turned as Grace entered the room, dusted off her hands, and came over.

'I'd better head off,' Grace said. 'Thank you for allowing me to intrude on your lives. I hope it has not been too traumatic for you. And I'm sorry for anything I said or did that upset you.'

Sophie gave her an apologetic look. 'No, it is me who needs to be sorry, Grace. You have done my uncle the world of good with your visit. It is nice to see the sparkle in his eyes once again.'

Grace pulled a piece of paper from her handbag and handed it to Sophie. 'My address. I would like us to keep in touch. Henri has said he would like me to bring Harry over in the spring. I would love to, if you wouldn't mind.'

'That would be swell,' Jenna said, joining them at the counter and placing a hand in Sophie's. 'Wouldn't it, *chérie?*'

Sophie looked from Jenna to Grace and for the first time there was warmth in her eyes.

'Yes. Yes, it would.'

Grace's drive back to the airport, past golden beaches and through rolling hills, was bittersweet. It was hard for her to leave Henri behind, she had barely begun to get to know him. At the same time, her heart ached to see Harry again. Going home also meant dealing with the fallout from what had happened with James. There were hard decisions she had to make. But she would keep Henri's words in mind and make them based on love.

THIRTY-FOUR

LILY

July 1942

I was glad it was only a short walk from the train station to Seafoam Cottage, along Beachfront Road. The tiresome commute from Brighton would have been even worse for my aching feet if there had been a long trek at the Dovecote end. I shouldn't have been complaining though. I was immensely grateful to Matron for allowing me to continue working, once Felicity was weaned and old enough to be left with Mrs Macnamara, who had conveniently retired not long after Felicity was born. The offer had been conditional on me transferring back to Brighton Municipal and Matron wanted me back full time. The hospital was overrun with the injured and dying so she needed all the staff she could get her hands on. But I couldn't bear to be away from Felicity any more than I had to, so we mutually agreed three days a week was enough for now.

I had grown to love Dovecote and it was my home now. It was small, and everyone knew everyone, but people just let you get on and didn't ask questions. Perhaps that was another consequence of the war – there were so many tragic stories that people no longer asked probing questions about each other's personal lives out of sensitivity. I certainly wasn't the only woman pushing a pram around Victoria Park who did not have a man at home, or who didn't know if the father of their child would ever be coming back.

I never imagined I could love another person with the ferocity and depth that I loved my daughter. My love for her father had changed me, but this? This was different. It went deep down into my bones, into the very fibre of my being. At times, it caught me off-guard and winded me. It was quite astonishing. Sometimes, during a quiet moment with Felicity napping on my knee or while playing with her on the floor, I would look at her and think about my mother. Had she ever felt such love for me? That she hadn't made any effort to contact me in the years since she'd let Daddy throw me out made me think not. If those melancholy moments struck me, I quickly brushed them aside. I had no regrets, and I knew I was loved by the people around me. My parents knew where I was if they wanted to apologise and meet their granddaughter.

As I passed the post box at the end of the road, the sun caught my eyes, making me blink and squint. There was someone outside Seafoam Cottage with their hand on the wave motif carved into the gate. I had just repainted the gate in pale blue as it had been looking rather weather-beaten. It was a man. A wispy cloud blocked the sun, and I got a good look at him. My heart pounded. Oh, dear God.

'Richard?'

He turned and my breath caught in my chest. For a brief moment, I was sure I was going to faint. The last I heard he was fleeing Singapore, headed for Ceylon. And now here he was, standing on my doorstep in Dovecote, his hair tousled by the sea breeze. Then I remembered – the last time I'd seen him, he had kissed me modestly and asked if I wasn't going to accept his proposal before he left, would I at least wait for him. I gave the glass pendant hanging around my neck a quick squeeze, reminding myself why I wore it and who it had come from, and shoved it down inside my uniform dress. My thoughts turned to Felicity. How was I going to explain it all?

'Lily?' He sounded unsure, as though he didn't quite recognise me. I suppose I had changed a bit. He looked good, a bit weary and world-beaten, but weren't we all. The years in the tropics had been kind to him. He almost glowed. He held open the gate as I reached it, his eyes not straying from mine. I didn't know how to greet him. Should I embrace him? Should he kiss me? All I could think about was the secret lurking behind the blue door of Seafoam Cottage. The secret that would most likely send him running for the hills. He was not an emotional man, I knew that. But I'd be a fool not to expect him to be frightfully angry and I was in knots knowing I was about to break him. Or perhaps not. Perhaps he had come to tell me he'd changed his mind, and he was releasing me from his proposal. It had been an awfully long time since he'd made it. My thoughts ran amok as we stood looking at each other for what seemed like an eternity.

'It's wonderful to see you,' he said eventually, awkwardly shifting his weight from one foot to the other. He appeared to be unsure of what to do next, just like I was. Then I was in his arms. His embrace was comforting and it was rather pleasant to be in a man's arms again, even if I wished they were Henri's instead of Richard's. That was wicked of me. I swallowed hard and inhaled his familiar scent. I had to be brave.

'I am so relieved you have made it back safely,' I whispered into his collar, meaning every word.

His arms relaxed and I took a step backwards. There was the sting of tears in my eyes, and he looked at me with concern.

'I wasn't sure this was the right place.'

I glanced at Seafoam Cottage, the windows glinting in the

sun. A robin was perched on the porch roof. 'Yes, this is my home.'

'It is very pretty.'

'Won't you come in?' I managed to say. 'We have a lot of catching up to do.' The gentle, loving look I got in return almost ripped my heart out of my chest.

His eyes didn't waver from me as I busied myself about the kitchen, turning the simple act of making a pot of tea into a drama worthy of Shakespeare. There was only silence from the floor above, so I presumed Mrs Macnamara had taken Felicity out for some fresh air, which settled my nerves a fraction.

It was only natural that there was a touch of awkwardness between Richard and me. After all, our relationship had existed solely on paper for the previous two years. At least that was what I told myself to disguise the fact that all I could think about was how I had lied to him, how I had betrayed him, and how I did not regret falling in love with Henri. With my back turned to him, I raised my eyes to Heaven and begged for forgiveness. Looking at him again, I tried to search his face for a hint of what he was thinking, or feeling, but he was terribly good at keeping such things well hidden. I only hoped I could say the same about myself and that my eyes or demeanour were not giving away that I was on tenterhooks waiting for the front door to open, forcing me to explain the summer of 1940.

'I'm sorry I don't have any cake to offer. We don't get enough in our rations to allow for anything beyond the necessary and the chap near Victoria Park has been having trouble with his chickens. They've stopped laying. Shell-shocked apparently,' I said, knowing I was babbling but desperate to break the growing tension. 'You probably didn't have any shortages in Singapore.'

Richard inclined his head to one side a fraction. 'There

were some. They import almost everything there, mostly from Malaya or from England, so the supply lines were disrupted. But we got by.'

'Yes, that's what we've been doing too. Just trying to get by.'

Richard opened his mouth, a serious look in his eyes. I wasn't ready to talk about us yet, so I cut him off.

'It did sound terrifically exciting in your letters. Do tell me more about it,' I said, praying he wouldn't see through the forced ease with which I spoke. His gaze softened and a faraway look shone in his eyes.

'It was paradise. The days were endlessly hot and sunny. Everyone I met was charming and spirited.'

'It sounds like you enjoyed it a great deal.' For some reason, a twinge of resentment began to grow inside me. It was all well and good him having a jolly time in the sun. On the south coast we'd been through the ringer and then some. It wasn't so bad in the summer, but the winters had dragged. The endless wet, grey days and long, dark nights were made worse by the blackouts. And this came on top of the shortage of decent food, not to mention the ever-present threat of being blown to Kingdom come, which had driven many to breaking point. I was about to make a comment about him enjoying Singapore so much he probably hadn't missed me, but I paused. If I said something like that, he would counter by asking me if I had missed him. Had I? Not nearly as much as I missed Henri.

'Yes, I did. It was such a shame it had to come to an end, but I suppose we were lucky to be spared the horrors of war for so long.'

'What did happen? The newspaper reports here were a little patchy on the details.'

'The Japanese army did what we thought impossible – they came through the jungle; virtually unchallenged. The government had deduced that any attack was likely to come from the sea, and the defences of the island were set up for that scenario.

They bombed us first, took out the airstrip, destroyed roads, infrastructure, sanitation. It was chaos. I was lucky to get out. On that last day, it was becoming clear that our armed forces had no choice; it was surrender or face total obliteration. We spent the morning burning documents and records so they wouldn't fall into enemy hands. It was a rather pointless exercise as the whole city was going up in smoke. Eventually, word came through that the surrender was imminent and we were told that if we could leave, we should. Did my message reach you?'

I nodded my head slowly. 'Yes, thank you for taking the risk to send it. I should not have been able to bear it had I heard the news without knowing you were safe.'

'I was far from safe, but I dare say I did better than anyone who was stranded there. The chaps that didn't make it out are probably in some God-awful prisoner-of-war camp by now.'

'How did you get away?'

'A fellow at the Department of Fisheries somehow managed to get hold of a launch. I didn't dare ask how. It was probably far from legal, and he made space for me. There were twenty-five of us, civilians, engineers, and government officials, crammed onto that tiny boat, with barely enough room to breathe. There were hundreds, thousands perhaps, of very desperate people trying to get into the docks. Some of what I saw I shall never forget. Nor speak of,' he added, catching my eye. A cold shiver ran up my spine at the haunted shadow in his eyes.

'I looked back as we pulled away, headed in the rough direction of Sumatra, and the entire city was on fire. As we passed Collyer Quay and Telok Ayer, I could see the warehouses and buildings from Finlayson Green to the Yacht Club and Fort Canning were a raging inferno. The oil tanks at Pulau Bukom and Pulau Samboe had been set alight and were sending thick black smoke into the air. The smell was horrific.'

He closed his eyes for a moment and when he opened them

again, he had pulled himself back to the present and was no longer on that awful boat. His knuckles were white from gripping the edge of the kitchen table. I placed my hand gently on his, but found I was at a loss as to what to say. His other hand closed over mine.

'The rest of the journey was long, hard, and largely irrelevant. The main thing is, I made it home. Home to you.'

I was prevented from responding by the click of the front door and the sound of footsteps on the terracotta tiles. Mrs Macnamara came into the kitchen and paused, startled, at seeing a man in her kitchen. She set Felicity down, her little chubby legs just about able to support her. She was getting more confident with walking and was fond of proudly showing off her new-found skill. She launched herself towards me, her plump arms stretched out for balance, and her pale-blonde curls bounced with each unsteady step. Her cheeks were rosy from the wind or possibly from more new teeth coming through, and her blue eyes were bright. She collided with my shins and wrapped her arms around my legs.

'Mamma,' she said in her little baby voice, and I bent to lift her onto my knee. At that moment, I glanced up at Richard and his face wore the look I expected. Confusion mostly, and shock.

Very brief introductions followed. Mrs Macnamara was familiar with Richard's role in my life; I had told her everything in the months leading up to Felicity's birth. I owed her that much in return for her incredible kindness and generosity. Also, it had been nice to offload to a friendly ear.

'Perhaps it would be best if I arranged Felicity's supper,' Mrs Macnamara said, displaying her uncanny ability to sense a strained atmosphere and diffuse it. I gave Felicity a kiss on her forehead and handed her over.

'Richard?' I said tentatively. 'I think perhaps we should go for a walk. There are some things I need to tell you.'

. . .

We walked in silence, not looking at each other, along Beachfront Road, past the train station and the shops on Queen's Parade that ran alongside The Promenade, the flowerbeds between the two now standing empty. Eventually we found ourselves in Victoria Park and we sat down on a bench overlooking the sea. The allotments expanded beyond the old cricket pitch and reached as far as the bandstand. It was nothing short of miraculous that the bandstand still stood in one piece. That much cast iron could have made quite a haul of grenades. I followed Richard's gaze over the razor wire that had been attached to The Promenade railings to stop people entering the beach. The Seaside Café was closed for the day, Rose, the owner, no doubt happy to get home to her daughter, and there weren't many people milling about. These days, people tended to get home and stay home. Being caught outside when the air raid siren went off and having to bolt for the communal air raid shelter in the cellar of The Royal Oak was to be avoided at all costs.

'Richard, I am sorry,' I began, but I ran out of words. He still wouldn't look at me. The confusion was gone, but I could see the muscles of his jaw working hard.

'Lily, I don't know what to say.' He rubbed his face with his hand and turned towards me.

'Will you let me try to explain?' I asked.

He nodded, his eyebrows inching closer together.

'I fell in love. That is the crux of it. I met a man, an injured French soldier, and we fell in love. Felicity is the result of that. There is nothing more to say.'

'Where is he now?'

'I don't know. The last I heard from him he was being sent back to France.' I tried to swallow the lump in my throat.

'Does he know about Felicity?'

I shook my head. 'I never got the chance to tell him.'

'And Mrs Macnamara?'

'Mummy and Daddy banished me from home and have not spoken to me since. Mrs Macnamara was the manager of Bayview, the convalescent home where I worked and Henri recovered from his injuries. Her husband was killed in a munitions explosion, and she offered me, and Felicity, a home. She has been very kind to me.'

A silence fell between us. Richard turned away and was looking out at the sea again, perhaps wishing he hadn't bothered to come home. It was starting to get dark and the light from the top of the lighthouse, dimmed in accordance with Admiralty regulations, cast a soft glow across the waves. I rummaged in my pocket for a handkerchief to wipe the tears that had sprung from my eyes. I hadn't cried about it all for almost a year. My thoughts were interrupted when Richard stood and faced me.

'I risked my life to come back to you. I could have stayed in Ceylon. I was safe there. But I made the decision to carry on, to undertake the most perilous part of the journey. Why did I do that? I'll tell you why – because I wanted to come home to you. This is a shock, Lily, a complete shock. I am saddened, disappointed, and, quite understandably, a little angry.'

All I could do was nod dumbly and acknowledge that he was entirely justified.

'I need time to think about this, Lily. I must admit, I am not entirely sure how I feel about you at this moment.' He turned and took a few steps away from me, before stopping and turning back. 'Are you still in love with him, this French soldier, this Henri?'

I forced myself to pause because my heart didn't need to, it answered immediately with a loud thud.

'I don't know, Richard. I am trying not to be because there is a good chance he could be dead.' I sniffled, another round of sobs bubbling in my throat.

'And me? You once told me you loved me. I presume this is no longer the case?'

'I don't know that either,' I said, without pause this time.

That was true. Seeing Richard again had jolted some old feelings, but could I honestly say, hand on heart, that I loved him? He made a sort of muffled huff-type noise and turned away again. I watched, in the fading light, as he walked up the path towards Victoria Park's gate. It occurred to me that I had no idea where he was staying. Presumably with his parents, if they were still in Hove. As he disappeared from view, I was left looking, through blurred vision, at the darkened windows and closed door of the Victorian pavilion.

THIRTY-FIVE
GRACE

October 2015

It might have been an overcast, grey day but as Grace entered Dovecote, passing Harry's school, the imposing gates of Dovecote Manor, and St. John's Church, a warmth radiated through her blood. As beautiful as Neuville-sur-Mer had been, there really was no place like home. Driving over the railway bridge, Grace checked the time. Ben and Harry weren't due back for an hour or two, so at the traffic lights she turned left into Courcey Road and wound her way up the sloping drive of Bayview Care Home.

'Hi, Heather,' Grace said as she signed the visitor's book. 'How is he?'

'Hi, Grace, good to see you. Did you have a nice time away? Your grandad has perked up quite a bit this week. He discovered that Betty Jones is a fan of ballroom dancing and they've spent quite a bit of time together. It is quite sweet, especially on the days when they think they're meeting for the first time.'

Grace shook her head. 'Betty and her mother lived next

door to Nanna and Grandad for years. I can't believe they don't remember they know each other.'

Heather gave Grace a sympathetic nod. 'It happens. We prefer to concentrate on the joy of new friendships that are made, without worrying about what may have been forgotten.'

Grace sighed but the sight of Richard in his usual chair by the window lifted her spirits. What made her smile was that instead of looking out towards the sycamore tree, he had been turned around so he was facing the rest of the room. He looked less lonely and, for the first time since he'd moved to Bayview, Grace wasn't hit by a pang of guilt about him being there. Betty was in her usual place near the piano and Grace gave her a little wave. The old lady wiggled her fingers back at her.

'Hi, Grandad,' she said as she approached.

'Hello,' he replied cheerily.

'You're in a good mood today. Heather was telling me that you have a girlfriend. Is this true?'

The smile that brightened Richard's wrinkled face warmed Grace up from the inside. It really didn't matter that this man wasn't her biological grandfather. He had been her grandad since the day she was born. He had fixed broken toys and hearts, applauded her achievements, and encouraged her through disappointments. He had been there for her through the toughest of times, and that was what mattered.

'Heather said Betty is a bit of a fan of ballroom dancing.'

'Who? Oh, yes,' said Richard. 'We have a lovely time dancing together.'

Grace wasn't sure whether much actual dancing went on, but she wouldn't have put it past him to give it a go.

'You know,' he continued, his eyes bright, 'it takes me right back to the dance halls of Singapore.'

Grace sat bolt upright.

'Ah, in those days we used to dance all night at the Tanglin Club or one of the grand houses. Hundreds of young people, having the time of their lives. Never a shortage of pretty girls either. Of course, it got rather hot. Even in the middle of the night, the humidity was brutal. There was one night the heat got to us and we dived into the club swimming pool.' He chuckled at the memory. 'Ah yes, Tommo and I got banned from the club for that. We would have gotten away with it if it weren't for Polly Stephenson making a fuss and squealing like a schoolgirl. I never did know what Tommo saw in her. She was pretty enough but had a head full of sawdust. It only took a word from Sir Shenton, and we were back in.' His face clouded over, and Grace feared that the memories were fading. 'Then the bombs started falling which put a stop to all that.'

They sat in silence for a while. Was there any reason to tell him where she'd been and who she'd met? On the one hand, if he became aware she knew the truth, maybe he'd talk about it, fill in the gaps in the story, tell her what happened when he came home and learnt about Felicity. On the other, what was the point? Would he even remember? Maybe she'd done enough damage and upset enough people, including Ben. Maybe it was better if both Lily and Richard were allowed to go to their rest thinking their secret was safe.

A rattling cough interrupted her thoughts. The sparkle had gone out of his eyes and in its place was that familiar blankness. Grace didn't know where his mind had taken him, but it was probably best just to leave him be.

Grace had barely pulled into Branwell Close and parked outside Ben's, when Harry launched himself out of the front door and down the driveway to her.

'Mum,' he cried, throwing his arms around her. 'I've missed you!'

'I've missed you too,' she said, giving his hair a ruffle. 'You've grown again. You'll be taller than me soon.'

'That wouldn't be hard, Mum, you're only short.'

Grace gave him a playful punch on the arm. He pretended it hurt.

'Go and get your bags and we'll head home.'

Harry ran back inside leaving Ben and Grace standing awkwardly on the path.

'Good trip?' Ben asked, avoiding eye contact.

'It was... interesting,' Grace said. She really didn't want to have to go through it all then and there. She needed time to get her head straight.

'How's James?' The bitterness in Ben's voice cut through Grace and she was relieved when Harry reappeared, laden down with stuff. Grace turned from Ben and opened her car.

'Say bye to Dad and get in the car, Harry. I'll be there in a minute.'

Harry gave Ben a hug. 'See ya.'

'See you soon, buddy,' Ben replied.

Once Harry was in the car and out of earshot, Ben turned to Grace. He ran a hand through his hair. 'I shouldn't have asked that about you and James when I called. You were right to hang up on me. I deserved that.'

'I really can't talk about it now, Ben. I'm tired and I just want to get home. It's been a tough week.'

Ben's forehead creased and he put a hand on Grace's arm. 'What's happened?'

'I'll tell you later. I just need to get my head sorted first.'

'Look, I know I reacted badly to finding out that James went to France with you, and I'm sorry that I did. I'm still here for you, if there's anything you need to talk about.'

Grace managed a nervy smile. 'Thanks. I might hold you to that.'

. . .

Grace had sent Harry off to bed after dinner. He had nearly fallen asleep in the car on the short drive back from Ben's. There was a chill in the cottage, having been empty for a week, so she lit the fire in the sitting room and pulled the heavy green curtains across the bay window. Henri's house in Neuville might have been light and airy and bright, but it could never be as cosy as Seafoam Cottage. Tired from the journey, and a long phone call with Rachel who, after an elaborate apology, demanded to be filled in on everything that had happened, she was just settling down with a cup of coffee when her mobile lit up with a message.

Hope you got home safely. I'll be in touch once I've got my head sorted.

There were several ways she could have replied to James's message but in the end, she thought it was probably better to say nothing at all.

THIRTY-SIX
GRACE

October 2015

Monday looked more like July than the dying days of October when Grace opened her curtains. The sunshine was deceptive and masked the decidedly cold wind that blew in off the sea. She was nice and snug in her winter coat as she drove Harry to school. Shame she'd forgotten her gloves – the steering wheel was freezing. On her way back, rather than driving down the High Street and back to Seafoam Cottage, at the railway bridge she turned into Courcey Road, down Temper Street, and into Branwell Close. Twice in two days. The neighbours might start to think she'd moved back in.

'Grace,' Ben said with obvious surprise when he answered the door.

'Hi, Ben. Sorry to interrupt while you're working but any chance you've got time for a chat?'

He tilted his head slightly. 'Always have time for you, Grace, you know that. Come on in. Excuse the mess.'

There were black bin bags stuffed with bits of wallpaper, a steamer, and a can of wallpaper adhesive dissolvent littering the hall carpet. Grace stepped around it all as she followed him into the kitchen at the back of the house. Half of the pine kitchen cupboard doors had been stripped of their varnish and sanded down. The other half were piled up in the conservatory. Calling it a conservatory was a bit generous; it was more of a lean-to with a corrugated plastic roof that looked like it would struggle to survive a strong wind.

'You're finally re-decorating,' Grace observed.

'Yeah, I figured it was time.'

'I could ask whether that shows that you're finally over me and moving on, but we both know that's already happened, huh.'

He shot her a nervous look.

'Relax, Ben. I'm teasing you. Kind of. Seriously though, it's about time you got rid of that awful wallpaper I made you put up, what? Ten years ago?'

'It must be that, yeah.' He put a cup of coffee down in front of Grace on the kitchen table. 'So, you said you wanted a chat. I'm guessing this is about Henri and him being your grandfather?'

Grace looked up at him, relieved for once that Rachel had done the hard work for her and filled him in on everything that she had told her about France. Grace had omitted the kiss with James and how she'd utterly broken him.

'Kind of.'

'Hmm,' he said, giving her a hard stare. 'Out with it.'

Grace knotted her hands together on the pine table. 'I have a confession.'

'You told James, didn't you?'

'I'm sorry. I know I said I wouldn't. But in all the tangle about meeting Henri, and everything that went on, it kind of slipped out. I said something off hand, and he wouldn't let it go. I tried not to tell him, but I had no choice. I am so sorry.'

Ben got up from his chair without a word and paced to the

end of the kitchen. He picked up a teaspoon and flung it into the sink. The clatter made Grace flinch. She watched silently as Ben leant against the kitchen counter and brought his hands to his face. He held them there for a long moment before letting out a very long breath and coming back to the table.

'What did he say, when you told him?'

'Understandably he was furious, and devastated, and so, so hurt that I'd kept it from him. I tried to explain why, and I think I got through to him. I don't know. He left France early, and I've not spoken to him since.'

'Grace, you'll have to allow me to ask that question again. The one I asked when I called.'

Grace squirmed a little. 'And now you know that I told him the truth about Harry, it's a reasonable question. The honest answer is no, there's nothing going on between James and me.'

'What happens now? Does he want to meet Harry? Because if he does, well that's a whole new issue, isn't it? It means telling Harry and I don't think I'm ready for that, Grace.'

'I have told James that if he wants to meet Harry, I won't prevent it. But that I'd have to discuss it with you, because to all intents and purposes you're Harry's dad and I'm not going to make any decisions without your approval.'

'Apart from telling him, clearly.'

Grace's face flushed. 'I'm sorry, believe me. The thing is, Ben, I've been thinking. Considering everything I've found out this last week, about Henri and Nanna, and my mother, I was wondering whether it's time to tell Harry anyway. Even if James *does* decide to walk away. We did say that we would, some day.'

Ben got to his feet again and walked over to the bookcase they had bought together when they first moved in. He picked up a framed photograph of him and Harry. Grace remembered the day she'd taken it. It had been a miserable, wet April

Saturday when Harry was eight. Ben had promised Harry they could go to Dovecote's annual Victoria Park fair and, because Ben always kept his promises, they went despite the rain. By lunchtime, the skies had cleared, and the sea was sparkling in the sun. She'd taken the surreptitious photo of the two of them sitting on the low wall between Victoria Park and The Promenade, stuffing their faces with dripping ice cream and laughing about something. There was melted chocolate ice cream all over Harry's mouth, but it couldn't hide the pure, childish joy on his face. It was one of her absolute favourite photos of them both. Ben put the frame back down on the shelf. He didn't turn to look at her. He rested his hands on the shelf and took several long, deep breaths. Eventually he spoke, still not looking at her.

'I don't care about James. I couldn't give a toss about whether he's hurting about all this, Grace, or what he does or doesn't want. All I care about is protecting Harry.'

'As do I. But I don't want to hurt you either. I won't say anything to Harry without your agreement.'

'You don't need that. He's your child, Grace, not mine.'

The venom in his voice seared her heart. 'Ben. Please.'

Ben finally let go of the shelf and turned to face Grace. The trace of tears on his face nearly broke her.

'Listen, Grace, Harry has a dad. He has me. Think very carefully about what you're considering doing. Not just to Harry, but to me.'

'Ben, I'm not saying this to hurt you. Really, I'm not. You've been Harry's dad his whole life, and you know how grateful I am to you for that. I'm just a little tired carrying this secret and I don't see that I, that we, have any choice.'

Ben swiped his hand across his face and leant against the wall, folding his arms across his chest.

'I've been dreading this day. I don't want to lose him, Grace.'

She got up and crossed the room to stand in front of him.

She looked him in the eyes. 'You won't. I promised you, right from the beginning, that he would always be a part of your life, and I stand by that. I do not want to take him away from you. I may be a terrible person, but I'm not that terrible.'

'You're not a terrible person, and I don't blame you for any of this. I don't blame anyone. We're in the situation we're in, and it is what it is.'

'Thank you,' said Grace. 'Even if I know you don't mean that.'

Ben unfolded his arms and wrapped them around her, drawing her close into his chest.

'I mean it. Look, you have to do what you think is right.' As he released her, he gave her the lightest of kisses on her forehead. 'This can't be easy on you either. Especially with what you found out about your grandmother.'

The warmth and understanding in Ben's words brought a lump to her throat.

'There is one thing that I'm going to insist on though,' he added.

'Anything,' Grace said, fighting against the hot pressure behind her eyes.

'That I be there when you tell him. I just want to make sure he knows I still love him and that I'll still be here for him.'

Grace nodded. 'That's fair. I'm sure you have work to do, I'll leave you to it.'

'Yeah, I'll probably lose myself in someone's tax return for the rest of the day.'

'Sounds thrilling,' Grace said.

'What? It is.' He opened the front door for her. 'Will you let me know when...'

She laid a gentle hand on his arm. 'I will.'

In her car, with her head resting on the steering wheel,

Grace let out a long sigh. It was done, and Ben, to his credit, had taken it better than she'd imagined. Now she just had to wait to see whether James wanted anything to do with Harry, or with her.

THIRTY-SEVEN
LILY

August 1942

Felicity was fractious and cried if I put her down, so I was doing my best to darn my uniform stockings with her balanced on my lap when the garden gate creaked, and the doorbell rang. With a huff, I lifted her to my hip and opened the door, expecting to find Sheila or Betty from next door, or the newspaper boy, on the step. My heart momentarily stopped when I came face-to-face with Richard. In the weeks since he'd left me weeping on the bench in Victoria Park, he had been in my thoughts almost constantly. During long, introspective and sleepless nights, the calm grace with which he met the news of my infidelity moved me deeply. I didn't deserve his forgiveness, his love, or even his friendship. I didn't deserve to ever see him again.

'Hello,' I said, my voice wavering.

'Hello, Lily. May I come in?' When I took a step to the side, he crossed the threshold, his gaze lingering on Felicity, who had laid her head on my shoulder, her thumb in her mouth. I led him into the front room. The sea breeze coming in through the open bay window ruffling the net curtains provided relief from the stifling heat of the day. We sat awkwardly at opposite ends of the couch, neither of us seemingly sure of what to say or do. The sun highlighted the fine layer of dust on the cream and brown tiled fireplace. I made a mental note to get the duster out before Mrs Macnamara came home from her Women's Institute meeting and spotted it.

Richard picked up the well-loved floppy brown bear that was folded in a heap on the cushion between us and held it out.

'Is this yours?' he asked Felicity.

She bobbed her head and reached for her bear. There was something in his smile as he placed the grubby soft toy in my daughter's outstretched chubby hand that made the butterflies loitering in my stomach take flight, and crash into my diaphragm. He raised his eyes from Felicity and looked directly at me.

'Lily, I have been thinking about you constantly for the last three weeks.'

I was about to interrupt to say I had been doing the same, but he held up his hand.

'Please, I need to get all of this out in one go, or I shall get myself tied in knots.'

I nodded, letting him continue.

'I've been reflecting on you, and your situation. It can't be easy for you. It must be difficult being ostracised from your family. I can also understand how what has happened came about, and I want you to know, I hold no ill-will against you for it.'

He got up from the couch and walked to the window, lifting the edge of the net curtain. The ray of sunlight highlighted the line of his jaw and reminded me I had loved that face, and it was still a face that lent itself to being loved. Having peered out at the sea for a moment, he turned to look back at me. There was a soft look in his eyes, that may have been regret, or just a dull sadness.

'I am in no position to pass judgement and I must offer my own apologies, and request forgiveness for also straying from faithfulness.'

My face warmed slightly. I had, over the years, wondered whether any of the glamorous, fun-loving women that featured in Richard's irregular letters had tempted him. If Richard was able to meet my infidelity with dignity and honesty, then I would forgive him any misdemeanours with equal charity and whole-heartedness.

'Lily, some would call me a fool for what I am about to say but it comes from the heart, and I mean every word.'

He paused and sat back down on the couch, closer to me this time. He reached out and took hold of my hand. His eyes were fixed on mine making me shake slightly.

'Lily, I love you. I love you more than life itself and I want to make things right for you. If you will have me, I will care for you, I will raise your daughter as my own and, most importantly, I will love you for the rest of our lives. I asked this question before I went away, and I ask it again now – will you marry me?'

THIRTY-EIGHT

GRACE

November 2015

The interval during the Year 6 class play couldn't have come soon enough. Grace's bum had gone numb from the hard wooden chairs that had been in use in the hall since before she'd been a pupil at Dovecote Primary School. They probably pre-dated even her mother's time. She glanced at Ben and he, very slightly, rolled his eyes. Harry's one-line part had been right at the beginning of the play, and now they were having to sit through the rest of the story of Guy Fawkes and his gunpowder plot until they could enthusiastically applaud him at the end.

'I heard a rumour there's coffee and biscuits in Harry's classroom,' Ben whispered as they shuffled along the row.

'Thank goodness. Oh,' she said, surprised by the sudden vibrating of her handbag. Her face blanched when she saw the display on her phone. 'It's Bayview, I'd better take it,' she said, her voice trembling slightly as she moved away towards a quiet spot by the window. The home never called this late, unless…

'Hello?'

'Grace? It's Heather. I'm sorry but Richard has taken a turn for the worse. I think you need to come in.'

Grace lowered the phone away from her ear in a bewildered haze. It couldn't be happening, not yet. Her eyes met Ben's. He was already making his way over to her, having abandoned their coffees, concern on his face.

'What's happened? Is everything alright?'

Grace shook her head. Ben knew without her telling him, she could see it in his eyes.

'Go,' he said. 'I'll take Harry home and explain it to him. Go.'

Bayview Care Home was in darkness as Grace pulled up under the sycamore tree, but Heather was making her way across the car park towards her.

'I'm really sorry, Grace. The doctor has said that there's nothing he can do, except make Richard comfortable,' she said as Grace climbed out of the car. Grace could only nod and follow Heather inside.

As they entered Richard's room, the doctor at his bedside took a step backwards, allowing Grace to get a look at her grandfather. Each of his breaths seemed a herculean effort. The doctor put his hand on Grace's arm.

'He's comfortable, and not in any pain,' he said before leaving the room.

Grace turned to Heather. 'Would you give Reverend Clive a call please and let him know?'

'Of course,' Heather said, pulling the door closed behind her.

Grace pulled up a chair and picked up Richard's hand. His skin was clammy.

'There'll be green leaves on that sycamore in the spring, just you wait and see,' he rasped.

Grace couldn't help but smile, remembering the conversation they'd had back in early October when he thought the tree was dying.

'Yes, I'm sure there will, Grandad.'

'I never should have told Lily about my affair with Maya. That's why she hasn't been to see me. It wasn't that I didn't love Lily, I did. But I was young and stupid.'

For a moment, Grace couldn't think where that name was familiar from. Then it dawned on her – his 'friend' Maya had featured in his letters. At least that evened out the score a little. She just hoped her grandmother's story hadn't been replicated on the other side of the world; she couldn't cope with finding out about any more extended family.

'I'm sure that's not it, Grandad,' she said.

He turned his head slightly, his eyes seemed to focus just a touch. 'Grace, you don't have to pretend, I know she's gone. And my darling Felicity too. I hope they both knew how much I loved them.'

Grace tried to speak but, even though she moved her mouth, no sound came out. His eyes fluttered before closing, and his chest stopped rising and falling. The years fell from his face as the world came to a grinding halt. Grace held the back of his hand to her lips.

'They did Grandad, we all did,' was all she managed to say before the sadness overtook her.

Harry was already asleep when Grace stopped at Ben's to pick him up.

'I'll take him to school in the morning,' said Ben, giving Grace a lingering look. 'Do you want to talk about it? I've made you a hot chocolate.'

'Thank you,' Grace said, taking the mug from Ben. 'I know I should have been expecting this, but still.'

'Knowing someone is unwell and fading doesn't make it any easier when they go though,' Ben said.

'I just wasn't ready to say goodbye. Not so soon after Nanna.'

They sat in silence for a while, sipping their hot drinks. As on the day of Lily's funeral, the silence was comfortable.

'I'll never know now what happened when he got back from Singapore,' Grace said, breaking the calm quiet.

'It's unlikely he'd have been able to tell you anyway,' said Ben, with a slight frown. 'But do you want to know what I think?'

Grace caught a glimpse of a spark in Ben's eyes. If anyone could guess at Richard's thought process, it was him. She nodded.

'I think he loved her so deeply and so completely that what she'd done wasn't important. All that would have mattered was that she loved him and that she agreed to spend the rest of her life with him. And the minute he saw Felicity, I'd say he fell in love with her too. Even though she wasn't his child, he would have loved her because she was Lily's.' Ben paused. 'He might have been a bit hurt, a bit shocked even, but the strength of his love for Lily would have eclipsed all those other feelings.'

There was a shine in Ben's eyes now and Grace held his gaze for a long moment, knowing his words had come from the heart.

'Thank you,' she said. The two small words seemed inadequate, considering everything Ben had done for her. For him being to her what Richard had been to Lily, and for being to Harry what Richard had been to Felicity. For being Ben.

THIRTY-NINE
GRACE

November 2015

Grace was a bit early for her meeting a few days later with Reverend Clive to discuss the funeral arrangements so, despite the ominous grey clouds overhead, she lingered on the High Street. The waft of fresh batter on the wind made her mouth water – a fish and chip supper might be in order. The yellow glow from Harrington's Bookshop beckoned her across the road. The jingling of the bell when she pushed open the door was an instant reminder of her visits to the shop on Saturday mornings, her grandfather in tow, and her pocket money jingling in her purse. She'd brought Harry here too, but by then the children's section had shrunk to near non-existence. In recent years it had grown again, thankfully. Taking in a deep breath of the scent of new books, she was drawn to the history section. She was reading the back of a book about the French Resistance when her phone beeped in her bag. It was a message alert – a message from James.

Hi, I'm heading down to Dovecote to see Mum and Dad at the weekend. Are you free to meet up for a drink tomorrow evening?

With trembling fingers, Grace tapped out a reply.

Sure, eight o'clock at The Royal Oak?

He didn't reply.

The Royal Oak was quiet for a Saturday evening, the typical November weather seemingly keeping the pub's regulars at home. Those who had ventured out were slowly steaming as the rainwater evaporated from their coats and jumpers in the warm, making the air slightly damp and giving off a vague whiff of wet dog. Declan had lit the fire and Grace and James took the table nearest to it.

'I'm so sorry,' James said when she told him about her grandfather's death.

'It was very peaceful in the end. I was with him,' she replied, and he nodded.

Grace picked at a flake of loose varnish on the table as a heavy silence sat between them. A pub in Dovecote on a miserable November evening was a different prospect to a sun-drenched beach bar in Neuville-sur-Mer.

'Look, Gracie, I'll be honest here,' he said, having taken a long drink from his pint followed by a deep breath. 'I'm still reeling from all of this, and I've not got my head around the fact that we made a human, and now there is a little mini-me running around and I know nothing about him. I keep thinking about all the things I've missed.' He put his glass down and looked her straight in the eye. 'It hurts.'

Grace shrank slightly under his gaze.

'I know. I'm sorry.'

'I don't know what I want to happen next or where I want this to lead. I mean, I can't just walk away, not now.'

The lump in Grace's throat prevented her from replying, so she pulled her phone from her handbag. She found the latest picture of Harry and pushed the phone across the table. James closed his eyes for a moment before looking down at the phone.

'That was taken by Ben on the beach in Wales at half-term. He's a mini-you. I think all he has from me is his mouth. It's the same shape as my mother's was when she was small.'

'No, I can see you in him. You used to smile like that when you got excited.' James nudged the phone back to her. 'Sorry about the eyesight. Has he needed glasses for long?'

'Just over a month. It's quite possible that my heart actually stopped for a moment when he chose that pair. When he put them on, I found myself looking at you. It was spooky.'

'I got mine when I was eleven too.' James let out a puff of air. 'Tell me about Harry.'

Grace took a big gulp of wine. 'He was the perfect baby. Although, he gave us a bit of bother by deciding that after a twenty-hour labour, he wasn't going to budge any further, meaning I had to have an emergency C-section. He was a healthy seven pounds and one ounce. I was in bits. He fed perfectly and slept through the night almost immediately. He was ahead of the curve on everything. He walked early, talked early. He has been a complete sweetheart since the day he was born. He loves computer games, football, cricket, and reading. He's better at English than maths, does alright at science, but if you asked him, he'd say his favourite subject...' Grace paused and looked up at James. She could see tears brimming in his eyes. What she was about to say next would probably make them spill over. 'Is history.'

James's hand was shaking slightly as he downed the rest of his pint.

'He's kind, sensitive and caring. He has so many friends. Everyone who meets him falls in love with him.' Her voice became wobbly, and her vision slightly blurred. 'He has a heart the size of a planet and I'm incredibly proud of him.'

As she wiped her wet cheeks, James reached over the table and put his hand on hers. Neither of them spoke for a long time.

The rain had passed leaving the sky clear and star-filled when they left the pub. Grace pulled her coat tightly around herself. Some of the shops along the High Street already had their Christmas decorations up and the moonlight made the streams of tinsel shimmer and flash. Harrington's Bookshop had installed a reclining Santa snoozing in an armchair in their window, and Dovecote Décor had miniature lighthouse ornaments dangling from their Christmas tree.

'You're seriously considering moving to Dovecote, then?' Grace asked as James fell into step beside her.

'Yeah, I am. London's too busy, and too expensive. I'm ready for a quieter life now. And I want to be closer to Mum and Dad. It's a fairly easy commute and I don't need to go into the museum every day. I can always read on the train. And I kind of like this little town. It's peaceful.'

'Yeah, it is. I never asked you where your mum and dad live.'

'Winman Terrace, it's bit further along the seafront, past Victoria Park and whatever that building is beside it.'

'At the end of Blythe Avenue?'

He nodded.

'The building next to Victoria Park is Dovecote Museum. It opened back in the seventies, I think. I've not been there in years.'

'I'll have to check it out.'

'Well, don't get too excited, it's not the Imperial War Museum.'

He had the good grace to laugh.

'It will be nice to have you nearby,' Grace said, immediately wishing she hadn't when he didn't respond. Despite the chill in the air, the warmth of the earlier touch of his hand on hers lingered.

As they passed the post box at the end of Beachfront Road, she stopped and turned to him.

'I meant that,' she said. 'It will be nice to have you close. James, I have to ask. Did finding out about Harry influence your decision to move?'

He bit his bottom lip and looked up to the sky. When he looked back down, he was half-smiling and there was a faraway look in his eyes.

'Subconsciously, yes,' he said.

'Does that mean that you want to be part of his life?'

'I'm still working that out, Gracie.'

'That's fine. I just...'

James reached out and put his hand on her arm. 'Are you going to tell him?'

Grace sighed. 'He's had a lot to deal with these past few months. Well, this past year and a bit, I suppose. He's been so resilient, so mature about everything. I don't know whether the time is right to load anything else on him. It's going to be a really big thing to find out the truth, and if I'm honest, my biggest fear is that he'll hate me for keeping it from him for so long.'

She started walking towards Seafoam Cottage. James followed. At the gate, she halted again.

'I need to know, James. I need to know what you want. For all our sakes.'

A slight frown creased James's forehead.

'I said earlier that I can't just walk away, and I mean it. But what's more important right now is that I don't want to. Gracie, seeing you after all this time has been insane, wonderful, confusing, and comforting. I'm a bit of a mess right now, but when I'm with you, some of that mess seems to be kind of fixed. Some of the questions that keep me awake at night no longer seem relevant. Some of the doubts I have just disappear. And I don't know if that's a good thing or not.'

'I have spoken to Ben.'

'How did he take it? Me knowing about Harry, I mean.'

'Better than I expected. I don't think you'd want to bump into him in The Royal Oak, but he was fairly calm about it. He has said if I do decide to tell Harry, he'll support me in that decision. He just wants to be there when I do, so that Harry knows Ben is still there for him.'

'He's a good guy.'

Grace let out a light chuckle. 'Yes, he is. And he cares so much for Harry. I know it's a cliché, but he really does love Harry as if he is his own child. I think that, over time, Ben may even have forgotten that he isn't.'

'Next time you speak to him, will you let him know that I have no intention of getting between him and Harry, if I, you know.'

Hearing James say almost the exact words she'd asked Jenna to tell Sophie made Grace's heart thud.

'Thank you. Yes, I'll tell him that.'

When their eyes met, there was a curious look in James's. It was the same expression he'd had in her hotel room the night he'd kissed her.

'I'd... um, well, I'll,' he said.

'Yeah,' Grace replied.

He didn't glance back at her as he walked away down the road and out of sight. Grace stared at the space he'd vacated for a long moment. This time she didn't wonder whether she'd see him again. The question this time was what would happen when she did. She shook off the tingling in her chest, she was only doing this for Harry, nobody else. With a sigh, she wiggled her key into the tight lock and let herself into the dark, silent cottage.

FORTY
GRACE

November 2015

A week had passed without any word from James, but Grace hadn't had time to linger over their last conversation. In a way, her grandfather's funeral was a distraction, albeit a tearful, sad, and tiring one. Once again, the people around her, Ben, Rachel, Reverend Clive, and Harry surrounded her with love and care and carried her through. She'd be sunk without them. James was back at the forefront of her thoughts. His indecisiveness was hard to cope with. The waiting was making her jittery. If James walked away now, she could rebuild, start over, pretend nothing had changed. But on the other hand, what damage could that do to Harry? The truth was bound to come out sooner or later and how would he feel knowing James had turned down the chance to meet him. It was out of her hands; there was nothing she could do but wait for James to decide the fate of everyone she loved.

Her dark thoughts were interrupted by the sound of Harry's key in the front door. Ben caught her eye as she walked out of the living room to greet them. Harry gave her a swift hug before bounding into the kitchen and rustling in the fridge for a snack. Grace had told Ben about her conversation with James, leaving out the moment where she'd been sure he was about to kiss her again. She was trying to forget that herself. It conjured up too many weird, mixed emotions. There was an unspoken question on Ben's face, and she shook her head.

'I just want to know,' she said with a sigh.

'I'm sure he has a lot to think about, Grace. I don't know what I'd do if it was the other way around, but he must have a lot on his mind.'

Grace examined her fingernails. 'I know.'

Ben squeezed her arm.

'Thanks,' she said, looking up at him. 'I've been thinking and I want to tell Harry.'

Ben rubbed his chin and bit his lip. 'I thought you would. Even though we don't know what James is going to do?'

Grace sighed. 'It's going to come out eventually, and there will never be a perfect time. I just think we should do it now in case James does say he wants to meet him. Surely, we should prepare Harry first?'

'To be fair, that does make sense. As much as I hate to admit it, you're probably right.' He raised an eyebrow and flashed her a half-smile.

'I'm always right.'

'Ha! As if.' Ben shook his head. 'But seriously,' he added, giving her a grave look, 'I've been thinking about it too and we don't *really* have a choice, do we?'

'Do you want to do it now?'

Ben grimaced. 'Let's just get it over with.'

Grace and Ben walked down the hallway towards the kitchen. At the door, Grace turned to Ben. 'Thank you,' she said. 'For everything.'

Harry was already sat at the kitchen table, a chocolate milkshake in one hand, a *Horrible Histories* book in the other. He looked up as Grace sat down beside him, and Ben pulled out the chair opposite.

'Am I in trouble?' he asked, his eyes flicking between Grace and Ben. He put the milkshake down.

'No, sweetie,' Grace said. 'But there is something that we need to talk to you about.'

'Oh. Okay. As long as it's not where babies come from. That's gross.'

Grace tried very hard not to laugh and a quick glance at Ben reassured her that he was struggling to hold it together too.

'No, nothing like that. Well, not exactly.' Grace paused. There was no easy way to say what she had to say. 'The thing is Harry, there's something that I never told you before, but I think you're old enough to know now. Before I tell you, I just want you to know that both your dad and I love you very much. The most important thing to us is that you are safe and happy and that's all we ever want for you. Do you understand that?'

Harry nodded, wariness in his eyes.

'Grace,' Ben said, giving her a warning look.

She shot him a frown.

'Harry, I know this is going to be a shock but Ben, your dad, isn't actually your real dad.'

The book slipped from Harry's hand, landing on the table with a dull thud. He looked from Grace to Ben and back again, confusion on his young face.

'I don't understand,' he said, his voice wavering.

Grace couldn't speak.

'It's true, Harry,' Ben said, seeing the hopelessness on Grace's face. 'I'm not your dad.'

'But there are photos of you with me when I was a baby?' Harry stopped, his eyes brimming with tears. He turned to Grace and gave her a look that pierced through to her soul. 'You lied to me.'

'I know, darling, and I'm so sorry,' Grace said, her voice cracking.

Harry pushed his chair back from the table and stood up. 'You lied to me,' he screamed. 'I hate you!'

Grace went to follow him, but the slamming of his bedroom door stopped her in her tracks. The only other sound in the house was Grace's uncontrollable sobs as she put her head in her hands.

Ben let out a muffled curse. 'I knew this would happen.'

'I'm sorry,' Grace whimpered. 'Please don't look at me like that.'

Ben was glaring at her.

'What did you expect, Grace? Look at what you've done to him. All because you had to go running off after some doddery old codger and dredge up a past that should have been left alone. This is your fault. You were the one who opened this can of worms by telling James.'

'I know,' Grace sighed. 'But I had no choice. You agreed we should tell Harry. You were the one who said we should tell him regardless of what happened with James.'

'Oh, no, you can't pin this on me, Grace. All of this is your fault. Because of you, our little boy's world has been shattered.'

'I said I'm sorry!'

They stood glaring at each other. Grace's tears had stopped but her heart was doing double time. They both drew long, deep breaths.

'Look, us having a go at each other isn't going to help.'

'You're right. Let's pull ourselves together and go talk to him. Here,' Ben said, pulling a tissue from the box on the shelf next to Lily's collection of cookery books and handing it to her. 'This was always going to be hard. We'll get through it.'

Having dried her eyes, Grace knocked softly on Harry's bedroom door. 'Harry?'

'Go away,' came the muffled response from the other side.

'Harry, mate, can we come in? Please?' Ben said gently.

'Fine. You're going to anyway.'

Grace returned Ben's tense glance and pushed open the door. Harry was laid on his bed, face down on his pillow. He sat up slowly and leant against the wall. Grace could see he'd been crying. She and Ben sat down either side of him and she reached for his hand. He didn't pull away, but he didn't look at her either.

'Can I try to explain?' she asked, and Harry nodded. 'Thank you. When I was young, just out of university, I was living with my boyfriend in London. His name is James Rutherford. He's a historian and a writer. We loved each other very much but we were very young. One day, James found out that he was going to be given a lot of money to go and work on the other side of the world. He was really excited about it, and he wanted me to go with him.'

'Did you go?' Harry asked, wide-eyed.

Grace shook her head. 'No, I didn't want to go where he was going. I wanted to stay in London and maybe get married. We had a big row and we split up.'

'How does this affect me?' Harry was frowning, as was Ben.

She frowned back at Ben and gave Harry's hand a squeeze.

'I'm getting to that. After James and I split up, I was angry and sad, and didn't want to stay in London any more, so I came back to Dovecote and moved back in here with Nanna and Grandad. But then, a little while later, I found out I was pregnant with you.'

'Oh.'

'I had to make some decisions. One of which was whether to tell James.'

'And you didn't?' Harry asked, his voice small and full of worry.

Grace glanced at Ben. 'No, I didn't.'

'I don't understand. Why? Did he not have a phone?'

'It wasn't that, sweetie. James had mentioned before that he wanted to have adventures, that he wasn't ready to get married or be a dad. I thought if I told him about you, he would give up his dream job and come back to look after me and you. I felt bad that I would be taking his dream away from him and I was scared that he might hate me for it.'

'I don't really understand.'

'I know. Looking back, I don't either, but at the time I was sure I was doing the right thing. I was home and safe in Dovecote and, as far as I was concerned, James was better off without me. Then my old secondary school boyfriend came to see me.'

Grace looked over at Ben, and Harry followed her gaze.

'Wait, Dad was your boyfriend when you were at school?'

Grace smiled. 'Yes, he was my very first boyfriend and I am sorry to say that when I went to London, I kind of broke his heart a bit.'

'Did she?' Harry asked and it was Ben's turn to smile. While Grace's smile had been warm and full of nostalgia, Ben's smile was bittersweet.

'Women will do that to you, mate,' he said. 'The ones you love.'

Grace blushed. 'We got back together. He promised to look after me, and to be your dad. We got married and then you came along. We were so happy, the three of us.'

'And then you broke up again,' Harry said, his eyes dropping down to his hands folded in his lap.

'Yeah, that happens too,' said Ben. 'Sometimes you realise that although you love someone, being married can be hard, and you're better off just as friends.'

'If it's that complicated, I am never getting married,' said Harry, rolling his eyes. He fell quiet for a moment and Grace could see him struggling with the thoughts in his head. 'So, James is my dad?'

'Yes.'

'And he doesn't know I exist?'

'He does now.'

'How come?'

'Well,' said Grace, 'you know how I went to France to find that old friend of Nanna's?'

'Yeah,' said Harry, frowning as though confused about how the two things were connected.

'James works at the Imperial War Museum, and he came with me to France to help me find Nanna's friend. While he and I were talking, I ended up telling him about you, and that he is your dad.'

'Why did you tell him?'

Grace looked down at her son. 'I don't really know. A lot happened in France, sweetie. A lot of things that made my head go a bit funny and made it hard for me to know what to think. While I was talking to James about it all, it just kind of slipped out.'

'What did he say?'

'He was very angry that I'd kept you a secret from him. I explained the reasons why I had, just like I've explained to you tonight. He didn't really understand either. I'd got it wrong about him not wanting to be a dad.'

'Did he ask lots of questions about me?'

'Yes, he did. I saw him last week and we had a long talk about you, how you like sport, and your favourite subjects at school. And about how alike you look. He wears glasses too, and his are just the same as yours.'

'Mum?' Harry asked slowly. 'What happens now? Do I have to meet him?'

Grace shook her head. 'You don't have to do anything you don't want to. If you decide that you don't want anything to do with him, then that is absolutely your right.'

Harry thought for a while, his fingers picking at a tiny hole in his jumper. After a long moment, he turned to Ben. 'But you're my dad still? Right?'

'Look, mate,' said Ben leaning closer to Harry, 'this doesn't change anything, alright? We're still going to hang out.'

Harry looked to Grace who could only nod.

'Harry, buddy, listen. I love you loads, you know that, and I don't want this to change anything,' Ben added.

In that moment, everything made sense. Henri was wrong. Family wasn't blood, it was love. It didn't matter who you were biologically related to, what mattered was who you loved and who loved you. Her family was a messy, disconnected one, but the love they shared bound them all together – her, Harry, Ben, Rachel, James, Henri, Sophie, and Jenna. Richard, Lily, and Felicity were all still part of her family, even though they were gone. As for her own father? Tony Lyttleton's actions proved the other side of the coin – just as family wasn't restricted to blood, blood didn't guarantee love either. The constriction in Grace's throat reduced enough for her to be able to open her mouth.

'Harry, listen to me. It doesn't matter that Ben isn't your biological dad. What matters is who we love and who loves us. Families come in all shapes and sizes and none of them are more right, or more real, than others. You can have two dads, that's fine.' She caught Ben's eyes and spotted the wetness in them.

'I think we did the right thing,' Ben said, doing up his coat at the front door a little while later. They had sat on Harry's bed for a good long hour, just holding each other, all three of them, until Harry fell asleep.

'Yes, I think so. Thank you for your help and for being here.'

Without warning, Ben wrapped his arms around Grace and pulled her into a tight hug. His scent was so familiar. 'Did you mean what you said about families?' he asked into her hair.

Grace pulled back out of his arms. 'Yes, I did.'

'That's good. And now?'

'Now I wait for James to decide whether he wants to meet Harry. But, more importantly, for Harry to decide whether he wants to meet James.'

'What happens if James tells you he wants to meet Harry, but Harry says he's not interested in meeting him?'

Grace sucked air in through her teeth. 'Then I tell James that I'm sorry, but my son's happiness comes first.'

'I hope it doesn't come to that. I'd like for you to be happy.'

'Do you know something? I think I am. And I think I would be no matter what happens with James. I have my family, and everyone knows the truth now. That's made me happy.'

At the front gate, Ben ran his hand over the waves carved into the wood and looked back. 'I love you,' he called to her.

'I love you too,' she called back, and she knew they both meant it.

FORTY-ONE

GRACE

November 2015

There was a dark patch on the right-hand side that needed a bauble. Grace squinted at the Christmas tree. There was still a week until December but, with the nights drawing in, and having still not heard from James almost two weeks after their meeting in The Royal Oak, Grace needed a bit of cheering up. Pulling the tree and decorations down from the attic had caused a slight heaviness in her heart; it wasn't going to be the same this year. As she lifted a red, sparkly orb from the box, Harry barrelled into the sitting room, throwing his backpack down on the floor.

'Careful,' Grace said as he launched himself down onto the sofa right in the middle of the pile of decorations.

'Oh, sorry Mum.'

Grace hung the bauble on a bare branch. 'How was school?'

Harry just shrugged. He was definitely entering pre-teenage territory. She busied herself with finishing the tree and turned to Harry for his approval when it was done.

'Sick,' was his one-word verdict when he looked up from his phone.

Grace vaguely remembered hearing somewhere that that meant good, or something.

'Do you want to put the star on the top?' she asked, holding out the glittery gold wire frame to him.

'Nah, you're alright,' he said, shrinking back into the sofa.

'Oh, I see,' Grace said. 'I guess it's not *cool* to end up with gold glitter all over you, huh? I've got news for you, kiddo, the sofa's covered.' She grinned as he leapt up and started wiping his hands over his trousers. 'Don't panic, there's a clean pair in the ironing pile. I won't send you to school tomorrow all sparkly.'

With an audible groan, Harry took the star from her hand and reached up as high as he could. He might have grown a bit, but he still couldn't reach the top of the tree. With a grunt, he clambered up on a chair and wedged the star onto the highest point.

'Happy?' he said, coming back down to ground level.

'Very,' Grace replied.

'Mum?' Harry said as Grace picked up the discarded empty decoration boxes and stuffed them back into their storage container.

'Yeah?'

'So, um, I was talking to Alice at school.'

Was that a slight hint of pink on his cheeks?

'And she told me that her dad isn't her real dad. She's always known but didn't tell anyone. Except me.'

'Oh, that was kind of her. You've not mentioned it all week, and I didn't want to push you, but how are you feeling?'

Harry flicked his left shoulder up, a movement that reminded Grace so much of James that it physically hurt.

'I'm okay, Mum. Really.'

Grace watched as Harry took one of the tree baubles in his

hand and turned it round, it was the bauble she and Ben bought when they'd taken Harry to Lapland when he was five.

'It's just that Alice said she sees her real dad sometimes and I thought maybe I might want to meet James, if you and Dad don't mind?'

Grace bit her lip and blinked. 'Of course we don't mind. We're happy to do whatever you want. When I spoke to James, he was still trying to get his head around it all.'

'So, he might not want to meet me?'

'I don't know, sweetie. I think he does, but it's a bit complicated.'

'How come?'

'It's a big thing for him to come to terms with. And I guess he needs to work out whether he can forgive me for keeping such a massive secret from him. He has also admitted that he, well, kind of likes me again.'

'Like he's in love with you?'

'I don't know if I'd go that far but I think there is something there. And that will affect his decision too.'

'Because you're not in love with him?'

Grace glanced at the tree and back to Harry. 'No, I'm not. We are friends, and that's what I think it's best we stay. It's been strange for me seeing him, but that's my fault. I was the one who got in contact with him. I've no one to blame but myself.'

'All this love stuff is really hard. I'm never getting a girlfriend. It all seems too much trouble.'

'Not even Alice?' Grace teased, unable to resist.

'Mum,' Harry groaned. 'Alice is my friend.'

Grace laughed as she put her arms around her son. He hugged her back.

'Do you want me to get in touch with James and hurry him along a bit?'

'Yes please,' Harry said. Stepping out into the hall he paused, resting a hand on the worn oak doorframe. 'Mum?'

'Uh huh.'

'Don't feel bad about all of this. It's weird but I'm kind of glad you got in touch with James. And if I can forgive you for keeping him a secret from me, I guess he can forgive you for keeping me a secret from him.' He gave her a fleeting smile. 'I guess what I'm saying is that it's okay.'

Grace's heart swelled at her son's maturity. She eyed her mobile sitting benevolently on the arm of the couch. She hadn't promised not to text James.

Hi James. Just to let you know, Ben and I have told Harry about you, and he has asked if he can meet you. I have told him that I'm waiting for you to decide what you want to do. I thought you should know that before you make a decision. I don't want to rush you, but it would be good if you could let me know soon, so that I can manage Harry's expectations either way.

There was nothing more she could do.

FORTY-TWO
LILY

January 1943

It was bitterly cold. The wind blowing off the sea had an icy chill that was funnelled through the lychgate and swirled around the church. But there could have been a force nine gale blowing and I wouldn't have noticed. Not there outside St. John's Church, with Richard's hand in mine.

'Here, put on your coat,' Mrs Macnamara said, handing me the white fur I'd borrowed from Dilys. 'You'll catch your death.'

'I don't want it on in the photos. This dress cost six pounds, nineteen and six, and a sizeable chunk of my clothing coupon ration. I want to be able to see it,' I laughed turning to Richard who had blanched slightly at the exorbitant figure.

What he didn't know was that my colleagues at the hospital had a whip-round and gave me three pounds towards it as a wedding present, and Matron had paid for my hat. Of course, had I swallowed my pride and got in touch with Mummy and Daddy, the cost would not have been a consideration. But my opinion of them remained unchanged – they had not been willing to support me in my darkest hour, therefore they did not deserve the privilege of sharing my brightest. I hadn't wanted a big white dress, it hardly seemed appropriate given the circumstances, even if I could have got hold of one. I hadn't wanted one made of parachute silk either, I found the idea quite morbid for some reason. No, my knee-length, rayon crepe lavender dress was perfect. I'd fallen in love with it the moment I saw it by chance in the window of a little boutique next to Brighton train station, on my way home from work. I loved everything about it, from the gold buckle belt at the waist to the gathering that came over my shoulders and across my bust, giving the optical allusion of a giant bow.

'It is a lovely dress,' Richard said. He looked as dashing as always in his best suit and tie. His sandy hair, which had lightened to blond in the Singapore sun, had regained some of its darker, reddish streaks. He gave me a small wink, making me blush. Mrs Macnamara fussed with the white lace on my skullcap hat, pinning an errant curl back into place.

'There,' she said quietly in my ear. 'You look beautiful.' She gave my arm a squeeze and stepped away as Richard and I smiled for Albert, the hospital porter who was acting as photographer for the day.

Albert fussed with the men, taking various pictures and generally fiddling about while I gathered Felicity in my arms. I wished I could have got her a new dress, but she looked pretty in her Sunday best anyway. Out of the corner of my eye, I saw Mrs Macnamara hand something to Richard, which he put in the inside pocket of his jacket.

'One of the ladies now,' Albert called stepping across the pavement.

I caught Richard's eye as he turned away from talking to his friend Tommo, and Dilys's husband Archie, for a moment. My heart swelled for the millionth time to the point where it could have easily burst. How had I ever not loved him? I had a fleeting thought of the glass and wire necklace tucked into a velvet pouch in my jewellery box. I glanced again at Felicity, who had wandered off and was pulling the heads off a patch of snowdrops. Henri was my past, Richard my future, and that was that. I pulled myself back to the present as Dilys, Mrs Macnamara, Matron, Sister Margaret, Sheila and Betty Jones, and a couple of my nurse friends gathered around me. Richard's mother stood awkwardly next to Sister Margaret. I don't think she had quite decided what to make of me, or Felicity. Richard and I agreed to let his parents reach their own conclusions. We wouldn't lie to them, but neither would we volunteer the truth. Mrs Macnamara had retrieved Felicity and was holding her on her hip.

'Polly, come on, you too. I want all the girls in this one,' I called out to Tommo's girlfriend who was standing nervously off to the side. She gave me a grateful smile and placed herself at the end of the group. What a funny thing she was.

We thawed out in The Royal Oak with tea and sandwiches, and a delicious almost-proper fruit cake that Sheila had somehow supplied. I dared not ask where she got the ingredients. Felicity had fallen asleep on my lap when Mrs Macnamara came over and sat down next to me. I was going to miss her so much. Her daughter in Aberdeen was expecting her first child and Mrs Macnamara had had enough of the coastal bombing raids and was moving up to live with her. Her son-in-law was in North Africa, so her daughter needed her. Seafoam Cottage had been put up for sale and Felicity and I had moved in with Sheila for a couple of days while Mrs Macnamara's furniture was packed up and moved out. I had wanted Richard to move into Seafoam Cottage the moment we got engaged but Richard, being Richard, decided that, for propriety's sake, he should remain at his parents' until we were married. He was never going to change.

'When do you go?' I asked, stroking Felicity's hair.

'My train leaves in about twenty minutes. I am going to miss you, dear, but I am less worried about leaving you now I know you'll be looked after.'

'I don't know how I can ever thank you for everything you have done for me, and for Felicity. Since you took me in, you've been a mother to me, a far better one than my own mother ever was.'

Mrs Macnamara squeezed my knee. 'It was my pleasure, pet. It's been marvellous having you around, and Felicity has been such a joy to look after. Now, I'll head off before we both make a show of ourselves by getting all teary.' She hugged me tightly and it was too late, I was already crying.

'You will write, won't you?' I said, through the lump in my throat.

'I promise.'

Richard had been terribly secretive about our living arrangements after the wedding. I'd become quite worried, but he reassured me that he had everything under control and that I would not be disappointed.

The only thing he had told me is that we would not be leaving Dovecote, which was a huge relief. I couldn't consider leaving my home. It would mean a daily commute for him to his office in London, but he said he didn't mind, it would give him time to read the papers. His father's rubber company was still under government control and Richard thought it would most likely remain so until the end of the war, if not after. So when he'd been offered a Civil Service job at the Ministry of Defence, he'd been delighted. I was ever so proud of him. He had a fine career to look forward to.

We were waved off from the pub in the late afternoon, just as the light was about to fade, and Richard took my hand in his.

'Close your eyes.'

'Richard, don't be ridiculous, how shall I see where I'm going?'

He laughed. 'Don't worry, I've got you.'

'Where are you taking me? And where is Felicity?' I may have had a little too much celebratory wine.

He raised my hand to his lips and kissed it. 'Sheila has taken Felicity home with her. She said we should have a proper wedding night. As for where I am taking you? I am taking you home, Mrs Morrison.'

Despite finding my way through Dovecote in many a blackout, I quickly became disoriented. We were going downhill, that much I could tell. And we were still near the sea, I could smell the pebbles and the air was salty. Richard pulled me to a halt.

'Open your eyes, Mrs Morrison.'

I did so and let out a gasp. We were standing in front of the gate of Seafoam Cottage. I blinked, not quite believing what I was seeing. But it was definitely Seafoam Cottage, with its white-washed walls, red-tiled roof and matching porch, pale blue window frames and door, the pittosporum in the front garden, the line of cast iron stumps along the front wall, and the gate with a wave motif carved into the wood.

'Richard! You didn't? No, we couldn't possibly afford it. How?'

He kissed me lightly on the cheek. 'Never mind all of that,' he said pulling a key from the inside pocket of his jacket and handing it to me. 'Welcome home.'

FORTY-THREE
GRACE

November 2015

With her latest column submitted, and trying to distract herself from James, Grace was making a start on her Christmas shopping. Workmen were stringing fairy lights up along the High Street, and there was a cherry picker by the train station, ready for the installation of the bigger lights on the lamp posts and across the road. Dovecote town council went all out at Christmas, and all the lights lifted the dark afternoons and evenings. She'd heard *Jingle Bells* in three different shops, picked up a box of Christmas cards from Harrington's Bookshop, and had popped into Las Gaviotas for a voucher for Rachel. It was a not-so-subtle attempt to reclaim a part of their friendship that had lapsed. Harry would want computer games and probably some new football boots, so she'd have to go into Brighton for those. She had no idea what to get Ben.

Her cheeks were starting to sting with the cold. She was about to stop by Aoife's Hair Salon to book a long-overdue trim before heading home, when she looked up and caught a glimpse of a familiar face, mostly covered with a thick scarf. The pedestrian crossing beeped. She didn't remember pushing the button.

'Hey,' she said. He'd been watching her cross the road.

'Hi,' James replied. 'I was going to come and see you.'

'Now you have,' Grace said, a little more awkwardly than she intended.

'Yeah. You got time for a coffee?'

Grace nodded and they crossed back over the road, heading for The Seaside Café.

James's glasses steamed up the minute they entered the café, so Grace guided him to a table by the window and went up to the counter. Janice had hung lights all along the counter and around the windows. Thankfully the Christmas music coming from the speaker by the door was quiet and not *Jingle Bells*.

'Grace. How lovely to see you,' Janice said with a cheerful grin. 'How are you doing, love? Missing Richard, I'm sure.'

'I am, Janice, and Nanna too. But we have to carry on, don't we? Can I have two lattes and, ooh, do I want a sticky bun or a mince pie? A mince pie, I think. It's nearly Christmas!'

'Of course, two lattes and two mince pies?' Janice was looking around Grace, no doubt eyeing up James. She wiggled her eyebrows.

'Yes please. No, it's nothing like that. Stop it, Janice,' Grace said with a grin. 'It's a long story, I'll fill you in some other time.'

'Shame, nice looking chap. Reminds me of someone.'

Grace said nothing as she punched her PIN into the card reader, her cheeks reddening. 'He's just a friend, Janice.'

'Of course. I'll bring the coffees over.'

'I'm sorry it's taken me so long to get in touch, Gracie,' James said, stirring his coffee. 'I spent a lot of time going around in circles, thinking about the same things over and over again and trying to work out what it all meant.' He looked up at her. 'And thank you for your text message. Knowing that Harry wants to meet me gave me the kick up the bum I needed to stop dithering and make some decisions.'

Grace held her breath knowing that the next thing James said was going to determine the rest of her life, and Harry's too.

'I understand. You had a lot to think about.'

'There's so much I want to say, and I had it all planned out. But it's all just gone out of my head.' He went to reach across the table before stopping and pulling his hand back. 'So, I'll keep it simple. Gracie, if you and Ben will let me, I would like very much to meet my son.' His voice cracked a little and Grace reached over and placed her hand on his.

'Can you do three o'clock on Saturday?' she said in a quiet voice, trying to swallow the lump in her throat. James didn't say anything, he just nodded, drew a wavering breath, and gave her a shaky smile. There was sheer terror in his brown eyes.

FORTY-FOUR

GRACE

November 2015

It was a good thing Harry spent Friday night at Ben's. Grace had lain awake most of the night worrying about what the next day would bring, and if Harry had been there, he would have picked up on her anxiety. The last thing she wanted to do was make the day any more stressful for him.

'How is he?' Grace asked when Ben answered the door.

'Fine. He's a bit nervous. His friend Alice came round for a bit last night and they were chatting for a while.'

Grace nodded. 'Alice is in a similar situation, although she's been in touch with her biological father her whole life.'

'It's nice that she talked to him about it. I think it helped. I wonder if we might be seeing more of her in the future, if you know what I mean.'

'Yes, I did wonder about that. Well, that's your department. Remember, we agreed "those" chats are your domain.'

'Yeah,' Ben scratched his head and Grace laughed at the concerned expression on his face.

'We'll get through it together,' Grace said. 'Like we have with everything so far.'

Harry appeared at the door, wearing his favourite hoodie. It was a bit worn, but he was comfortable in it, and that was the main thing. Today of all days.

'We've not done too bad a job, have we?' Ben asked, giving Harry a nudge. 'You're an alright kid.'

Harry groaned.

'Come on, sweetie. We best get going,' Grace said.

Harry looked up at Ben. 'Are you sure you can't come?'

Ben looked from Harry to Grace and back again and put an arm around Harry's shoulder. 'No mate, sorry. This is something you're going to have to do without me. It's best if it's just you and Mum.'

Harry sighed, with obvious disappointment. 'I'll see you later, then.'

Ben and Grace exchanged nervous smiles. 'Will you let me know how it goes?' Ben asked, his voice low. 'I'll be here all day if he, you know, wants to come round for a bit. Or whatever.'

'Thanks, Ben.'

Grace's stomach was doing somersaults as she pulled into the car park by the railway bridge. It had been a relief that Harry wanted to meet James in the chain coffee shop at the top of the High Street, because they were doing special Christmas hot chocolate, rather than The Seaside Café. Considering the curious look Janice had given James on Tuesday, Grace could have done without her being witness to this already fraught meeting. She also wanted to avoid Janice putting two and two together. If, and when, she told people who James was and how he fitted into their lives, she would do it on her own terms.

Next to her, Harry was quiet and thoughtful. She tried to

make small talk, but the most she got was one-word answers. She paused before getting out of the car.

'Harry,' she said softly. A pair of serious, dark eyes looked over at her. 'So, um.' She couldn't go on. There was so much she wanted to say but the words weren't there.

'Mum, it's okay. This is all a bit weird, but I want to do this.'

'I'm sorry it's taken so long,' she said.

At the exit of the car park, Harry came to a sudden stop and Grace's heart plummeted. Was he going to change his mind?

'Mum?'

'Yes, honey.' Grace's voice wobbled.

'What if he doesn't like me?'

'Of course he's going to like you!' Grace said.

'But Mum, seriously, what if he doesn't?'

Grace put her hands on Harry's shoulders and dipped down to look into his eyes.

'That's not going to happen because everyone likes you. And listen, just because you're meeting James today, doesn't mean you have to see him again, ever. It's entirely up to you.'

'But wouldn't that make him sad?'

Grace's grip on his shoulders tightened a fraction. 'You let me worry about that. The main thing is that you're comfortable and happy.' She pulled him into her and gave him an extra-squeezy hug. 'Ready?' she asked.

'Let's do this,' he replied, linking his arm through hers.

James was waiting exactly where he said he would be, right outside the coffee shop. As they got nearer Grace glanced at Harry. He was watching James with wide eyes.

'Hi,' she said. She turned to her son. 'Harry, this is James.'

Harry and James looked at each other for a long moment, and Grace held her breath. Seeing them together really highlighted how much Harry was a mini version of his father.

'Hi, Harry,' said James. 'It's really good to meet you.'

Harry took James's proffered hand and shook it.

'Hi. It's nice to meet you too,' he said.

In an instant, Grace saw him not as the child he was, but as the smart, confident young man he would become. A rush of pride swelled in her, and she released her captive breath.

'I don't know about you guys, but I'm freezing,' she said. 'Who wants a hot chocolate?'

'Do you like computer games?' Harry asked, spooning whipped cream and marshmallows off the top of his hot chocolate into his mouth.

'Um. I've not played any for ages. I did have a Gameboy when I was younger. I don't think I was very good at it though,' James replied.

'What's a Gameboy?'

'It's a really old hand-held computer game machine that came out when I was about your age,' Grace said, handing Harry a napkin. 'Back in the dark ages.'

'What about football?'

James grimaced. 'I watch it sometimes.' He glanced at Grace, and she could see a touch of panic in his eyes.

'Didn't you play cricket once upon a time?' she asked, hoping she remembered that correctly.

'Yeah, I did. I was a terrible batsman, and a mediocre bowler,' he said, shooting her a grateful look. 'Your mum told me you like cricket, Harry.'

Harry put down his spoon and fiddled with the handle of the mug. 'Yeah. Although I had to miss the last match of the season. I hurt my wrist.'

'Oh, that's a shame. What happened to your wrist?'

Grace sipped her coffee and watched, hiding her amusement at the slightly green tinge that spread over James's face, as

Harry enthusiastically, and in meticulously gruesome detail, told him about his trip to A&E.

'It sounds like you were very brave,' James said, looking rather relieved, when Harry had finished.

'I guess. I mean at least it wasn't as bad as what happened to Lucy Simmonds. She fell off the swings at school and broke her leg. The bone was sticking out of her skin and there was blood everywhere. Alice said Josie Mackie was sick all over herself when she saw it. Jake fainted, the wuss.'

'Harry,' Grace admonished, grimacing.

He just shrugged and grinned, clearly enjoying grossing-out the adults.

'Why don't you tell James what you're learning in history.'

'Oh yeah! We've been doing World War One this term. It's alright. But I'm looking forward to doing World War Two next term. No one else in my class has a great-grandad who was in the French army.'

'Oh wow. Henri told us a lot of his stories from the war when we met him.'

Harry nodded. 'Mum said we can go to France and meet him at half-term.'

James looked up at Grace. 'You're going back?'

'Yes, I promised Henri I'd bring Harry over.'

'That's lovely.' He turned back to Harry. 'And of course you'll have to come to the Imperial War Museum. I can give you a personal guided tour.'

Grace put down her coffee cup. 'I think there's going to be a school trip arranged.'

James shot her an apologetic look.

'So that's Harry,' Grace said a little while later when he'd excused himself to go to the bathroom. 'I did tell you he was a mini version of you.'

There was a slight shine to James's eyes when he removed his glasses and fussed about cleaning them.

'Thank you for allowing me to meet him, Grace. Honestly, I'm a little stunned. I hope I'm meeting his expectations, if he had any. Did I overstep the mark when I mentioned the IWM? I'm sorry. We're taking this one step at a time, I know. He may not even want to see me again.'

Grace shook her head. 'It's fine. I think he'd probably love a personal tour. But, yes, one step at a time.'

Harry came back but didn't sit down again and Grace took that as her cue to wrap things up.

'We should be getting going,' she said. 'This one's got homework to do.'

'Urgh, Mum,' Harry groaned.

'Yeah, I should be heading off too. I said I'd pop in to see Mum and Dad. It was really nice to meet you, Harry,' James said.

'Yeah, you too,' Harry said, with a shy smile.

As the three of them left the café, Harry ran ahead, and James put his hand on Grace's arm.

'If you and Harry want to do this again, you know, some time, then I'd like that.'

'I'll let him know and I guess we'll go from there.'

'It's up to him. No pressure.' James was looking down at his feet. 'I think I might go for a bit of a walk before going to Mum's. Get some sea air.'

Grace gave him a gentle look. 'That's a good idea. I often find a wander along the beach works wonders for getting my head straight. I'll be in touch.'

'Bye, Harry,' he called, and Harry turned and waved. 'See you.'

'Yeah, see you.'

As he walked away Grace blew out a long breath and ran to catch up with Harry.

. . .

'Mum?' Harry asked as Grace was about to turn out his bedroom light. Normally he considered himself too grown-up to be tucked in but tonight he'd allowed her to put him to bed.

'Uh huh?'

'Can we go to the Dovecote Museum soon?'

Grace's heart was in her throat. 'Sure, how about next weekend?'

Harry nodded. 'Do you think James might like to come too?'

'I think he would. Do you want me to ask him?'

'Yes, please.'

'Then I will. Night, night, sweetie.'

'Night, Mum.'

Grace turned out the light and pulled the door shut behind her. She rested her head against the door and raised her eyes to the ceiling mouthing a relieved 'thank you'. Having poured herself a stiff drink, she picked up her phone, and dialled Ben's number, knowing he'd be pacing the floor waiting to hear how the meeting had gone.

FORTY-FIVE
GRACE

December 2015

The sea and sky were a matching shade of December grey, and The Seaside Café was warmly inviting as Harry tugged at Grace's arm, ushering her past to the Dovecote Museum. A blast of warm air from the heater inside the museum was a welcome one. James was waiting by the small reception desk, and he waved as they approached, shedding scarves and hats, and unzipping layers of coats.

'Hi,' he said giving Grace a hug. Harry hung back and James gave him a smile, which Harry returned, much to Grace's relief.

'This place is great,' James continued as they moved into the main body of the museum. 'I mean, for a small town like Dovecote to have its own museum, is pretty special.'

'The last time I was here was probably on a school trip when I was about Harry's age. I seem to remember their being lots of fossils and not a huge amount else. But I think Rachel and I spent the time hiding in the loos reading Judy Blume books, which was probably a more useful education.' Grace laughed, she'd forgotten the hours she and Rachel spent flexing their chests chanting 'I must, I must increase my bust'.

'Mum, come look,' Harry called. He'd gone straight to a large square Perspex case in the middle of the room.

'Oh wow,' Grace said as she saw what Harry was looking at. 'It's a model of Dovecote.'

James bent to read the inscription on the display. 'It says here this is how Dovecote looked in 1941.'

'The beach has wire all over it,' said Harry, poking at the Perspex.

'There would have been explosives buried on the beach, in case of invasion. So, the wire was to stop people wandering down there and getting injured,' James said.

'Can you see our house, Harry?' Grace asked and Harry's eyes widened. He ran a finger along the case until it hovered over the tiny model of Seafoam Cottage.

'It looks the same, they even have the tree in the back garden. But no grass.'

'A lot of people dug up their gardens during the war,' James said. 'They needed to grow fruit and vegetables.'

'As there weren't any in the shops because of rationing?' Harry asked.

'Yeah, that's right. You see that poster over there.'

Harry looked where James was pointing.

'That was the advertising slogan they used to get people to grow as much of their own food as they could.'

'"Dig for Victory",' Harry read, inching closer to the poster. 'Oh, there's a gun over there. Mum, come look!'

Grace was still investigating the model of Dovecote. 'Why don't you two go ahead? Guns and gory stuff aren't my thing.'

James looked at her with widened eyes and she gave him an encouraging nod.

'Go on,' she whispered. 'This is your chance to impress him.'

She watched them for a moment and, once satisfied that Harry was alright, looked back at the model. It really was incredible how little Dovecote had changed. She could pick out the train station and the bridge over the tracks, St. John's Church, Dovecote Primary School, and Dovecote Manor, with its little cottage nestled in the trees, at the top of the cliff. And there, back down the High Street and along Queen's Parade was Victoria Park, complete with a bandstand and miniature cricket pavilion. There was even a little café on The Promenade. The museum itself had once been a square of posh-looking houses. Her eyes drifted north, away from the beach and up the hill to Bayview. In 1941, it had still been two separate red brick buildings, and Grace's eye lingered on the model bench under the sycamore tree her grandad used to stare at. To the east of Bayview, where Churchill Drive and Temper Street now led to the secondary school and Ben's house, was just open fields, dotted with a couple of farmhouses and some model cows. It was the Dovecote of her grandparents' youth, and it gave her a warm fuzziness in her stomach that it wasn't all that different from her Dovecote of the present.

Looking up from the model, her eyes caught sight of a picture on the far wall. She went over and read the caption on the card underneath it.

Bayview Convalescent Home in 1941. British and French soldiers evacuated from Dunkirk were some of the first wartime casualties to recuperate at Bayview, having been treated at Brighton Municipal Hospital (later Brighton General). The building became Bayview Care Home in 1973.

Grace studied the picture more closely. There were two figures stood outside the building on the right: a short, stocky woman with curly hair, and a tall, thin nun. Unquestionably, the women in Lily's wedding photo.

In this video filmed in 1987, a year before her death, retired nurse, Dilys Armitage, talks about her experiences as a nurse at Bayview between 1940 and 1943.

Grace tried to get the video to play but it seemed to be stuck. She'd have to come back another time. At that moment Harry came running up, breathlessly excited.

'Mum, it's so cool. There's a whole anti-aircraft gun back there, and a dummy in uniform with his leg blown off. I didn't like the gas mask though, that was totally creepy.'

Grace pulled a face which James mirrored.

'It's pretty gruesome,' he said. 'Where's that?' He inclined his head towards the photograph.

'That's Bayview Care Home. It's where Nanna looked after Henri and where Grandad moved to when he got too ill to live at home.' Grace let out a short, sharp laugh. 'No wonder Nanna wasn't all that keen on Grandad moving there, it must have held a lot of memories for her.'

James nodded and drew a deep breath. 'Indeed.'

Grace pulled herself together. 'I promised Harry we could go for a wander around the Christmas Market in Victoria Park, if you wanted to join us? There's a mulled wine chalet.'

'Sounds good to me. If you don't mind, Harry?'

Harry shook his head. 'I don't mind. You can tell me more about how people were injured and killed by explosions!'

Grace shot James an open-mouthed stare and he shrugged, almost apologetically.

It had gotten late, and the Christmas lights decked over the maze of wooden huts in Victoria Park gave off a warm, yellow glow in the dark. Harry had bumped into his friend Jake the minute they'd walked into the Christmas Market. They were trying their luck at a game which seemed to consist of trying to shoot wooden elves with tiny plastic baubles fired from a giant candy cane. Grace and James huddled on the bench overlooking the beach next to the drinks stall, bathed in the golden glow of the Christmas lights, each cradling a cardboard cup of steaming spicy wine. The reflections of the lights, strung up between the lamp posts on The Promenade, sparkled on the black sea.

'Have you heard from Henri lately?' she asked, blowing the top of her mulled wine. It was too hot to drink but was doing an excellent job as a hand warmer.

James took a tentative sip of his and grimaced. 'Ouch! Too hot,' he said. 'Yes, I had an email from him the other day. Well, from Sophie.'

'How is he doing?'

'Much better. Sophie said he's fully recovered from the chest infection he had in October. She said she's not seen him this sprightly in years.'

Grace laughed. 'Ah, that's a relief. I'll pop a Christmas card in the post. Harry had some school photos taken on Monday. I'll send them one.' She nearly asked James if he wanted one too, but that might have been a bit weird.

'Henri's asked me to help him write his memoirs.'

Grace couldn't tell whether the pink tinge on James's cheeks was due to embarrassment or the cold.

'That's lovely. So, you'll be going over to see him?'

'For sure. Probably a few times. I could come over with you and Harry in the spring.' He looked down at his feet. 'If you wanted?' he added quietly.

Grace didn't get a chance to reply as Harry bounded up at that moment carrying a large, stuffed reindeer toy.

'Where on earth did you get that?' she asked, aghast. The thing was almost as big as Harry and hideous, with a garish Christmas jumper and a bright red nose that Harry was squeezing to make light up.

'I won it. I knocked over fourteen elves. Listen.' Harry squeezed one of the antlers and a tinny, muffled tune came out of the reindeer's mouth.

'Is that supposed to be *Jingle Bells*?' James asked and Grace sighed.

At the intricately filigreed gates of Victoria Park, they paused.

'I'm this way,' James said, pointing to the right towards his parents'. Grace and Harry were going the other way, back down Queen's Parade to Beachfront Road. 'I've had a lovely afternoon,' he said, giving Harry a grin.

Harry smiled back. 'Me too.'

'How's the house hunting going?' Grace asked. 'Any luck?'

'Oh, yeah, I meant to say. I think I've found somewhere. It's only a rental for now, until I can sort out somewhere more permanent. Just around the corner from here, on Courcey Road. Mum and Dad said I could move in with them, but I prefer my own space.'

'No way! That's where Rachel used to live before she moved in with Dad,' Harry said, hopping up on the low wall that surrounded the park and tightrope walking along it.

'Rachel's moved in with Ben? Already?' James had one eyebrow raised.

Grace shrugged. 'Yep. They did ask me if I was okay with it.'

'And are you?'

'I guess. Are you asking me if I'm over my ex?'

He blushed again. 'No, of course not.'

'Say bye to James, Harry,' she said, with a grin.

'Bye, James,' Harry replied. 'Maybe we can hang out again soon?'

'If your mum agrees, I'd really like that.'

'Fine by me,' Grace said, trying and failing to keep the quiver of relief from her voice.

She turned away and tucked the hideous stuffed reindeer under her arm. James called out.

'Gracie. Sorry, I forgot to say. If Henri wanted to include your grandmother, you, and Harry in his memoirs, would that be a problem?'

Grace glanced back at the Christmas Market for a moment, then swallowed the lump in her throat and shook her head.

'No, not a problem,' she said softly. 'Actually, I think it would be a rather lovely thing for him to do.'

James nodded and the edges of his lips curled upwards in a small smile.

'I think so too.'

Walking back along Queen's Parade, Grace's mind was whirring. Did the soft look in James's eyes and the blush on his cheeks mean what she thought it did? Did she hope it did? Why did watching him walk away leave her with a slightly hollow sensation in her stomach? And how soon could she arrange to meet up with him again?

FORTY-SIX
GRACE

December 2015

Grace couldn't decide whether to applaud the commitment or curse the stubbornness of the under-thirteen's football coach, who decided not to cancel the morning's training. It was a week and a half until Christmas, the school term was ending in three days, and it was snowing. Not nice fluffy snow either; it was that wet stuff that melted the instant it hit the ground and stung your face. The poor weather was unfortunate especially as it was James's first time on the touchline, and it had been Harry's idea. Grace got the feeling Harry was testing James, seeing how invested he really was, how far he would go and what he would put up with, and whether James would give up three Saturdays in a row for him. James deserved extra points for showing up this morning, that was for sure. Grace glanced over her shoulder. There was no sign of Ben. Maybe she shouldn't have told Rachel that James was going to be there.

'Get in under here, you're getting soaked,' Grace said, lifting the umbrella slightly to allow James to duck under it. It wasn't a large umbrella so they had to stand close together. The sleeves of their puffy jackets were squashed between them and the pressure of James's arm against hers warmed Grace more than the insulation of her jacket.

'Thanks. I'm clearly ill-prepared for Saturday mornings on the touchline. I have much to learn.'

Grace turned back to the game. Harry was somewhere in the melee of boys running around after the ball like a swarm of bees. The coach was trying to lure them back into some sort of formation, but the boys were far too preoccupied with trying to knock each other over in the mud to pay him any attention. Out of nowhere, the football came flying right at her. Somehow James managed to catch it before it hit her square in the face. A lanky boy with straggly, dark hair trotted over, reclaimed the ball from James, muttered a barely audible 'sorry', and trotted off again.

'Nice reflexes,' she said, lowering the umbrella. It had stopped trying to snow. That was the thing about living by the sea. The weather didn't hang around for long. She pulled a pack of wet wipes from her handbag and handed one to James so he could wipe the mud and grass from his hands. 'A mother never leaves the house without a pack of wet wipes, no matter how old her child,' she said with a grin.

'For which I'm grateful,' he replied, wrinkling his nose.

Grace turned her attention back to the action on the pitch as James meandered off to find a bin, so didn't realise someone was behind her until they spoke.

'Hey!'

Grace turned and did a double take.

'Rach. Hi. What are you doing here? Oh.' The penny dropped. 'Let me guess, Ben has sent you to pick up Harry so that he didn't risk bumping into me. Or rather, into James.'

Rachel grimaced. 'Yeah. And to be honest I've been sat in the car for the last half an hour, waiting for it to stop raining, or snowing, or whatever it was doing. Don't get me wrong, I love Harry to bits, but this isn't really my natural habitat.'

'You'd better get used to it,' Grace snapped. Harry would be disappointed that Ben wasn't there, but clearly that was less important to Ben than avoiding, what would be at worst, a slightly awkward meeting. Rachel was looking down at her hands.

'Sorry. I didn't mean that to sound as narky as it did. I'm mad at Ben, not you,' Grace sighed.

Rachel raised her eyes. 'I know. And you're right, I'm going to have to step up, aren't I?'

'All in good time. It's a big adjustment for you, suddenly having to take a child into consideration. It took me a while, and I gave birth to him.'

'So did James not... oh.'

Grace turned as Rachel's question died on her lips. James had returned and was hovering behind her.

'Rachel, meet James. James, Rachel,' Grace said gesturing from one to the other. 'I was sure you two had met before, but maybe not.'

'No, I don't think we have. Hi, Rachel, nice to meet you.'

'Hi. Ben, um, he, um, got caught up in something, otherwise...' Rachel's voice faded out again.

'It's fine. I get it. Honestly. If I were him, I'd probably try to avoid me for as long as possible too,' James said with a slight shrug.

Rachel turned to Grace. 'How long does this go on for, anyway?'

Just as she asked, the coach blew his whistle and the kids surged back to the middle of the field and gathered in a circle around him.

'That's the final whistle. They're doing a little end of term prize-giving. If you want to...' Grace inclined her head towards the centre circle where the other parents were starting to gather.

Rachel looked at the sodden grass and down at her shoes.

'I don't think mud and high heels are a good combination,' she said. 'You go on, Grace, I'll wait here.'

'I would but, um.' James paused. 'There's already been a few questioning glances in my direction. Best not draw attention to myself,' he added with a slight shrug.

As she crossed the squelching grass, Grace glanced over her shoulder to find James and Rachel chatting amicably. What were they talking about? And did it have anything to do with the way James looked at her? She'd taken the risk of telling Rachel about the afternoon at the museum and Christmas Market. She may have also mentioned that it was only Harry's presence that stopped her from inviting James back to Seafoam Cottage for a coffee.

'Can I have a word?' Ben asked as he stepped over the threshold of Seafoam Cottage the following evening. Grace shut the door against the bitter wind blowing over the sea wall. Harry gave Grace a quick, silent hug and disappeared up to his bedroom. Grace turned her attention back to Ben, standing in her hallway, frowning darkly. She led him into the sitting room.

'What's up?' she said, her mind still on Harry's peculiar mood.

'I think Harry's a bit upset. I think it's James,' Ben said. 'He's been in a mood all weekend.'

'Did he say it was because of James?' Grace asked, her heart rate rocketing.

'No. He wouldn't tell me what was wrong,' Ben said, not sitting down, but pacing the room, avoiding Grace's eye.

Grace glanced up at the ceiling. Computerised music filtering down told her Harry was on his console, which was fine. He didn't have any homework as all they were doing at school for the last two days of term was watching films and having a Christmas party.

'So, you're presuming it's about James, then?'

Ben gave her an exasperated look. 'What else could it be?'

'Oh, I don't know, Ben. Maybe his *dad* letting him down.'

'What?'

'He was really disappointed you didn't turn up to football practice yesterday. He tried to hide it, but I could see it. He wanted you to be there, so you could see him getting his little award, and you weren't. Why?'

Ben didn't reply, he just rubbed his forehead.

'You know, I'm glad James was there. That cheered Harry up a bit,' Grace snapped, instantly regretting descending to such petulance.

'Oh great, so now you're happy with James taking over. I knew this would happen. That he'd want to push me out. What's next? A cosy little family holiday? Has he told Harry to call him "Dad" yet?'

'Don't you dare, Ben,' Grace hissed. 'And keep your voice down.' She closed the sitting room door. 'James is not pushing anyone out. You chose not to show up yesterday. You promised Harry that us telling him about James wasn't going to change anything, that you'd still be there for him. But you weren't. And if Harry is, justifiably, annoyed with you, then I don't blame him. I'm annoyed with you. If your relationship with Harry is being damaged, then that's all on you.'

'I just don't know if I can bear to be in *his* presence.' The way Ben said 'his' was loaded with poison.

Grace let out a deep, frustrated sigh. 'What is your problem, Ben? Huh? What have you got against James? If you want someone to be angry at, it should be me. James didn't ask to come into Harry's life. I was the one who contacted him, who told him about Harry, who said that I'd welcome him into our lives. He's done nothing wrong, and I won't stand by and let your fragile ego upset Harry. Also, that comment about a cosy family holiday is a bit rich coming from you, who whisked Harry away for a week with Rachel at the earliest possible opportunity. If I were you, I'd take a good long look in the mirror before you accuse me of letting someone else muscle in on anyone.'

There was a hint of wariness in Ben's eyes. Grace didn't often go off on one at him.

She softened her stare. 'Look, Harry and James are getting to know each other, slowly, and it's going really well. They like each other. Whether you like it or not, James is a part of Harry's life now, and there will, inevitably, be times when Harry wants or needs you both to be there for him. So, you can either pull yourself together and get a grip, or you can tell Harry that he can no longer rely on you. Your choice.'

Ben said nothing as he opened the sitting room door and stood in the terracotta-tiled hallway. Grace drew a few steadying breaths and followed.

'Ben?' When he looked around, she could see a shine in his eyes. 'If I arranged for you and James to meet, would you come? You and Rachel and me and James, for a drink, nothing more. Just half an hour.'

'I'll think about it.' His voice was gravelly.

'Give James a chance, Ben. If not for my sake, then for Harry's.'

Ben glanced at the staircase, with a brooding look in his eyes before turning away.

'Ben?' Grace begged. 'Please.'

'I said I'll think about it.' And he was gone.

Grace leant against the wall of the hallway and let out a long sigh. Once again there was nothing she could do but wait.

FORTY-SEVEN
GRACE

December 2015

Saturday evening, three days before Christmas, and almost the whole town appeared to be in The Royal Oak. Grace spotted a few familiar faces as she led James through the crowd. Aoife, her hairdresser, was sat at a table with Jez, the carpenter who'd fitted her grandparents' new kitchen a few years earlier. Janice was stood at the bar talking with Sue and Terry who lived in Dovecote Manor at the top of the cliffs. At the tap on her shoulder, and she turned to find Heather behind her.

'Heather. Hi,' she said giving her a quick hug. 'You finally got a weekend off!'

Heather grinned. 'Only because I'm working all over Christmas.'

'Do you mind?'

'Not really,' Heather said shaking her head. 'We have a bit of a laugh.'

'It was lovely last year when we came to visit Grandad on Christmas Day. It was good to see him with a paper crown on, having a good time.'

'Well, we try. We all miss him, Grace.'

Grace touched Heather's arm. 'Thank you.'

'Merry Christmas,' Heather said with a wink before turning away and disappearing into the crowd.

Grace heaved a sigh and gave Declan behind the bar a wave.

'I don't reckon we'll get a table,' James said over the chatter and the Christmas music.

'Don't worry. Declan's reserved one for us.' Grace grinned at James's surprised look. 'Declan and I go way back. We were at school together. I let him snog me behind the bike sheds once. He's still repaying the favour.'

'I wish I could say I don't believe you, but I do.'

'Go on and sit down at that table over there,' Grace said, indicating a small rectangular table at the back of the pub. 'I'll get us a drink.'

'How are you doing, Declan?' Grace shouted across the bar.

'All good, Grace, all good. Merry Christmas and all that. Who's the fella, then? Do I have competition again? Here's me thinking I might have a chance this time!'

'Merry Christmas. Give us two large Merlots, please.' She glanced over her shoulder at James who was drumming his fingers on the table, slightly wide-eyed. 'There's always a chance, Declan,' she added with a wink as he passed the glasses to her.

'Ah, if only that were true,' he chuckled. 'Well, I hope he's good to you, otherwise I'll have to have words.'

'We're just friends, Declan.' Her chest ached at her own words.

'Where's Harry tonight, then?' James asked when Grace sat down next to him at the table.

'Jake, his best friend, is having a Christmas party sleepover.'

'That's nice.'

'Yeah. I'm a bit concerned because he let slip that his other friend, Jake's cousin Alice, is going to the party. I think Harry has a little crush on her, so I hope she's not staying over too.'

'I think it's probably a little too soon to be worrying about things like that just yet.'

'Yeah, I know. But it's a mother's prerogative to worry about her child, no matter how ridiculous.'

James gave her a nudge. 'I will admit I'm glad we're doing this in public. Just in case.'

'Rachel told me she's had a chat with Ben, and he's promised to be on his best behaviour. Don't worry, he's a big softie really. He just cares so much about Harry.'

'I know. I just hope I can convince him I'm not trying to muscle in. I've seen quite a lot of you and Harry over the past few weeks. I hope Ben's not felt left out?'

Grace shook her head. 'Not at all. He took Harry to watch the football during the week. They're still having a great time together.'

'That's good.'

Grace looked up as the crowd shifted and Rachel emerged from the melee, followed by Ben who, on spotting Grace and James, froze. Rachel put her hand in his and almost dragged him across the pub. They paused at the bar where Ben ordered a glass of white wine for Rachel and a pint for himself. Rachel leant in and said something to Ben which made Ben's shoulders relax away from his ears a fraction. He swallowed half of his pint in one go.

The two men stood looking at each other for a long moment.

'Hi. I'm James,' James said extending a hand. After the briefest of pauses Ben took it.

'Ben.'

Grace and Rachel let out long, synchronous breaths as everyone sat down at the table. Grace and James on one side, Ben and Rachel on the other. How many times had Grace and Rachel's positions been reversed when Rachel's latest flame made up the four? Rachel's hand settled on Ben's knee. Grace smiled at them. They were happy together, and they both deserved that. Ben had an odd look on his face. He kept looking at James, shaking his head.

'What?' Grace asked.

'I can't get over it,' Ben said, with a bemused half-smile. 'How Harry is the absolute image of you, James. It's like seeing into Harry's future. Funny how over the years I kind of just didn't notice, or maybe I chose not to see that there was, obviously, nothing of me in him.'

'The good news is my dad is nearly seventy and still has a full head of hair, so hopefully I've passed those genes on.' James smiled awkwardly.

'Everyone ready for Christmas?' Grace asked, trying to steer the conversation into safer waters.

'I think so,' Rachel said. 'It's quite nice to be letting someone else do the hard work this year though.'

Ben glanced at Grace.

'I know I've said this before, Grace, but Mum and Dad want you to know you're more than welcome to come to theirs with us and Harry,' Ben offered.

'You're not going to be on your own, are you?' James added. His knee was resting gently against hers. Had he noticed?

'It's fine, don't worry about me. The plan is for Harry to stay with me Christmas Eve and Christmas morning, and then I'll drop him round so the three of you can go the Curtis's for lunch. It'll be a tight enough squeeze around that dining table as it is without me.'

Ben shrugged. 'I think Mum's invited one of her bridge club ladies who was widowed in August as well.'

'See.' She turned to James. 'It's fine. Honestly. I'll put on my pyjamas and watch a Cary Grant film.'

Ben and James rolled their eyes in unison and Ben laughed.

'She made you sit through all those old films as well?'

'Many times,' James said with a grin. He shifted slightly and his knee fell away from hers, leaving her cold.

'Shall I get some more drinks in?' Rachel asked, looking around at everyone's empty glasses.

'I'll come with you,' Grace said. James and Ben would have to be left alone at some point. It may as well be now.

'Thanks for getting Ben here, Rach,' Grace said as they stood at the bar waiting for Declan. Grace caught Janice's eye and they gave each other a wave.

'He's alright with it, you know. It's just taken him a bit of time to work it all out. You know what he's like better than I do.'

'I know how much he loves Harry and I do understand his reaction. It was the same with Sophie when I met Henri. It's only natural to be afraid of losing the people we love.'

'That's not a reason to avoid getting involved with them though,' Rachel said, with a superior look. Grace's cheeks grew warm.

'I don't know what you mean.'

'Yeah, you do. You can't let worrying about what might happen in the future, prevent you from letting things happen in the present. I've got eyes, Grace. I see the way James looks at you, and the way you look at him. But I know you, you'll be worrying about what it might mean for Harry.'

'I'm not sure how it's happened, Rach,' Grace admitted, picking up the two glasses of red wine.

'You're preaching to the choir, Grace. I mean, six months ago, who would have thought we'd be where we are now?'

'And what if it all goes wrong?'

'Then we will be there to help you pick up the pieces.' Rachel tossed her chestnut-brown hair. 'And anyway, I prefer to think what if it all goes right?'

'So, we've got it all sorted out,' Ben said when Grace and Rachel sat back down. 'James said it took him hours to defrost after Saturday so, as he's not a fan of freezing to death on football pitches or in stands, I'll be responsible for Harry's sports education, and teaching him inappropriate football chants. James's going to be in charge of museums, art galleries, historical monuments, and all that stuff.'

'And Ben's going to take care of all maths homework, because I am useless at numbers,' James added.

'Sounds good to me,' Grace agreed. 'What does that leave me with?'

'Everything else,' said Ben.

'And keeping us in check and on our toes,' James laughed.

Grace and Rachel rolled their eyes at each other. 'Lord, help me,' Grace said.

FORTY-EIGHT
GRACE

December 2015

The pub had quietened down a little and, when Rachel and Ben left, Grace and James moved to a small table by the fire. When Ben and James wished each other a Merry Christmas, Grace had finally relaxed and thanked her lucky stars that even if they would never be best friends, at least Ben and James weren't going to be sworn enemies.

'So how did the move go?' Grace asked when James returned from the bar with another round of drinks.

'Good, thanks. I've still got a lot of boxes to unpack, and I don't think I'll be getting my Christmas tree up. I have no idea where the decorations are. I'll probably find them some time next year,' James chuckled.

'Harry and I could come round tomorrow evening and give you a hand. You can't not have a Christmas tree! I've had my tree up since November.'

'November?' he said, laughing. 'That's way too early. Yours must have been the first one up in the whole of Dovecote.'

Grace shrugged, but she was smiling. 'Probably. I don't care. I wanted a bit of sparkle, that's all.'

James looked into her eyes and Grace's knees went a little weak. 'Are you sure you don't mind being on your own on Christmas Day? Especially as it's your first one without Lily and Richard.'

A lump immediately formed in Grace's throat which she struggled to swallow.

'I'm sure my mum could fit you in round theirs. She always cooks enough for a medium-sized army.'

'Thank you, that's very kind, but I think I'll pass this time.' It was a very tempting offer, but Christmas Day was not the day to meet James's parents for the first time in fourteen years or so, especially considering the circumstances. Had he told them they had a grandson?

'Before I forget,' James said reaching into his bag and pulling out a rectangular present wrapped in dark red paper, with a gold ribbon. 'I didn't wrap it, Mum did.' He passed it across the table and Grace took it, her pulse quickening as her fingers grazed his just a fraction. 'It's for Harry. I didn't put a label on it in case you don't want to tell him it's from me. It's a book about the French Resistance. I asked someone on the school liaison team at work what would be good for someone Harry's age and they recommended it. I thought it might be interesting, considering Henri's history.'

Grace put the parcel down on top of her handbag. 'Thank you. That's very kind. I will let him know it's from you. Of course I will.'

'I didn't know the etiquette,' James said with a nervous shrug.

'We can't pretend it's from Father Christmas. Harry told us he didn't believe in him last year. It broke me a little bit. I think I was more upset than he was.'

'Gracie, can I ask you something?'

She tilted her head slightly. 'Go on,' she said with some trepidation. It sounded serious.

'It's nothing to do with me, but when Rachel and I were talking about Henri at Harry's football training last week, she mentioned that you'd heard from your dad, just after Lily died. I don't remember you ever talking about him much.'

Grace put down her glass. So that was what they'd been talking about. Typical of Rachel, she just couldn't let it go. Ever since Grace had shown her that card, Rachel had been dropping Tony Lyttleton randomly into conversations and Ben had started doing it too. It drove her mad.

'Did she ask you to talk to me about it? She and Ben have brought him up a few times since all this kicked off.'

The way James looked down at his hands answered that question and Grace sighed.

'He sent me a sympathy card. It was the first I'd heard from him in nearly thirty years.'

'Do you ever think about getting in touch with him?'

'The thought briefly crossed my mind. He put his email address in the card. But, no, I don't think so.'

'Even with everything that's happened over the past couple of months. You know, with Henri and with me?'

'I threw out the card.'

'Yeah, Rachel mentioned that. You said Henri told you he was sorry that he never knew about your mother, and that he regrets he might not have much time with you. I've missed out on so much of Harry's life, which I will always regret. Thankfully I can rectify that, so long as you and Ben will allow me to. Don't you think your dad deserves the chance to get to know you, to spend time with you and Harry, before it's too late?'

Grace put her head in her hands and rubbed her eyes. The smoke from the fire was making them watery.

'It's not the same, James,' she said, her voice shaking slightly. 'Neither you nor Henri can be held responsible for not being there. Neither of you were aware your children existed. My father knew about me. He chose to walk out on me, chose not to contact me for three decades. He knew where I was the whole time, and he made the choice not to be part of my life. Anyway, like I said, I chucked the card, so I don't have his email, even if I did want to get in touch with him.'

'You didn't have any way of contacting Henri and look what you achieved.'

'I had you.'

'Yes, but this time you're not looking for a ninety-year-old French war veteran. Your dad will be easier to find, he's probably on Facebook.'

'It's just a whole other thing, James. I don't think I have the emotional bandwidth for anything that traumatic. And anyway, I just don't want to. As far as I'm concerned, I have no reason to contact him. And he knows where I am if he wants to apologise and meet his grandson.'

'I get that. But if you do change your mind, you know I'll be there for you.'

'You will? Oh. I mean, thanks.' Grace blushed.

If there was a moment Grace could no longer deny that she was in love with him, it was right then.

The night was bitterly cold when they stepped outside The Royal Oak. Grace wrapped her winter coat tightly around her and fished a pair of gloves from her pocket. James wound his scarf around his neck and zipped his coat right up over it.

'Come on, I'll walk you home.'

'Are you sure? It's the wrong direction for you and it's a bit cold.'

'I don't mind. It's a nice evening. Nice and clear, I mean.'

They walked slowly, and in silence for a while, the faint strains of Christmas carols drifting in the frigid air. As they crossed the High Street they found the source of the music – a brass band was playing softly outside the station, collecting for charity. Grace slipped her arm through James's, and they stopped to listen for a while. James dropped a note into the collection bucket and they walked towards Beachfront Road.

'How are you really doing?' James asked, the streetlight casting an orange glow on his skin. 'I mean coping with the loss of both of your grandparents?'

Grace blinked a bit and glanced out at the inky blackness where the starlit sky met the sea. In the distance, the lighthouse shone its beam on the rocks below.

'You know, I think I'm getting there. I don't have that same intense heaviness on me all the time any more. I'll always miss them, Nanna especially. And with Grandad, I have kind of been saying goodbye to him for the best part of a year, so it's a bit of a relief. If that's not a terrible thing to say.'

James glanced at her. 'No, it's not. It's completely understandable. And I'm glad you're feeling a bit better.'

Her healing had started in France when she'd sat with Henri as he told her what Lily's letter had only just revealed to him. The way he thought of her and Harry being a bit of him left in the world, made her realise that her grandparents, and her mother, lived on in her and in her son, and that was comforting.

She laughed lightly. 'And also finding out that Nanna and I had similar life stories has brought us closer, even though she's gone.'

'Do you think she'd be happy with how everything has worked out?'

Grace tucked a stray strand of golden-blonde hair behind her ear with the hand that wasn't holding on a little too tightly to James's elbow.

'I think she would. And I think she'd be most pleased that Harry is getting the chance to do what my mother never did.'

'I think she'd be very proud of you for everything you've done to right past wrongs.'

'I hope so.'

'Can I ask you something?' James said as they reached the gate of Seafoam Cottage. The fairy lights she'd strung around the roof of the porch twinkled and the light above the front door bathed the garden in a soft white glow.

'Sure.'

'I know I asked you this back in Neuville, but quite a lot has changed since then, so I want to ask again. Do you have any regrets?'

'About life in general, or about anything specifically?'

James gave her a lingering look. 'In general, I guess.'

Grace thought for a moment. 'There is a lot I could have regrets over, mostly about you, and us. But, if I've learnt anything over the past few months, it's that there isn't really any point to having regrets. We can't change the decisions we made in the past. And who's to say that they were the wrong ones. I can't know how things would have worked out if I'd chosen differently. We can't alter our past. The only thing we can change is the future.'

She hesitated. James didn't interrupt. Instead, he pushed open the gate and they stepped through into the garden. She had to let go of his arm as he followed her up the path to the front door. It was like losing one of her own limbs.

'But I know I made mistakes. I hope I'm doing a decent job of putting them right. And that I've learnt enough to not make the same mistakes in the future. Does that make any sense?'

'Yeah, it does and you're right; regrets are a waste of time and energy. Far better to concentrate on looking forward.'

'So, you don't have any regrets either?'

A fluffy snowflake landed on Grace's nose. James brushed it away with a touch so gentle it sent a shiver through Grace's body. He took a step towards her and looked right into her eyes. She could barely breathe.

'I have one,' he said, his voice low and quiet. 'I regret not trying harder to see you after you left me all those years ago. I should have told you more how much I loved you, how much you meant to me. Maybe if I could have done that, then things would have been different.'

'I knew, James. I really did.'

'And as for not making the same mistakes in the future...'

'Hmm?' Grace said, her heart thumping.

The snow was falling heavier now, silently sprinkling the grass and the daisy bushes with flecks of white. There were flakes in his hair and on his coat.

The instant he kissed her, every worry and doubt evaporated and she let herself be flooded with a warmth that was a lot like coming home.

FORTY-NINE
LILY

June 1945

Felicity was sleeping, exhausted from the street party earlier in the day, and Richard was out celebrating Tommo's engagement to Polly Stephenson. He would be late back, but I didn't begrudge him it. It was hard for him; everyone was in a celebratory mood, but he still worried about his former colleagues and friends caught up in the ongoing war in the Pacific. Just a few days ago, word had filtered through that Maya Carson's father had been killed in a prisoner-of-war camp. The last thing he'd heard of Maya was that she had been sent to America. I was glad she was safe. I wouldn't be in a rush to meet her, but I wished her no ill-will. At least no more than Richard would wish on Henri.

I re-read the letter that had arrived and, with a sigh, sat down at the square table in the bay window of the sitting room to formulate some sort of a response. I flicked on the lamp, pulled a sheet of paper from my pile, unscrewed the lid of my fountain pen, and listened to the waves lapping against the sea wall for a moment.

Seafoam Cottage, Dovecote, 2 June 1945

My dearest, darling Henri,

I cannot tell you what joy and happiness it brings me to hear that you are alive. I have held you in my thoughts and prayers continuously, although I feared the worst. I was very touched by your letter and have read it many times. It is with the deepest, and greatest regret, that I have to ask you not to come. I am sorry to write these words, I wish things were different. If you will indulge me, I will explain.

In the months following the wonderful night we spent together, I found out that I was expecting a child. I knew this child was your child, Henri. There had been no one else. I gave birth to our daughter on the fifteenth of March 1941. I named her Felicity, after the French for happiness, because that was what holding a living memory of you gave me. I have enclosed a photograph taken of Felicity and me. As you will see, she has a lot of you in her. She is a healthy, sunny child, who delights and charms everyone who meets her.

Her arrival was not welcomed by my parents who banished me from their house. As a result, I have not spoken to them for many years. I faced a difficult future, until Richard returned from Singapore. I am sure you remember me telling you about Richard, who had proposed marriage to me, and to whom I did not give an answer. On his return, he found me and my daughter living with Mrs Macnamara (whom I am sure you will remember from Bayview), and when he professed his enduring love for me, forgave me for my love affair with you, and asked for my hand again, I accepted.

Richard and I were married in January 1943 and are very happy. I love him dearly, and he is the most wonderful father to Felicity. We have settled into a nice, quiet routine, the three of us in our cottage by the sea in Dovecote. Although I am reminded of you daily in the places we spent time together, and in our daughter's smile, I have promised my life to Richard, and I intend to keep that promise.

I know this is not the response you would have been hoping to receive and I am sorry to have to let you down like this. As much as I love Richard, there will always be a place in my heart for you and I shall never forget you for as long as I live. I shall close by wishing you happiness, health, long life, and, most importantly, love.

With best and warmest wishes,

Lily x

I folded the page before the tears brewing in my eyes spilled out and blotted the ink. I kissed the photograph of Felicity and tucked it safely between the folds. I carefully wrote the address on the envelope before sealing it. Popping out to put it in the post would have to wait until the morning.

EPILOGUE

GRACE

August 2016

There was a warm breeze blowing in the open bay window of Seafoam Cottage, carrying with it the swish of the waves and the raucous screeching of the omnipresent seagulls. Grace sat at the square table and looked at the blank email, her chin resting in her hand. She'd filled in the email address but couldn't decide how to greet the man she hadn't spoken to in almost three decades. She would certainly not be opening with 'Dear Dad'.

She yawned, rubbed her eyes, and flicked to an open Word document. James had convinced her to have a go at writing Lily's story down, seeing as he was writing Henri's. So far, she'd jotted down a few memories, and a rough outline of everything she knew about her grandmother's life. Would it come to anything? Even if it didn't, it was a nice way to remember her. She looked up from her laptop as a car pulled up outside.

'They're here,' she called up the stairs. Two doors slammed and two pairs of feet stomped along the landing and down the stairs. Harry had had a bit of a growth spurt during the summer and was now up to Grace's shoulder. He was looking more like James every day. James gave her a light kiss on the lips as Harry ran to the door and flung it open. A thin woman in a simple black dress with dark hair pulled into a tight bun, and a woman with a wild mop of grey curls wearing bright yellow dungarees, climbed out of the car.

'Hey, we made it!' Jenna cried, and Harry ran to give her a hug. They had formed a bond on their spring trip to Neuville. Harry called Jenna his cool aunt, and Sophie his scary aunt. Grace had not told Sophie that.

There were air kisses and hugs all round. Grace had a tear in her eye as she watched Sophie help Henri out of the back of the car and into the wheelchair Jenna had a firm grip on.

'Ah Grace, I have finally made it back,' Henri said with a laugh. 'It has only taken seventy-six years.'

'It's wonderful to see you again.' Grace sniffled, giving him a gentle, but warm, hug.

He drew a deep breath. 'It is good to be here.'

'Come on in, everyone,' James said, holding the wooden gate of Seafoam Cottage open. 'You could probably use a rest and a cup of tea after your journey.'

Henri scowled as if about to argue but then relented. '*D'accord*, one cup of tea, but then I want to see Dovecote again.'

They wrapped Henri tightly in blankets and set off up Beachfront Road and along The Promenade, Harry acting as tour guide pointing out landmarks like the post box and the train station. Grace walked alongside as Henri took in everything and offered his own memories.

'The beach, of course, was closed. It was a shame, but it was not safe, so it was how it had to be. *Alors*, I remember this place!'

'This is Victoria Park,' Harry said proudly. 'I play cricket on the pitch over there.'

'The gates are new,' Henri observed.

'The gates are, in fact, very old,' James said, as he and Jenna caught up with them. 'They were taken down in 1939 to be turned into aeroplane parts, but they were never used. At the end of the war, they were found in some old chap's shed and put back up.'

Henri looked at Grace with a slightly glazed look in his eyes. 'Is there still a little wooden house in the corner?'

'Do you mean the pavilion? Yes, it is still there,' Grace said, unable to hide the surprise in her voice.

'Can you take me there?'

They stopped outside the pavilion, and Henri looked up at the low roof and timber walls for a moment, before beckoning Grace closer. She bent down and he whispered in her ear.

'Do not tell my niece, but Lily and I made love on the floor in this building.' He let out a light chuckle. 'Your mother was conceived that night.'

'Oh,' Grace said, her cheeks warming.

'I know it does not sound very romantic, but it was. The darkness, the distant sound of the waves. It was beautiful. But come, there is much to see. We are going to my old convalescent home, are we not?'

Grace gave the pavilion a quick glance, she would never look at it the same way again.

To avoid having to manoeuvre Henri's wheelchair up the steep driveway, James had dashed back for his car and driven Henri and Sophie up to Bayview. Henri was already installed on the bench under the sycamore tree when Grace, Harry, and Jenna arrived, a little out of puff from walking up the hill. Heather came out to meet everyone and to ask if anyone wanted tea.

Grace sat down next to Henri, while Sophie, James, and Jenna talked to Heather about the history of Bayview and what it would have been like when Henri had stayed there.

'We kissed for the first time here, on this bench,' Henri said, stroking the wooden arm. 'Probably not this exact one, but one very similar. I remember the view so well. The beach, the lighthouse. It is all so very fresh in my mind. It could have been yesterday.'

'My mother's ashes were scattered in the sea from the rocks around the lighthouse.'

Henri nodded slowly. 'That is lovely to know. I think I should like my ashes scattered in the sea too.'

Grace gave his hand a squeeze. She glanced behind her. The others were still chatting, and Harry had wandered off and was playing with a large ginger cat who was sunbathing on a windowsill. Grace leant closer.

'I have one more secret for you,' she said softly. 'Something only James and I know. We haven't even told Harry yet, but I want you to know.'

The old man raised a bushy white eyebrow.

'I'm having a baby,' Grace said quietly. 'It's early days.'

'Little one, that is wonderful news!' Henri nodded, a wide smile stretching his lips. 'Really wonderful news. You have given me even more reason to keep living. I am ninety-seven years old, Grace, but I should like to be a hundred.'

James placed a warm hand on Grace's shoulder, and she turned and nodded at him. He grinned at the wetness of her eyes.

'Happy tears,' she said.

James bent over her shoulder and put his mouth close to her ear. 'I love you,' he whispered.

. . .

The last stop on their tour of Dovecote was St. John's Church, or rather the cemetery behind the church. At the grave by the path, under the shade of an ancient oak tree, Henri stood from his wheelchair, supported by Sophie. He bent his head for a moment, and then looked up at the headstone on which two names were engraved.

'I am going to see if I can get my mother's name added, Henri. Even though she is not buried here, I think there should be some sort of memorial to her. Don't you?' Grace said softly.

Henri simply nodded. James leant down and placed the flowers Henri had insisted on bringing next to the headstone. He and Grace stepped away slightly and Grace nestled into his side, as he draped his arm around her shoulder. Grace drew Harry into her other side, and they watched Henri place a hand on Lily and Richard's headstone. Jenna slipped her hand into Sophie's.

'I am sorry it has taken me so long to come back to you, my love,' Henri said, his voice cracking. 'But I know you were well looked after and very well loved.' He paused. 'Richard, I thank you from the bottom of my heart for raising my daughter, and my granddaughter. I am eternally grateful to you for them.' He pulled a handkerchief from his pocket and wiped his eyes. 'My darling Lily, my heart has belonged to you since the first day I saw you and will forever.' He drew a breath. 'There is so much I want to say to you, so much in my heart that I cannot form into words. So, I will say simply this – I love you.'

A LETTER FROM LAURA

Dearest Reader,

Thank you so much for choosing to read *My Grandmother's Secret*. I really hope you enjoyed spending time with Grace and Lily and their loved ones. If you enjoyed *My Grandmother's Secret* and would like to find out about all of my latest releases, you can sign up at the following link. Your email address will never be shared, and you can unsubscribe at any time.

www.bookouture.com/laura-sweeney

One of the best things about writing fiction with an historical element is the research that has to be done to ensure that readers really feel as though they are there in that time and place. I owe a huge debt of gratitude to the Imperial War Museum and their wonderful archives, which brought the historical events mentioned in this book to life for me. Reading the first-hand accounts of people who were at Dunkirk and who witnessed the fall of Singapore was a humbling experience and one I shall never forget. The photographs that Grace looks at in the IWM are real photos and can be viewed on the IWM's online archive (catalogue numbers NYP68075 and HU104615). If you are ever in Lambeth, London, I really recommend popping into the museum.

I really love hearing from readers, so please get in touch via my social media.

Thank you so much for your support.

Laura

www.laurasweeneyauthor.co.uk

X x.com/laura_c_sweeney
instagram.com/laura_c_sweeney
bsky.app/profile/lauracsweeney.bsky.social

ACKNOWLEDGEMENTS

It is often said that it takes a village to raise a child, and the same is true for bringing a book into the world. It may be my name on the cover (which is an immense thrill) but so many people have helped in myriad ways to produce this baby you now hold in your hands.

First thanks must go to you, dearest reader, for picking up my new-born and holding her so carefully. Without readers we authors are just typing into the void, and I sincerely hope you have enjoyed my book (or if you are reading the acknowledgements first, like I do, I hope you enjoy it).

Humongous thanks to my incredible, delightful, and patient editor Imogen Allport, whose vision and insight have moulded my words into a real, proper book. This book would not exist, literally, without the hard work and dedication of the team at Bookouture.

When I started writing I had no idea what I was doing, and I have been incredibly fortunate to find wonderful people within the writing community who have taught me everything I know (and from whom I will continue to learn). Thank you to Jericho Writers and particularly to Debi Alper for being the first person, other than my mum, to read my work, and for being so encouraging. Sweary thank yous to Jo, Sarah, Kathy, and everyone at Writers' HQ for all the encouragement and gold stars, especially in the lockdown days. Special thanks to Julie Cohen for giving me the most valuable single piece of writing advice. Thank you to Robbie Guillory, this book's first midwife.

Writing can be a lonely occupation, but I have been lucky enough to make brilliant friends amongst the writing community who have supported and encouraged me and peeled me off the ceiling on more than one occasion. Love and hugs (in a field) to my Primadonna posse: Kali, Louise, Laure, and Anna. Special thanks to my fellow BookCamp mentees; being a debut novelist is a strange and exciting experience and I couldn't have done it without you (sorry for the long WhatsApp messages) – you are all brilliant, talented writers and I am very lucky to know you all. Special thanks to Imogen Martin for being my sounding board. Thank you to Alex for putting up with my catastrophising with super-human patience, and for opening a bookshop near me thus enabling my book-buying addiction – I blame you entirely for my never-reducing TBR pile.

Last, but by no means least, thanks to all my friends and family who have reminded me that there is a world beyond writing (I know, that's a scary thought) and for helping me navigate it. Jo, Emma, Laura, Kirsty, Kate, Bébhinn, Kate, and the T&C gang, I love you all dearly.

Mum and Dad, thank you for instilling a love of books and reading in me at an early age, and for everything since. Loughlin, you're the best sib a girl could ask for. Love you.

PUBLISHING TEAM

Turning a manuscript into a book requires the efforts of many people. The publishing team at Bookouture would like to acknowledge everyone who contributed to this publication.

Commercial
Lauren Morrissette
Hannah Richmond
Imogen Allport

Cover design
Debbie Clement

Data and analysis
Mark Alder
Mohamed Bussuri

Editorial
Imogen Allport

Copyeditor
Deborah Blake

Proofreader
Liz Hurst

Marketing
Alex Crow
Melanie Price
Occy Carr
Cíara Rosney
Martyna Młynarska

Operations and distribution
Marina Valles
Stephanie Straub

Production
Hannah Snetsinger
Mandy Kullar
Ria Clare
Nadia Michael

Publicity
Kim Nash
Noelle Holten
Jess Readett
Sarah Hardy

Rights and contracts
Peta Nightingale
Richard King
Saidah Graham

RAISING READERS
Books Build Bright Futures

Dear Reader,

We'd love your attention for one more page to tell you about the crisis in children's reading, and what we can all do.

Studies have shown that reading for fun is the **single biggest predictor of a child's future success** – more than family circumstance, parents' educational background or income. It improves academic results, mental health, wealth, communication skills, and ambition.

The number of children reading for fun is in rapid decline. Young people have a lot of competition for their time, and a worryingly high number do not have a single book at home.

Our business works extensively with schools, libraries and literacy charities, but here are some ways we can all raise more readers:

- Reading to children for just 10 minutes a day makes a difference
- Don't give up if children aren't regular readers – there will be books for them!

- Visit bookshops and libraries to get recommendations
- Encourage them to listen to audiobooks
- Support school libraries
- Give books as gifts

Thank you for reading: there's a lot more information about how to encourage children to read on our website.

www.JoinRaisingReaders.com

Printed in Dunstable, United Kingdom